# THE HATE VOW

BOOK ONE OF THE QUICKSILVER TRILOGY

## NICOLE FRENCH

This is a work of fiction. Names, characters, organizations, places, events, and incidents are either products of the author's imagination or rendered fictitiously. Any resemblance to real people or events is purely coincidental.

Copyright 2019 Raglan Publishing.

ISBN: 978-1-950663-00-2

Cover design by Raglan Publishing.

Photography by Sara Eirew Photography.

Model: Lucas Bloms.

*To every reader who has been asking for this story for more than a year.*
*Thanks for the push. You are all more inspiring than you know.*

*xo, Nic*

# PART ONE

## THE QUESTION

*There once was a girl from Chicago*
*Whose lips were as red as a cardinal.*
*To kiss her was bliss,*
*But her bite was to risk*
*Being maimed by her killer bravado.*

"Jane's Limerick"
—from the journal of Eric de Vries

## PRELUDE

Tick. Tock. Tick.

The gong of the antique clock rippled through the air at exactly 10 a.m., Eastern Standard Time. Eric knew this because it was synced to his watch, and his grandmother, Celeste de Vries, *always* had the correct time. She was nothing if not punctual. And she demanded the same from everyone else.

Normally he wouldn't have minded the familiar old clock. It might have even been a comfort, considering he hadn't heard it for so long. But today he was hungover like a piece of wet laundry, a headache splitting his temples in two. Now, that wasn't particularly odd for his average Sunday morning. Usually he'd be wrapped up in a pair of shapely legs—sometimes two pairs if he'd played his cards right the night before.

But emergency tea with the de Vries clan matriarch? At ten in the morning? In New York, four hours from his apartment in Boston? Not Eric's *modus operandi*. Not by a long shot.

It didn't help that he hadn't seen his family in close to ten years, and the last time wasn't pretty. "Call me when someone's dying." Famous last words to Celeste de Vries, the formidable head of the de

Vries family. Right before he stormed out of this very penthouse to make a life of his own, separate from this tangled web of power and manipulation.

Well. She did.

"Madame will see you now, Master Eric."

Eric looked up to find Garrett, Grandmother's butler, waiting for him in the hall. It was amazing. The man really hadn't changed in a decade, despite being as ancient as ever. Eric was thirty-two, with the filled-out chest, occasional gray hair, and three fine lines over his forehead to show for his time away. But Garrett was just as much of a well-maintained antique as the Ming vase sitting in the foyer or the salmon-colored wainscoting of the penthouse's halls. He was an anachronism, something frozen in time. A butler in New York City in the twenty-first century. But that was Grandmother. Tradition or death.

"Thanks, Garrett." Eric followed the butler to the parlor at the southeast corner of the apartment.

Yes. His grandmother had a parlor nestled in a maze of hallways crisscrossing the complete top floor of a building she owned on Eighty-Seventh Street and Park Avenue. In New York City, one of the most crowded places on the planet, his ninety-pound grandmother occupied more space than the mayor.

Nothing in that room had changed either. Not the priceless antiques, the Chesterfield furniture, not even the family portrait that was painted twenty-five years ago at her famous rose garden in the Hamptons. There was Eric's father, mother, and him as a child; next to his aunt, uncle, and their daughter, Nina; plus a whole host of extended family, all presided over by Grandmother, sitting in the middle of them like a brood hen.

Their smiles were the opposite of genuine. The kinds of smiles where people stare imperiously at the camera without showing their veneered teeth. Blue and gray eyes vacant in the summer sunlight. Despite the life blooming all around them, everyone was dead inside.

A flood of memories washed over Eric. Him at five, in knee socks and a sweater vest, trying not to fidget while Grandmother lectured all the ways he was expected to fulfill his destiny as the heir to the family fortune. Nina, his younger cousin, listening curiously while she tugged at her braids and clutched a stuffed panda.

Eric at eleven, arguing over playing fucking polo in Westchester instead of baseball in Central Park like he wanted. Like his father, deceased just a few months prior, had promised. Nina had cried and been shuttled to her etiquette lessons.

Eighteen, howling his decision to attend Dartmouth instead of Princeton like the rest of the de Vries clan. Nina, watching with wide eyes while she focused on her homework. She would attend Smith, of course, like her mother, Violet.

And the last time. Twenty-two, fresh out of school with a degree in English instead of finance. Eric was expected to take the reins of the family business, but instead he gave it the finger and went to Harvard Law instead. He had enough money in the trust from Father's death to pay for it himself. Okay, so it wasn't much of a rebellion, trading one white-collar career for another. But he did it himself, and did it without being held under the cranky, wrinkled thumb of the resident tyrant of the Upper East Side.

Celeste Annika Van Dusen de Vries.

"Grandson."

Her voice also sounded exactly the same: sharp, but rough around the edges, like a serrated knife. But when Eric turned toward the leather armchair under the original Van Gogh, he found the one thing that had changed completely: Grandmother herself.

She was never a big woman, but now she stooped like a vulture, withered like a half-sheared, weather-beaten branch. She wore a scarf around her head—Hermès, no doubt—though wisps of white hair slipped under its edges. She still wore matching Chanel coordinates, but the tweed pantsuit hung off a frail body that seemed mostly skin and bones. When she breathed, something rattled in her lungs from across the room, like a brewing storm.

"Sit down, Eric," she ordered, gesturing toward the couch with a thin fingernail still polished a tasteful, girlish pink.

"Grandmother." He greeted her with a stiff nod, but obeyed. Old habits die hard. "It's...a pleasure to see you again."

It was not. But Eric's manners were too well-entrenched to say anything else. He might not have forgiven her for what she did, but he was too well-bred to be rude. *Fuck.*

Grandmother balanced her hands on the oxygen tank in front of her, then appraised her grandson openly. Eric willed himself not to look away or fidget with his clothes. *You're a man, Eric. Remember that.* Because he was not the scrawny twenty-two-year-old she last saw. Since telling his family where they could stick it, he had gone to the best law school in the world, worked his ass off at a top-twenty firm, and then started his own shop with one of his best friends. Eric was proud of what he had accomplished without his family's money or connections. He didn't need this frail woman's approval anymore. He didn't need any of them and hadn't for a long time.

"You've grown up." Grandmother waved at Garrett to bring in the tea. "You've done well with your little law firm, I understand. Although I see it hasn't taught you to stop dressing like a pauper."

Eric crossed one foot over his knee, ignoring her jibe at his T-shirt and jeans. He generally preferred more tailored looks, to tell the truth. A whole rack of designer suits hung in his closet at home. Armani. Boss. Tom Ford. Burberry. He liked a nicely cut lapel, a well-chosen pocket square. He had a tailor in Boston on speed dial. The worn denim and concert T-shirt were for her—He knew they would piss her off.

"I *have* done well," he agreed. There was no point in being modest. Since he, Skylar Crosby, and Kieran Beckford started Copley Associates two years ago, the firm had gone from three attorneys to ten, and they were looking to hire two more. They'd already developed a reputation for being ruthless and savvy in a city chock-full of lawyers.

Grandmother nodded. "Yes, yes. Although I'm sure it's helped to have the Sterling *and* de Vries names behind it, hasn't it? Nothing like new money to get things started. Isn't it Sterling's wife, that little no-name from Brooklyn who nearly ruined Ellen Chambers's family, who's your partner? Pity. His first wife came from such good family."

Her eyes gleamed in that way they always did when she talked about other members of her "station." Always conniving, always judging. She wasn't stupid. She likely knew all the details of Eric's business arrangement with Skylar and her husband, Brandon Sterling, a former investment magnate and now-inventor. Brandon divested from his companies six years ago to play in his lab, but the guy still had one of the biggest stock portfolios on the eastern seaboard, and his new company's legal needs initially kept Copley afloat. In Grandmother's estimation, Sterling was a fish worth watching.

Or, Eric wondered vaguely, was Brandon a whale? Would that make his grandmother Captain Ahab?

Instead of answering, Eric remained quiet. He knew that game, and he wasn't there to play it. It would be easier, though, if he actually knew why he was there at all.

Garrett wheeled in the tea tray and fixed them cups while they eyed each other over the porcelain. By the time he parked it on one side of the room, even Grandmother was ready to be done with the silence.

"Leave us, Garrett." It was not until the old man was gone that she turned again to Eric, taking a deep breath through her oxygen mask before speaking. "I'm sure you're wondering why I requested your presence."

"'Request' is a bit generous, but sure. I'm curious."

He had received a phone call two days ago from her personal assistant, who simply said Eric was expected for tea. To deal with an emergency. That was it. He could have ignored it, just like he ignored all of the embossed invitations for Christmas dinner or sporadic phone calls to join the family at the Hamptons. They had an arrangement. She could pretend Eric hadn't told his entire family to stay the fuck out of his life or he'd air their dirty laundry to the press. And he could pretend they didn't say anything to him at all.

But this was different. The assistant's voice, curt and cold, had simmered with desperation.

Grandmother took a leisurely sip with shaky hands. "You might be stubborn like your father, but you were never an idiot. Clearly I'm not in good health."

Eric pressed his lips together. "Of course. I'm sorry to—"

"Let's not play coy, Eric," she interrupted. "You loathe this family —you made that perfectly clear when we saw you last, and have continued in the years hence."

Eric gritted his teeth but didn't argue. When your family works together to split up you and your fiancée because they don't think she's good enough for them, you get pretty pissed off. And when their actions cause her to kill herself, well, that's pretty fucking unforgivable.

So, yeah. He had a bit of a grudge.

"What do you want, Grandmother?" he asked, setting his untouched tea on a gilded tray balanced on the sky-blue ottoman. "Julie said it was an emergency."

"Isn't it, though?" She gestured at the oxygen tank and her dilapidated body. "I'm dying, Eric, since apparently your senses are failing you. The doctors, fools, all of them, say I have six months, at best. Cancer, apparently. It's so...pedestrian, isn't it?"

"I'm sorry to hear that. Did you ask me here for some kind of absolution? You want forgiveness for what you did to Penny? Because I'll tell you right now, it's not coming."

Eric swallowed hard, but ultimately, was unmoved. He knew it was cold, but he had truly lost all love for this woman a very long time ago. It was she, after all, who led the crusade that caused Penny to slit her wrists that terrible morning in May.

Grandmother just scoffed, waving her paper-thin hand. "No, no," she said. "I expect that's a lost cause, particularly since I don't regret it. Not her death, of course, but that wasn't really our fault. We couldn't have known she was so...delicate."

Eric's face flamed. He was determined to keep his cool when he arrived, but he should have known better. Grandmother took sadistic pleasure in getting under people's skin.

So instead he rose. "I think that's enough." Without a backwards glance, he started out of the room, not giving two shits whether or not his sneakers left tracks on her precious floors.

"Eric, stop right there!" Her voice rang out, though it was quickly swallowed by the thick Aubusson carpets. And damn it, there was something in it that made Eric obey once again. A terror. A weakness he'd never heard before. Not coming from her.

Slowly, he turned around but remained in the doorway.

"I'll be gone in six months," Grandmother said. "And just who do you think is going to get all of this?"

She meant the opulence around them. The de Vries fortune was older than Manhattan, having started with a New Amsterdam shipping company that became one of the biggest conglomerates in the world. The name was on containers and boats worldwide, although no de Vries had done more than sit on the board of directors for nearly a hundred years. But money made money, and the de Vries family had more than just about anyone.

Not that Eric wanted a goddamn cent.

He crossed his arms and glared. "I'm not going to help you play inheritance games with your kids, Grandmother. You want Mother and Aunt Violet to jump through hoops, you talk to them about it. Or talk to Nina, your other grandchild. The one who actually speaks to you."

"That would be all fine and good if I intended them to have it, but I don't." Grandmother paused to take a long siphon of oxygen, then offered a smile that could only be described as sickly sweet. "It's for you, Eric. All of it."

Eric's heart stopped. Completely. He was dead for at least two full seconds.

"What?" he finally croaked. "But that's...you have one other child. Who is alive, I might add."

"Violet is not a de Vries," Grandmother said. "And therefore, neither is Nina. Now, before you say anything, they've always known that's how it would go. Girls can't continue the family name, Eric. Astors and Gardners can't own a company called De Vries Shipping. But you can, my boy. You're the last one."

It was true: Eric was, in fact, the last in a long line of de Vries men. His father was the only son of Jonathan de Vries, Grandmother's husband. They were both gone—Grandfather to lung cancer well before he was born, and Father to a freak sailing accident when Eric was just a child. It wouldn't have mattered if his mother married again or had other children. None of them would have been de Vries. They wouldn't have had pure blood. Eric was the one and only man in the family who still bore the name.

"I don't want it," he said finally. "I don't need this family's money or the company. I meant it when I said I was done with all of you."

Again, Grandmother just snorted. "You have no idea what you're saying. That's a seventeen-billion-dollar corporation you're tossing away like old crudité. You'd attend board meetings as chairman—a controlling shareholder, that's all—and let the money do its work." She snapped her papery fingers. "Simple."

Eric's jaw opened and closed like one of those nutcrackers that always adorned the massive Christmas tree Grandmother set up every year in the ballroom. He knew his family's net worth was estimated to be high by Forbes, but never as high as that. Seventeen *billion* dollars?

"Why me?" he asked thickly. "Just because of a stupid name? Have one of the cousins change theirs if it means that much to you. Carla went to business school, for Christ's sake, and she's just as much a de Vries as I am, even if her last name is Gardner now. Nina's probably dying for the job too—she always did bend over backwards to please you. This family is everything to you. Why would you hand seventeen billion dollars over to someone who turned his back on it?"

But Grandmother just quirked an eyebrow and shrugged—an oddly casual movement for her. "Tradition was important to your grandfather. And your father too. So was strength of character, and you appear to be the only one in this family who has it besides me. I've watched you over the years. You're a force in corporate law now, which would be a boon for the company. Your father would be proud."

It was the only guilt trip that ever worked on Eric—the invocation of his dead father. He knew the pictures on the mantle by heart. The clean-cut man who always showed his teeth when he smiled. Who did things like sail across the Atlantic and learn to fly prop planes. Who swept Eric's mother off her feet with random trips to Paris or obscenely expensive jewelry. The man had swagger. He was everything that, as a boy, Eric wanted to be. Everything that, as a man, he was not.

Well, except for the swagger, maybe.

"Of course, I'm not just going to *hand* it to you." Grandmother shook Eric out of his memories.

And there it was: the caveat. There was always one.

Eric clenched his jaw. "Let's have it."

She took another gulp of oxygen, intentionally drawing out the conversation. "I want to know the de Vries name will go on," she said. "It's what they both would have wanted; therefore, it's also my dying wish."

Eric's mouth dropped again. "Are you for real? Is this a joke out of some Thomas Hardy novel? Dying *wish*?"

Grandmother grinned again. It was alarming. She'd lost some teeth, and others were badly decayed, likely from the chemo. A woman like her wouldn't go without a decent set of veneers or dentures with any company whatsoever. She must have really been in pain.

"I assure you it's very real," she said. "Marry, Eric. Within six months. And stay married for at least five years, long enough to produce an heir, if you can. Should you succeed, the company is yours. And if you truly don't want it after five years, you may abdicate your position to your aunt Violet or your cousin Nina." She sucked in another round of oxygen, like the thrill of the announcement was too much for her. "Say no, and I'll sell everything, leaving the family penniless but for their current trusts. And as you know, those have never been as generous as they would like."

His first instinct was to tell her she was off her goddamn rocker. Even with one foot in the grave, she was still up to her old tricks, playing with people like marionettes. And if it were just him she was trying to manipulate, Eric probably would have said so. But his family didn't deserve to have their entire future ripped from them. Nina, to whom he'd barely spoken in ten years—What would her life be like? And as much as he couldn't stand his mother or aunt, weak and self-absorbed as they were, they didn't deserve it either. None of them deserved to be pawns in this Machiavellian game Madame de Vries was playing.

"Marry," she repeated. "And as the good Lord said, 'be fruitful and multiply.'"

The words rang through Eric's head like the gong of the grandfather clock, chiming on and on. Any instinct he ever had for marriage died with Penny, seeped out of her veins and down the bathtub drain along with her life.

Eric just wasn't the marrying type. He was more the never-let-them-into-his-apartment type. The screw-them-and-leave-before-it-gets-light type. And even if he weren't, there was no one who would be willing to go along with this crazy scheme. No one he could stand long enough to try.

Except...one. One woman whose wit and audacity could possibly make this arrangement bearable. She was one woman in the world Eric could ever see himself marrying, even if it was just for show.

Jane Lee Lefferts.

A woman who completely and utterly hated his guts.

# ONE

"You ready, baby girl?"

I scrunched my eyes shut in pure, unadulterated anticipation. I might have been way too close to thirty for my
liking, but in that moment, I was like a child locked in her bedroom
on Christmas morning. The utter sweet-tooth who has to wait until
last to have a piece of cake at a birthday party. A lottery winner about
to collect their winnings.

"I'm so ready I'm about to pee my pants," I declared to Frederick,
my hairstylist for the last five years.

"Please don't," he said in a British accent that I was pretty sure
was as fake as his name, considering it seemed to change regions
every couple of months. "More because you will ruin those fabulous
leather pants, and I thought those were the centerpiece of your
makeover, darling."

Two years ago, Freddie here sounded like John Lennon. Last
month, he was Eliza Doolittle. Today he was more like Posh Spice.
But Frederick could pretend he was the Queen of England for all I
cared. The man was the best colorist in Chicago. You don't fuck with
your colorist, my friends.

"Just do it," I said as I stared into the mirror, knees shaking in anticipation. With a beige towel over my head and the way my nose was all scrunched up with excitement, I looked more like a Shar-Pei than a twenty-nine-year-old half-Korean former lawyer. I grabbed my glasses off the counter and shoved them on. I wanted to see the goods.

With a flourish, Frederick whipped off the towel, and suddenly my face was surrounded by jewel tones of purple, turquoise, blue, green, and most of all, pink—glorious, carnationy, Pepto Bismol-branded *pink*—all falling around my shoulders in a waterfall of rose-hued color. A wet, un-styled, waterfall, but oh my *God*, a flood of damn *color* after years of plain, boring black.

"Aaaaahhhh!" I screamed, wringing my hands like a teenager while Frederick smirked behind me.

"Like it, love?" he asked.

Please. He knew I did, the cocky fake Cockney.

"Like it?" I parroted while I clapped my hands together. "*Like* it? I freaking *love it*, you sarcastic gay monkey! I *FLOVE* it!"

Frederick grinned. "Well, calm yourself so I can blow it out properly, will you? Then you'll *really* see what it looks like, mmkay? Now then, off with the specs."

Obediently, I ripped off my cat-eye glasses while the blare of the hair dryer started. I hadn't colored my hair in five years, since I started my first job out of law school at the Cook County State's Attorney's office in Chicago. Five years of abiding by strict court dress codes that made me look like a funeral director on her way to the library. Five years I had to shop at Ann Taylor, Banana Republic, and Macy's while my soul slipped away with every swipe of my credit card.

So this. *This* was almost enough to make up for the fact that after five long years, the state had tossed me to the curb like old garbage. It helped me ignore the fact that as of yesterday afternoon, I was out of a job and out of an apartment, with no way to pay over two hundred thousand dollars' worth of student loan debt. Everyone said a law degree from Harvard was supposed to be the ticket to success. Ha. Right. Everyone lied.

Maybe I should have seen it coming. I started fresh with one state's attorney who was now moving on to greener pastures (it was nice to have a congresswoman's name and number on my resume, I guessed). But when the next SA arrived, I ignored the way everyone else in my office started sending out resumes. I assumed that if I just kept my head down and did a good job, I'd carry over. I was an idiot. One year into the job, and it was the red wedding in there. Except it wasn't people who were murdered—it was our burgeoning careers.

I was the only one who didn't have a job lined up when the bloodshed occurred. And yet...the only thing I could think was *fuck me, I can dye my hair again.*

I blinked into the mirror, watching with glee as Frederick made quick work of the blow-out, brushing me free from the chains of public service tyranny. He twisted his brush around the candy-colored waves, and when he finished, I looked like a character from Jem and the Holograms. Truly outrageous indeed.

*All that glitters is not gold, Jane Brain.*

A sudden lump formed in my throat, the way it did whenever my dad's voice, complete with the clichéd sayings and corny nicknames, popped into my head. It was happening less and less frequently these days, nine months after his death. Heart attacks kill. Who knew?

*Clothes don't make the man either, pumpkin.*

I could still see his half-disapproving, half-amused expression. The way his lips curved under his thick gray beard while he crossed his stocky, gingham-covered arms. The way his eyes twinkled with humor under his ridiculous bucket hats. *Whatever you say, Santa Claus,* I'd tease him during the months when he'd been eating too many of my mother's dumplings. *Who would you be without your red suit, huh?*

But Dad would just smile because he knew his point was made. *It's the inside that counts, Ms. Austen,* he'd say, calling me after my namesake, my mother's favorite author. And immediately, I'd feel guilty for teasing him about his belly. I'd feel guilty for thinking disparaging thoughts about his hat. After all, this was Carol Lefferts we were talking about. Psychologist to war vets. Captain of community service. The entire reason I had not only pursued a law degree instead of fashion, but used that degree for a career as a public servant.

*Sorry, Dad,* I thought as I watched my reflection. I couldn't shake the feeling that even now, he was disappointed in me. After all, I was hiding from the career he had always encouraged me to follow. And now, without a job, with no future ahead of me, I was the worst thing of all in his eyes: a loafer. A dilettante. A waste.

"Puh-*lease* tell me you're going out tonight to show off this fantastic work of art I've created," Frederick said after he turned off the dryer. He tousled my hair around my face and looked expectantly at me through the mirror. "Hair this sexy deserves an orgasm, love. You know it's true." He leaned over. "I live vicariously through you now that Colin and I tied the knot. So, come on, give me the dirt on my Jane's latest conquest."

I smiled grimly. This was a request I heard a lot from my coupled-off friends, of which there seemed to be more and more these days. It was a parlor-trick—if, you know, people actually had freaking parlors. Tell the sad married people all about your sex life so they can pretend to have one. Or maybe it was just that their lives made *me* sad.

I knew exactly one couple who seemed to have better sex the longer they were together, and that was probably because Skylar and Brandon basically combusted whenever they didn't see each other for more than a few hours. I mean, I was happy for my best friend, but she and her husband bordered on codependent. It worked for them, but that would drive me *crazy.* It wasn't natural. The fire was supposed to go out when you were together for that long, not create a damn inferno.

But what did I know? Maybe I would have wanted to see a guy for more than one night too if he was a billionaire with a six-pack.

Who looks like that at forty-two? Really? I didn't know how my best friend did it, but she basically fell in love with Tony Stark. If I didn't love her so much, I'd have hated her for it.

Frederick waited impatiently as he fluffed my hair. Once upon a time, I'd have been ready to play this game. I was the *best* at this game. A year ago, I had stories to tell, probably ones from the night before. When the sun went down and the courthouse was closed, I lived my life as God intended a young, sexually active woman to live: without fear or boundaries.

But here was my dirty little secret. I hadn't actually taken a dip in the sea since Dad's funeral. The worst of the grief had passed. But my mojo? She hadn't come back.

But that didn't mean I didn't have memories I could rehash.

"Go forth and rock," Frederick said after I finished telling him about James Carvey, the public defender I met at my first trial out of law school. The entire day was like pure foreplay—all that sparring, cross-examination of each other's witnesses. Shaking my hips back and forth as I offered my closing statement. By the end of it, I was about ready to combust right there in front of the judge. And when the verdict came, we didn't even care. James and I were locked in a closet in the basement of City Hall within an hour.

It was hot. And then it was done. Just how I liked it.

Or at least, how I used to.

"See you in six weeks, Freddy," I said after I paid.

"You better," he said. "I don't want to see those roots, girl."

Now it was back to my mother's condo, where if I was smart, I'd spend the rest of the day sending out resumes so I'd be able to afford a new apartment before I killed my sire. But who wanted to be responsible with new hair the color of a bag of Jolly Ranchers? Fuck that. Tomorrow I could go back to being Sad Sally. Now was the time for Tinder. Time to celebrate the *present*.

And with that thought, I walked out of the shop and right into my past.

A chest of hard muscle. The smell of cologne and fresh linen.

The face of the one person who almost convinced me to go against my better nature and settle down.

"What the fu—oh!" I looked up, fixing the glasses that were knocked off my nose. "Eric?"

He was the last person I ever thought I'd run into on a random street in Chicago. The man with a mouth sweeter than chocolate and a dick that tasted even better. The man who ordered me around like crazy, and more than that, made me love it. The man who, five years ago, utterly shattered my heart.

Eric de Vries.

———

ERIC. Eric in Chicago. Eric wearing a gorgeous gray linen suit, with a jaw like an ice sculpture and eyes like a storm cloud.

Eric Sebastian Franklin Stallsmith de Vries standing in front of my hair salon exactly 984 miles from Boston.

I scowled. I hated that I still knew that. I hated that five years after we split up, I still knew the exact distance between me and the only man who made me forget about every *other* man out there. Because for a short period of time, he really was all I could see.

Rich.

Entitled.

Blue-blooded.

He hid it as best he could, but Eric's Upper East Side pedigree was one of the worst-kept secrets at Harvard. You can't really mask that kind of breeding, and Eric always radiated the calm, poised confidence only people from very wealthy backgrounds have. He was a mystery in every other way, and there were rumors he had done something terrible back home, which was why he wouldn't talk about his family. Like, ever. But unlike the other trust fund brats at Harvard, Eric actually worked his ass off. He built his own legacy after school rather than depending on jobs from his family. Regardless of what happened between us, I always respected him for that.

Dad would have respected him too.

*Dammit.*

We met during our first year in law school, about one month into our second semester. Total opposites who fell into bed one night after binge drinking the way only overworked, overstressed Ivy League students can. I woke up the next morning in his apartment, wondering what the hell had happened to me. This wasn't unusual. It wasn't the strange apartment that got to me. It was the feeling like I...I don't know...belonged there.

I kept trying to figure it out—by going back, that is—for exactly one month until the stressors of our torts class got to both of us, and we chucked each other to the curb. Two and a half years later, we reunited in another frenzy—there was no other way to put it—that crashed and burned like a NASCAR explosion. It was bad. Horrific. Life-alteringly horrible.

That was five years ago.

And now...holy shit, he looked good. Eric was always a tall, handsome fucker, if a little on the gawky side. Well, that gawky boy had definitely disappeared since the boy exited his twenties. All that was left was the handsome, and he was one hundred percent *man.*

Eric had the kind of face that could change on a dime. Fair and blond, but not overwhelming. One second, he'd look as ordinary as could be; the next, you couldn't stop looking at him. Skylar always chalked up that shift to his "lady-killer smile," but Eric had a whole repertoire of scene-stealing expressions. And the most effective wasn't the smile that could light up a room (though it could). It was the one where he looked at you like he wanted to spank you black and blue—and he knew you wanted him to do it. Bad. From Boy Scout to YES, DADDY in less than a second.

A shiver practically tossed me two steps forward. Whoa. That was a trip down memory lane I hadn't visited much in the last five years.

So, I did what I did best. I deflected. "What the hell are *you* doing here?"

Eric cracked a sly smile and raised an eyebrow. Something else that hadn't changed: that infuriating unflappability. "Nice to see you too, Jane."

Once again, my vision was clouded by another memory—that wide, soft mouth, drifting over my navel just before he—*Stop it, Jane.* What in the hell? Nine months of the Sahara Desert, and all of a sudden, I was a river. Of memories and mojo alike. I couldn't go there. Not with him. Not now. Not ever.

I folded my arms. But when I didn't say anything, I was finally, *finally* rewarded with something more than a smirk when Eric rubbed the back of his neck and straightened the collar of his starched white shirt.

"I'm here to see you," he admitted. "Skylar told me you were having your hair done today." He glanced over my now-flaming rainbow pink tresses. At least that looked amazing.

"Skylar told you..." I murmured to myself, only then remembering our conversation the night before. "God, Anne of Green Gables is such a damn blabbermouth. She can't ever keep her mouth shut. So, what, you just hopped on a plane to witness my makeover?"

This wasn't random. That much was obvious. It wasn't like Eric and I had never seen each other in the last five years. We had morphed into used-to-fuck acquaintances locked in an antagonistic truce because Skylar Crosby, his partner and my best friend, was an important part of both our lives. I still visited Boston whenever I could, especially now that Skylar and Brandon had two adorable kids to whom I happened to be godmother. And the Crosby-Sterling household loved to entertain their Auntie Jane. When Eric and I had been forced to be around each other, we'd maintained wide circles, wary and mostly tolerant. You know, like cats. The ones who might pounce on each other in a dark alley. And tear each other's fur out.

But generally, Eric and I just avoided situations where we both might be present. He got them full time, so when I was in town, he made himself scarce. Our feline truces were few and far between.

Eric cracked another smile at the nickname. Skylar tended to be a bit of a know-it-all and had bright red hair, just like the titular character of L.M. Montgomery's classic.

"Well, I was in town, and I asked her what you might be up to," he said. "Do you always tell her when you're having your hair done? Seems a little codependent to me."

"Says the guy who stalked me to the salon," I retorted. "God, look at us. We look like fucking Spy vs. Spy, do you know that?"

Eric looked down at his light gray pants and white Oxford shirt, then back at my all-black ensemble. It was a little warm for them, but I was enjoying the fact that I could wear leather pants, a black concert tee, and my favorite combat boots in the light of day again. We were dressed like opposites. Yin and yang. Except, you know, for the pom-pom hair.

I bit my lip to keep from laughing.

"I'm wearing perfectly appropriate clothes for mid-May," he returned, though his mouth twitched again. "No one said you have to walk around looking like the grim reaper on acid."

"Whatever you say, Zack Morris."

Eric mimicked faux horror. "*Saved by the Bell*? Really? You've lost your touch, Jane. I am way better dressed than Zack Morris."

I just shrugged. He really made this too easy. "Fine, Preppy. You look like Zack Morris after he dropped out of school and started selling used cars."

We chuckled, letting the string of jokes settle. The truth was, I missed this kind of back-and-forth. Most guys couldn't take my particular brand of caustic humor. It always amazed me how women were constantly accused of being the more emotional sex, because most men I knew could barely take a joke.

Eric, on the other hand, never seemed to mind. He wouldn't always trade barbs, exactly. He just sort of absorbed it all without a response, which, of course, just made me taunt him more. If it bothered him too much, he had ways of making me pay for it later. Ways that frequently included rope or some kind of restraints; maybe a gag if he was feeling creative. Hell, sometimes I *wanted* the payback. Eric would get this gleam in his steely eyes, and I'd act like a toddler about to knock over her block tower. Then I'd call him "Petri dish" and find myself with my hands tied behind my back, ass in the air in about fifteen seconds...

I shivered again, this time with a shock of delight. More memories. *Shit.* When I said I wanted my mojo back, that was not what I had in mind.

"So, what do you think?" Eric interrupted my daydream. "Do you have some time for coffee?"

I blinked. "What? Oh, um...wait, why are you even here? You couldn't have just called me like a normal person?"

He swallowed visibly while he shoved his hands into his pockets a little harder than normal. Inwardly, I threw a mental fist into the air. I was getting under his skin. *Ha!*

"It's not really the kind of thing I can talk about over the phone."

*Color me intrigued.* I tipped my glasses down my nose, noticing for the first time the signs of clear distress. Two days of stubble on a normally clean-shaven jaw. His shirt was slightly wrinkled from travel—had he come straight from the airport? And his deep gray eyes, which still sparked as he watched me, bore tiny wrinkles at the sides and dark circles underneath. Something was wrong. Very wrong.

"Is that so, Petri dish?" I said, using the old nickname I gave him in law school. It was the best I could come up with. Eric got around even more than I did in those days. He was basically an STI incubator.

But there was no twitch in his mouth at the jibe, no sudden appearance of the dimple I used to lick from time to time, and immediately, I regretted it. Not just for the way it clearly irritated him, but also for the next wave of memories that washed over me. The bad ones. Starting with the last time he was in Chicago.

Eric showing up to tell me he loved me after one of our many breaks. The other dude lying in my bed from the night before. Me flying back to Boston to beg him to try again. And after I finally thought we might be able to make it work...finding the red, fake-satin thong shoved in the bottom of his sheets. Every fear I'd ever had about committing to a man who had already slept his way around half of Boston bubbled upward until I was shouting at him loud enough for the entire building to hear.

He wasn't good enough for me. He wasn't worth my time.

Now on the street, Eric didn't move, just kept his hands in his pockets and waited, patiently as ever, for me to respond. Eric would wait. He'd always wait. As long as it took for someone to talk.

Some things never change.

I flipped my hair over my shoulder with more attitude than was strictly necessary. "Fine," I said. "There's a cafe around the corner. We can talk there."

# TWO

I couldn't help it. I kept sneaking glances at him as we walked the few blocks down to the Red Rose Cafe. He just looked... shit, he looked so good. My mojo wasn't just back, she was slamming her foot down on the gas of a 1960s Mustang so she could stock up on post-sex cigarettes. This was a problem.

Eric still had the talent of making the most normal clothes look like he'd walked off the cover of *GQ*. In the mid-May sun, he wore a simple white button-up shirt and perfectly tailored gray slacks that would be dad pants on anyone else, but looked indecently good on his long, muscular legs and what right now appeared to be the tightest, most grabbable ass this side of the Rockies. Jesus. Men in suits were Skylar's thing. I preferred joysticks in jeans, the kind that were wrinkled from two days on the floor, not perfectly ironed slacks. *Slacks*. Ugh. Just the stupid word was a total boner-killer. And yet, here was Eric, making me want to tackle him down the next alley just to see what he wore underneath them.

I needed to stop immediately. I did *not* need to go down that rabbit hole again, since the last time I got involved with this man, he broke my heart into a million pieces. Once a player, always a player. A wolf in sheep's dad pants.

I tripped again.

"Everything all right?" Eric asked. His stupid gray eyes twinkled. Like a fucking Disney character.

"Ah, yeah," I said as I stared at the sidewalk. "Just clumsy. You remember."

Eric shrugged—that nonplussed shrug that always made me want to throttle him—and we continued down the street and into the cafe.

By the time we ordered our drinks—black coffee for me, a "bone-dry" cappuccino for Eric, because he was clearly still a particular, pretentious bastard in the most random little ways—the unperturbed facade had evaporated again. In fact, Eric looked more nervous than I'd ever seen him, and that included the weeks before we took the bar exam and we were boinking like bunnies to get rid of the tension. He didn't even notice when the barista wrote her number on his cup sleeve.

"Don't tell me you're taken," I said. "She was hot to trot for you, Casanova. She'd probably give you a blow job in the stock room if you asked nicely."

Eric just smiled grimly—no teeth—but didn't give the number a second look. Always the well-trained gentleman, he held the door for me to walk outside. It was a gorgeous spring day in the Windy City, and I wanted to take advantage of it. It wasn't because being outside gave me more things to look at than Eric's soul-deep eyes or the wall behind them. No, that had nothing to do with it.

"All right," I said after we sat at a sidewalk table. "Spill."

Eric surveyed the street. "Couldn't we go someplace more private? This is kind of personal. What about your place?"

I snorted. "My place currently consists of the couch in my mother's condo. If you would like to meet Yu Na Lee Lefferts, be my guest. But beware, she is the equivalent of the Bermuda Triangle for boyfriends. Once you go in, you may never escape."

He just blinked. "We could go to my hotel room..."

Me and Eric. Alone in a hotel room? With the way I was feeling, there was absolutely no way I could trust myself alone with the man. And by the doubt in his voice, I was guessing he felt the same way.

"Hey, you came to me, Don Draper," I pointed out. "What's the big deal? You worried you're going to get caught? Got a wife at home who wouldn't appreciate you sitting with the town whore?"

The words spilled out before I could help them. He wasn't wearing a wedding ring, but maybe he had taken it off. I didn't know why the idea bothered me so much. Although I'd had my share of accusations thrown at me for my, uh, extracurricular activities, I didn't usually internalize them that way. The world was a shitty place for women like me—women who wanted to have just as much fun as men. I tried not to let it bother me, but apparently, sometimes it did.

"Don't talk about yourself like that, Jane." Eric's voice didn't raise a decibel, but the authority was clear. He didn't move, just stared at me for a long time across the table, daring me to challenge him.

And I couldn't. Not just because he was right, but because that dark expression whisked me right back to other times when he made that authority even more...known. Five years ago, when one steely look had me running for the bedroom to enjoy the *many* talented things he could do with that mouth. Particularly when I said and did things he told me explicitly not to say and do. Things that had me on my knees. Or tied up to the—

I shook my head. *Stop it, you horn ball.* So what if I'd never been able to recreate anything like it since (and not for want of trying)? Eric and I were bad news together. Drove each other crazy. We were either fucking or fighting—there was no in between. Neither of us were relationship material. It was as simple as that.

"Fine," Eric said, pulling me out of my X-rated visions. "It's like this. I'm in a bind, and I need some help."

He then proceeded to tell me the craziest story I'd ever heard about his grandmother, his dead father, and a plan to blackmail him and his kin out of a whole lot of money if he didn't get married within six months and try to produce an heir within five years.

"Produce an *heir?*" I repeated loudly when he was done. "Who are you, Prince William of the shipping industry? You have to protect your family's divine right to trade routes?"

"Shhhh!" Eric sat up straight with a glare that had me squirming all over again. "The whole fucking city doesn't need to hear this, Jane."

"Let me get this straight," I said, setting my hands on the table. The cluster of rubber bracelets on my wrist fell forward, their silver clasps clinking lightly. "You're not just Eric de Vries, generically wealthy Harvard graduate. You're Eric *de Vries*, as in *De Vries Shipping*, heir to one of the largest companies on the planet. Have I got that right?"

Again, that shrug. A tacit denial of my utter shock. It was a nonverbal form of gaslighting, and it had *never* ceased to infuriate me.

"It's just a name," he said.

I scowled. "You don't need to act like I only found out you drink whole milk instead of two percent, Mr. First-in-Line. It's *not* just a name. And we're not talking a few measly million, are we? We're talking, shit, we're talking Jackson Anderson-levels of cash, aren't we? As much as Brandon, even?"

Again, that stupid shrug. Now I wanted to punch him on that razor-cut jaw of his.

"*More?*" I demanded, though the word was faint. "How—how much?"

Eric expelled a long sigh. "Jane, you can look up this information easily on *Forbes* or *WSJ*."

"Yeah, but I want to hear it from the super-rich horse's mouth. How much does it cost to buy eternal playboy Eric de Vries with a sweet church wedding?"

His eyes shot up, nearly black—whether from the insinuation or the challenge, I wasn't sure. "Seventeen billion dollars." The words escaped between clenched teeth.

*What?* I tried to speak, but all that came out was a choked squawk like a dying turkey and a spray of coffee. Eric dabbed at the mess with distaste, but relaxed once he was sure nothing had marred his pristine clothes. Then he just sat there, a solid statue next to my quivering ball of shock, waiting patiently for me to process the magnitude of the numbers. All seventeen billion of them.

"Good God, you're really not just a random rich kid," I finally managed after coughing twice more. "You're a fucking dynasty." I looked up in alarm. "But who requires a marriage contract to grant an inheritance? The Tudors? Is your grandmother completely batshit or only beginning her decline into dementia?"

"She's an old, rich, dying sociopath," Eric said dryly. "So, it pretty much amounts to the same thing. But it's not about the money. The firm's doing fine with Skylar and Kieran, it really is. I don't need or want to chair the board of directors of DVS."

"Okay," I said. "Then why do it? You already told your family where to stick it once before, though for what, I don't know. Why pander to this medieval bullshit? You don't even like these people."

It wasn't a story I knew a lot about, but I knew some. Something had happened that Eric couldn't forgive. He had lost someone, somehow. One of the many little pieces that had broken off his stalwart personality in the dead of night.

———

*"I NEVER THOUGHT I'd feel like this again," he said as he traced a finger around my cheek. "I never thought I'd ever have this again..."*

*We lay together in his bed, streams of moonlight through the blinds striping our bodies. Both of us glistened in the wake of pleasure, but my heartbeat picked up all over again. I didn't dare ask more. He never mentioned anything about his past. Ever.*

*"And I really never—" His hand dropped, but before he could pull it away, I captured it and pressed his palm against my cheek.*

*"Never what?" I asked. My voice was a breath. I was almost afraid to hear the answer.*

*Eric's eyes glossed, but they speared right through me. "Never thought it could be so much more."*

———

"I DON'T EVEN *KNOW* MOST of them," Eric agreed, yanking me out of the memory. "They are terrible people, all of them. But I don't think that means they should lose everything they have. No one deserves that."

He shrugged. Again. I wanted to smack him. Feigned nonchalance about something that arguably deserved more "chalance" than anything. He should have been the chalantest of chalant people right then. And yet he sat here, acting like his grandmother's ridiculous request was on par with taking out the trash or doing an extra load of dishes.

"Okay. I mean, it's your choice to sacrifice five years of your life, I guess. But...how come you never told me before that you were the crown prince of New York City? Jesus Christ, Eric. You once invited me home to meet these people. Were you ever going to tell me who they really were?"

One more shrug. I scowled.

"I would have gotten around to it," he replied. "But who they are didn't matter then. It matters now."

"Honestly, Petri. I feel like I never even knew you." It was meant as a joke, but the words didn't hit as lightly as I wanted. Maybe because they echoed the moment when things really ended before.

———

*"I FEEL like I never knew you at all."*

*I stared at the red panties dangling from my index finger. They* were thin, polyester. Lined with lace that had a few threads of over-stretched elastic fraying off the edges.

"Jane. It's not—it's not what you think. Those were from before you and I—"

"You and I what, huh? Before you and I split up for the nineteenth time this summer? Or got back together for the twentieth? Before what, Petri dish?"

Eric's face clouded with a look that normally would have portended me on my knees, arms tied behind my back, within the next five seconds. But my face must have said something very different, because the ferocity disappeared, leaving only irritation.

"I said, don't call me that," was all he replied.

"If the shoe fits again, might as well put it back on, don't you think?"

"I don't even know what that means, Jane."

"It means you've been a whore since I met you. A tiger doesn't change his stripes. A rose is still a rose by any other name. Pick your fucking cliché; it all means the same thing. People don't change."

I hurled the underwear at him, and the stupid ass didn't even move, just let the cheap, faux-satin smack him in the face before it fell back from whence it came: Eric's immaculate white sheets. He stared at the lingerie for a long time, but when he looked up, that mask had resumed its place. The mask that made him look like he didn't care. Like nothing mattered. Like everything wrong in the world could slide right off his golden shoulders.

I turned around so he couldn't see the sheen covering my eyes.

"Well, how's this for another cliché?" he asked as I shoved my things back into my overnight bag. "Takes one to know one. Right, pretty girl? After all, it was maybe one week ago that I found you with another man. How long had we been broken up, Jane? Five minutes?"

I straightened and pulled my bag over my shoulder, willing myself not to cry as he invoked the name. That name. The one that meant, in no uncertain terms, that I belonged to him.

*Except right now, it went the other way. Right now, it meant I belonged to...no one? Everyone?*

*I swiped under my eyes before turning back around. No man had ever been worth my tears before—this one certainly wasn't.*

*I stared at the panties: gauche, bright, plasticine. Eric was as tall and stolid as ever, arms crossed and head tipped with that subtle superiority that made me want to punch him in his stoic, straight nose. My heart turned to stone.*

*"Key words: broken up," I said as calmly as I could. "I never did this to you. I never did it, and I never would."*

*His condescension dropped along with his arms, and apologies flew from his mouth, a tumble of anger and sorrow and frustration that were so unlike his normal collected self. But I didn't stop to listen. My heart was already out the door.*

---

I SIGHED. I didn't really want to think about that pair of red panties in his bed. God, I really hated that word. It was worse than slacks. *Panties.* Panties were different than underwear. Underwear was what I wore. It was cotton, comfortable, made for normal people who didn't want to pick fabric floss out of their ass every ten seconds. *Panties* came in all the colors of the rainbow—or my hair. They came in lace, satin, polyblend spiderwebs that itched and pinched so you could look the perfect picture of a male fantasy. Trussed and tied up for *his* pleasure—certainly not yours.

I knew we weren't technically together at the time. We weren't official like that ever, just people who fucked on weekends. And talked a lot. And maybe even considered moving back to Boston to be together. But that shit still hurt, and at the time, I didn't really care that it made me a hypocrite. It hurt that it wasn't my underwear I found. It hurt that I was no longer the only girl he had ever brought back to his place. And it hurt even more because the other girl he did bring back wore fucking *panties.*

I realized, in that moment, just how easily Eric de Vries could hurt me. And I promised he would never, ever do it again.

"You knew me better than anyone, Jane." Eric's words were frank and open. Disarming.

I blinked. "Did I?"

He nodded. "By a long shot."

I sipped my coffee, looking for something beneath his words. But there was nothing but honesty in those deep gray eyes.

"Which is why," he continued, "I'm hoping you'll be the one to do it."

I frowned. "The one to do what?"

Carefully, he set down his cup, folded his hands on the table, and looked straight at me. "The one who'll marry me."

I sat back, suddenly confused. Okay, not just confused. Fucking bewildered. Flabbergasted. Bamboozled. And every other weird, old-fashioned word that would explain just how crazy disorienting it was to hear *those* words coming out of *his* mouth. After that entire story, somehow, I'd missed one central piece. That he was actually sitting there, wanting my help to fulfill the terms of this ridiculous contract. Eric de Vries was asking me to marry him.

"It was five years ago," Eric continued. "We were stupid twentysomethings. The timing was off. Now, we've grown up, become more accomplished, and there's nothing keeping you from coming back to Boston and marrying me."

"Wait, wait, wait...you're asking *me* to be your...bride?"

The statement was so preposterous that I immediately burst out laughing and collapsed on the table so loudly that a number of passersby startled. Eric just sat like a statue, rubbing his brow, which only made me laugh harder.

"Me?" I repeated between gulps of breath, though I was nowhere near done laughing. "Marry you? Playboy, consummate-bachelor, super-bro lawyer, and soon-to-be shipping magnate *you*? You don't even believe in marriage!"

It was the one thing we'd always had in common. I believed in marriage. Just not for me. And Eric felt the same. We were birds of a feather that way. We knew ourselves well enough to know that regardless of what others did, neither of us was ever going to be the type that could be with someone forever.

Eric checked his watch. "We've been over this. I do now. I have to."

"Still, even if you wanted to have a sham marriage and fuck around like other men of your 'station,' those men don't marry women like me. They marry the 'ee'-girls."

He quirked a brow. "'Ee'-girls?"

I snarked. "Yeah. Future Stepford wives. The ones whose names all end with the sound 'ee.' Lindsay. Katie. Sherry. Laurie. They have black Amex cards and love their pearl necklaces—and I don't mean the dirty kind. Well, not unless you give them some Tiffany's first. Then you'll get a nice, prim BJ before they let you come all over their surgically perfected tits."

Eric didn't reply, just crossed his arms and listened. I ignored the way the movement made his forearms flex under his rolled sleeves. What did he do, bicep curls while he gave his opening statements? No lawyers were that fit.

"And you...you want to take me, confrontational, unfiltered, half-Korean, candy-haired *me*, home to *marry*?" Now I was crying, and I had to take off my glasses to wipe away the tears and keep them from spoiling my eyeliner. "Oh, God," I creaked. "Oh, God, that's good. Can you imagine it? They'll think I'm a mail-order bride. I'd be the end of your poor grandmother. Your uptight family would *freak!*"

When I finally stopped crying-laughing, Eric had a very satisfied look on his face. He leaned over the table, bending down so we were eye to eye, then reached out and twirled a strand of my newly dyed locks around his finger. The tug pinched slightly, sending a current of something other than mirth down my spine.

"That's kind of the point...pretty girl."

That shut me up. "What?"

Eric smiled, and it was the first time I had seen that *panty*-kryptonite in five years. Good God, I'd nearly forgotten that curious, bright smile that transformed his face from someone average and almost plain into someone who could get into any girl's pants in a matter of minutes. Sweet and full, but with an impish edge that let you know he was completely capable of trouble. It had worked on me plenty of times in the past. Hell, it was working on me right then. *Shit*.

He leaned even closer so I could smell again that intoxicating combination of cologne and fresh linen. Like a magnet, I couldn't help but mirror the action until we were almost nose to nose. *Pretty girl*. How long since I had heard that?

"It'll be mutually beneficial," he said as he dropped my hair and took my hand. "Jane, you're the only one who could make it bearable."

His fingers were long, and a few more memories flashed through my head of the things I knew he could do with them. He curled two into my palm and applied just a bit of pressure like he used to some-where...*else*. Hot damn, Batman.

"I can save my family's fortune and stick it to my grandmother at the same time," he said. "What's not to like about that?"

"Right. Well. As funny as the Christmas cards will be, I'm not sure I want to be a tool for you to engage in some delayed teenage revenge," I said, transfixed by the way his thumb pressed into my finger pads, one at a time. "What's—what's in it for me?"

"Twenty million dollars."

I froze. "Come again?"

Eric replaced my hand on the tabletop and sat back, crossing his arms once more with a satisfied half smile. The action made his biceps bulge. Lord above.

"Twenty million dollars," he enunciated. "You move back to the East Coast. We get married. You live with me for five years. That's it."

I grimaced. "How romantic."

"None of this is romantic. That's also the point. I don't need someone who is going to get attached, Jane, who thinks I'm her knight in shining armor. I need someone who knows the score. Who knows exactly what kind of person I am."

"You mean the fact that you're a heartless bastard?" I shook my head. I really had no filter around the man, for better or for worse.

But his face remained immovable. "I wouldn't call it that," he said softly. "But...sure. Someone who knows what I'm capable of and what I'm not." He nodded, agreeing with his own words. "And at the end of five years, you walk away with twenty million to do whatever the fuck you want. Practice law or don't. Design clothes. Open up that shop you used to dream about."

My jaw dropped. I hadn't thought about that pipe dream for a *very* long time. I was honestly shocked he even remembered.

Eric took a drink of his coffee, scowled, and set it back down. Clearly it was not up to Mr. Fresh-Roasted Beans's impeccable standards. Then he folded his hands on the table and fixed me with another one of those deep gray, infuriatingly unreadable stares.

"Come on, Jane...say what you want, but you and I always did have a good time."

For once in my life, I was speechless. I had literally nothing to say. It was ridiculous. I couldn't just up and move my life. I had friends. Family. *Family who drive you crazy*, my subconscious reminded me. Since my father had died, my mother was close to sending me to the funny farm.

The fact that Chicago never really seemed to fit, even though I grew up and went to college here, wasn't helping. My best friends lived in Boston. Who were my friends here? A hairdresser I saw every six weeks and some work acquaintances I no longer worked with? I'd been too focused on my career to be that social beyond a one-night stand. Or twenty.

And now...what career? *You just got canned, you idiot, and you owe hundreds of thousands of dollars that you have no idea how to pay off.*

"Jane?" Eric said, pulling me out of my sudden panic.

I looked up, filled with surprise at my own conclusions. This was crazy. I couldn't really be considering this. Could I?

"Well?" Eric looking more nervous than I'd ever seen him. And that was counting when, ironically, he also asked me to meet his family as his then-girlfriend. Talk about blowing us both out of the water. "What do you think?"

I downed the rest of my coffee, wishing that it were laced with something stronger. Then I opened my mouth, prepared to say, "Absolutely not, you can take your weird fake-marriage and go fuck yourself." That even if I could use that money to pay off my loans and so much more, nothing was worth sacrificing my dignity and driving myself crazy by being married to *Eric* for five whole years. Petri dish. A penis in a suit. No.

But sometimes, we surprise even ourselves.

"I'll think about it," I said instead of "hell fucking no." "I'm due for a trip to Boston anyway. Give me a week, and I'll tell you then."

# THREE

"I still don't understand. Why do you have to go to Boston now? You have to find a job, Jane. You have to work."

I swiped another three dresses off the rack behind my mother's couch and tossed them on top of the suitcases. I flipped through the other clothes that had been hanging there since I'd had to vacate my apartment. Almost all of them were black, with a few red, and a couple olive green pieces. None were particularly nice, with the exception of one red and black number I got a few years back. I stared at it for a moment. I'd received it by virtue of association when I attended a gala with Skylar and Brandon. My one brush with the world of the rich and famous.

Eric had gone too. The look on his face when I walked out wearing it flashed through my memory. He didn't need to *say* "pretty girl" in that moment, but his expression had told me exactly what I could expect later that night.

I left the dress on the rack.

I grabbed two other dresses that were acceptable and tossed them on the pile, suddenly in a hurry. I *really* needed to see my best friend right now. So much that I didn't really care if I was maxing out the last of my credit card to do it. Skylar's curt, cut-through-the-bullshit sensibility was exactly what the doctor ordered.

It had been three days since the chat on the sidewalk. Three days since Eric had stared at my mouth, making small talk for another thirty minutes before he went back to Boston. Three days of nothing but one short message asking when I thought I'd be coming to town to discuss the "agreement."

Like it was a real estate transaction, not a marriage proposal.

"I need a nicer shoe to go with these," I muttered to myself. Then, finally, I turned around to where my mother stood on the other side of the couch, glaring at the contents of my suitcase. "*Eomma*, do you have a pink heel that would go with my hair?"

The glare lifted to me, and I swear, if I hadn't already been wearing glasses to protect me from her death rays, she might have straight-up turned me to salt. I was pretty certain at one point that my mother was part basilisk. It was a little eerie, reading about the giant snake in *Harry Potter* that could kill people with a glance and being reminded of my mother's formidable stare. Harry Potter beat the snake, but could he have beat Yu Na Lee? Hard to say.

"Okay, okay," I said to the suitcase when she didn't reply. "No pink heels. Message received. I'll check out The Garment District when I get to Boston."

"Jane!"

I turned around again. "What? You *do* have a pink heel? *Eomma*, make up your mind. My flight's tomorrow."

With that, she flew into a rush of Korean, of which she was fully aware I could understand about one word in ten. My Korean was never that great—especially since Dad never learned it either. You just don't pick up the family lingo in quite the same way when no one speaks it in the house unless they're angry, but you do learn the classics. Especially when they are aimed at you on a regular basis.

"*Eomma*, slow down," I said as I folded my clothes into the suitcase. "You're going to give yourself a heart attack. What is wrong? Why is it such a big deal that I'm leaving right now? We've been at each other's throats since my lease expired, and literally *all* you've been talking about is how much you need space. I would have thought you'd be jumping at the chance to be rid of me."

"What's wrong?" she demanded with a face flushed beneath the mask of makeup she wore daily. "Four days you been with no job. One month you been on my couch. Now you show up yesterday with hair like a lollipop, and you're packing your bags. What are you trying to do to me?"

I rolled my eyes. Leaving the cap off the toothpaste. Forgetting to turn off the lights in the kitchen. My mother talked about everything like it was a life-or-death situation. Yu Na lived like a soap opera heroine, and without my father to calm her down, the habit had gotten worse.

I turned around. "*Eomma*, it's *my* hair. It's *my* life. Why is this about what I'm doing to you?"

"Because it is embarrassing, that's why! It was bad enough when you were younger, coming home with ripped jeans and spiky hair. Bad enough you had to ruin good clothes from Macy's or dye your hair like crayons. But I think, she will grow out of it. My Jane will grow up, like her mother and dad taught her the right way to be. And it took you a long time, but you did. Finally. Now...you are almost thirty, Jane. Too old for pink hair and running away!"

Self-consciously, I touched the messy bun piled on the top of my head. I had my mother's hair color—black-brown—but whereas hers was straight, mine was unruly unless I took the time to dry it properly. She made it sound like I looked homeless with this hair color, but in all fairness, I hadn't done it yet this morning. Like her, I wasn't usually one to step outside without makeup and a nicely coiffed head. I was the daughter of an esthetician, after all. And it was just eight in the morning. I hadn't even had coffee.

"The hair looks fabulous," I informed her for the tenth time since she'd seen it. "And since, as you remind me, I *am* almost thirty, I'll wear it any way I damn well please. Just like I'll get a job when I'm good and damn ready, and I'll visit my friends whenever I damn well like. Without my mommy's damn permission!"

"How do you talk to your mother like that? Damn this, damn that. Where is the respect?" She tossed her hands up toward the ceiling. "What am I going to tell my friends? They ask about you all the time. They say, Jane, is she married yet? No, she don't have a boyfriend, so how can she be married? But I tell them, she has a good job. A lawyer in the city. Now you don't have that. No money. No apartment. What do you have now? Pink hair and a bunch of ugly black clothes, sleeping on your mother's couch. What kind of life is that?"

I threw a pair of gladiator sandals into the suitcase a little harder than necessary. I really, *really* needed to get out of this apartment. I would have stayed with my cousin in Albany Park, but her spare room was now occupied by a baby. Everyone really *was* growing up. Except me.

"That's enough, *Eomma*. If I want to be berated by your friends, I'll play *godori* with you guys or watch the soaps with Jiyeon. I'm going to live my life the way *I* want. So kindly can it, or butt the hell out."

When I turned back around, my mother was gawking at me like I'd just told her to lick a toilet seat.

"What," she said, "would your *father* say to that?"

*Easy now, Plain Jane. You know how she gets.*

And there it was. I knew it would happen sooner or later—the constant reminder that now, in death, my father was likely ashamed of me. That in these moments, it was up to me, not her to assert control. That he knew I could do better.

His memory had been urging me to take care of her, to *manage* this situation since he died. Though my mother had no problem invoking his memory when it suited her inconsistent arguments, the reality was that her worries extended beyond my life to hers as well.

See, we learned a lot from Dad's death.

Lesson One: VA psychologists don't make much. And Dad only had a measly pension and never took out a life insurance policy.

Lesson Two: It's a lot harder to get a job when you're fifty-three than twenty-one. And most nail salons weren't interested in hiring an out-of-practice esthetician with a lapsed license. Getting work took my mother a while.

Lesson Three: The house in Evanston was worth a lot more than when my parents originally bought the place in 1980-something. And that, unfortunately, came with property taxes that my mother couldn't afford, especially on top of the lavish funeral she insisted on having. The sale of the house covered the funeral, this small apartment in Skokie, and enough for her to grieve for about six months before she had to go back to painting nails for a living. Reality came for her too. There was no way around it—my mother was bitter.

It didn't help that on top of being the provider, Daddy was also the peacemaker between *Eomma* and me. The diffuser between two women with opposite values and identical tempers. He loved us both and had made it possible for us to tolerate each other.

Not anymore.

*Just walk away, peanut. You know she doesn't mean what she says.*

"Daddy would probably tell me to ignore you," I shot back. "Which is exactly what I'm going to do. In Boston." I finished zipping up the bag with a flourish and stood up. "I'm going to take a shower, and then I'm going out. And when I'm done, you and I are *not* going to talk about this again."

"Why?" Like a jumping flea with coral lipstick, she followed me into the kitchen. "Why do you have to go to Boston *now*, Jane? You need a job! You need a place to live! It makes no sense when you have no prospects."

For a second, I almost told her. Just to get her off my back. Just to see her head explode in surprise confetti of dyed-black hair and rouged cheeks when I broke the news that not only did I have a prospect, but he was probably the best goddamn prospect in the entire world.

For three nights, I had considered Eric's indecent proposal. But I still didn't know what to do. I needed the person who cut through the shit in my life like I did for her. I needed to look my best friend in the face and ask her what she thought about this bullshit, especially since it was coming from someone she also knew very well. Eric was her friend and her business partner. Skylar would tell me the truth.

*So then why fight, kiddo? Jane Brain, you're better than this.*

It wasn't fair. I knew that. I couldn't have this fight with my mother if she didn't know everything. But I couldn't tell her. Not yet. Part of me didn't want to know what she would say. On the one hand, she might jump for joy. After all, who wouldn't want her daughter to marry into obscene wealth, especially when the both of us were dealing with our fair share of money issues? But on the other hand, she might be ashamed. It was bad enough that I acted absolutely nothing like an ideal Korean daughter would. I wasn't sweet. I wasn't obedient. And I wasn't quiet.

Acerbic. Discordant. Loud.

Disappointment. That was me.

*Let's not play that game, Jane Brain. Your mom loves you. She just doesn't know how to show it.*

How many times had I heard my dad say that? Guilt squeezed my stomach. But it still came back to the same conclusion: what would Yu Na Lee Lefferts think of her daughter selling five years of her life for twenty million dollars? Just how shamed would she feel?

I stood there for a minute, staring at the contents of her fridge. Leftover rice. Three types of kimchi. Cheap cuts of chicken for two. She bought for both of us now, not just herself. My anger faded.

I turned around and surprised my mother when I wrapped her in a hug and kissed the top of her head like she was the child, and I was the parent.

"Jane!" she squawked, but her squawk was laced with love.

I released her. "It's just a week, *Eomma*, and then I'll be back. I have a Harvard law degree and five years at the Cook County State's Attorney's office behind me. I'll figure something out, I promise."

Slowly, while I held onto her short, squat body, the sharpness in my mother's face softened too.

"Okay," she relented. "But you shower and fix your makeup, okay? You look like one of those people in the circus with that hair." She picked up my hand and clucked her tongue as she examined my nails. "And before you go, I'll give you a manicure."

# FOUR

I magine my surprise when I walked out of Logan arrivals the
next morning to see a tall drink of water in a Tom Ford suit
waiting in front of baggage claim. Imagine my further surprise
when he presented me with an emerald-cut diamond ring and a
blood red rose to go with it. Five different women gasped, and at least
one squealed like *Babe* the pig.

"Get off your knees, you asshole," I said before his knee even
touched the dirty airport floor.

Eric smirked. "That happy to see me, huh?"

"Are you really that desperate for me to say yes? What do I look
like, a Hallmark heroine? Stop that, Petri, you'll ruin your suit."

Eric rose with a cheeky grin that bewildered our audience. "I'm
offended. I came here like a gentleman to give my maybe-fiancée a
ride." He fingered the still-open box in his hand. "You might as well
take this."

I ignored him as we made our way through Logan. "You know I
hired a shuttle to take me to Brookline, right?" I held up my phone
app, already ready. "You owe me twenty-five dollars. Stopping at ten
houses on my way to Skylar's isn't cheap, you know."

"You're so sentimental," Eric remarked drily, though he did what I said. He flipped me two twenties, which I snatched.

"I can be sentimental," I retorted. "Just not with garbage manipulation. Did you really think I was just going to hand you five years of my life with that trite little stunt?"

"If you had, I probably would have taken it back."

I rolled my eyes. "Games, games. You're an asshole, you know that?" Eric just laughed.

"Now, get rid of that," I told him, waving away the tiny velvet box containing something that sparkled under the fluorescent lights. "And toss that rose in the trash."

He dropped the rose in a bin as we passed, but tucked the box into his jacket pocket.

"Don't pretend like you're not a sap at heart, Petri," I said as I followed him out to the curb, where a Town Car was waiting for us, rumbling beside a grouchy police officer. "I've seen all those poetry books in your bedroom."

"I'll never be ashamed of being well-read, pretty girl," he said with a sideways grin. "Especially considering how much you used to like those books too."

———

*Now I am all*
*One bowl of kisses,*
*Such as the tall*
*Slim votaresses*
*Of Egypt filled*
*For a God's excesses.*

*I lift to you*
*My bowl of kisses,*
*And through the temple's*

*Blue recesses*
*Cry out to you*
*In wild caresses.*

*And to my lips'*
*Bright crimson rim*
*The passion slips,*
*And down my slim*
*White body drips*
*The shining hymn.*

*And still before*
*The altar I*
*Exult the bowl*
*Brimful, and cry*
*To you to stoop*
*And drink, Most High.*

*Oh drink me up*
*That I may be*
*Within your cup*
*Like a mystery,*
*Like wine that is still*
*In ecstasy.*

*Glimmering still*
*In ecstasy,*
*Commingled wines*
*Of you and me*
*In one fulfil*
*The mystery.*

ERIC CLAPPED *the book shut and tossed it to the ground before turning to me with satisfaction. And it was well-earned. I was speechless.*

*"Lawrence," he said as he drifted a hand over my collarbone.*

*"Wow," I said. "I never knew...I mean, you hear the shit college students write in their creative writing classes—"*

*"Hey, I was one of those college students once."*

*"Of course you were, Eric. Of course you spent your time in college swimming in bullshit verses instead of studying econ like a good boy. What? Playboy wasn't good enough for you?"*

*"Poetry," he said, "is better than porn. It's nothing if not erotica. The rhythm." Kiss. "The play." Kiss. "The tension." He delivered two slow, deliberate kisses along my collarbone. I couldn't help it. I arched toward them.*

*A finger drifted down my sternum, playing between my breasts and down my stomach.*

*"We make poetry all the time," he whispered as he watched his finger's progress. "You and me. You are this bowl of kisses, and look at me. Filling you up." His hips thrust lightly toward me, reminding me of how many times he had done just that.*

*I peeked up at him. "You are so gooey."*

*He just licked his lips, then leaned down, and with his tongue, followed the path his fingers had started.*

*"I don't think so, pretty girl," he said. "Just ready to fill you with kisses again."*

———

A CHILL SLID over the back of my neck as the echo of the verse faded. It felt now, as it had for years, that those kinds of moments had always been for his pleasure, not mine, no matter how much I loved them at the time. At one point, I had thought they were the only way Eric could ever say how he felt, and how I could bear to hear it. But now...well, I knew just what kind of heartless bastard he really was. Cool. Calculated. A complete asshole.

Eric de Vries was about as sentimental as a colonoscopy. I needed to remember that.

"Where to?" he asked as he shut the car door behind us.

My thigh tingled when his hand brushed it.

"Where else?" I asked as I stared out the window, dearly needing the grounding of the blasé gray exterior of the airport. "Your office. I need to see Skylar."

––––––––

"THIS IS INSANE."

An hour and a half later, Eric and I sat in front of Skylar Crosby's desk, looking at each other like a pair of naughty teenagers who had been sent to the principal's office.

Skylar had a way of making people feel like idiots. Imperious—I'd heard more than one person call her that when she was out of earshot, and it served her very well as a family law specialist. After we finished law school, she began as a divorce attorney and soon after started her own shop with Eric and another shark, Kieran Beckford. Skylar didn't put up with anyone's shit. Ever.

"But—but—you *hate* each other!" she exploded like a sputtering, redheaded teapot. "I've barely been able to get the two of you in the same room for five fucking years! Eric, anytime I bring up Jane's name, you change the subject. You say you have plans. Last time we invited you both to dinner, you literally booked a trip to London for the weekend just to get out of it."

Eric raised a finger, but Skylar cut him off. "Eric, I heard your assistant making the travel reservations, you idiot. It was *after* I asked!"

I snorted, but she immediately swiveled to me.

"And *you*! You *still* call him Petri dish because you think he's such a manwhore! How many variations on that nickname do you have for him, Jane? Ten? Twenty?"

"Thirty-four," I whispered, earning a curious look from Eric.

"Exactly!" Skylar practically shouted. She took some deep breaths while the color of her face faded from a tomato-red to a more normal flesh tone.

"I don't hate her, Crosby," Eric said mildly. "I'd hardly have asked her to marry me if I did."

"Sky, I'd probably marry an *actual* Petri dish for twenty million dollars, and so would you, so wipe that judgmental smirk off your face," I added. Her indignance made me want to grab that ring out of Eric's pocket and shove it on just to piss her off again.

"I'm not judging—"

"You're *totally* judging," I snapped. "You're Judge Judy. I feel like I'm on an episode of *Night Court* with a very special message at the end. And I'm over it. Eric and I are grown adults who both think the institution of marriage is an antiquated sham." I turned to find Eric fighting a smirk. "Right, test tube?"

He shrugged as if I hadn't addressed him like another lab experiment. "Sure."

"So, then. He's asked me a question. I just have to decide if I want to help him game the system for a few years." Again, his face flickered to mine mischievously. It made me want to smack him and kiss him at the same time. "Lab rat, can I screw who I want?"

Infuriatingly, his jaw didn't drop. In fact, he showed no signs that the question—or the name—bothered him at all. Fucker.

"So long as we keep it on the down-low, sure, why not? We can sleep with whomever we want," he replied, though that half grin reappeared. The subtext was clear: *including each other*. Well, Eric had another thing coming. That smug sonofabitch wasn't getting anywhere near my magic garden.

"And at the end?" I prodded. "It's done? We both walk away, clean and simple?"

Eric nodded. "We'll be like roommates," he said. "And at the end of a five-year lease, you'll be free."

"Except you'll have a *baby* to take care of," Skylar inserted. "Did you ever think of that?"

"She just said I have to stay married long enough to procreate," Eric said. "She never said it had to happen."

"And you think your grandmother is going to be okay with that?" she asked.

"Honestly, Cros, she'll probably be dead before it's an issue," Eric said, and it was hard not to flinch at the chill in his voice.

I swallowed. "What the prodigal son here is trying to say, is that no one is having any babies. So, let's not count chickens, all right?"

"It sounds like you've already talked yourself into this," Skylar huffed.

Eric turned to me, victorious. I just glared at him.

"Not at all," I said, enjoying the way his triumph faded. If he thought he had me wrapped up, he could think again. "I'm just trying to get my bases covered. Know what I'm *really* deciding to do."

"Well, I think you're both idiots. Getting married for twenty million dollars. Who does that?"

"Give me a break," I retorted. "Don't pretend like you didn't win the jackpot with Brandon."

Eric snorted. Brandon Sterling was worth at least a few billion and adamantly refused any sort of prenup when he married Skylar. The hilarious thing was that he married the one person who would probably hurl all his money to the bottom of Boston Harbor if she could. I had a front-row seat to that shitshow when it first started. Skylar slapped him exactly three separate times—once because he tried to surprise her with a trip to Paris. My friend was amazing, but she had some serious issues with money, despite now having gobs of it.

"You know that Brandon's money had *nothing* to do with why I married him," she snapped, understandably defensive. That was an accusation she'd never totally be rid of. You don't go from being a garbage collector's daughter to the wife of one of the richest men in New England without people throwing around the term "gold digger" behind your back.

I shrank, feeling appropriately guilty. "Sorry, Sky. You're right."

Part of me wondered if I should insist again that Eric do this with one of the unnamable girls who would probably drop everything in their silicone-lifted lives to pretend to be his wife. This wasn't me. I had watched my friend struggle to adapt to the world of the ultra-rich. It had made her a target, and it was really only after she and Brandon had both withdrawn from it that they found calm and happiness together.

But she had also never worried about where she was going to live. She had coasted through school on the money her mother had left in a trust. Skylar had been raised by humble people, but she'd never been in a situation like mine where she had to make a choice out of real necessity, not just personal desire.

The student loan statements in my purse suddenly felt like they weighed several pounds. So did the very low balance of my mother's bank account.

A large hand landed over mine on the chair arm. Eric didn't say anything, his face as unreadable as ever. But his thumb stroked lightly over my knuckles, offering a smidge of...what? Comfort? Foreplay? Manipulation?

I pulled my hand away.

"Look, Sky," I said, with an edge I couldn't quite hide. We'd been in this office for over an hour now, going round and round while Skylar poked and prodded and cross-examined everything about the arrangement. I was done. "We didn't come here to ask your permission, and I haven't made a decision. I just wanted your advice on the prenup, all right?"

"My *advice* is that you need to walk the fuck away." Skylar shook her head, sending a few strands of bright orange hair into her face. "Do you...Janey, I'm sorry, but I have to ask. Do you *really* think this is appropriate given everything you've been through this year?"

I stiffened. God, if it wasn't my mother bringing up his memory, it was my best friend. What happened to letting the dead rest?

*The dead are never gone, Jane Brain.*

Eric turned. "What is she talking about?"

I couldn't meet his eyes. "My dad passed. About nine months ago."

All levity vanished. "Ah, shit. Jane, I'm sorry. I didn't know."

"No, you wouldn't have, so really, don't worry about it." My words were fast. Too fast. And because I had no desire to see anything resembling kindness on Eric's smug face, I glared at Skylar. "And it *was* nine months ago, so it's not like I'm wearing black out of mourning, Sky. This isn't a snap decision out of grief."

"But—"

"Goddammit, Mr. Rooney, are you going to be my lawyer or not?"

Skylar's green eyes blazed. "*What* did you just call me?"

Eric snorted, but passed it off as a cough. I smirked. With her red hair, bullet-sharp gaze, and sanctimonious attitude, Skylar totally resembled the principal from *Ferris Bueller's Day Off*. It was one of my better nicknames, especially since she was lecturing us like we were errant teenagers.

"We could go with Principal McGee," Eric suggested. "I think she had red hair too, Cros."

"Oh, *Grease*. Yeah, I see it," I said as we both appraised Skylar, who was starting to resemble a tomato again. "I could get you your own xylophone to play on your voicemail too, Sky."

"Is going back to Anne of Green Gables too easy?" Eric offered. "You mentioned that the other day, but I don't think she was ever a principal. Was she?"

"Why, Eric," I said as he turned to me. I tugged on my thick, multi-colored braid. "I didn't know you were so well-read in tween girls' fiction."

"I have a cousin. We were bored stiff at the Vineyard one summer."

Eric's eyes twinkled with each traded barb. This kind of back-and-forth was never our problem—we always had it in spades, even if he ended up the butt of my jokes. And then he'd repay me, tenfold.

I couldn't lie. I'd been thinking about it since the second I ran into him outside the salon. The strange thing about Eric and me wasn't just that neither of us seemed to have a problem coming back for more (when we were easily bored with other partners). It was also the way certain...tastes...came out when we were together.

He said he wasn't a dom, but he sure acted like one sometimes. And I'd never call myself a submissive, but something about Eric made me want to prostrate myself on the floor. Like it or not, Eric was the closest thing I'd ever had to a real relationship. Otherwise, sex was a long series of one-night stands. Men who wanted to believe I loved them for a night before they took what they wanted and let me take mine too. Fun, sure, but shallow, and not exactly the stuff dreams were made of.

It took exactly one night after a long day of studying before Eric and I were doing things together neither of us had ever done before. Maybe it was the stress of the bar exam. Maybe it was three years of tension between us. But the second he called me *pretty girl*, it was like a direct line to my G-spot. I wanted him to gag me. Bind me. Fill my mouth with something besides insults. He knew it too, and more than that, he *liked it*.

You don't get to that point with a one-night stand. Though I'd tried a few times, I'd never been able to find it again. Someone who knew how to bring that out of me. Who knew how to take what he wanted and take care of mine too.

Eric winked. That gleam was back, though not as bright as I remembered. I shifted in my seat—my thighs were getting a little damp and tight underneath my black mini skirt. This was supposed to be strictly business. Purely platonic. A marriage of convenience.

Except. Eric crossed his legs, and the fabric of his Italian-cut pants pressed over powerful thighs and a bulge that looked a little bigger than was strictly decent. Shit. He was feeling it too.

I shook my head. *Get a hold of yourself, you idiot.* Eric and I blurred the lines between love and hate too many times—that was, at its core, our biggest problem. It was a mistake I wasn't going to make again.

"I think I liked it better when you hated each other," Skylar grumbled, still annoyed by the mean principal comments and completely oblivious to the sexual tension that had just bloomed in her office.

"Cheese and *rice*, Sky, you're not talking us out of this!" I cried, more loudly than necessary, conveniently ignoring that I hadn't decided to do anything yet anyway. Hadn't I flown here for her honest opinion?

"Janey, I'm *not*. And obviously I'm going to serve as your legal counsel, so give me a dollar now so this conversation counts, all right? I'm going to make sure your prenup is iron clad so Grande Dame de Vries doesn't try to weasel out. If for some reason—and I think we know there are many—things don't last five years, you both need to have your dumb asses covered for even trying. A stepped payout scale, maybe."

I sighed. Yes, this is what I needed. Skylar's disturbingly practical mind. "I'm not deciding anything, so do what you think is right. I'm not sure I want to be judged for my poor decisions every step of the way. Otherwise, I'd hire my mother." Suddenly, I was exhausted by this conversation. By the idea of any of it.

Skylar just shook her head virulently. "I'm doing it, or else Kieran is." She shot Eric a knowing look. "Your choice, hot shot."

Eric blanched. I sympathized. Kieran was one of the scariest people on the planet.

"Fine, John Grisham," I said wearily. "You. Just try not to lord it over me too much, all right?"

"Good." Skylar held out her hand for the crumpled dollar I fished out of my purse. "I happily accept you as my client. Now please take my advice, and *don't do this*."

"Skylar!"

"Fine, fine." Skylar sat back, her hands held up in surrender. "I had to try. Now, two more things. If you do actually go through with this idiotic plan and don't make Jenny your flower girl, I'm going to throttle you both. And, Eric, I'm going to need to take Jane for lunch to harass her some more. Actually, I'm going to need the rest of the afternoon, so *you* get to take my appointment with George Barrett."

Eric groaned. "Skylar, come on. I took Kieran's meeting with him last month, and I had him the month before. I can't."

"Yes, you can," Skylar said as she grabbed her purse off the back of her chair. "You want me to get your messy marriage scheme figured out? I get to take the bride-to-be to lunch."

# FIVE

I woke up the next morning in the giant guest room in Brandon and Skylar's house in Brookline, with the pitter-patter of little feet serving as my alarm clock. Except they weren't really pitters or patters. They were quick, jerky taps up the hardwood stairs and down the hall, followed by loud, elephant-sized thumps. Brandon chasing Jenny, their daughter.

"Jen. *Jenny*. It's time to go, hon."

"No! I want to see Aunt Janey before she and Mama go to work!"

I pulled my sheets up to my chin and smiled. Jenny was basically a mini-me of Skylar—small, spunky, with bright red hair and a genetic ability to piss off her dad but command his devotion all the more for it. I loved my goddaughter to death, if only for her attitude.

She was *really* getting under his skin this morning, if his emerging South Boston accent was any indicator.

"Peanut, Jane's asleep. She was up way too late last night with your ma. It's time to go."

"No!"

*Come on, peanut. Up and at 'em.* I smiled, hearing my own dad's voice in the common nickname. It was from that, after all, that I'd acquired my penchant for them in the first place.

"Jenny, I'm not playin'. You need to get your ass downstairs in three...two..."

"Daddy." Her voice dropped to a near-whisper, but was still loud and clear. "You said *ass*."

I didn't have to be in the hall to imagine Brandon's face as his daughter corrected his language. The guy might have been a billionaire, but he had a mouth like a trucker from Dorchester, the neighborhood in the South End where he was born and raised. Brandon Sterling was as Boston as they came, but if you gave the guy a beer, or apparently, women in his life who pushed his buttons, he went from Ted Kennedy to Marky Mark faster than you could say "Red Sox."

"I said *arse*, Jen," he corrected her. "It's different."

"How is that diff'rent?" she asked in her tiny, four-and-a-half-year-old voice. "It sounds the same to me."

I snorted. When Brandon was stressed, the middle r's in his sentences basically disappeared, so "arse" really did almost sound like "ass" coming from him at the moment. Over the years, it sort of became a game for me and Skylar to see which of us could bring out that accent first. Skylar always won.

"Arse is British, pea," he said. "So, it's the fancy kind of ass."

"So, can I tell Teacher Mandy that *she's* an ass when she tells me to clean up the Pick-Up Stix?"

"Hell, no—I mean, heck, no, Jen. No!"

"Daddy!"

There was a bit of a scuffle, but I could tell by Jenny's tinkling laughter that she wasn't totally upset when Brandon picked her up, and from the sound of it, smothered his daughter in kisses.

"Don't tell your mother," he said. "Now come on, pea. I'll be right here when you get back."

I lay back into the pillows, listening as his footsteps and Jenny's giggles receded. The sounds were oddly familiar, taking me back years. Back to when my dad and I would share similar conversations.

When he'd be leaving on one of his many business trips, and I'd wrap myself around his ankle, letting him drag me across our long wood hallway as I clung to his leg, giggling helplessly while his laughter filled the air. I'd beg him to stay, and he'd promise me a treat—a sundae, a walk in the park, maybe even a movie. And he'd promise he'd be back. He'd always come back.

Until nine months ago, when he didn't. He'd left for his last appointment at the VA, collapsed on his desk, and ended up dying there before the EMTs even arrived.

*Peanut, you can't be worried about that now. It's the past, Jane Brain. Time to move on. Grow up.*

Christ, this really was one hell of a hangover. I usually kept those moments firmly shoved to the other, nonconscious side of my brain, but just then, they rang like a gong. Fuck. Lunch yesterday led to dinner that night with Skylar, Brandon, and their kids, which turned to another two bottles of wine after the little ones went to bed. I was pretty sure all of us were probably nursing substantial hangovers this morning, but I'd freely admit that I had easily consumed at least a bottle by myself. Anything to take the edge off the game of good cop, bad cop the Crosby-Sterlings played for three hours trying to convince me *not* to get married.

My headache surged. Raggedy Ann and Andy probably worked off their hangovers running around the nearby reservoir—both of them were exercise junkies. I had no such morning discipline.

My phone, plugged in on the nightstand, buzzed loudly while L.L. Cool J proceeded to shout "Mama Said Knock You Out" until I slapped a hand over the speaker and picked it up. I didn't even like that song, but since my mother hated all things rap and made a face like a screwed-up lemon when I told her about that one, it was only appropriate that I made it her ringtone. It was hilarious, really. Yu Na Lee Lefferts had no idea how appropriate a metaphor of boxing was for the way she'd been coaching me since I was little.

I rolled over. "*Eomma*, it's eight in the morning. What the what?"

"What the what the what? What does this mean, Jane?"

My mother's shrill voice screeched through the speaker, forcing me to hold the phone a solid four inches from my ear. Ten bucks said she had forgotten I was in Boston for the week already. She had been like this since Daddy died—scatterbrained and anxious. Without someone to fret over in her own home first thing in the morning, she had to transfer that nervous energy somewhere. And that somewhere was usually me.

"Where are you, Jane?" she demanded. "Four times I call you last night. Four times!"

Yep. Ten bucks some cosmic force was coming my way.

I set the phone on the bed and put her on speaker so I could cover my eyes with a pillow. "*Eomma*, I told you. Boston. Skylar. One week, remember?"

"Boston? You just saw Skylar two months ago. You need to come *home*."

I examined a pink strand of hair while my mother prattled on about how I never told her anything, why did I do this to her, did I expect her to follow me around everywhere...Yeah, I stopped listening pretty quickly.

"Jane? *Jane!*"

"*Eomma*, what?" I asked irritably, switching to my side and rubbing my forehead. The room was blurry, and my head throbbed. I had absolutely no desire to bicker with my mother this morning.

"You are almost thirty, Jane. Roaming the world is no good. Bad enough your father never got to see you have babies. How are you going to have any now when your eggs are dried up like raisins, eh?"

Good lord. Was the woman a witch? How the *hell* did she even know that was on the menu when I hadn't even mentioned the real reason I was here.

"*Eomma*, stop," I croaked, glad she couldn't see my face as I sat up and glared at the phone. "You act like I'm a decrepit old hag. I lost my job. I'm just taking some time to see friends and figure out what my next move is. Take a second to be free."

"Free? What does this mean, *free*? What man is going to want a girl with no home, no job, no nothing, huh? Are you going to travel like a gypsy? Is your man going to catch you in the air like a butterfly?"

"You mean like you?"

A thick silence dropped. Shit. I knew better than to reference her past life as a flight attendant. Flying made her think of Korea, and all the people she had left there to be with my dad. Who was now gone, leaving her alone with a recalcitrant, pink-haired daughter.

*Come on, pumpkin. Where's your compassion? For yourself too.*

"*Eomma*, I'm sorry," I said quickly. "I was wrong. Please forgive me." To show her I meant it, I repeated the three phrases in my halting Korean. I knew enough to kowtow to the Queen Bee. I knew enough to make amends.

The silence continued, and I waited with her, knowing that she would push until the last possible moment before finally:

"It was *my* husband that died, Jane."

I ground my teeth together. It always came back to this. Like she had some kind of monopoly over our grief because she was the wife, and I was only the daughter. Like I wasn't allowed to feel sad. I wasn't allowed to mourn.

"Well, he was *my* dad," I said. "For some people, that might count for more. Blood and all that."

*Jane.*

His voice was only a word, but his disapproving face appeared right in front of me. I smacked my forehead and closed my eyes.

Once again, there was a long silence. *Fuck.* I was an asshole. A real, bona fide asshole. They should give me a certificate.

"You need to come home," she said finally. "Be a good daughter for once."

I flopped back into the pillows. "*Eomma*, I'll be home when I'm home."

"No, Jane, you have to come *now*."

"No."

"Yes!"

"No!"

"*Yes!*"

"Why?!" I exploded. "I'm gone for a few days, and I obviously drive you crazy! Watch your soaps. Get your nails done. Play some cards. You could just en*joy* yourself, for Christ's sake. Tell me, why the hell is it so damn urgent that I come home right this very second?"

"Because I have something to tell you."

"Oh my God, then spit it out!" I shouted.

Silence. Nothing important to say, and she wouldn't shut the hell up. Something with legitimate gravity came along? Suddenly she was Fort Knox.

*Careful, peanut...*

"*Eomma*," I tried again. I leaned toward the phone, staring at it like it was a crystal ball that would reveal what in the fucklord's name she was trying to say. "Just tell me. What's so important?"

The babble returned. "I pray and I pray, and I don't care what they said, I have to tell you, you need to know...no, you need to come back, Jane. Come home. I will explain."

But I sat there, feeling crazy in the middle of these posh surroundings while the whole of me started to shake. This was crazy. *She* was crazy. There was something wrong with this woman, something that had broken in the last year, and now she was siccing her misery on me.

"Jane..."

Across the room, I stared at myself in the mirror. My hair was matted in the back, and I had dark circles under my eyes. Eyes that weren't deep brown like my mother's—or my father's blue—but something closer to hazel. I had always chalked that up to being mixed. *Hapa*, like some friends from Hawaii called themselves. But as I stared at my face—the nose that was a little too long, the lips that were a little too full, cheekbones that were a little too sharp—I searched for remnants of Carol Lefferts in my face. A telltale stamp that he had left behind.

And I found nothing.

"I don't have time to walk you through another breakdown, *Eomma*," I said with a mouth full of sandpaper.

"Jane. Come home. We will talk—"

"I'll see you in a week."

———

SKYLAR AND BRANDON were both gone by the time I padded downstairs. After spending most of the morning applying half-heartedly for jobs in Chicago (and perusing a few in Boston, and yeah, New York), I left the big house in Brookline and spent the rest of the afternoon poking around my old haunts in Boston, doing my best to ignore the decision I still had to make. I had coffee at Trident while I indulged in a novel (first one I'd read in years). Listened to the newest punk records at Newbury Comics, then took the Red Line to Porter Square and poked around some of the new boutiques that had appeared in the up-and-coming area. I visited Boston plenty, but I rarely had time to be alone here. I really did miss it.

Skylar and I met for drinks that evening, but I could tell she was in a hurry to get home to see her kids. I, however, still felt...restless. I wasn't ready to go back to the Mansion of Marital Bliss and melt into pea soup out of jealousy. So, when she returned to Brookline, I resumed my wandering of the city under the moonlight and the streetlamp light that bounced off the cobblestones.

Okay, yeah. So I *was* jealous. Maybe I was annoyed that now, when I was twenty-nine, I was basically in the same place I was five years ago. I sacrificed the last five years of my life doing what I was *supposed* to do. I put away baddies in the great city of Chicago. I was the do-gooder that Dad taught me to be. Like a superhero, I used my superhero powers (which came by way of a Harvard degree) for good.

But what had that gotten me? Five years later, I was jobless. Homeless. Futureless. And...fatherless.

I considered the warm house in Brookline. Brandon and Skylar had thrown themselves into building the kind of safe haven for their family that neither of them had growing up. They would let me stay there as long as I liked. But it wasn't *my* safe haven. It wasn't *my* family.

I kicked a stray rock as I meandered through Government Center. I had thought, for the longest time, that family wasn't in the cards for me. I was Jane. A weirdo. If some people marched to the beat of their own drum, I had my own damn orchestra. Family. Marriage. Commitment. Me and these things...we didn't get along.

Except once. Once I had considered it. Once I had thought that maybe, just *maybe*, I had met someone who didn't care that I had a tendency to speak before I thought. Eric had once made me feel like I was enough. Just me. Skin and angles. Big mouth, small tits. Spikes and high heels. Jane. Enough.

Until I wasn't.

A flash of red. Fake silk. White sheets. Eric's guilty face. My broken heart.

I turned to a shop window in Quincy Market and examined my reflection. I was casually dressed in jeans and my favorite black ankle boots, but my hair looked wild, a mane of color floating over the black and white polka-dotted top that spilled off one shoulder in a way that was very day-to-night. I pulled out my lipstick, drew on a fresh coat of red that matched my glasses frames, then blew myself a kiss in the window.

I had other ways of feeling like I was *enough*. I didn't need a man, or any other person for that matter, to make me feel valid. And if I had a restless itch, which seemed to be coming on tonight, I had ways of scratching it myself before going back to doing my favorite thing in life: whatever the hell I wanted.

# SIX

Don't ask me how I ended up in the North End that night. Also don't ask me if it was because a certain Alexander Skarsgard lookalike lived there. By the time I stumbled into Marleigh's, a lounge on the quieter end of Hanover Street, I'd already consumed three other gin and tonics at two other bars and had promised myself that if I didn't strike gold there, I was going home.

No one seemed right. No matter what, I couldn't break this damn streak. They were either too stupid or too stupid. Too boorish or too condescending. This was Boston, so people either had no education or too much. No money or all the money in the world. There was no in-between.

The thing about Boston too was that it was basically all ladies. When a third of the city falls between twenty and thirty-five, and close to half of that number are students, and more than half of them are girls, the odds are definitely in the dudes' favors. If they offer more than Cup O' Noodles for dinner, most girls are dying for a ring. Wear a collared shirt, and she'll be yanking that collar into her bedroom before midnight.

The flipside was certainly not true. Here I was—a lawyer from the best school in the country. Educated, smart, cute as fuck (if I do say so myself), and a certified kick in the pants. But if I wanted to get laid, the guy either had to be drunk enough not to care about any of those things, or he had to be arrogant enough to think he was better.

And tonight, I wasn't really in the mood to pretend.

"Buy you a drink?"

The stool next to me at the long mirrored bar was suddenly occupied by a guy who looked like he should be named Stuart. I didn't know why, but in his worn flannel shirt topped with suspenders, his carefully groomed beard, and the thick tortoise-shell glasses, he just looked like one of those hipsters who fronted jangle-pop bands and ironically assumed the middle names they got from their grandfathers. Stuart Jenkins. Or Barry McPhonyName. Something like that.

"I suppose," I said. "What's your name?"

"Henry," he said, signaling the bartender. "Henry Fellowston."

Close enough.

"I'm Jane," I said, offering a hand. "What's your story, Henry?"

You know what? I don't remember what he said, so I'm not going to tell you. And you know why? Because he was boring. This was made worse by the fact that the second Henry started talking, a few people stepped away from the bar, clearing it all the way down its reflective top and revealing one of the few people on the planet who had never had a problem holding my attention.

Eric.

He wore a simple outfit of black pants, white shirt, and a skinny black tie, and his bright hair gleamed even under the dim lights. Simple, but classic. Well cut.

It made sense now that Eric came from money, of course. If I hadn't been so sex addled, his spare, yet pristine apartment would have told me everything. What kind of law student has a closet full of Tom Ford and Zegna? How did he always know the right thing to say and do at those events we attended with Skylar and Brandon? At one point, I remembered people approaching him and asking if he was getting involved in the business too. I had thought at the time they meant Brandon's brief flirtation with politics, since Eric was a new associate at Brandon's law firm. But now...now I wondered if they were asking because they knew who Eric really was.

While Henry blared on and fucking on about the differences in hop species—apparently this guy went full-on cliché and brewed craft beer on his rooftop—I couldn't stop staring as Eric accepted his customary two fingers of top-shelf vodka—hell, yes, I remembered that—and smiled at the female bartender.

My heart sped up. My newly sweaty hands knotted together. *Dammit.*

Our repartee, unspoken, already echoed through my mind. How easy it would be.

*You look like a waiter, Gaston. Are you ready for my order?*

He'd turn slowly, that familiar twinkle in his eye. *I have an order for you, pretty girl. Can you take it?*

Why couldn't it ever be like that with anyone else?

I watched, suddenly riveted by the sight of Eric making casual small talk with both bartenders—female *and* male. It was like watching an animal in the wild. *See the preying jackal in his native habitat. When he thinks no one is watching, he interacts with other jackals too with charm and ease. But is it all a show to lure the female into his den? Only time will tell...*

"Uh huh," I said as Henry began a diatribe on malt preferences. "Please say more about that."

Eric smiled at the lady bartender. She *was* very attractive, and my polar opposite. Tall and blonde, with boobs that practically smacked her customers in the face. Eric laughed at some kind of joke she made, and jealousy practically hurled me off my stool. Fucking hell. Why did I *care* so much if he laughed at someone else's jokes?

*Because he used to laugh at yours.*

It was the one thing I offered, wasn't it? I wasn't blonde or buxom. I wasn't anyone's idea of a cover model. I was smart, quirky, and sometimes a barrel of laughs. Men like Eric didn't love women like me, but they could be entertained by them. And for a second, I hated myself for ever settling for that. I had never been anything but a passing dalliance for him. And wasn't that why he was asking me to marry him anyway? To make it *bearable*, he said? Translation: to entertain him.

Fuck. That.

The male bartender slid an arm around the female's waist and kissed her on the cheek. She cupped his face, and I watched as Eric smiled at them, not with that predatory look I remembered, but with genuine affection. The male bartender fingered the woman's hand, and a ring on her left hand reflected in the bar top. Eric grinned, then stood up and kissed the woman on the cheek and shook the man's hand. I recognized the way his mouth formed the word "congratulations." And the way he clearly meant it.

Oh, hell.

"Jane?" Henry pulled me out of my stupor.

"Hmm? What?"

"I said would you like another beer? I could get us a flight so you could really see the differences in hops I was talking about. It's a lot better than the stuff you're drinking, I promise."

I blinked down at my half-empty PBR. This guy really was nice. Henry was probably the kind of guy I should be seeing if I wanted a relationship at all. I bet he made his own compost too and grew rooftop kale in Somerville. One day he'd build a chicken coop in the alley and bring the eggs to his neighbors out of the goodness of his heart.

He'd be a great boyfriend for a while too. Dutifully learn all my favorite indie rock bands, call me his "partner" instead of something horribly gendered word like "girlfriend," and no matter what, he would probably always request very politely whenever he wanted to remove a piece of my clothing before we made tender and compassionate love approximately twice a month. And he would always, *always* remember lubricant because there was no way in hell I'd ever be the slightest bit turned on without it.

*May I please remove your bra now, Jane?*

I shuddered.

"Um, you know what..." I said, but I couldn't even finish the sentence. Poor Henry. Someday he really would make some woman a wonderful partner. But that woman wasn't me.

And then, in that strange way that everyone does when they know someone is watching them, Eric turned. His eyes zeroed in on mine, and the side of his mouth quirked in recognition. Because there was nothing else to do, I raised my pint glass, which was now almost empty. Henry the beer guy was still jabbering away, but I had no clue about what.

Eric picked up his glass and raised it in a silent toast. Then, almost imperceptibly, he tilted his head.

No one would have known it for what it was besides me. A call, a summons. That minuscule movement carried all magnitude of promise. Once I would have jumped at the thought of it. Found the nearest empty room I could and willingly surrendered to whatever the man had planned. To my knees. Against the wall. Bound. Gagged. Whatever he wanted, because it would inevitably become what *I* wanted too.

The man somehow always knew my desires before I even thought of them.

Eric blinked. His steely gaze hadn't moved, and as the bartenders stepped away to help other customers, I found myself smiling. Eric was alone.

"Hey, where are you going?" Henry asked, his voice a distant blur as I slid off my stool.

I slapped a ten-dollar bill in front of him. "For the drink," I said. "Your next one's on me."

While Eric watching with an inappropriate display of satisfaction, I patted Henry on the shoulder as if he were nothing more than a puppy and started toward Eric as if in a trance.

*Pretty girl.*

The term floated back to me once again. I couldn't let him go there, but by the way he was watching me, silvery gaze sparking over his glass, it would be pretty hard not to.

It was, one might say, a challenge.

"You look like a waiter, Gaston," I recited as I joined him at the bar. "Are you ready for my order?"

"That depends," he said without missing a beat. "On whether you've checked the menu."

I smiled. He grinned, but this time, there was nothing innocent about it.

"Who's this?" the lady bartender asked, reappearing with all her boobular awesomeness.

Eric wrested his gaze away. "This is Jane, Viv." He turned to me. "Jane, this is Vivian. She and Tom, her fiancé, own Marleigh's. I come here a fair amount—"

Vivian snorted. "Try every night. I mean, I like the business and all, but you should probably step out of your box sometimes, Eric."

I sniggered. "Still don't like breaking your routines, huh, Petri?"

"Petri?" Vivian blinked between us. "Who is *Petri*?"

Eric hid his eyes under one palm. "Jane, really?"

I leaned in. "Tell me, Vivian. Does Howard Hughes here have a tendency to pick up random tail at your fine establishment?"

Vivian raised a blonde brow at Eric. "She knows you well, DV."

Eric just groaned into his hand. "Yes," he said. "She does."

"We go back a ways," I told her. "I know *all* his dirty secrets."

"Well, as his bartender, I'd like to think I know a few too." Vivian glanced at my nearly empty glass. "Need another?"

I nodded, and she left to refill my glass. Eric just watched me, his face settling back into a placid non-expression.

I looked him over, taking in his shirt, the way the slim-cut tailoring showed off a narrow waist, broad shoulders, and those damn biceps all over again.

"Have we been doing a few extra sets of pushups to impress the ladies, Casanova? I don't remember you being this jacked."

"I try to take care of things when necessary."

He was smug, which told me I wasn't hiding my admiration very well. Asshole. What right did he have looking like that? Did men take a secret class in college that taught them exactly how to roll their sleeves up *just* haphazardly enough to make a woman's mouth water? Did they share tips on how hot and bothered a well-placed forearm would make her?

Bastards, all of them.

Vivian returned with my beer. Eric examined the PBR with obvious distaste and told Vivian to put it on his tab along with another drink for himself.

"Yes, I still like my PBR," I said as I took a welcome sip. "So you can take your condescension and shove it, Eric."

"I didn't say anything," he murmured, but accepted his next drink from Vivian too. This one had olives.

"Dirty martini with Beluga Gold Line," she said, and Eric nodded appreciatively.

"Damn," he said after he took a sip. "Tom's really trying to expand the clientele, isn't he?"

Vivian shrugged. "He's shooting for the after-work crowd. He thinks that if a smug son of a bitch like you shows up three or four times a week, there are others who'll do it too."

I snorted again, but Eric didn't answer. It seemed like Vivian enjoyed baiting him too. I liked her already.

"So how do you two know each other?" Vivian asked.

"I added my sample to the dish," I said. When Vivian just looked confused, I elaborated. "We used to hook up sometimes. And after that spectacularly crashed and burned, our relationship became one of boisterous animosity."

Eric just sighed.

"You're kidding," Vivian said almost gleefully. "No offense, DV, but she doesn't really seem like your type."

I hated how much the comment stabbed.

"Then whose type does she seem like?" Eric asked, a little too sharply. Was it possible he was just as annoyed by that statement as

I was?

"Well, that guy's, to start." Vivian pointed a rag at Henry, who was now talking hops and malts to another unsuspecting lady. She looked about as interested in them as I had been.

All three of us watched with almost academic curiosity as Henry pushed his glasses up his nose and gestured emphatically at the row of beer samples between him and the girl.

Eric turned back to Vivian. "What's the difference?"

"Come on. Don't tell me you don't see it. You're...look at you. Every weekend I see you in these pristine shirts without even one wrinkle. With your shiny hair and your fancy watch. That guy looks like her. A little, I don't know, rough around the edges, no offense, Jane. A little rock and roll."

I guffawed. "He is the furthest thing from 'rock and roll,' I can promise you that. He's basically Gordon Lightfoot."

Vivian giggled. "I sound like my mother when I say that, but you know what I mean."

"I'm sorry for laughing," I said. "But I promise you, that guy is about as rock and roll as the Osmonds."

Eric was still staring hard at Henry. "He just doesn't look like a rock star from right now, Jane. He looks like he should be on the cover of Spin Magazine circa 1997." He took another sip of his drink as Henry pointed excitedly at one glass of beer. The girl was looking around the rest of the room.

Vivian snorted. "Enlighten me. Why 1997?"

"Yes, Petri. That's an oddly specific year," I chimed.

"The ill-fitting flannel shirt. The overgrown monk hair. The horn-rimmed glasses I'd bet five dollars he picked up at the Goodwill. I'd bet you five more they don't even have a prescription."

I chuckled. "I see it. Henry does kind of have that nineties emo look going for him."

"Henry? Is that really his name?"

Vivian shrugged. "If he's nineties, then so is Jane. She kind of reminds of Gwen Stefani. Like she should be his lead singer."

We all looked down at my outfit. Thin black and white shirt slipping off one shoulder again, an arm full of silver bangles, and the loud pink hair that I'd blown into waves. I guess the reference worked. Gwen Stefani wasn't Asian, but she did have pink hair at one point. And we both liked red lipstick.

Eric seemed extremely interested in that last aspect of my outfit too, but when I looked up, he glanced away and took another sip. "He looks homeless. Like he lives on someone's couch. And nowhere near good enough for her."

"Who, the girl over there?" Vivian asked.

"No," Eric replied. "Jane."

# SEVEN

We were the last ones there when Vivian and Tom
started closing up the bar, winding Saran wrap around
the tops of the bottles while Mazzy Star serenaded
people out the door. Maybe it was the three more pints of PBR that
made everything seem funnier than it was, or the vodka that cracked
Eric's careful mask and had him loosening his tie halfway down his
shirt. Maybe it was the look on his face—half annoyed, half adoring—
every time I stole one of his olives and chucked it at him for no
apparent reason. But soon I found myself on the tail end of one of the
best dates I had had in a long time.

The best date...that wasn't even a date.

I honestly couldn't remember what we had talked about for the
last three hours. Hell, I couldn't even remember the last time I had
talked to *anyone* for three straight hours. Not Skylar. My mother. My
cousins. No one.

And what had we even discussed? Nothing and everything. Our
jobs. The shitty music from 1993 this bar insisted on playing. The
ridiculous outfit Henry had been wearing when he walked up to me.

*Who wears suspenders and a belt?* we asked, again and again. The more we asked, the funnier it seemed.

We laughed. Joked. Drank. Even danced a little before camping at the bar again. And slowly, I let myself enjoy the fact that Eric's gray-brown eyes didn't waver downward when I spoke. I let myself fall into the simple grace of his smile, and though we never touched, sink toward the magnetic warmth of his body. I had forgotten how easy it was to just...be...with him. If I wasn't fighting it.

"Seriously, though," I slurred after finishing the last of my beer. "You were such a damn dainty little princess. Between the specialty coffee and the perfectly mixed martinis, you're basically the *dauphin* of France, even without the heir thing."

"Princess?" he said, shimmying slightly on his stool for a second. "Come on, Jane. James Bond drank martinis. Shaken, not stirred, amIright?" His words were blending into one another too. "I dress up as Bond every year at the firm's Halloween party, you know. My secretary said I do a great British accent."

He smacked his lips, and those gray eyes twinkled as he nodded fondly at his own memory. He no longer looked the picture of pristine perfection, but somehow, the rumpled, rolled sleeves and the way the back of his shirt had come out of his pants made him look *that* much more delicious

Loosened by vodka, Eric winked at me. I almost fell off my stool. *Goddammit.*

So, I did what I always did when I felt out of my league with Eric. I teased.

"Pinkies up, James," I said, gesturing at his fingers, which were pinching the fragile stem of his martini glass. Long fingers. Agile fingers. Fingers that had once given me no less than three orgasms in one night. *Back to back.*

I quivered in my seat.

Eric just looked at his glass. "Real men know how to drink cocktails, Jane. You want some PBR-drinking Neanderthal, maybe you need to go find your emo friend again. Grab him by the suspenders."

*Ha.* So he was still bothered by that.

"Maaaybe I should," I retorted, swinging around on my stool, as if I was genuinely interested in Captain Kangaroo and his lumbersexual beard. As if that guy had one tenth of the sexual charisma of the man sitting next to me. As if anyone else but Eric (or maybe Bond) could make holding a Martini glass look like a rated-R sex act.

It was a ploy that might have worked better if we hadn't been the only ones left. A second later, I was twisted back around, suddenly caged by Eric's arms. His used-to-be lanky, suddenly wiry, steel-trap arms.

All humor had disappeared, replaced by a lazy, slanting smirk and an imperious gaze that lit a fire deep within my belly.

"Who do you think you're fooling, pretty girl?" he purred, tipping his head to the side to examine me. "There's no one here but me."

I opened my mouth, ready to launch another comeback at him, but none came. In my beer-soaked haze, all I could see was his mouth, full and wide. All I could smell was his cologne, that hint of Tom Ford, plus a clean, surprisingly earthy scent that zipped to the back of my head and the bottom of my heart with a twang. My mouth didn't close. And Eric, damn him, stared straight at it.

He raised a hand like he owned the place. "Viv, we're going to need another round."

"No can do, you idiot," Vivian called from the till. "Last call was thirty minutes ago. Finish your drinks and take your girl home, DV."

"DV?" I perked up, and the spell was broken. A giggle burst from my chest. "Did she just call you DV?"

Eric sat back and shrugged. "She's been calling me that all night, you lush. It's an acronym. For, you know, my name. De Vries."

"You do realize that's really just VD spelled backward? Good God, that's *brilliant,* Petri!" I slapped my hand on the bar, tickled, well, pink with my epiphany.

"God." Eric tipped back the rest of his drink and yanked it away from my grasp when I tried to grab the final olive. "Oh, no, Lefferts. I'm eating this one."

The bar's overhead lights flickered on, and both he and I squinted painfully.

"My eyes, my eyes!" I moaned, though I was already laughing.

"Viv!" Eric twisted around, blocking his eyes. "You could warn us!"

"I did warn you, *VD*. Thirty minutes ago. Go home!"

I started giggling uncontrollably. Eric just rolled his eyes, but this time, his full mouth bit back a bigger smile.

"Damn," I said as I set my empty glass on the bar top. "I honestly don't remember the last time I closed out a bar. God, I'm getting old."

"Time flies when you're having fun, right?" Eric replied. "I can't tell you how relieved I was to see you sitting over there. You saved my night, Lefferts. I was bored to damn pieces."

"Please, Petri. People don't change that much, and the only thing that's really different about you these days is that you have a bigger paycheck. Nicer clothes. Better hair. You didn't come in here looking for me. I just happened to be in your line of sight."

I started looking through my purse for nothing in particular, ignoring the way that particular statement cut into my chest. Dammit. I'd fallen into that trap, that special Eric trap. The one where he made me—and countless other women—feel like the only girl in the room. Like I was special, when I was undoubtedly not.

He had looked up because he was cruising for his next victim. And he had summoned me because I was a challenge. It was as simple as that.

Eric watched me for a moment, then passed a hand back through his hair, which, like the rest of him, was beautifully mussed. "I'll have you know I come here for the excellent cocktails, not the easy tail. If that's all I wanted, I would have left you with your date."

*Sure. Right.* Like I was going to believe that.

I rolled my eyes and stood up. Okay, and maybe I swayed a little. "I...need a walk."

"There are more enjoyable forms of exercise." When I looked up, he wasn't even trying to hide his leer. Or his glass-cut jaw. Or that goddamn sparkle.

"You," I said as I pushed a finger into his chest, "didn't use to be this corny, Petri dish."

My finger, though, didn't move. It just kept pressing. Into that divot. Between those chest muscles. Which I suddenly discovered were a lot more...defined...than I remembered.

*Stop it. Stop. It. I am not going there. I don't care that you suddenly learned how to trim your stubble so it looks like your jaw was chiseled by Michelangelo himself. I don't care that you look like you could still make me forget the days of the week with those well-honed bedroom skills of yours.*

*Not. Going. There.*

Eric just shrugged—*again*—like a cataclysmic level of sexual tension hadn't just passed between us.

"I had to try. I wouldn't be living up to that fucking nickname if I didn't, right?"

He stood up and checked for his wallet and keys, leaving me wondering if I was the only one who had felt it. *Shit.*

"Come on, Lefferts, let's walk it off."

Walking...that was unfortunately a bit more difficult. It took about four steps outside for both of us to trip on the uneven cobblestones on Hanover. I thought I had done pretty well, going with three-inch heels instead of four tonight. And these were block boots, not stiletto. I should have been fine, even after ingesting the equivalent of a full pitcher of PBR by myself.

But the cobblestones disagreed. Vehemently.

"Whoa!"

Eric caught me as I basically went flying into the street, clasping my shoulders between his broad palms as he set me upright. His scent floated past all over again. Damn him. Damn Tom Ford. It's like that guy bottled sex pheromones and had the audacity to call it cologne instead of Jane Lefferts Kryptonite.

"Steady, girl," he said. "Come on, let me help."

"What am I, a horse? Get off me!"

I batted at him, but Eric just tucked one of my arms under his and forced me to walk alongside him until we were back on the sidewalk. It didn't take long for me to stop fighting it. His large, solid bicep *did*, after all, make it easier to walk. Right?

We continued through the crooked streets of the North End, finally ending up by the harbor, where a few other last callers were doing the same thing we were—walking off their booze, restlessness, and sexual chemistry. A few were unlikely to make it back to their apartments. More than one couple pawed at each other on park benches.

"Don't fall in!" I called as we passed one couple who were practically horizontal over the pier railing. They didn't stop. I bit my lip as we passed, trying to ignore the ache flowering in my lower belly. It had been humming there all night.

"Remember when that was us?"

Eric was watching the same couple with...was that longing in his gray eyes? He chewed absently on his lower lip for a minute and squeezed my hand a little harder.

"A bit, yeah," I said. "We had a little more style, though. You were never one for PDA, to start."

"I had you in that alley in Allston once. Behind the bakery, remember?"

"Had me? What am I, a pastry?"

The right side of his full mouth tugged up in a smirk. "What do you want me to say? I pounded you like bread dough?"

"I believe the term is 'fucked,' sir," I proclaimed. "It was a shag fest. Especially the summer while we were studying for the bar. So, yes. We *fucked* in that alley in Allston. But it wasn't really public because it was so dark. And late enough that they were already baking the croissants for the next morning. You got me one after we were done, if I remember correctly. And coffee. A true gentleman."

Eric flipped his free hand and mimed as if he were tipping a top hat and we were strolling around in an Edith Wharton novel, not stumbling-around, drunken Bostonians on a cool spring night.

"I would never do anything so pedestrian as fuck, Jane," he said. "Especially not with you."

"Oh, really, Jeeves? Then what would you call it. 'Making love'?"

Eric smirked again. "What's wrong with 'intercourse'?"

"I mean, it's fine, I guess. If you're Mrs. Cleary, my ninth-grade health teacher."

Eric tipped his head from side to side, like he was weighing the options. "You know, of all the euphemisms I can think of for sex, there aren't a lot of expressions that cover the whole bone-melting, earth-shattering, life-changing...actions...we did." His eyes flashed. "At least in my opinion."

I arched a brow. "Oh? 'Making whoopee' doesn't get you there?"

The smile broadened. "How about 'Blitzkrieg mit dem fleis-chgewehr.'"

I guffawed. "Point for the obscure German metal reference. What about the 'beast with two backs'? If we're averting pedestrian, there's nothing better than Shakespeare."

Eric nodded, eyes shining with approval. "The Bard's got a few good ones."

I chuckled. "Oh, fucking hell. I should have known better than to start with the poetry. Do you really still quote that crap offhand?"

"Why not? It's better than what most assholes have to say. 'Lady, shall I lie in thy lap?' sounds a hell of a lot nicer than 'wanna screw?'"

"Hamlet, eh? 'You are keen, my lord, you are keen.'"

Eric stopped, assuming a posture that once again took me back five years. Hands shoved in his pockets, eyes closed, nose tipped up while he searched his memory. I was jerked back to those moments, right after we'd both basically given ourselves up to the beast from Othello. He'd suddenly shift from a beast to a poet, quoting lines from his favorites. It matched his other pretentions, of course, and from anyone else, I might have found it insufferable. But from a man who, generally, was so apathetic and immovable, there was something very addictive about hearing words born of passion in his deep voice.

"'It would cost you a groaning to take off my edge,'" he said with a rakish lift of his brow. But then he continued with the rest of the verse, which had a distinctly less playful mood. "'Doubt thou the stars are fire'...'doubt that the sun doth move'...'doubt truth be a liar'—'"

"You're out of order," I said, cutting him off before he could get to the fourth and final stanza of the poem Hamlet writes Ophelia.

"'Never doubt my love,'" he finished anyway, just as his eyes met mine.

We locked gazes for a few seconds, and then he looked away.

I gulped. "That doesn't happen until the second act." My voice wasn't nearly as strong as I wanted.

*Remember*, I told myself. Sure, for all his calculated moves and pragmatic career choices, Eric was a poet at heart. Surprises, surprises. But these were surprises he must have shared with countless other women before and after those brief months we shared. There was absolutely no way I was the first woman ever privy to his...talents.

"Besides," I said as I scampered a few steps ahead of him. "They're both mad. Crazy. Hamlet and Ophelia both, am I right?"

Eric's eyes opened, and he smiled serenely. The moonlight made his teeth gleam, and my heart twisted in my chest.

"Crazy," he agreed. "Yeah." Then: "It *was* a good summer, wasn't it?"

He waited a long time, but I didn't answer, just looked out at the harbor as we continued to walk. *Never doubt my love.* The words kept echoing through my head, a verse unfinished.

"Hey," Eric called me back. "Wasn't it, Jane?"

I stopped and turned around. "Well, yeah. You know it was, at least until the end. You don't need me to say it to pad your ego."

His eyes weren't shining anymore. Suddenly they burned, and that sense of déjà vu was back. Only now it wasn't Eric's inner angel I was remembering—it was the inner demon that appeared just as quickly.

"Maybe I just needed to know *I* wasn't crazy for remembering it that way, pretty girl."

The words just slipped out, like they had before, and in a second, just as I had at the end of the bar, when a single tip of his head had me gliding across an entire lounge like a robot, I froze in his thrall. The light breeze blew off the harbor, but Boston wasn't asleep. We were at the edge of the North End, and the sounds of other late-night denizens of the city echoed off the cobbled streets, just as they had for years in the heart of this city.

Eric took my hand, and I let him. I let him weave his fingers in between mine. And then I let him stop, let him tug me around to face him. His eyes sharpened and dropped to my lips. He took a step toward me, then another, and for a second, every memory I had of us flashed through my mind. Once, it would have been so simple—or as simple as it ever was with Eric. A few words, a quick signal. My pretenses would drop, like some kind of magic password released them, and I'd go from mouthing off at every little thing to doing whatever he said...or bearing the punishment for it. Gladly.

*Pretty girl.*

That had been the phrase. The cue, which came as naturally to me as anything else had with him. With Eric, both my mind and body had acted on instinct; perhaps the phrase worked so well because it wasn't true. Because I wasn't pretty—not like Skylar or probably most of Eric's family was. I was angles and length, wide-set eyes, a mouth that was a little too big, breasts that were a little too small. I was loud and without decorum, steel edges and torn knees.

But no sooner would he say it, and I'd become someone else, someone I'd never really been with any other. My hands, my arms, my mouth, my voice...everything moved in concert with the man who used that name.

In those moments, we made poetry together. Or so I wanted to believe.

"Pretty girl..." He whispered it this time, then watched with complete and utter joy as my face tipped toward his.

For a second, I stood there, suspended. My mind swam, and I inhaled, suddenly surrounded by his scent of cologne, soap, linen, Eric.

*Easy, there, Jane Brain. Don't run away with yourself.*

Dad's voice, strong and serene. And followed, surprisingly, by my mother's, the complete opposite.

*Jane!* My mother hissed from a thousand miles away, warning me to keep my head, keep my heart away from men like this. Telling me to play it safe. Telling me to be more like her.

"Jane." Eric's voice was deeper. More immediate. And yanked me back to the here and now.

Tomorrow. Tomorrow I could make the necessary decisions. I'd tell him no. I'd go back to my staid, boring life. Find another job I barely liked, learn how to put up with my mother, and carve out a space for myself that was right back in the limbo I'd endured for the last five years.

Tomorrow I could go back to that life, if you could call it that at all. But tonight...tonight I could do something else.

"Fuck it," I whispered, and kissed him.

# EIGHT

They say don't stick your fingers in a socket because you'll get a shock. Well, I shouldn't have kissed Eric de Vries, because it was like being caught in a lightning storm. His taste, his touch, the currents of *life* that flowed through this man galloped through me in less than a second. Every cogent thought in my head disappeared except one:

*Need. Him. Now.*

Was I playing with fire? Sure. But my self-preservation, which had never been my strongest sense to begin with, had pretty much evaporated at that point. What did it matter anymore if Eric and I had another one-night stand? What did anything matter? Right now, the world was flat, down was up, right was left. I was living with my mother, mourning my father, and actually considering getting married for a price tag. Letting Eric work his voodoo on my confused, fucked-up brain seemed like the most correct thing in the world.

Besides, *he* started it with all that pretty girl crap. He started it the second he stalked me to a salon in Albany Park. As my brain moved into that sweet space where it stopped pushing so damn hard and just let things be, something in the air shifted. And then his lips—

those full, suckable lips that always seemed halfway to growling no matter what—responded to mine, and my brain stopped working too.

He just...transformed. He stopped being calm, collected Eric de Vries. And turned into...him.

Gone was the placid face as his hands ran up and down my back, grasping my waist, my ass, my legs with purpose and intent, hard enough to make me moan. His mouth, stunned at first, turned ruthless, sucking and plundering with every brutal kiss. It was like both of us hadn't just been starving for the evening, but for the last five years, and now we were making up for it. We weren't a meeting of two like minds. This was a fucking thunderstorm.

He grabbed my ass and squeezed again, hard this time, and I moaned into his mouth. Two more minutes, and I wasn't going to care if we were in the middle of Fenway Park. Eric would be able to tell me anything he wanted me to do...and I was going to do it. Sneak onto one of the boats bobbing in the harbor. Bang on the door of Marleigh's to use that mirrored bar of theirs. Hell, I'd dart behind a dumpster in the mood I was in. I just wanted the man. Inside me. Yesterday.

But instead of jumping him like I wanted, I pulled away, gasping. Eric's chest heaved, his tie hanging from it like a hangman's noose, his mouth swollen and red, like it had just been bitten. He stared at me like he was going to lunge all over again. Like I had done to him. And he was definitely finding it hard to breathe too. *Good.*

My lower lip slipped between my teeth, and Eric winced. Other memories came flooding back. His hand on my ass whenever I did that. *Bite it*, he'd say. *Bite it again, pretty girl.* I would, of course, and he'd find flesh with a scintillating crack. Two, three, four. He'd make me count, shout them with him. *You drive me crazy*, he'd tell me at the end. So I'd do it once more.

I blinked at him and slowly let my lip free. Even in the night, I could see Eric's eyes dilate.

"Come here," he ordered, and yanked me back to his waiting mouth.

It was like the last five years hadn't happened. Like Eric and I were just out of law school all over again, young and green and fucking unable to keep our hands off each other. His lips molded to mine frantically, and my hands traveled up and down his extremely hard body. This didn't feel like the body of someone who sat behind a desk all day. What did he do, full-body planks while he read depositions? Narrate opening statements from a captain's chair?

But I didn't care as his hands cupped my face, my neck, my waist, playing over my small curves like they were all he needed in the world. Even part of me, down to my bones, seemed to cry for his touch. It didn't matter that it was past two o'clock in the morning. It didn't matter that we were making out like kids in the middle of Government Square, where all of Boston could stare at us. As our tongues twisted around each other again and again, all I could think, feel, sense was that I needed to fuck this man. I needed him inside me. Right fucking now.

Need.

What?

*What?*

I exploded back all over again, feeling like I'd been punched in the gut. I knew that feeling. That wasn't just lust. *Need* went beyond getting your rocks off. *Need* was something much more visceral. It sank right to the heart of things, and what I truly *needed* was to stop that feeling immediately.

If only he didn't taste so damn good...

"Jane—" Eric managed to croak as I held up a hand. Somehow, I managed a step back. "Jane, what are you doing?"

"We...need...to...stop," I gasped.

He stared at me, incredulous, as if I'd just asked him to give me a kidney. "Are you *kidding* me right now?"

I shook my head, still gasping for breath. At least I wasn't alone. With his normally neat blond hair a tousled mess and his chest heaving like he'd just crossed a champion finish line, it was clear that I wasn't the only one who had just run a marathon with that kiss.

"Eric," I said again. "Come on. We can't."

He groaned. "So we're back to this."

"Back to what?"

"This fucking push and pull. Will we, or won't we?" He pushed his hands over his face and yanked at his hair. "Fucking *fuck*."

"Be reasonable," I said, more to myself than to him. "You just asked me to marry you. As an arrangement. We start sleeping together, and it's going to complicate things so much more. You know I'm right, Counselor."

Eric turned. "And if I hadn't?"

My brows knitted together. "If you hadn't what?"

"Asked you to marry me. If you were just here visiting for the weekend, going back to Chicago tomorrow? What would you do?"

I swallowed heavily. We both knew the answer to that. I'd yank his tie the rest of the way off and beg him to bind my wrists. I'd lift my skirt and yank down his pants and taste him right here just because I could.

I'd take one night. And then I'd be done. Because I'd know that was all he could give.

My answer must have shown clearly on my face, because Eric stepped toward me with clear intention.

"I'll give you what you want, Jane," he said, low and sure, like he was soothing a scared animal. "One night only, like you always said. I'm not trying to use you. We just both know that *this*"—he gestured between us—"isn't going away unless we deal with it. So we might as well just get it over with and move on."

The fucked-up thing? My heart skipped and fell at the same time. Because I did want him. More than anything. I was so tired of trying to figure everything else out in my life, and I knew that in Eric's bed, I wouldn't have any space to think at all.

But for one night only, right? And the next morning, he'd go back to being as aloof as possible. And I'd have to remind myself that to him, I was only ever going to be a good time. A means to an end. A way to retain his fortune and have a little fun while he was at it.

Well. I hadn't said yes. And two could play at this game.

"You promise?" I said as I took a step forward too.

Eric's hands dropped to his sides. "Don't play with me right now, Jane."

I took another step closer but remained just out of reach. "I mean it. A good time, right? And one night only? That's where it ends?"

One more step. I bit my lip again. This time on purpose.

Eric's eyes grew darker. "Is that what you want?"

"What I want..." I entered his space, slipped a hand up his chest and around his neck. Our foreheads touched, and his scent swept over me, a crazy, intoxicating combination of soap, cologne, and a hint of vodka.

I couldn't think. I couldn't breathe. All I could do was want.

"Be careful, Jane—" Eric whispered as his dark eyes traveled over my face.

"Be careful with what?" I whispered back, suddenly entranced by the small divot in his chin. *Should I? No, I shouldn't.*

But I did anyway. I licked it. Eric hissed.

"Once upon a time," I said as I slowly drifted my mouth around the edges of his lips, "you used to know how to quiet this crazy mind of mine. You knew how to own it. Did you forget?"

Eric was a statue, but his eyes were stars. "Absolutely not."

I closed my closed, almost like I was meditating. When I opened them, Eric's lips grazed mine.

"Then do it," I murmured against his mouth. "For one night... make me your pretty girl again...Mr. de Vries."

Gone. My self-control was gone. It was nearly depleted when I kissed him the first time, but the second his name slipped out of me like that, I knew I'd given up the ghost. For the next few hours, at least, I was his.

*Oh, the relief.*

Eric slipped a hand around the nape of my neck and then stared at my mouth for a good five seconds. My lips throbbed with want, but he didn't move. In fact, he seemed to enjoy the delayed gratification—either his, or more likely, mine.

"What do you say?" he said, his husky voice barely above a whisper.

He didn't want me to ask. He wanted me to beg.

I blinked, a slow sweep of lashes behind flickering lenses. "Please."

Eric swallowed heavily and pulled at his collar, though it was already unbuttoned. "Come with me."

———

IT TOOK ABOUT five minutes for him to drag me back to Hanover, hand firmly around my neck. I didn't care that my boots were scraping on the sidewalk—if I couldn't walk, I had no doubt that Eric would have carried me at that point. Picked me up and slung me over his shoulder, without a care for my squawks or other pedestrians' gasps. *Hmm*, that was a thought.

We tore down the street, past Marleigh's, which was now completely closed, and two more blocks down to a large brick building, where a door was immediately held open by a portly man in a green suit with brass buttons. God, Eric was such a snob. Of course he'd live in a building like this now, with a fucking doorman. He probably didn't even know his name.

"This is Jane, Paul," Eric said as we swept inside. "She's with me."

Okay, so I was wrong about that one.

His touch dropped from my neck, and he took my hand instead. And sure, maybe I sent him a sideways glance before smiling brightly at Paul, who waved politely, but said nothing. And sure, maybe I puffed out my chest a little when Eric said it like that: *she's with me.* I didn't want to think about how good it felt to be with him like that again. To be *claimed* like that again.

We rode the elevator in silence up to the seventh floor, and I followed him down a long hall, my hand tightly in his grip. Eric stopped outside the door at the far corner, keys dangling from his fingers. I waited without a word. But instead of opening the door, Eric turned.

"Are you sure about this?" he asked.

I quirked a brow. Eric almost looked like he might smile. But instead of fighting back with yet another snarky reply—the kind that would have earned me a quick slap on the ass five years ago—I just blinked.

"No," I admitted. "I don't know what we're doing. I don't know what tomorrow is going to look like. I don't know what I'm going to say about all the...questions...I still have to answer. But, Eric?"

I paused. Sometimes you don't know you want something until it actually happens. Like a name. Like the look on his face when, instead of calling him Richie Rich or VD or Petri dish, his given name came out of my mouth. The hunger on his face was threaded with something else that resembled an emotion both of us had once felt, but only one of us had said. And as I saw it, I realized then how badly I missed it. How badly...how badly I had missed him.

Something in me broke.

"What is it, Jane?"

Before I could continue, Eric reached out and gently pulled off my glasses. My vision wasn't the worst. I was nearsighted, so I could actually see him pretty clearly up close. He knew that. He used to say, once upon a time, that he didn't want anything between us. After he had made me lose all my senses, he would lie on his side and stare at my eyes. Memorizing, he said, their strange mix of greens and blacks and browns and yellows. Memorizing their beautiful chaos. Just like me.

*Oh*, fuck. There went my heart all over again.

Eric folded the frames and tucked them into my purse.

"Tonight, I don't...I don't want to think," I said. "Is that all right?"

I didn't know what was going on. This wasn't the confident, nofucks-to-give Jane I worked so hard to be. Gone was the almost Napoleonic bravado. I couldn't have made a joke if I wanted.

Most of the time, I wrapped myself in humor like it was some kind of armor—it took a lot to break through that. But just like he had always done, Eric managed to pierce my careful defenses with little more than a few guarded words and some patience.

He examined me for a few moments, then pulled me closer. Our bodies met, from chest to knees, and I closed my eyes at the sudden sensation of this tall column of muscle pressed against me. Wondered if I'd be able to handle it when there was nothing at all between us.

"You got it."

Eric's deep voice slid over my aching skin. Then he reached around my trembling body and unlocked the door.

# NINE

Despite his taste for the finer things in life, Eric had lived modestly when I knew him before. Student housing through law school, and then a tiny two-bedroom a few blocks from here that he actually shared briefly with Skylar before she and Brandon got married. I had no idea where he lived between then and now, but it couldn't have been this place.

Then again, what did I know? Maybe he had owned it the entire time.

"This is where you live?"

I wandered into the apartment with wide eyes, honestly unsure of where I should even set my purse. The Lucite entry console? The sleek silver counters? Maybe the white leather armchair positioned by a single bookshelf. Everything was sterile and utterly charmless.

I turned around to where Eric was placing his keys in an empty glass bowl by the door. "You really are a Petri dish. This is basically a laboratory."

The entire apartment was white, silver, and glass. It wasn't huge —these places in the North End never were. But what it lacked in space, it made up with perfection. The stainless-steel counters in the kitchen were spotless under rows of bright white cabinets, the four-person dining table with steel legs and blonde wood looked like no one had ever eaten there, and the row of *Harper's* magazines on the glass and steel coffee table in the lounge were neatly fanned in front of an immaculate white, mid-century modern sofa. It was the opposite of my former homely studio, my parents' messy house in Evanston, or the plastic-covered chaos of my mother's condo. He had obviously paid someone a lot of money to create this ice palace.

Eric untied his half-Windsor knot as he strode into the kitchen, his black boots clipping across gleaming parquet floors. The Boston skyline twinkled against the clear night sky through picture windows.

He fixed himself another finger of vodka, then turned to where I stood, somewhat nervously, in the middle of the room, much to conscious of the fact that I was the only drop of color in it.

"Like one?" he asked, holding up his glass. Both strands of his tie hung down his chest, waiting to be tugged.

My head felt fuzzy, but the PBR was wearing off. *Beer before liquor*...I thought hazily.

"No," I said, to my surprise. I couldn't stop staring at his tie. Thinking of all the things he could do with it. Then I looked straight at him. "You know what I want." No use beating around the bush.

Eric's eyes didn't leave mine as he sipped on his vodka. His expression was blank, and again, the urge to shatter that smug demeanor coursed through me. Why did he always have to look like that? Like nothing *ever* bothered him? Especially since the whole world seemed to bother me?

"I have to leave on Monday," he said. "That's when I told her I'd be there. Or, I suppose, that's when she said I have to start."

I blinked. That was not what I was expecting. "She?"

He took another long drink. "Grandmother."

I frowned. "You know, I really didn't come up here to chat about dear old Granny and her maniacal marriage plot."

Eric emptied his drink, then set the glass in the sink with unnecessary force. "No, but we're going to have to." When he looked up, his eyes had lost all humor. "I gave you a week, Jane. You've had time." His head tipped to one side. "Tell me, and I'll give you what you want."

My jaw dropped. "You're kidding. You're going to hold out on me *now*, VD? After all that damn foreplay? Two minutes ago, you had your hands all over my ass, and now you want to play hard to get?"

His mouth twisted into a smirk that was half delicious, half infuriating. "That's right."

I watched irritably as he rounded the kitchen island to where I stood, taking one measured step at a time.

He tipped my chin up, forcing me to look at him. "I need an answer, Jane."

I swallowed. Monday was in two days. "Don't give a girl much time, do you?"

The hand on my chin didn't move. "*I* don't have much time, Jane." For a second those deep gray eyes shuttered. "Such is life, I suppose."

I swallowed. "Well, then. I'd better decide, hadn't I?"

He stared at me, hard, and then his hand dropped. "Jane. Cut the bullshit. Yes or no?"

I kept my chin where it was—lifted and defiant. His hands flexed by his sides. I could only guess what he wanted to do with them. It was too easy to imagine.

———

*"TURN AROUND, PRETTY GIRL."*

*I did. I had defied him enough tonight, and my ass was a bright shade of pink to show for it.*

*Eric smirked as I placed my hands neatly on his counter, pushing myself out slightly for his viewing pleasure.*

*"That's a very nice view," he remarked, circling halfway around me and back again. Though I couldn't see his face, his gaze seared my skin.*

*Soft lips grazed the back of my thighs, drifting across the delicate skin like feathers.*

*"So beautiful," he murmured as he slipped a hand between them. "So...fucking...beautiful."*

*I arched into his touch as one finger breached my entrance.*

*"You like that?" he asked from below. "You want more?"*

―――――

"JANE?"

I blinked. "What?"

His brows knit together in irritation. "Yes. Or. No?"

I exhaled and walked toward the windows. Below, Hanover still bustled in spite of the late hour. Boston was a city full of young, virile bodies trapped on its historic grounds. I watched as one pair toppled into a dark corner. The spot between my legs throbbed.

"Jane."

God, he was annoying. Stubborn, really, like a dog with a bone.

I turned, leaned back against the window, and crossed one ankle over the other. Eric approached, placing one hand on the glass over my shoulder so he could loom over me, a dark Adonis lit only by the sparkling lights of the city below.

I glanced up at his hand. "Sure you want to leave a print like that?"

His face didn't move. "Your answer, Jane."

"What do you think...Petri?"

A second later, I was whirled around, my wrists cuffed behind my back by one of Eric's large hands while the other wrapped around my chin, forcing me to look out the picture window.

"I think," he said, staring at our reflections with an intensity that I couldn't believe I had forgotten. "You need to stop fucking around."

"Let go of me," I said, struggling, but not. Just enough to make him fight a little. Give him something to control.

Which he did. The grip on my wrists turned iron, while his other hand flicked open my jeans, then slid down the front with a harsh shove that had me gasping already.

"Is this what you want?" he demanded as he tugged the material roughly to my ankles, suddenly baring my legs to the cold of the glass, the harsh chill of the room, and the warmth of his body behind me.

"You know what I want. And it's not to be held hostage by your arrogant ass."

His hand found my ass with a loud crack, and I jumped as he pushed me against the glass. My breathing came up short, and it wasn't because I was scared. It was because I was turned on. *So fucking turned on.*

"Say that again," he said as his palm now soothed the flaming skin.

"That again."

*Smack.* I jerked, wanting to punch him and beg him for more at the same time.

Again, another soft caress. "You really want this, don't you?"

I twisted to look over my shoulder. "Don't I?"

He was finding it harder to mask his frustration. I only found it more erotic, and if the long, hard bulge pressed against me was any indicator, so did he.

He jerked me back against him, his teeth grazing my earlobe. "You are playing with fucking fire here, Jane. Don't toy with me. Or have you forgotten what I'm capable of?"

In my experience, most men treated the clitoris like a light switch or El Dorado—it was either too common to treat nicely, or they acted like it was a mythical land no one could find, their fingers dancing around in itinerant, drunk circles until the girl faked it or took care of herself.

Eric, however, knew exactly what to do. Slip his fingers under the cotton edge of my underwear. Dip his fingertips into the sensitive, damp folds. Toy lightly, tickle until my breath came short. Explore, little by little, not with the tips, but with the pads of his fingers one at a time, and then, when he found the right spot, move two fingertips in a firm, insistent rhythm that quickly drove all rational thoughts out of my mind. This was just one of Eric's many gifts.

I groaned, smashing my entire face against the window when he dropped my wrists. It was all I could do to remain upright—I needed the brace of his body behind me to keep me standing. One of Eric's hands slipped around my hips and down, past the flimsy material and into the warmth that awaited him. He found my clit with practiced skill—like it had only been five days, not five years—and began to rub in those slow, delicious circles I had craved for so long.

"That's it, isn't it, pretty girl? God, you're shaking." His mouth hovered next to my ear, his breath hot, his lips grazing my earlobe. "I'd never forget this pussy. I'd never forget you."

"Jesus," I moaned against the glass, my breath clouding it next to my face. The man was a genius. That was all there was to it.

His other hand slid up my thigh from behind, taking a minute to massage one ass cheek, then the other. He pulled it away, and for a second, I braced myself for a quick slap.

"No, not this time, pretty girl." His deep voice vibrated against my neck. "But you want it, don't you? You always did."

"D-don't get ahead of yourself," I said, but my retort was weak. I was too busy melting. He was completely correct. I did want it. This was exactly what I needed. The shadow of grief that had been shading me like a veil for the last nine months was finally being chased away. Here in the dark, the world was bright again. Here, with Eric's slow, careful movements, I could finally—

*Smack!*

I jumped with a squeak, as pain and, yes, desire shot through my body.

Eric rubbed his hand over my ass again. "That was for your smart mouth," he said. "Don't forget who's in control here." The fingers on my clit continued their steady drive while his other hand slipped between my thighs, up, up, farther and farther until finally his thumb tickled my soaking wet entrance.

"You want it, don't you?" he growled as he toyed with me. "My finger? Or do you want my dick instead?"

"Ummmmm."

The man was literally driving the words from my mouth. I, mouthy Jane Lefferts, could no longer speak in complete sentences. Fucking Eric. Fucking delicious, finger voodoo, god of sex *Eric*.

"Tell me," he said as two of said digits slipped just inside. His other hand moved slightly faster, harder over that tight bud. I emitted a long, low moan.

"What do you want, Jane?"

I exhaled through my teeth, gritting them tight as he drew me toward the edge and pulled me away again just by adjusting his fingers' cadence. Slower. Faster. Then slow again. "I want...Jesus *Christ*, Eric..."

There was a low chuckle behind my ear, and then I felt the wet of his tongue as he traced its edge, then dipped inside there too. He was penetrating me, just slightly, in two different places, but not enough. It wasn't nearly enough.

"Your dick," I blurted, jerking my hips back toward him. "Fucking *hell*, Eric. I need your cock. Like, right fucking now."

The chuckle returned as his fingers pressed harder, even faster now, and the fingers at my pussy slipped all the way in, forcefully enough that I jumped.

"I want you to come first," he said. "I want to watch you fall apart in my hands before I split you in two, pretty girl."

His hand drove now, pumping mercilessly while his other absorbed the pressure outside, coaxing my ecstasy forward. I rocked against them, urging him to fuck me harder with his hands. Higher... higher...oh, God, here it came...

"I'm going to come," I moaned as I felt myself starting to topple over.

"Are you?"

'Y-yesssss," I breathed, feeling that imminent ledge approach. It had been so long...

And then—his hands disappeared.

My body throbbed. It ached. But his body, his hands, his long, solid length pressed against my thigh—All of it evaporated. And I was left plastered against his fishbowl windows with my pants down to my ankles while his footsteps receded.

I twisted around to find Eric walking down the far hall, adjusting himself as he went.

"Hey!"

He didn't answer—just kept striding toward his bedroom.

"*Hey!*"

When he still didn't answer, I shimmied after him like an awkward penguin, managed to get my pants back up, and then jogged across the apartment to catch him at the end of the hall.

"Eric!"

When he *still* didn't turn around, I kicked him. Right in the stupid, irritatingly round, perfectly placed tush. With my boot. Really, fucking hard.

*Then* the bastard whirled around. "What the fuck, Jane? Did you just kick me?"

"Right in the ass, yep! I *literally* just kicked your ass. Because who the fuck brings a girl that close to an orgasm and leaves her high and dry?"

Eric shook his head, like he couldn't believe it. "Like you're going to do to me? You just came to Boston to toy with me, didn't you? You don't give a shit about my problems, about this shitty situation. I ask you one fucking question, yes or no, and you're *still* toying with me. Well, two can play that game, gorgeous."

My mouth dropped. "Are you *serious* right now? Who's been playing games, asshole? You flirt all charmingly, get me all hot and heavy, when really you were just trying to manipulate me into a marriage contract so you can get your precious billions. Is that what the banter was for? All the 'you know me better than anyone' bull-shit? The kiss too?"

Eric stormed toward me, forceful enough that I wanted to back down, but my pride wouldn't let me. Because fuck him.

"No," he growled. "*That* was because I couldn't fucking *not*."

He whipped my arms around my back and walked me backwards toward another window, this one looking out onto a quieter street at the end of the hall. My knees buckled as my ass slammed into the edge of a wood console. A few seconds later, my boots were hurled over his shoulder, and my pants were yanked completely off. I was hoisted bodily onto the sleek wood surface.

"You really haven't changed, you know that, Lefferts? Always want to fight."

He kissed me again, and this time it was hard, not soft; fast, not slow. His hands cuffed my wrists on either side as he yanked me into him, attacking me with his tongue, his body, everything he had.

"Is that what you want?" he demanded, breathless and chilly before he devoured me again. "A quick fuck? Someone who'll use you and put you out of your misery?" His breathing hitched, and his low voice was growing uneven. He was angry. Just like me. "Or is it the fight you want? Well, like it or not, Lefferts, no one loves to fight you like I do."

"Can't quite keep your cool anymore, can you, Petri?" I jabbed back before nipping his lip.

Eric yelped, but delivered each kiss, bite for bite, bruise for bruise. His hands flew everywhere. "You're a pain in the fucking ass, Jane."

"You look like the dad from *Full House*."

Another growl. "You look like a Powerpuff Girl fucked a Betty Boop impersonator."

I yanked on his tie. "Cartoons? Really? Come up with something better than that, you polo-wearing twat."

The hand in my hair twisted. "Please. You have ten different colors in your hair. You look like Rainbow Brite on acid."

"Better than being a poster child for the Gestapo!" My hand slid roughly into his pants and took hold of him—anger, it seemed, turned Eric the fuck on. Well, that made two of us.

"Fuck!" Eric shouted, and then, in about four seconds, kicked his shoes away, ripped his pants down, applied a condom from his pocket, and shoved into me with another animal cry.

"You bastard!" I yelped as I clawed at his shoulder. "Take what you want, is it? Is this how marriage is going to be too? Fuck the foreplay, and use the girl?"

It was all for show. He knew it. I knew it. My cries were the only vestiges of control I had, since the simple shape of Eric's long, slightly curved cock was doing its work better than I remembered.

"You're so full of shit, Jane," he said as he found his punishing rhythm—one that included my head banging against the glass behind me, and a screech of the console legs on the floors. "You love every fucking second of this. My dick. Your pussy. Stretching you. Punishing you. You love that my fingers are going to leave bruises all over your ass in the morning, and your neck will be covered with bite marks. *My* marks."

His teeth sank into my neck, just under my ear, hard enough that I yelped.

He thrust even harder.

"Fuck. You," I gritted out, even as I snaked a hand around his neck to hold him in place. If he stopped, I really *would* kick his ass.

"*You are*," he retorted as he continued to split me in half. Just as promised.

And then it hit me. One, two, three more harsh thrusts. My body, which had already been brought to the brink before he'd walked away so cruelly, couldn't fight the tidal wave that crashed through me.

It was always like this with him. It was why, even when I couldn't stand him, I could never forget him.

I didn't just come with Eric. I fucking hurtled.

"GoddammitmotherfuckerholySHIT!" I shouted loud enough that my throat hurt as my head slammed against the window behind me. Profanities spilled out of me one after another, again and again as Eric rattled through me.

He came with a shout, his iron grip on my body tight enough that there *would* be fingerprints, just as he promised. Both our tensed, angry bodies shook until every inch of animosity escaped, one violent shake at a time. It was like the glass walls didn't exist, and all the energy, the anxiety, the *hate* we both felt was free to fly out to the city, disintegrate into the atmosphere.

And all that was left, shared skin on skin, lips on lips, was satiety. Contentment. Bliss.

Eric.

# TEN

"You're an asshole," I mumbled sometime later.

"I know," he said in a voice still searching for breath.

Maybe it was seconds. Maybe it was years. But my voice was weak, and my nose was happy. God, I loved his smell. I sagged against him, finally satisfied. I felt like one of those big predatory cats that don't eat for days, then gorge themselves until their bellies drag on the ground. That was me. An overstuffed pussy.

I snorted. If I could speak at all, I'd have made the joke out loud. Eric, in his blissed-out state, would probably have understood. Hell, he'd probably have started purring just to jump in.

Still, there was truth to the analogy. I hadn't known it until then, but it was like there was an animal pacing inside me most of the time, and only Eric knew how to let it out. He gave it the space to be fierce, to yowl, to roar as it needed. And then he and his slacks-clad ass tamed it, so I was nothing but a sleeping feline. Goodbye, leopard. Hello, house cat. Meow.

Tomorrow I'd hate him for it all the more. But right now, I was in an exceptional state of bliss.

"Clearly you've been keeping up your skills," I remarked, immediately annoyed by how much the idea bothered me. Like I had a claim on him. Like I should care at all where he'd been for the last five years.

He stood up straight so he could look down at me, and I watched with some sadness as his mask of indifference reappeared. "You just can't help yourself, can you?"

I worried my lips together, but looked away. Maybe he was right. Maybe I couldn't.

When he pulled out, though, instead of walking away, he swept me off the console and carried me in his arms like some idiotic romcom character. And I, in my sex-hazed stupor, was too tired, too sated, too *tamed* to fight it as he toted me into a large, equally pristine bedroom and carefully laid me down on one side of the giant, cloud-like bed. I burrowed into the delicious, thousand-count sheets I remembered from years before. It was the little things that betrayed his tastes.

*It's the little things you miss.*

Eric left to clean himself up. When he returned, I watched dazedly as he started getting ready for bed, pulling his shirt the rest of the way off. Damn. He really *had* filled out.

Like he could feel me staring a hole through his psychotically defined abs, he looked up, startled like a wild animal. Then a slow, satisfied smile spread across that square jaw. "Enjoying the show?"

I propped my head up on one hand. "I can't complain." I pointed up and down his body. "I don't, um, remember all of this business."

He looked down at his chiseled physique. "I wasn't so bad back then."

"No, but you didn't look photoshopped either."

He chuckled, but didn't respond as he finished undressing. It was almost like he was doing it deliberately slowly. Turning around, he paused like a model on a runway in front of his closet. So I could get clear views of his ass in those tight black boxers. Enjoy the way the lean muscle in his back rippled in the moonlight. Observe the way his abs crunched deliciously when he bent to pull on his pants.

He stood up fully and turned back, giving me another head-to-toe view of his sculpted body. Good lord. It was like staring at the David —well, a fiery-eyed, ass-slapping, much better "equipped" David.

Eric padded to the bed and sat on the edge. "Are you planning to sleep in your shirt, Lefferts, or should I take your clothes the rest of the way off? Not that they don't look good, but seems like they would be kind of uncomfortable."

"Who said I'm sleeping here?" I asked, though a yawn was already overtaking me. This bed felt like a cloud and the daze of alcohol and sex was setting in. A few more minutes, and I'd be completely immobilized, regardless of the way my blouse was bunched around my ribs.

Eric chuckled, then crawled on his knees so he was close enough to undress me. Noodle-limbed, I let him remove my socks and lift my shirt over my head, then retrieved my other clothes from the hall. I put on my underwear and tucked myself under the covers while he folded the clothes and set them neatly on another white chair in the corner of the bedroom. Then he returned to the other side of the bed.

He didn't pull me close—he knew me too well for that. We hadn't exactly made love—just scratched an itch both of us had. And maybe tore off some skin in the process. Instead, he set a hand on my hip and turned me over, then draped us both with his comforter so we were cocooned in the plush cotton.

"We probably shouldn't do that again," I whispered, suddenly mesmerized by the way his chest gleamed in the moonlight like it was covered in dew.

Eric's eyes flashed, then closed. When they opened, they were collected again. "Yeah. You're probably right."

"Not that it wasn't good. It was. I...I just think it complicates things, you know?"

He didn't reply, just continued to watch me with that unreadable face. But I found my vitriol was gone, at least for the moment. I knew in the morning, I'd feel real regrets, not just the ones I *thought* I should feel. Right now, I had the space to ask the questions my pride wouldn't allow earlier.

"I just need to know one thing." I turned my back and studied the way the moonlight striped the ceiling through the blinds. "Why me?" I glanced back to see his expression.

Eric's forehead crinkled with a few more worry lines at thirty-two than he'd had at twenty-seven. It was the only real sign of aging I could see. And I couldn't lie. They worked for him, just like every other change.

"What do you mean, why you?" he asked finally.

I sighed. "That song and dance about me knowing you better than anyone? It's bullshit. I don't know you at all. I didn't know about any of this, and I bet there's a lot more about your history I'll learn if I say yes. So why me, Eric? Really? And don't you *dare* say it's for shock factor. Or for the hate sex. I'm not a dancing monkey or your courtesan."

He snorted. "I wouldn't have called you either one of those things, Jane. Give me some credit."

I flopped back to my side. "And you better not say it's because I'm funny."

He shook his head, but his mouth quirked deliciously. I found myself wanting to tackle him all over again. *Down, girl.*

"No, it's not that either, although I *usually* enjoy that too. But if I wanted to marry someone for laughs, I'd find a poor comedienne." He shook his head. "I was engaged once before, you know."

My eyes flew wide. "What?"

His mouth pressed into a firm line, and the worry lines reappeared. "It's not something I particularly like discussing."

"Well, tough shit, J. Edgar. Start talking."

Eric gave me a hard look. "'Bright star, were I as steadfast as thou art...'"

I screwed up my face. "Lemme guess: Shelley?"

Eric shook his head. "Keats."

"And that's supposed to mean..."

He sighed. "It means, have a little fucking patience, Jane. This is going to take a minute to get out."

So I waited. And waited. And waited. Did I mention that waiting wasn't particularly my strong suit?

"Penny was my girlfriend in high school," he said. "She was...she was a scholarship student. A girl from Astoria whose parents owned a diner." He rolled onto his back and stared up at the fifteen-foot ceiling. "Penelope Kostas," he said softly.

"She was Greek?"

He nodded. "She was. And sweet. And smart. And not particularly rich. And definitely not from the Upper East Side." He snorted. "Not even close."

I digested this carefully. Eric had been in love. *Eric*, king of the one-night stand, date for every night, dipped his quill in every fucking ink jar in Boston...had once been in love. Who would have thought? I wouldn't have believed it, but the reverence in his voice was clear, and the dreamy, far-off expression on his face couldn't be mistaken for anything else.

*He said it once to you too, Jane Brain,* came my dad's voice out of nowhere. Which was funny, since he had never even met Eric. I had never even mentioned him to my parents.

"She came with me to Dartmouth," Eric continued. "She attended a community college across the river and waited tables in Hanover during my last two years. Her parents were furious. Well, both of our families were upset."

"I bet," I said. "All that work to get their kid into prep school, and she follows your sorry ass to collect fifty-cent tips from legacy frat boys? Fun."

His mouth twisted sadly. "Yeah. Well. I asked her to marry me during my senior year. It only seemed right, and I did love her, regardless of whether or not we were too young. The plan was to move back to the city so she could finish at CUNY while I took up my rightful place at DVS. That, at least, made her parents happy."

"But not yours?"

"I think my dad would have liked her," Eric said. "But since he died when I was a kid, I'll never know."

I quieted again. How did I not know this about him either? How had we spent an entire summer fucking and three years of being classmates without knowing such fundamental things about each other?

"But the rest of them...no," he said. "They hated her. My cousin. My mother. Aunts, uncles, everyone. And most of all, the matriarch herself: my grandmother."

"This is the one who wants you to get married now?"

Eric nodded again. "Ironic, isn't it?"

It was, I had to agree.

"So, what happened?" I asked. "Obviously you didn't get married."

"What happened?" he asked, his voice soft enough that it almost sounded threatening. "What happened was, they made her life a living hell."

I frowned. "Like, how?"

His jaw ground for a second, and a muscle flickered in the side of his cheek. "Little things. They'd invite her to lunch, but no one would be there. Or they'd tell her to dress the wrong way for a party. A costume instead of black tie. Once someone spilled red wine all over her dress. That sort of thing."

I tipped my head. "Oh, nice. Your garden-variety bullying, then."

Eric nodded. "I hoped it would die down the longer she was around them, but it didn't. They started to be more overt about it. Tell her to her face she was trash. Refuse to let her in at functions or family gatherings or make her take the service entrance. Later, they would convince her I was doing terrible things on the side too. That I didn't love her. That I was ashamed of her. That she had no right to be a part of 'their' world. Fucking vultures. All of them."

I was quiet as he bit the words out. The hatred Eric so clearly nursed for his family was unnerving. "That's awful."

Eric worried his jaw for a moment. "It was. So many small, seemingly insignificant moments, but they all came together, you know? Years of it, until one day, Penny believed it all. And that was when I came back to our apartment and found her lying in the bathtub with her blood running down the drain." And then, finally, he turned, with eyes that looked black as the night outside. "She slit her wrists. Left me a note on the bathroom sink. She was sorry, she said. But she knew it was the best thing for me."

My hands flew over my mouth. "Holy shit. Oh my God, Eric. I'm...God, I'm so sorry."

I could imagine it, though I hated to. A young, strapping Eric, eyes full of love for this girl, walking in to find her dead. How his heart must have ripped in half. Had he cried? Howled? Run to her?

My chest shook as each potential action coursed through me.

Eric remained completely still. "So, you see," he said after a few minutes. "There's no love lost between me and my family. Because they took the only thing I ever loved to begin with."

For a second, I hated her. I hated a dead woman, because the bitter pill of jealousy sitting on my tongue made me hate the fact that the world's biggest player, the ice-cold, empty-chested lothario of the Northeast did in fact have a heart. Had in fact met one person he could have loved.

*Except he did say it to you, peanut*, my father's voice reminded me again.

I shook the thought away. That wasn't love. A summer of sex? Endless fights and a string of breakups? That had never been love.

I was a terrible person.

"I'm so sorry," I said again. "Eric, I really am. I hope...I wish... God, I wish there was something I could do."

Finally, his eyes softened a little. "Jane, there *is*. I've already asked you to do it."

My face screwed up with confusion. "I don't get it. How is marrying you going to help this situation? This...God, it's an utter tragedy. But it happened ten years ago. Maybe...maybe it would be better for you to move on, you know?"

Eric sighed. Again, I felt terrible. Who was I, a woman with her dead father chattering in her head, to dictate the limits of anyone's grief?

"This story is why I'm asking *you*, Jane," he said, turning onto his side. He took my hand, stroking the ridges of my fingers and lingering over the left one. The one that could bear a ring. "I'm asking you because I respect you. And because you're the only person I've ever met who would be strong enough to bear it. Them. Their ways. Their fucked-up forms of pressure." His hand returned to my hip and stroked lightly. "It's bad enough they're roping me back into their lives like this. The fuck if I'm going to give them the satisfaction of marrying one of them too." He sighed, and then his mouth quirked again. "You don't give a shit about what anyone thinks of you. I always envied that about you."

"But..." I pressed my lips together. No, I shouldn't say it...it was so pathetic, so ridiculous. It would sound like I wanted his approval, which I *didn't*. Did I? "But you don't even like me," I bit out, recalling Skylar's rant. "I drive you crazy. Why would you want to marry someone you can't stand?"

Eric blinked. "Is that what you really think? That I can't stand you?"

Out of nowhere, my lower lip trembled. Fucking *hell*, were those tears threatening now?

I looked back up at the ceiling. "I don't know. You've certainly acted like it."

"We might spar, Jane, but I think that's a strength."

"You said I was a pain in the ass."

"You are. But in the best possible way, I promise."

I turned back. "So I'm not a total nightmare."

One side of his mouth hooked up, a sly smile that was forgiving. Even warm. "No," he said. "You are definitely not a nightmare."

I smiled back. I couldn't help it. "That's good to know."

His smile widened, brightening the whole of his face. "Then it's settled," he said. "I can stand you, and you can stand me. Now the only question is whether you'll marry me."

———

WE FELL asleep in the cozy nest of his bed, facing each other without speaking, letting the haze of memories and attrition settle over us like a blanket until we drifted off. But a few hours later, I woke again as the sun was peeking over the harbor, just evident over the rooftops of the North End.

Careful not to disturb the sleeping, golden god next to me, I slipped out of the bed, wrapped myself in a thin blanket, and crossed to the window to watch the sunrise. From here, Boston glittered. I felt like a queen surveying my kingdom. I kind of liked it. Queen Jane.

There was a rustle behind me. I turned.

"Hey," Eric said groggily, pushing halfway up. "Everything all right?"

"I don't need more time," I said from where I stood at the window.

"Oh?"

I touched my hand to the glass. It was cool against my fingertips. "I thought about it. And my answer is yes. On one condition."

Eric's reflection tipped its head. "What's that?"

I turned, full of determination. Not to fight him. To fight my own instincts. "You keep that pretty girl stuff to yourself from now on."

Eric studied me for a moment. The early morning light cast a golden glow over his body, and for a moment, he seemed larger than life, a figure lifted from my ultimate fantasies, waiting to welcome me home.

My heart twisted.

"You sure?" he asked. There was nothing sarcastic in his tone.

We both knew what we had. Sex, hate, and maybe a little bit of fondness for one another in between those. And respect, apparently, nicknames aside. But if we got married, something was going to give.

How many friends did I have—Skylar and Brandon notwithstanding—who complained about how much "changed" once they married their husbands? Who talked about how marriage turned them into objects? House cleaners and trophies. Babysitters and models.

They stopped being people. They lost themselves.

All it took was a few minutes on top of a console to forget my name. What would happen if I was married to the person doing that?

I had no idea. I just knew I couldn't lose the most important thing I had—my sense of self.

So I nodded. "Abso-fucking-lutely. You and I know *that* is not a good place for us to revisit. This isn't going to work if we do."

Eric didn't say anything, just continued to watch me from the bed. His eyes were black in the early morning light, the sunlight creating deep shadows over his perfectly chiseled cheekbones, the square pectorals, and the carved muscles of his deltoids and biceps. The man was a work of art. A work of art I had no problem defiling.

That itself *was* the primary problem.

"I'm serious, Eric," I said as I returned to the bed and sat next to him. "You try that dominant shit on me at *any* time and can kiss your billions goodbye. No more sex. This has to be a business transaction. You help me out, and I help you out. And maybe at the end we can come out friends again. Okay?"

"And if I do?" he said just as directly. "If I promise? You'll do it? No games, no push-and-pull?"

His voice was deep, but trembled slightly. It wasn't until that moment I realized the real stakes here. I was going to marry the new head of one of the most powerful families in the world. Which meant I'd be at the head of it too. It didn't matter if this promise was false. It didn't matter if we were lying or not. If we were going to do this, it had to be all the way. With a partnership that no one, not even we, could shake.

"Yes," I said. "I'll do it. If you promise."

Somewhere, a gull voiced its lonely cry amidst the ships bobbing in the harbor. A foghorn blew in the distance, likely from a massive shipping container. Maybe even one of his.

"All right, Lefferts," Eric said solemnly. "It's a deal. You marry me in six months, I won't touch you unless you ask. On my honor."

I blinked, but he didn't. He meant every word he said.

Cautiously, I held out a hand. Eric examined it, and we shook, like a couple of gangsters in a bad film.

"Deal," I said. "Let's get married."

# PART TWO

## THE TENSION

*Please open that*
*Big*
*Red*
*Mouth*
*One more time so I can*
*Crush*
*Those lips like two cherries. I'd destroy*
*Yournameyourbodyyourmindyoursoul*
*Just like*
*You once destroyed mine.*

"Taunt"
—from the journal of Eric de Vries

# INTERLUDE I

The helicopter landed in midtown at half-past eight, carrying a man in a simple, but immaculately cut black suit, a garment bag containing another, a briefcase with EdV engraved into the soft leather, and a paper sack with two bags of single-origin, light-roasted Ethiopian coffee beans and an Aeropress.

The briefcase was a gift, sent from his grandmother two days prior, when he'd called in the early morning hours to tell her that everything was settled. He was getting married, and he would be joining the family on Monday, off to start a newly created position with the CEO that would essentially require him to shadow the day-to-day operations of his family's dynasty. Considering how quickly the briefcase was delivered and the fact that, with the engraving, Grandmother had likely commissioned the custom leather piece weeks ago, he was almost loath to accept it. It meant he was a foregone conclusion; it was designed to convey his grandmother's wry intelligence as much as congratulations.

The coffee was his own. He knew it would probably seem neurotic to his new office. Staff loved to gossip, and his entry into the company would cause ripples of it for months as people observed his every quirk and reported them to their friends at happy hour. But he didn't care. Most offices had terrible coffee, and just because DVS would soon be his didn't mean they would know how to caffeinate properly.

Another man in a black suit stood at the end of the helipad, waiting for Eric to approach. His suit wasn't as nice as Eric's. Too boxy around his linebacker-sized shoulders with a cheap black tie that didn't match tonally. Eric noticed these things.

The bodyguard touched a Bluetooth headset lodged in his ear and made a comment under his breath before turning to the new arrival. "Mr. de Vries."

Eric nodded and allowed the man to take the garment bag and the coffee, but not the briefcase. "Tony."

Tony was the other gift: head of the security team Grandmother had insisted upon the second she was told her grandson had decided to obey the terms of her offer. For his protection, she said. As the new heir to De Vries Shipping and its subsidiaries, Eric would be walking around with a target on his back. But Eric knew the truth. Tony was a babysitter, pure and simple. A spy.

"No Ms. Lefferts?" Tony asked as they walked through the port. "Mrs. de Vries thought she might accompany you. She is eager to meet her, I believe."

Eric shook his head. That hadn't taken long. When he informed his grandmother about the arrangement, her response had been curt: she wanted a name, a date, and the name of her lawyer. Now she was siccing bodyguards to fetch more information.

"Jane's tying up a few loose ends," he said. "She's coming for Sunday dinner next weekend."

The thought pricked his skin. Once, five years before, he had tried to bring this girl home. Girl. Woman. She'd probably be indignant at the former and scoff at the latter. What the hell was he *supposed* to say? Female companion?

Eric smirked. Fucking hell, he fought with her when she wasn't even there. She'd probably like that.

But the last time he'd asked had been a catastrophe—this, at least, was more civilized. A quick, brutal fuck followed by a heart-to-heart about a life Eric would have preferred to keep in the past. But instead of running with a string of curses, like he'd expected, Jane had instead extended an oddly formal handshake, and the following day, Eric had received a notice from her lawyer establishing contact. And since the lawyer was Skylar, that meant the letter was walked from the office next to his.

It was one of Skylar's iron-clad prenups that were quickly making her famous around Boston's elite.

There was no way Eric should have agreed to anything without Grandmother's permission. So of course, he did right away. And immediately had to endure another meeting with Kieran, the other founding partner of their small firm, to discuss the terms of his five-year leave.

———

*"IT'S STILL YOUR FIRM,"* Skylar said. *"You're not selling your stake, and that's final."*

*Eric nodded, grateful for the gesture. His share of Copley's billing was a pittance compared to his new salary at DVS, but it was still nice to know that his percentage of the firm's earnings came from his own efforts, not a tangled inheritance.*

*"I'll be back," he told her. "It's just time to learn and eventually oversee the business. I'm not stepping on as CEO. Just shadowing."*

*Skylar didn't look so sure, but she nodded.*

*"I wondered if Celeste de Vries would pull something like this at some point," Kieran remarked as she sipped on what had to be her sixth espresso of the day, leaving a bright red lip print on the edge of the porcelain cup.*

*Eric's favorite part of working with Kieran was their shared passion for good coffee. Otherwise, the woman scared the shit out of him and just about everyone else. It shouldn't have surprised him that his partner had done her homework.*

*But he jerked his head up anyway. "You knew?"*

*Kieran rolled her eyes. "Why do you think I agreed to start this place with you and Skylar? The two of you were still as green as the dollars in your trust fund, Eric. But between Brandon's billables and the fact that your name alone gets us half our corporate clients—don't argue with me on that point, you know it's true—this firm was never going to fail." She shrugged. "It was just good business. And if you enrich our relationship with the New York business elite, even better."*

*Eric frowned. "You're not thinking De Vries Shipping is going to be a new client, are you? I might not work there yet, but I can tell you right now they won't hire outside of New York State. It wouldn't make any sense."*

*Kieran turned to Skylar. "When did he get slow?"*

*Skylar just shrugged. She was uncharacteristically quiet, and Eric wondered for the tenth time that week what kind of conversations had been happening with a certain pink-haired houseguest.*

*Kieran swiveled her chair. "If you're the chairman of the board at DVS, our profile is going to go through the roof, you idiot. Sending you off on this little sabbatical will be genius for our bottom line. We'll be able to compete with Kiefer and Grove. I'd bet you five hundred dollars that we'll need to hire at least ten new associates by next September."*

*"I have a bit more news, to that end," Skylar said. "Brandon offered to step in last night. Fill your shoes, as it were. Or at least take on your pro bono stuff and some of mine if, um, Jane wants me to come down here and there."*

*At that, Kieran's jaw dropped. "You're kidding. I'm going to have to deal with his smart ass every day of the week?"*

*Skylar chuckled. Kieran and Brandon were best friends, having grown up together in South Boston, but they definitely had a love-hate relationship, more like recalcitrant siblings than anything else. No one got under Kieran's skin like Brandon.*

"You've said a million times that my marriage to Brandon gets us business," Skylar pointed out. "What do you think actually having him here is going to do?"

"Make a damn mess, probably. Brandon hasn't stepped foot in a courtroom in years," Kieran returned.

Skylar shrugged. "We can put him on contracts. But I doubt he's forgotten how to do this job. He used to be the best litigator in Boston."

Kieran couldn't argue with that.

Eric turned back to Skylar. "Does that mean Jane's coming tomorrow after all?" He ignored the way his chest thumped at the idea. He didn't really care that much if she did. Or at least, he'd keep telling himself that.

Skylar shifted uneasily and shook her head. "No, no. She has to go back to Chicago to pack. But I'm planning to come next weekend with her. I just...want to make sure she settles in all right. Dealing with... those types...can be daunting."

Eric didn't have to ask what she meant. Skylar's mother was a Chambers, a similar clan to the de Vries on the Upper East Side, though they didn't have anywhere near the social clout his family had. Janette was a piece of work, though, and had definitely put Skylar through the wringer five years back. Eric sympathized with her worry for Jane. Really, he understood the threats even better than she did.

So he didn't argue. The truth was, when—if, because until she was there, he wouldn't actually one hundred percent believe it—he brought pink-haired, smart-mouthed Jane Lefferts to Park Avenue as his fiancée, all of New York was going to explode. Jane would need an ally. Eric wouldn't be enough.

———

TONY STOPPED outside a stolid black Rolls-Royce and opened the shiny back door.

Eric stared at it. "You've got to be kidding."

"Sir?"

Eric looked up. "I'm thirty-two, Tony, not eighty-two. This is the same car my grandfather drove. It's time for an update, don't you think?"

Tony cleared his throat. "This car is two years old, sir."

Eric sighed. *Jane would get it.* She would have taken one look at this fucking behemoth and made some crack about Mr. Burns and Tony being Smithers. The thought brought a whispered smile to Eric's face.

It was worth it. Even after getting ridiculously high off their give-and-take, realizing that fucking her was even better than he remembered, and promising he wouldn't touch her again for the next five years...it would all be worth it if she would be there to keep him from feeling dead inside while he sold his soul to this company. Pissed off was better than dead. Crazy with lust was better than dead.

Anything was better than that.

Tony walked around to the driver's seat while Eric slid into the back seat. Fucking hell, this city was a noisy cesspool. Already, Eric missed the comparatively quieter streets of Boston, the way the sturdy brick buildings of the North End insulated him from the sounds that, in New York, made him feel like he was in an echo chamber. At least the leather interior was butter soft. And the way New York's cacophony was practically muted after all the doors were closed might have been worth the near-three-hundred-thousand-dollar price tag this car carried.

It still made him look like an oil baron, though.

"Mr. de Vries, hello!"

A cheery, chestnut-haired woman popped her tiny brown head from around the passenger seat, making Eric jump. With her pointed nose and fluttering brown eyes, she reminded him distinctly of a hummingbird.

"Jesus," he muttered, clasping a hand to his chest. "Who are you?"

"Bridget McAvoy, Mr. de Vries. I'm your executive assistant. Mrs. de Vries interviewed and hired me two weeks ago."

Ah, another spy. Like the briefcase, another sign the old bat had been preparing for this long before he said yes. To her, he never had a choice. The idea was infuriating, but just as Eric opened his mouth to fire the girl for it, she started talking at a mile a minute.

"So, I tagged along with Tony to go over your schedule for the day. You're very busy, you see, and I also wanted to get a feel for when you thought you'd prefer to start most days. Today you have the morning blocked out with the CEO and the CFO, followed by a debriefing with the tariffs VP, Mr. Hartley, and then after that you've got two other meetings with George Clarkson and Alex Pham, followed by an appointment with your real estate broker, then your tailor, then—"

"Tailor?" Eric interrupted the avalanche of scheduling. "The others I get, but why a tailor? I have plenty of suits."

"Ah, Mrs. de Vries said you would need their services to represent the company f-fully," Bridget said meekly.

Her gaze traveled over him, as if searching for validation. Eric bristled internally but didn't move. She'd find none. He happened to like nice suits, and this particular Calvin Klein was one of his favorites. He wasn't interested in being remade into a version of his grandfather with a bunch of stodgy old Greenfields.

He shook his head vehemently. "I'm not a paper doll, Bridget, and I have a closet full of perfectly adequate menswear."

"But—"

"Cancel the tailor. I have one in Boston we can fly in if we need him."

Bridget bobbed her head nervously and used her stylus to scratch a note onto the iPad. "All right, then. After that, you've got drinks with the mayor—"

"Nope."

"—followed by a board meeting at Lincoln Center—"

"Absolutely not."

"—and a dinner gala for the Children's—"

"No."

Bridget looked up like she was speaking to a small child. "Mr. de Vries."

But instead of getting angry, Eric smiled. Bridget quaked. He had to stop himself from rolling his eyes. He really didn't know what it was about women that made them respond that way to something as simple as a smile, but at this point in his life, it was getting, well, boring.

At least Jane didn't do that. She'd probably tell him to stick his smile back in a test tube.

Now the smile widened for real.

When he first moved to Boston, a cocky shit of twenty-two, the city was his oyster, and all the girls were pearls. Eric had absolutely no problem hopping from bar to bar, bed to bed. The chase was as much fun as the catch, and Boston, with over thirty-five colleges and over one hundred and fifty thousand students milling around, was basically a prime place to go hunting. Girls from Cambridge, girls from Southie. Girls from Watertown, girls from Somerset. Tufts girls, BU girls, MIT girls, BC girls. UMass, Emerson, Suffolk, Northeastern, and yes, Harvard. All of them useful distractions from the broken heart he was trying to mend.

Jane would have probably made another cutting remark right about then about how he'd lived up to that irritating fucking nickname, Petri dish.

Was it her insecurity?

Was it because she liked the reaction it would provoke?

With Jane, he never knew.

But it took one to know one. If Jane hated his habits, then she'd have to hate herself. It took about five seconds at an orientation mixer to recognize each other for what they both were: players. It took another fifteen minutes to get back to Eric's apartment, and twenty more for them to collapse on the bed, gasping for breath.

Rinse and repeat.

And two years later, when it happened again. And again. And again.

The memories came flooding back.

————

*TOO MANY DRINKS. Sex in the air. Overloaded with stress, their friends' drama, the pending bar exam, and new jobs. It had started with a night out. Dancing in a crowd of sweaty people. A cover of "Rock the Casbah" blasting from the stage. And when Jane turned around to look at Eric, some unknown barrier had broken.*

*He had to have her again. And that was it.*

————

FROM THEN ON, every time she visited Boston, she was in his bed, usually tied up, or provoking him into doing something else. The way her skin turned pink from his hand went from a novelty to a compulsion. She was the first woman who was literally game for anything—anything he wanted to try, she was a willing participant. The challenge was intoxicating. Addictive.

And then...something unbelievably stupid happened. What started out as a casual, stress-reducing fuckfest quickly turned into something else. They should have known better. You can't really fuck your friend without falling in love. And you can't fall in love without breaking someone's heart.

Three months later, they were through. Eric should have known it was coming—for all their similarities, he and Jane were like oil and water. She was loud and outspoken, whereas Eric tended to keep things to himself. She dressed like every day was a Cure concert. He almost never wore black unless it was a suit. So even though it hurt— and yeah, it *fucking hurt* when they ended—Eric had to admit that it was probably for the best.

Except when she left, he missed the girl.

He missed the too-skinny, spiky-haired, nose-ringed, punk-listening know-it-all who liked nothing more than to call him names and make fun of his idiosyncrasies. Was it just the give-and-take? The banter? He couldn't have said. But if he was *really* being honest, for five years, that feeling had never quite disappeared.

*No one wants to fight you like I do.* God, it was true.

Eric pressed his forehead to the cool glass of the window while Bridget chattered. These little flights down memory lane happened from time to time—usually when he was tired or had too much to drink. They were easily chased away with vodka or women, but he didn't have access to either at the moment.

He didn't need to rehash the disintegration of the relationship. The misunderstandings. The betrayals. The feeling like being stabbed in the chest every time some random thing of hers showed up in his apartment. One of her rubber bracelets. A half-used blue dye kit. The well-thumbed copy of *The Bell Jar*.

New York flew by, a blur of gray and black and white and yellow —buildings, pavements, people, taxis. With every passing block, Eric's mood grew darker.

"Mr. de Vries?" Bridget's voice woke him out of his trance.

"Hmm...sorry. What?"

She was holding out a plain white envelope, her twittery bird face blinking nervously.

Eric glared at it. "I have messages already?"

"Just...just one. It arrived this morning. Same-day delivery from Paris, if you can believe it."

The skin on the back of Eric's neck prickled as he accepted the letter and opened it. Inside was a simple sheet of white paper. He unfolded the note, and immediately, dread wrapped around his rib cage and squeezed like an old friend he hadn't seen in years as he clapped eyes on the familiar slanted handwriting. Familiar, but certainly not wanted.

---

*Triton,*

*Imagine our surprise to learn you were back from the dead after committing such unnecessary self-regicide.*

*We rejoice at the return of our brother. And look forward to giving you a proper welcome at Portas. Soon.*

*Noctis silentio tuetur.*
   *—Titan and the rest of Janus*

---

Eric swore. It was under his breath, but Bridget clearly heard him —her fawn-like eyes widened at the string of sudden profanity.

"Ev-everything all right, Mr. de Vries?"

With a sick feeling in his stomach, Eric crunched the note into his fist tightly enough that his knuckles turned white, then shoved it into his briefcase. When he caught his reflection in the rearview mirror, he wore an expression he had not seen for a very long time: an odd combination of fear, dread, and rage, all at once.

He gave Bridget a tight, flat-lipped expression, but said nothing.

The Rolls pulled to a stop in front of the old stone building four blocks from South Street, where three twenty-foot steel letters—DVS —guarded the revolving glass doors. Eric didn't wait for Tony to let him out, just stepped onto the sidewalk, full of people, and gazed up at the building that he had once hoped would never be his destiny.

For a long time, he stared at the behemoth letters. When he was a child, he had climbed on them, imagined they were towers where fair maidens were captured. Now he was on his way to the top floor to claim his place in the tower where he would be trapped for the next five years.

The letter in his briefcase felt as heavy as a rock.

"Fucking hell," he muttered to himself. "Just call me Rapunzel."

Except there would be no prince to save him. The only way out was to jump.

# ELEVEN

I couldn't deny it. Sometimes it was really, *really* nice having friends with money.

Both Brandon and Skylar had insisted on coming with me to New York prior to my big debut with the de Vries clan. It wasn't necessary. I knew that. Eric assured me that he'd cover anywhere I wanted to stay. But their kids were staying with Skylar's grandmother, so the weekend was a bit of a getaway for the two of them too. They'd gone all out with a giant suite at the Plaza—two master bedrooms with their own entrances, split by a living room bigger than my old studio. Skylar wouldn't hear of me being anywhere but next door, and Brandon refused to sleep in a single room.

I stretched out in the tufted-back, king-size bed and reveled in the pillow-topped mattress and the fact that absolutely nothing smelled like pickled vegetables or Febreze. Listen, you try spending five weeks on your mother's sagging couch and tell me a suite at the Plaza isn't heaven. I could have died right then and been happy.

Aside from the hotel room, though, I actually didn't like New York much. I'd visited with Skylar a few times in law school, since she was originally from Brooklyn and would bring me home on holidays to hang with her family. New York—well, at least Manhattan—just felt like a sanitized version of Chicago, and without the cool lake on one side. Chicago had better Italian food by a long shot, and yeah, I'll say it: better pizza too. What's wrong with these people? Who wants thin crust pizza so floppy you have to fold it in half to eat? Especially when you can get a full meal in one slice of deep dish?

The shopping, though. You can't be a fashion addict and not like that. Would being a de Vries would give me access to Fashion Week? Hmmm. Maybe there were other perks to this gig that I hadn't considered yet.

Sometime after nine, I dragged myself out of bed, shoved my hair in a knot, popped on my glasses with the vintage gold Dior frames, and padded groggily into the suite's living room. Skylar sat curled in one of the plush armchairs with a cup of tea while she paged through a brief. Through the wall of windows waved Central Park, where a wash of green was dotted by the pink and white flowering trees of late spring. Okay, so one more point to New York. It wasn't Lake Michigan on a crisp June day, but it was definitely pretty.

"Morning, sunshine," Skylar said, not looking up from her brief. "Breakfast is over there."

"Coffee," I mumbled as I padded over to the room service tray on a small dining table. There were two plates of food, still covered and warm, containing eggs and sausage. I grimaced. No, thank you. The other plate contained fresh fruit and a box of Froot Loops. I grinned. My friend knew me so well.

"Where's Brandon?" I asked as I sat down at the table and poured my cereal into a spare bowl. Don't judge me. The only good cereal is the sweet kind.

"He got up to run around the park." Skylar joined me, taking her plate of scrambled eggs. She checked her watch—a very pretty Bvlgari that was a push present from Brandon after Jenny was born. Well, that and a trip to Italy, but who was keeping track? "He'll probably be back any minute. Dinner tonight is when?"

I swallowed a massive bite. "Seven. Eric said he'd pick me up here at six." I rolled my eyes. "Like I need an escort. You guys are all ridiculous."

Skylar narrowed her eyes but didn't respond while she munched on her toast. "Okay, then." She swallowed. "I was thinking we should go shopping today."

I frowned. "*You* want to go shopping?"

My best friend was many things, but a clothes horse was not one of them. When we were roommates, I'd usually have to choose her outfits like she was a freaking toddler whenever she went on a date. Otherwise she was more likely just to lounge around in her favorite old jeans and a T-shirt.

Since marrying Brandon, her style had grown up, though not without my continued guidance. She preferred simple, elegant pieces and over the years had increasingly taken advantage of private stylists to supplement her wardrobe of suit separates and the occasional evening gown. But those ugly old jeans—which she was currently wearing—were still her favorites.

"Not for me," she said. "For you. Since you're actually meeting your future in-laws today, you might want to make a good impression."

"You sound like my mother," I grumbled, then stared down at the old plaid pajamas and the ripped T-shirt I'd worn to bed with a bit of shame.

I had some nice things. I loved clothes, even made my own sometimes. Skylar knew this—I had practically sewn the girl's wedding dress together before she and Brandon eloped. Therefore, I resented the insinuation that I didn't know how to dress to meet Eric's stuffy family.

"Well, I wasn't going to meet the countess in my pajamas," I said before reaching across the table to pour myself some coffee. She wasn't royalty, but I couldn't think of Eric's grandmother as anything else. "I think I can handle it."

"Black suits for court don't count."

"They aren't all suits."

"It's almost summer on the Upper East Side. You shouldn't be wearing black anything."

I snorted. "Says the one-woman funeral service. Skylar, you have more black in your closet than Wednesday Addams."

"Yeah, but this is different. *I*'m not trying to make a good impression on a family who probably spends more on clothes each year than most people spend on their mortgages. Think about Janette. She never wears black."

Janette Chambers, Skylar's estranged mother, was born and bred on Park Avenue, a person who floated in and out of her children's lives and nearly sabotaged Brandon and Skylar's entire relationship in an attempt to extort money from them to save her own fortune. In other words, a terrible person. A graceful, beautiful, eminently stylish, but nonetheless horrific human being.

She also, if I recalled correctly, usually looked like springtime incarnate.

I grimaced. "They can't *all* be like her." My denial was weak. After hearing Eric's story about Penny, I wasn't sure I believed myself.

Skylar nodded. "Sure, they can. They can *all* be like that. Why do you think I agreed to a big fancy wedding? I wanted to fit the hell in."

"Sky, you eloped in a hospital chapel."

"Yes, but we *planned* a big church wedding."

"And you wouldn't shut up about the fact that Brandon bought you a fifteen-thousand-dollar dress to wear for five hours," I argued back. "You yourself thought the whole thing was ridiculous. At least I'm not fighting it. Planning this wedding, even if it is fake, is actually something I'm looking forward to. It's going to be fun to deck myself out in yards of couture."

I sighed. Truth? I bought four stacks of bridal magazines for the flight back from Chicago, looking for patterns to knock off. There was no way I or my mother could afford a couture wedding dress, but maybe I'd get lucky and one of the houses would want to dress the newest addition to Eric's family. And if not, if I started now, maybe I could sew a knock-off myself. I was scared shitless of almost everything else about this ridiculous arrangement, but the fashion? I could handle that.

Skylar shrugged off my points. "It was insanely expensive, but I did like the dress. And, by the way, I'm buying yours too. You're not walking down the aisle in something you made on your sewing table, I don't care how talented you are."

I bit my lip, annoyed she read my mind. "Thanks a lot."

"I'm sorry, Janey, but you don't get to go *Pretty in Pink* this time. It's just not going to work."

I stuck out my lip. I resented that. I made way cooler clothes than that ugly pink dress. "It's just one dinner. And my style is way better than Molly Ringwald's ever was."

Skylar gave me the same look she gave her daughter when Jenny asked to stay up all night. "Do you really think it's going to end with one dinner? You'll meet his family and 'poof,' six months later you'll be married?"

I paused mid-stir of my coffee. "Well..."

"Jane, you read the style section every week. I know you know what a society wedding really looks like."

I gulped. Shit. Despite paging through bridal shots yesterday, I really hadn't thought about this, but Skylar was right. Engagement parties. Rehearsal dinners. Two and three and four receptions. The weddings of the rich and famous were gauche, months-long affairs. Maybe ours wouldn't be like that. My mother and I certainly couldn't afford it. But the more Skylar spoke, the more I realized I truly had no idea what kinds of things were going to be expected of me in the months to come.

"Do you know if they have any other events planned this summer? Stuff you might be expected to attend?"

I cleared my throat. "Um...just a few. Dinner tonight with family and close friends, and another thing out on Long Island in a month or two. That one is a big barn dance for New York's high society."

Skylar arched a thin red brow.

I rolled my eyes. "Don't be so pleased with yourself, you Cheshire cat. Okay, so there's going to be a party. But you're forgetting one thing."

"What's that?"

I gestured around my face and body. There was a lot to see—the rainbow pink hair, the ornate glasses, the lips I usually painted red. "I'm pretty sure he's asking me to do this *because* of the shock-and-awe factor. I don't have to fit in. Eric said."

"Eric's a guy," Skylar retorted. "He doesn't know what kind of bullshit double standards women deal with or how they talk to each other. It's all very under the nose, but these people have a way of making you feel like nothing without even saying a word. After all, didn't you say that they basically drove his fiancée to her death?"

Slowly, I nodded, and sympathy glowed in Skylar's green eyes. She had been in the same place only five years ago, learning to maneuver through her husband's world of uptight New Englanders who wanted to keep him for themselves.

"Trust me on this, then," she said. "It's not lace and satin—it's armor. And it's going to give the vultures one less reason to pick you apart." She reached out and squeezed my shoulder. "You helped me through this process, remember? I don't think I would have stayed with Brandon if it hadn't been for your perfect combination of sass and confidence. So, let me help you, Janey. Let me buy you a couple of dresses, all right?"

I opened my mouth to say no, but visions of Eric's judgy-as-fuck family looking down their long Dutch noses stopped me. I was already going to be an oddity—more than likely, his family was already pissed off that the family's black sheep was being handed the keys to the empire. Marrying me was just the cherry on the fuck-you sundae. As far as they knew, I wasn't just going to be a blemish on their spotless blonde family tree. I was going to poison the damn thing.

Well, if I was going to go about ruining bloodlines, I might as well do it looking fierce as fuck.

"All right, Counselor," I abated. "You've just won your case."

Skylar grinned triumphantly, but before she could respond, the heavy front door to the suite opened, and a very sweaty Brandon bounded in, his sharp blue eyes landing immediately on Skylar. I swear, the man had built-in radar when it came to his wife.

It took him less than a second to reach her.

"Brandon!" Skylar half whispered, half screeched as the man proceeded to bury his face in her neck. Her dismay was clear, but her pleasure was even more evident. Please. She acted all tough, but Sky couldn't get enough of this sort of thing.

Should I have felt uncomfortable, watching my friend get accosted by her husband while I enjoyed my morning joe? Maybe. But honestly, you want uncomfortable, try a blind date in a sex club full of middle-aged, vinyl-clad doms trolling for their next sub. Yes, that once happened. People see spiky hair in a personal ad, and they think you'll do anything. It was...uninspiring. Too many assless chaps, not enough chisel, if you catch my drift.

"Red," Brandon murmured as he lifted her easily out of her seat. "We have no kids around for two whole days. *No. Kids.*"

"Brandon, Jane's here. I was trying to convince her to go shopping —ah!"

My eyes? They practically rolled out of my head when, instead of letting her finish her sentence, Brandon basically did his own version of *The Kiss*, that World War II photograph of the soldier sucking the nurse's face off in the middle of Times Square. Really, though. Skylar was going shopping for a few hours, not embarking on the S.S. Punch A Nazi.

"Brandon, Jane is right next to us!"

Brandon twisted around with a frown. "Oh. Hey, Jane. I didn't realize you were up."

I raised my mug in salute. "Hey, not like I haven't seen it before.

After all, I had a front-row seat to you rabbits learning each other's love buttons the first time around."

Skylar's face flushed the same color as her hair, but Brandon just smirked as he touched his nose to his wife's.

"I told you," he informed her in a low, foreboding voice. "This is happening whether she's here or not."

Brandon kissed her again with a growl that gave me shivers—not because he turned me on the way he clearly did Skylar, but because the implied threat reminded me of someone else who used to growl at me that way.

Someone whom I had told in no uncertain terms he was not to look at me like that again.

Someone whom I was now supposed to...marry.

I ignored the pang in my stomach at the thought. That feeling? I'd learned to live with it over the last five years. But that didn't mean I liked it.

Skylar grinned over Brandon's large shoulder. "Sorry," she mouthed as he carried her toward their bedroom. Still, her green eyes danced.

I grinned right back at her as I got up from the table. She wasn't getting off that easy. "Is boy-o here snipped yet, Sky? Because I'm pretty sure he could get *me* pregnant over here the way he's looking at you."

"Jane!"

This time it was both of their glares that sent me scampering back toward my bedroom. Brandon's staunch refusal to get a vasectomy was a topic of contention between them, and it was *way* too easy to bug the guy about it. Skylar, after having suffered miserably through one pregnancy, had absolutely refused to carry a second baby (they adopted Luis, their second). I happened to know that my friend had no interest in having a third kid—after all, they were already practically raising her younger siblings alongside their own children—but I was pretty sure Captain America there wanted another. Actually, I was pretty sure he'd knock up Skylar every year if she'd let him.

"Sky...just rap on my door when you're ready to go," I called. "What do you think, Brandon? Fifteen minutes? Or will it only take ten?"

"Try at least ninety!" Brandon shouted, chasing me away completely.

As much as I loved giving Brandon shit, he was paying my way here. I could at least try to give the guy a break.

———

"WHAT ABOUT HERE?"

I looked up and down at the storefront window, not even bothering to mask my disdain. "St. John? *Really?* Skylar, we are not scheming, middle-aged actresses on *Days of Our Lives.*" I looked her over. "Come on, you have money. You don't dress like this."

Skylar sighed. We'd been tromping up Madison Avenue for thirty minutes, and my friend had yet to suggest a shop where the patrons' average age wasn't at least sixty-five.

I tried again. "Maybe we should—"

"Don't say it."

"Come on, Janette knows where to—"

"Absolutely not. Jane, we are not inviting my mother to stick her ridiculous and probably fake nose into this situation."

We stood there, staring at each other in the middle of the street while a mix of taxis, Town Cars, and Teslas drove past.

"Fine," I said. "Then we'll go straight to the source. One of these broads ought to know what to wear to dinner with Grandma on Park Avenue."

I looked around the street, searching for good potential. Immediately, I spied a group of well-manicured women holding disposable coffee cups and pushing strollers that probably cost more than a car payment.

"Ah ha!" I said. "The mommy brigade."

"Jane—"

"Stop being such a scaredy-cat," I snapped before striding right up to the women as they approached us. "Excuse me. Hello, excuse me!"

Despite being only a few feet away, I had to practically shout before any of them stopped. Like they were connected by some electronic cord, the women all stopped at once, and their faces swiveled together toward me.

"Yes?" asked the one closest before she pursed her perfectly plumped lips together.

She was tall, but petite. Lithe, but still curvy. Her style was effortlessly put together with whites and denim, but the kind that looked like it had never been worn before, and her dark brown hair hung in gentle waves, framing rose-petal skin and possibly enhanced lips. If they were fake, her doctor was the best. Just like everything else about her.

The woman's bright blue eyes scanned my outfit, which, as Skylar had pointed out again when we were dressed, was decidedly *not* Upper East Side. Black cigarette pants, patent-red platform sneakers, and a canary yellow sweater that was perfect for the slight nip in the air that morning. Punk with a side of Bettie Page, my personal style idol. With my hair plaited down my shoulder in a fishtail braid and my makeup on point beneath a pair of heart-shaped red glasses, I thought I looked fabulous. Maybe not Park Avenue, but fabulous nonetheless.

But to the mean girls of the Upper East Side, I was just a misfit.

"I really am Andie Walsh," I murmured to myself.

"What?"

"We were just wondering where ladies like you shop." Skylar stepped in with a concerned look for me. "My friend has an event tonight that she's shopping for."

"Your friend?" asked the woman with another skeptical glance at me. "Have you checked the Village? Maybe Brooklyn?"

The women behind her snickered.

"Well, the event is up here," Skylar pointed out sharply. "My mother is from here, but we just didn't think her taste was the best."

I wanted to snort. I knew what she was doing. As much as she hated them, Skylar was offering her bona fides to these haughty bitches.

"Oh?" asked Blue Eyes. "And who *is* your mother?"

"Janette Chambers," Skylar stated through clenched teeth.

"Oh!" The woman's eyes popped open, suddenly as bright as the sky, and her tone changed completely. "Didn't her daughter...so that would make you..."

"Skylar Sterling," Skylar admitted, barely audible.

Now my eyes flew open. I happened to know my friend hadn't taken Brandon's name legally—she was too fucking independent for that, and she also loved the way Crosby sounded professionally.

"*Oh!*" Suddenly every one of these women was clamoring across the sidewalk, abandoning their strollers (and the children in them) so that it was virtually impossible for other people to pass. They practically fell over themselves trying to shake Skylar's hand. Obviously, Brandon wasn't an unknown entity in New York. Skylar's cheeks were pink, but I recognized her smile as the creepy one she wore when she was uncomfortable. Suddenly, there wasn't much more I loved about my friend besides the fact that she abhorred this world.

"So yeah," she said. "We were just wondering where the best shops were. You know, if we're not looking for St. John." She winked at me. I chuckled.

"Oh, gosh, yes, I can give you a bunch of recs," said the blue-eyed leader, who then introduced herself as Caitlyn. Five minutes later, she and her entire posse had provided Skylar with about fifteen recommendations, including names of salespeople. Meanwhile, I hovered on the fringes, trying not to get pushed into the street.

"Are you shopping for anything special?" asked Caitlyn. "What's the event, exactly?"

"Actually, we're here for my friend's engagement," Skylar said, pulling me into the center of the group. "We hear that Celeste, Jane's future grandmother-in-law, is a little picky."

"Wait...Celeste de Vries?"

All four heads swiveled back to me. Caitlyn stepped forward. Suddenly we were back in high school. They were a pack, and she was the ringleader. What did that make me? The lone wolf, or prey?

"You're not...you're not Eric de Vries's fiancée, are you?" she asked with a tight smile, almost as if she couldn't believe she was saying the words as she scanned me again with new care.

"Well, um—"

"She is," Skylar put in firmly. "This is Jane Lefferts. We've all been friends since law school. At Harvard." More pedigree dropping. This time mine.

"*You're* marrying Eric de Vries." The woman—Caitlyn—said it like it was a foreign language phrase. Slow and not quite enunciated correctly.

I folded my arms—and no, it wasn't just so I wouldn't tug my multicolored braid self-consciously. "That's right."

Now all four pairs of the women's eyes turned to my empty ring finger. I resisted the urge to stick it in my back pocket. So I had thrown his gaudy, boring engagement ring back at him. So what? I agreed to marry him, not wear ugly jewelry.

"Well, that's...just lovely," said Caitlyn. One of her friends snorted next to her. She smacked her. "I was actually invited to the dinner at Celeste's. I'm a close family friend, you see. Nina, his cousin, is one of my very best friends. She was actually maid of honor at my last wedding."

Now I glanced at Caitlyn's empty ring finger. Her "last" marriage must not have lasted long. Vaguely, I wondered how many she'd had.

"So, I'll see you there...Janine?"

"Jane," I supplied.

"Jane," she repeated, again like the most basic name in the world was foreign. "Nice to meet you. You too, Skylar!"

Her friends just giggled as they turned back to their forgotten kids, a few of whom were starting to squall.

"Con-congratulations," a few of them stuttered with red cheeks, like they were holding back laughter. "Have fun tonight!"

"Oh my *God*," one whispered as they turned away. "Did you see her *hair*?"

Skylar and I stood there, watching them and waiting for my ego to reflate. They looked so casual, but every one of those women were wearing items I'd seen in *Vogue*.

"Why do I get the feeling that if we go to any of the shops they just named, the salespeople are going to say, 'that's *very expensive*' about everything I look at before telling me to leave?" I murmured. "I see what you mean now. Armor."

Skylar sighed at the reference to the famous scene from *Pretty Woman*, but didn't argue. I supposed that was exactly the kind of bullshit she wanted to help me avoid anyway. "I'm glad. But also... not. You still don't have to do this." She looked worried.

"No, I'm not backing out now. I just need better armor." I cast another look up and down the street, then tossed my coffee into a waste bin. "But we're not doing it here. I can costume design with the best of them, but you're right, I need to do this quick and dirty. Let's go to Soho. There are just as many designer shops, but people downtown won't look at me like I'm an alien."

# TWELVE

"First will come cocktails," Eric said for the fourth time since picking me up in the massive black Rolls-Royce that apparently carted him around now. The car was ridiculous. It made him (and me) looked like cartoon villains.

"Then hors d'oeuvres," he continued. "Then dinner, followed by a light dessert course, and a nightcap afterward if she's feeling all right. We'll see."

"Eric, I *know*. Stop fretting. I'm not a fucking barbarian, you know. I've been to enough of these kinds of things at Brandon and Skylar's to handle myself."

The car stopped, and we waited as the hulking driver named Tony lumbered around to let us out.

"Thanks, Smithers," I said.

Behind me, Eric snorted.

"What?" I asked.

"Nothing," he said. "Tony, I'll call when we're ready to go, all right?"

"Of course, Mr. de Vries."

"Look at you," I said as I followed Eric on a literal red carpet toward the entrance of a posh brick building lined with engraved stonework around the base.

"And don't worry about the forks, you know?" he said. "Just eat with the ones I use, and you'll be fine."

I stopped. "Oh my *God*, can you stop? I'm not a total Neanderthal. Or are you forgetting those bullshit etiquette courses they made us all take during orientation at Harvard?"

"You know they got about half of that wrong, right?"

My eyes about bugged out of my head. "*No*, I did not!"

Eric resumed his mask. "Hey, it's fine. Like I said, just use the ones I use."

"Fucking forks," I muttered as we turned back to the door.

"And try not to say 'fuck' so much."

My glare shut him up. Instead, he greeted the doorman as we passed. "Hey, Gracie."

"Evening, Mr. de Vries." The portly gentleman in his dark blue uniform tipped his hat at me like a Frank Capra character. "Miss."

"Gracie, this is Jane, my fiancée," Eric said amiably. "She's here to meet Grandmother."

The doorman emitted a long low whistle. "Good luck to you, miss, if you don't mind me saying."

Eric nodded, then turned to me. "You're also going to need this."

I watched, incredulous, as Eric pulled a familiar velvet box from his jacket pocket.

"What are you doing?" I asked. "I told you I don't want—"

"It's not the same one," he cut in. "Look."

When he opened it, Gracie the doorman gave another whistle.

"Ve-ry nice," he pronounced. "That's some rock you got there, kid."

"Thanks, Gracie," Eric said before he turned back to me. "Come on, put it on so we can go up. She really hates it when people are late, and we should have been here ten minutes ago."

The ring sparkled under the streetlamp. The sleek platinum contained rows of tiny diamonds around the finger and a sharp, marquis-cut, jet-black diamond that looked as much like it could take someone's eye out as join them forever in holy matrimony. Brutal and beautiful all at once.

I stared at the ring, then at Eric. "It's not even the kind of jewelry I like."

That was a lie. It was *exactly* the kind of ring I would pick out for myself. I just wasn't going to give him the satisfaction of knowing that.

"Well, I tried to find a rubber and leather engagement ring, but Tiffany's was all out." Eric's mouth twitched like he wanted to laugh, but instead, he glanced again up the side of the building, like he expected a camera to be pointed at us from above. He sobered, then stilled me with a glance. "Jane, we're going in there, and I'm introducing you as my fiancée. It's going to look strange if you don't have a ring. Just wear it, all right?"

I opened my mouth to argue, but found I couldn't, still remembering the look on that girl Caitlyn's face when she zeroed in on my bare finger. Hadn't I allowed Skylar to dress me up like a doll all afternoon so I wouldn't feel out of place with these people? If he thought the ring would help, then why not? We both needed this to work.

Irritably, I held out my hand. "Thank God I got a manicure."

Eric slid the ring on with satisfaction I wanted to smack away. His fingers, though, lingered over the shiny red polish that matched my lipstick. "It looks good."

It *did* look good. Enough that I had to admire it for a solid minute.

Behind us, Gracie the doorman sniffled.

Eric turned around. "Really, Gracie?"

"You're just so darned beautiful," Gracie responded as he dabbed his eyes with a stained handkerchief. "I love that you let me share the moment with you fine kids."

Eric rolled his eyes. "Come on, let's go before we need an umbrella to fight the waterworks."

He guided me through the gilt lobby of the nicest apartment

building I had ever been in. Marble floors, not one but *two* concierge desks, and a huge chandelier casting a million prisms of light dancing around the walls. It was hard not to stare.

"This way," Eric murmured as he guided me, hand at my lower back, toward the bank of elevators at the far end. Yet *another* service representative stood there in a navy waistcoat and white gloves to match Gracie's.

"Alex," Eric greeted him.

"She's expecting you, sir," replied Alex as he escorted us into the farthest elevator, waited for the doors to close, and pressed the button for the penthouse.

"This really is a beautiful piece," I said as we rode up, still admiring my ring.

My nerves were back. I had spent exactly three hours today getting ready for this dinner. Hot-rolling my hair into perfect waves that I clasped to one side. Steaming out the floaty, green chiffon wrap dress that gave me an illusion of curves. Trying on shoe after shoe before finally settling on the pair of white pumps that I was still trying to convince myself were more *Gossip Girl* than *Working Girl*.

Eric smirked. "Not the kind of jewelry you like, right?"

"Shut up." I shoved him on the shoulder. "Where did you get it? It looks vintage." This ring definitely wasn't your average Tiffany's purchase.

He shrugged. "A dealer helped me out."

We rode a few more moments in silence, and it was then I realized just how much thought Eric had put into this evening. The ring. The escort. He even looked like he had dressed for the occasion—not just for his grandmother, but also for me. He was in another one of his suits, of course, but this one had a slightly more rock and roll vibe to it. Cut with slim notched lapels in a deep maroon gabardine combined with a starched white shirt and skinny tie that brought out the dark in his eyes. He had allowed his hair to muss a little more than usual and hadn't shaved, making him look more like a rake than ever.

We actually sort of looked like we...belonged?

"Go ahead," he whispered, noticing me noticing him. "Just say it."

I bit my lip. "You look like a movie theater attendant in that jacket."

His lips quirked as the elevator came to a stop. "You look nice too."

But before I could reply, the doors opened, and Alex the operator tipped his head—not actually making eye contact with me—as Eric guided me onto the landing of a very, *very* posh apartment.

"Well," Eric said. "Here we are."

Nothing—*nothing*—could have prepared me for the grandeur of this place. It was like walking into a hatbox that also served as a preservation center for world-class colonialism. The foyer, lined with green flowered wallpaper, contained a massive circular table bearing the biggest array of lilies I had ever seen. The light naturally drew the eyes to the domed ceiling, which glowed with gilt molding around a giant chandelier. Gilt. As in gold. This family was so rich that they literally used gold as paint.

"Holy shit," I murmured as I took it all in.

"Sir, may I take your coats?" A dry British accent interrupted my staring.

"Oh, she has a Smithers too," I remarked under my breath before sticking out my hand. "Hi, I'm Jane."

The butler—I assumed that's what he was, though he was ninety if he was a day—stared at my hand as if I'd offered him a bag of old tissues.

"Garrett, this is my fiancée, Jane Lefferts," Eric said.

Garrett stood up a little taller but did not take my hand. I took it back, wiping it slightly on my skirt. Eric removed his jacket and helped me with mine as well, then handed them both to Garrett, who very, very slowly stowed them in a coat closet before guiding us down a long, wainscoted hallway lined with several pieces of artwork I could have sworn belonged in the Louvre.

"Sheesh, what crawled up his ass?" I muttered as Eric guided me with a hand at my back.

"About forty sets of silver," he whispered back.

I gulped. He was joking, but just the idea of forty sets of silver reminded me of a very simple fact: I was *not* in Kansas anymore.

We turned a corner—this freaking apartment was basically a labyrinth—and rounds of voices filtered down the hallway.

"How many people are supposed to be here tonight?" I asked, thinking of Caitlyn what's-her-name.

Eric's shoulders tensed. "It was only supposed to be her, my mother, my aunt Violet, and my cousin Nina. Maybe a friend or two. Not the whole damn family."

"And you haven't seen them in…"

"Almost ten years." He spoke through clenched teeth, and before I could reply, his hand snatched mine so quickly I started.

"What are you—"

"We're engaged, Jane," he said with a sharp look. "Time to act like it." And then he straightened and pulled me into a room full of pastels and gray summer suits.

They were shiny. Bright. Every person here gleamed with unnaturally bright teeth and jewelry that reflected in the mirrors mounted over the ceiling. For a moment, I was reminded of Versailles and the Hall of Mirrors. Was this how it had been with the wealthy of France too—light bouncing off every surface, sequin, glass, and ring? Was it possible that the rich made their *own* particular light, even in the dark of night?

The chatter quieted immediately when we entered.

"Oh my God…" someone murmured from the back.

There were at least forty people in attendance—four or five patrician gentlemen and their wives, a smorgasbord of younger folk whom I guessed included Eric's cousins and possibly some friends. Everyone was immaculate, neutral-toned, and oozing entitlement. Eric and I were basically Starburst candies next to this crew.

"Who…is…this?"

Like Moses and the Red Sea, the crowd parted in half to reveal a very frail old woman making her way toward us on a walker while a housekeeper or some kind of assistant carried an oxygen tank with her. Despite her poor health, she was dressed to the nines in an exquisite pink Chanel suit, her gray hair immaculately set in an up-do—*a wig*, I thought, considering what Eric had told me about her condition. Well, if it was a wig, it was a damn nice one.

"Grandmother," Eric said in an odd, stiff voice. "May I introduce Jane Lee Lefferts. My fiancée."

Celeste looked me over with beady gray eyes that were the exact same shade as her grandson's. She was withered and small, but I found it hard not to shrink in front of her.

"She has pink...hair," she remarked. "Among a few other colors."

From the back of the crowd, there was an audible giggle.

"Why, yes, I do," I replied, trying to make light of it. "I can give you the number of my colorist if you like it."

"It looks like a carnation. Eric, I loathe carnations."

Eric sighed. "Jane, this is my grandmother, Celeste."

"You may call me Mrs. de Vries," she corrected him.

"Mrs. de Vries, then," I said as friendly as I could manage.

In return, all I received was a stare like an ice statue's. "And she's Oriental."

Ouch. Really? I didn't even know people used the term Oriental anymore unless they were talking about a rug sale.

"Jane's Korean, Grandmother," Eric said, but not as gently as I would have expected.

"Well, half, that I know of," I joked.

His hand squeezed mine harder. I squeezed back.

"Are you adopted, then?" Celeste asked sharply, sending another machete slash through my attempts at humor.

The room was now completely silent as forty pairs of eyes witnessed my interrogation. I glanced around nervously. None of them would meet my gaze.

"Ah, no. No, I'm not," I said. "My, uh, mother is from Korea, and my father is originally from Ohio. They moved to Chicago after they got married."

"But your name is Lefferts." Her brow wrinkled even more as she considered the fact. "Bruce, dear, what kind of name is Lefferts?"

A man on the other side of the room shrugged. "German, maybe?"

"It's Dutch, actually," I supplied as helpfully as I could. "Just like yours, right?"

"North or South?"

I blinked. "I'm sorry? In Chicago? North. I was raised in Evanston, actually."

But Celeste de Vries rolled her old, beady eyes and shook her head. "You said your mother was from Korea. I asked North or South *Korea*."

"Ohhh," I replied. "Right, right. Sorry, I'm just so used to my mother calling it Korea, so I do too, you know?"

"No, I don't know," Celeste replied. "Do you know this, Eric?"

Eric only looked blank.

"It's two separate countries." She turned back to me. "And she still hasn't answered the question. South Koreans are allowed in this country. North Koreans are essentially enemies of the state, are they not? So which is it? North or South?"

"Ah, South, ma'am," I said, feeling suddenly like I was on the stand myself. "My mother is originally from a small town outside of Seoul, I believe."

"You believe? You mean you don't know?" Her knife gaze traveled up my body, taking in my shoes, my dress, my clutch, my hair—everything that I had actually tried—well, relatively so—to normalize for the evening. Then, without saying another word, she turned back to Eric. "Is this really the best you can do?"

There was another smattering of laughter from the back of the crowd, but I was too shocked by the conversation to look for the culprits.

*Maybe he wants her to say these things. Maybe he wants her to end this now.* The neurotic voice popped into my head before I could stop it. For once, my father's calm timbre was nowhere to be found.

Eric scowled. "Grandmother, Jane and I have known each other since law school. Almost eight years, all right? You wanted me to get married, and this is whom I've chosen. You can deal with it or not."

"That hair," she croaked. "We can't have that in the style section. What would the Astors think?"

"Jane can wear her hair however she damn well wants, Grand-mother," Eric piped up. "And if you don't like it, well, we can stop this game right now."

By this point, the room had gone completely silent once more, and heads were turning left and right as if they were watching a tennis match.

"Eric, be nice."

A droll female voice spoke up behind Celeste. It belonged to a woman with bobbed blonde hair and two rows of neatly strung pearls. She was a remarkably well-preserved woman, who, anywhere else, would probably pass for maybe a few years older than me, but in this crowd, that probably meant she was verging on sixty.

"I'm just trying to get to know her, that's all," Celeste answered smugly. She was getting under Eric's skin, and what's more, she liked it. "Let the poor girl get to know us. We have standards, of course, for being in this family. You of all people should know that."

"Oh, I do," he gritted out. "If you recall, that's why I left in the first place."

"*Eric.*"

The blonde woman who had just spoken detached herself from a few other similarly Botoxed ladies and joined the three of us. A murmur arose as the crowd of family began to chatter, though I noticed glances continued to dart back at our strange quartet.

Eric turned to the woman stiffly. "Mom."

*Mom?* I jerked my gaze to the woman with new interest. Her gaze met mine but revealed nothing. No emotion. No gratitude to see her son. No response to me. Nothing.

Well. Now I knew where Eric had learned the art of the mask.

She kissed him awkwardly on each cheek, but Eric just squeezed my hand, making no move to reciprocate his mother's greeting. She stepped back and smiled at me, not quite warmly, but several degrees above the glacial expression of her mother-in-law.

"You must be Jane," she said as she air-kissed my cheeks.

"Jane, this is my mother, Heather," Eric said.

"Dear Grandmama only looks out for us, you must understand," Heather said as she stood back. Next to Eric, it was obvious that they were related. "Nina is around here somewhere with Violet, my sister-in-law. Ah, there she is." She pointed to a girl in the far corner who looked like she could be Eric's sister. The girl waved listlessly but made no move to greet Eric any more than he did her. It was strange, really, how none of this family seemed happy to welcome back its heir.

"Now, tell us, Jane, what do your parents do?" asked Heather.

I did my best to smile. "Well, um, my mother is a housewife, although she recently went back to working at a salon. She used to do nails, you see, after she was a flight attendant. And my father, he was a psychologist at the VA before he died last year."

"Oh, dear, I'm so sorry."

"So," Celeste spoke again. "She has no family—"

"Well, that's not entirely true—" I cut in.

"No manners—"

"What? Wait, what did I—"

"No class—"

"Well, my dad *was* a psychologist, so, we weren't exactly destitu—"

"And no style."

I opened my mouth with another smart retort, but this time, her sharp eyes zeroed in on me fully. And I was stunned. Because I *had* style. I dripped style, my friends. Sure, maybe it was different than the average Anne Klein-wearing, Barre-loving New Englander, but I had lived and breathed fashion since I was a kid. I literally couldn't remember a day after Aunt Flo first visited that I hadn't worn lipstick.

Instead, I focused on the here and now. And the here and now was awkward as *fuck*. Heather stared at her Manhattan like the ice was going to reveal the future. Celeste stared at me like I was going to pull my dress over my head and run around like a banshee. And Eric just stared at everything but us, looking desperately like he wanted to disappear.

And me? For once in my life, my bravado deserted me. I just stared at the carpet like Charlie fucking Brown, and the only other noises were hums of light conversation and the clinks of ice in people's glasses.

"Jane?" A sweet female voice cut through the awkward silence. "Oh my gosh, Jane, it really *is* you!"

The entire room swiveled again. Celeste's carefully painted eyebrows shot up an inch as Caitlyn, the woman I'd met on the street, emerged from the corner where Eric's cousin stood, dressed tastefully in a blue sheath dress that I recognized from Calvin Klein, her tawny brown hair cascading over her shoulders in perfect, effortless waves.

"Caitlyn?" Celeste asked. "Do you *know* this young woman?"

"Um...what?" Eric looked like he wanted to know the same thing. "You know Caitlyn Calvert?"

"Oh, Celeste, yes," Caitlyn said. "We're friends. I mean, we only met today, but my *goodness*, she has the best street style. I couldn't forget Jade if I tried."

"It's Jane," I tried to say, but my words were swallowed quietly by Celeste's glare.

Celeste looked like she could not possibly believe this, but did not say anything. As Caitlyn continued talking, the rest of the room seemed to relax and turn back to their conversations.

"Oh my gosh, is this from the new Alice + Olivia collection?" Caitlyn asked me. "I saw that, but I couldn't believe anyone would be adventurous enough to wear it."

I tugged self-consciously at my handkerchief skirt, with its layers of chiffons delicately embroidered with flowers. I had loved this dress when Skylar and I found it this afternoon, but even with her compliments, Caitlyn made me feel like a sideshow act.

"Um, yes," was all I could say. "It is."

Eric looked sharply at me, clearly as surprised by my lack of response as I was.

"I *love* it," Caitlyn gushed. "Come on, you'll have to tell me all about how you came up with such unique styling. I just go with what works, you know. Classics, so they say. Come on, I'll introduce you to Eric's cousin." She turned to Eric with a sweet, yet sly expression. "That is, if Desi here will let me take you away."

Eric blushed. He actually blushed. And immediately, I was pissed. Celeste and Heather watched him curiously. Clearly they noticed it too.

"Desi?" I asked. "Who is that?"

"It's just a nickname," Eric said before taking a long drink of a martini he accepted from Garrett, who carried none for me.

"When we were little, our nannies used to bring us to the park together. But sometimes, especially when Ana Lucia was sick, Rosa would let us watch TV instead. It was always *I Love Lucy* reruns, and so when we started to talk, Eric and I started calling each other Desi and Lucy. Everyone used to say we were just like an old married couple, didn't they, Des?" Caitlyn shrugged. "It just stuck."

Eric chuckled. "It's true. How long did I call you that? Until what, high school?"

"Probably until you met Penny and broke my heart." Caitlyn faux-elbowed me in the waist. "I was his first, you know. At the tender age of seven."

My eyes popped open, and immediately Eric started shaking his head while Caitlyn giggled into her drink. "She means first kiss, Jane."

"Oh, ha," I said weakly. "I, um, thought that was kind of young."

As Celeste and Heather looked at me with horror, I decided this was now *really* the most awkward conversation ever.

Caitlyn tittered. "Oh, lord, *no*. But we definitely had crushes on each other, didn't we, Des? I guess when you've been friends for that long, it's bound to happen."

Eric just offered a tight smile. He didn't hold my hand anymore—instead, he was more intent on holding his drink. I didn't know why that bothered me so much.

"Gosh, that takes me back. I haven't thought about those names in so long." Caitlyn reached out to squeeze Eric's arm, and like she was moving in slow motion, all four of us watched her smooth, French-tipped fingers toy with his sleeve. "It's so good to have you back, E. We missed you."

Suddenly, I was suppressing the urge to vomit. I was grateful to Caitlyn for saving me from Eric's grandmother. And she had also managed to deflect the crowd of people surrounding us. Truly, I had no reason to be nursing a completely irrational hatred toward the girl. She was nice. Very nice. *Too* nice.

"Do you think you'll be in New York for good, E?" she was asking.

*Stop calling him E. He's not a rave drug circa 1999.*

"A good long time," Celeste put in. "Eric is taking over the company."

Eric shrugged. "I'll only assume the chairmanship, provided the board votes me in. So, I'll stay as long as it takes me to learn enough of the company to take over Grandmother's position," he said. "Then maybe Jane and I can return to Boston."

"You can't possibly be chairman and live in Boston," Heather said, a little too sharply. "Come, Eric, that's naive. Even for you."

Eric's expression was like cut glass. His mother looked away and took another drink of her cocktail.

"Well," Caitlyn said as she continued to finger his sleeve. "I can only hope it's a nice, complicated job. I'm dying to know what's happened since you've been gone. I want to know all there is to know about you now, Desi. Oh, and you too, Jade."

She gazed up at Eric like I wasn't even there, and Eric, the bastard, looked right the fuck back. It took the two of them about five full seconds to stop, and only when I cleared my throat loud enough to sound like an advertisement for cough medicine. Celeste smiled for the first time, baring a set of pearly dentures.

"Oh, my!" Caitlyn jumped, pressing her hand to her heart as if I'd genuinely frightened her. "You sound like you need something for your throat. Come on, let's get you a drink, all right? Then I can introduce you to the whole gang!"

And with that, her hand left Eric's sleeve, and I was whisked away to find a much-needed cocktail while I mingled with my new family. But I couldn't help noticing that every time Caitlyn thought I wasn't looking, she would find wherever Eric was standing in the room. And then she would just watch. And wait.

# THIRTEEN

At exactly ten o'clock the next morning, following the horrifically awkward five-course dinner that lasted until approximately the end of the next ice age, Eric, Skylar, and I were shown into the salon once again to await Celeste for a purely nonsocial visit: the prenup discussion.

Skylar carried her briefcase and was dressed in full lawyer-garb, right down to the chic black suit and thick tortoiseshell glasses that were similar to the ones I wore that morning. My clothes, however, were decidedly more casual—a comfortable green crepe jumpsuit I had sewn myself and black ballet flats fitting for the balmy June day. With my hair tied up in a topknot with tendrils escaping here and there, I looked and felt like a goddamn spring flower—and a fair bit more comfortable than last night. *Note to self: your clothes are still better than any designer crap.*

"You look nice, by the way," Eric told me again as we entered the salon. "I like that...whatever that thing is you're wearing."

I turned, making my hoop earrings swing. "Will you stop it?"

"Stop what?"

His frown made an adorable crease between his eyebrows, and he shoved his hands into the pockets of his gray pants. With the navy and white gingham shirt, he looked, as ever, like a damn J. Crew ad. Preppy and sexy at the same time. Of course it would be right when my libido woke up for the first time in almost a year that I'd have to spend my days with the off-limits Don Juan of the Upper East Side.

"Stop being so nice," I said. "Last night. And you've been doing it all fucking morning too. It's annoying."

Behind us, Skylar snorted as she started setting out papers on the coffee table. "You know, it's not too late to back out," she said drily. "No one has to risk mariticide yet."

"Shut up, Skylar," Eric and I spoke in unison.

She just snorted again.

Eric rolled his eyes. "It's called being thoughtful. I just figured—"

"You figured that I can't handle myself with your family. But you said yourself that I was the only one cut out to deal with them, right? Now, did I or did I not survive dinner just fine last night?"

It hadn't been so bad. I felt a little like a zoo animal, and the passive aggressive comments about my hair or ethnicity never seemed to stop, but that was nothing a few drinks couldn't cut the edge off. And sure, there was the weird sensation that everyone was talking about me behind my back, or the moments when I was pretty sure Caitlyn Calvert wanted to eat Eric instead of the Chilean sea bass in front of her. But it was fine. Small potatoes. Not worth stressing about.

I poked Eric hard in the chest, ignoring the way his skin barely gave. Lord, the boy really was as hard as a rock. What did he *do* that made him like that? Most lawyers I knew were the general consistency of playdough.

Eric stepped back, hands held up in surrender. "Fine, fine," he said. "You want me to be a dick, I will."

"Good," I said. "It makes it easier to remember just why I'm doing this."

As we waited, I drifted around the room, which looked a bit different than it had last night. The furniture had been replaced in the center—a settee, a couple of art deco-style davenports, and a Chesterfield-style chaise lounge next to a bay window. Now that the walls weren't crowded with people, I noticed the art—was that an original Gustav Klimt?—and the smattering of family portraits. Most of them were stiff, the kind you'd hire a professional photographer to take in a studio, except the surroundings were obviously private homes. Of course—a backdrop like this room would be infinitely better than some bland studio. And people as rich as this hired photographers to come to them, not the other way around.

"Adam Novak did that one," Eric said, coming to stand next to me while Skylar set up.

"Seriously? The *Vogue* photographer?" I stared at the family picture in which Eric looked about five. It was in the middle of a blooming rose garden, and hardly anyone was smiling. Celeste de Vries sat in the middle of all of them, preening like the Queen of England.

Eric nodded. "I figured you'd know who he was, considering how obsessed you are with fashion."

I cast him a look, but he continued examining the portrait. Most people, even Skylar, didn't treat my love of fashion as anything other than a hobby. Most people didn't even remember.

I peered closer. "How old are you here?"

"Six, maybe seven."

"Awwww," I cooed, peering closer.

There were a dozen kids in the photo, all of them girls except Eric. I recognized a few from dinner last night. Eric sat in the front, right at the knee of his grandmother, her frail hands drifting just over his head like a halo. His position was clear. If she was the queen, he was the crown prince. It was becoming clearer to me just what he had walked away from at twenty-two. Not just a family, but an entire empire. He had been groomed for the job since he was born. And then, just when it was supposed to happen, walked away completely.

I also wondered, considering the somewhat chilly reception we had enjoyed last night, how many of his family members truly thought he was doing them a favor by returning.

"Your dad," I wondered as I drifted a finger over the picture. "What was he like?"

Eric cocked his head as he looked fondly at the portrait. "Well, I didn't know him that well. I was only ten when he died. It was a sailing accident. He got caught in a storm by our house on Long Island."

"*Ten*? Holy smokes," I murmured. "Eric, I had no idea." Was that because he hadn't told me, or because I hadn't asked?

It was disturbing that I couldn't answer that question.

He gave me a queer look. "What's funny about that is that you've known me for almost eight years now, Jane."

"I know," I agreed.

"There really is a lot we don't know about each other, isn't there?"

For a second, I thought he might call it all off. Maybe he'd realize what a truly ridiculous venture we were about to begin. It surprised me how much I disliked the possibility.

"Yes," I agreed slowly. "But I'd like to know now." I turned, hopeful. "I'd like to know better my betrothed, sir." I said it in a mocking tone, but it wasn't a lie.

Eric sighed. "I didn't see him much, but when I did, we had fun. He used to take me sailing around Long Island during the summers. And if I was still awake when he came home, he'd usually be up for a game of Uno."

The man in the picture looked a lot like Eric now—handsome, preppy, fair, and blond. His smile was practically blinding, magnetic in a JFK, Camelot manner only certain wealthy families from the Northeast emanate. Beside him, the entire family seemed to glow in the sunlight of a summer day.

"What do you think he would have thought of all of this?" I wondered aloud. "Knowing his son isn't marrying for love?"

"Oh, he probably would have found it ironic," Eric said as he gazed at another photo—this one a portrait of just his father.

"Ironic? Why?"

I received a sharp look. "Well, it's not like it was never said, right?"

―――――

*A KNOCK SOUNDED on the door. I groaned. Who in the hell was banging on Suejean's door at 9 a.m.? My cousin was working a forty-eight-hour shift at the hospital, and she never had company.*

*The lump of person next to me snorted, then chuffed like a wildebeest in a nature video.*

*"Hey, what's up?"*

*"I just need to check something...Grrrrreg?" I guessed.*

*He didn't answer. I assumed the name was correct. I also didn't particularly care.*

*The knock turned to a pound. "Jane! Jane, I know you're in there!"*

*At the sound of a voice which, after the week before, I was sure I was never going to hear again, I shot out of bed like a cockroach scuttling under the fridge. Holy shit. What was he doing here?*

*"Where you going?" snuffled Maybe Greg, whose hand had emerged from the blankets like some kind of primeval monster rising from the deep. I watched it traverse the sheets toward me.*

*"Ah, mailman," I said as I edged away. "He gets feisty if we don't pick up our letters personally."*

*"Jane!" The pounding grew louder.*

*"The mailman knows your name?"*

*"It's a very personalized service," I said. "Be right back." I tied on the thin pink robe I'd had since high school and darted out of the room to the door, patting at my hair, which currently stuck out at all angles. Not exactly the picture of effortless sexual charisma I would prefer this "mailman" to see.*

*I opened the door to find Eric pacing my cousin's hallway, looking a far sight from his normally impeccable self. His short blond hair was standing up on one side, like he'd slept on it funny, and his navy pants and white button-down were a wrinkled mess.*

*He turned when I opened the door. "So, you are here." His eyes narrowed. "I was starting to think you'd found another place to sleep last night."*

*"What are you doing here?" I asked, closing the door a bit behind me.* Stay in the room, Maybe Greg. Keep your monster in its cave.

*His gray, sleepless eyes closed for a moment, then reopened looking like bright, iron stars. "You," he said as he approached me. "You're not allowed to end things like that."*

*I crossed my arms, shooting for defiance, but couldn't quite manage it. "Eric—"*

*"No." He stopped pacing. "It's bullshit, what you pulled. I'm not some one-night stand with an asshole you picked up in a bar."*

*I cringed. He didn't know how right he was.*

*"You and I, we're special," he rattled on. "And the second I own up to that, you cut and run. Well, I'm calling you on your bullshit, Jane. What gives?"*

*This time, my defiance didn't have to be feigned. "What gives? God. This is just like you. You expect me to drop everything to come to your beck and call. Did you forget that you also asked me to stay in Boston? After we had both taken the bar exam in two separate states?"*

*Eric groaned. "Jesus Christ. Is that what this is about? I'll move to Chicago if that's what you want."*

*"No, it's not what I want! And that's the entire fucking point. I would never ask you to give up your career, but you, just like every other man on the planet, think it's completely acceptable to ask that of a woman. Love doesn't mean asking each other to give up anything, Eric. That is the fucking point!"*

*I was practically shouting by this point, and I was sure that Suejean's neighbors were going to poke their heads out any second to ask me to kindly shut the hell up. What was it with him? We were either fighting or fucking, wrestling constantly for power neither of us* seemed to know what to do with. I couldn't stop, but I knew it wasn't healthy. None of this was healthy.

Instead of yelling back, Eric remained quiet, though no less intense. I realized then that for the first time, he really was more interested in talking than maintaining his careful facade of comportment. He looked a mess. And he looked me right in the eye.

"Fine," he said at last. "If you're finally willing to accept that what we are is more than just a way to blow off steam while studying for the bar, then maybe we're actually getting somewhere. That I can work with."

Did I think that? What did "more" mean? I stood by my previous words. Even if this was...something more...what right did that give us to hamper each other's careers? That wasn't the kind of relationship I wanted, even if I had one to begin with.

But before I could answer, the door behind me opened.

"Jen? Jenna? Um...hon? D'you have a towel or somethin' I can use?"

Eric and I both turned to find ~~the creature from the lost lagoon the lump from the bed~~ last night's sexual partner scratching his head like a Shel Silverstein illustration, wearing nothing but his size too-small white boxer briefs that were just tight enough around the waist to give the guy a muffin top. Hot.

I pressed my lips together. I didn't even want to see the look of horrified disdain I knew was plastered all over Eric's face.

"Linen closet is in the hallway across from the bathroom. Kthanks-bye." I shoved Maybe Greg back into the apartment, slammed the door shut, then whirled around to face Eric, who was indeed staring at me with unmitigated disgust.

"Nice, Jane," he said quietly. "Really nice."

I watched for a moment as he turned and slumped his way back down the hallway. And then, something about the sight of Eric walking away like that broke me. I sprang into action.

"Eric, wait. Hey, will you just hold on a second!" Struggling to keep my robe in place, I jogged after him, giving Mrs. Stewart, Suejean's neighbor, a weak smile as I passed. "Dude, stop!"

I grabbed the cuff of his shirt, yanking him back just before he turned down the stairwell. When he turned, his brow was furrowed and his eyes were squeezed tightly shut.

"WHAT!" he exploded, boomeranging back at me like he'd been released from a slingshot. "What do you want from me?"

"A second to listen!" I shouted back. "Jesus Christ, Eric, this is not my fault. You don't get to be mad like this because I'm doing what normal grown-ups do—what you do on a nightly basis, I might add—and exercising my right to be a healthy sexual human fucking being!"

He just shook his head and rubbed his neck. "This is bullshit."

"Oh, is it?" I demanded, poking him in the chest. "Be honest. You're telling me you of all people have been celibate for the last week? We broke up!"

"And whose decision was that?" he snapped. "I asked you to come meet my family, and you hopped on a plane faster than Usain Bolt."

"Well, who asked you to do that?" I demanded. "We were having a good time! We knew the score. We knew this whole thing had an expiration date. And then you had to go fuck it up by doing something like a big family invite!"

"And do you know why?" he shot back. "Do you have any fucking idea why I wanted you to do that? It's because I love you, Jane. I fucking love you! Do you get that? Do you even understand what it means to say that to someone?"

I stumbled forward, suddenly feeling like I'd been punched in the gut. Eric caught me, hands curved around my shoulders as he held me up. All anger drained from his face, and what was left was a mix of fear, hope, and something else.

Was that love? Was that what it looked like?

"I love you, pretty girl," he whispered. "I came here to tell you that. And to ask...to ask if you...do you love me, Jane?"

My mouth trembled, unable to open fully or shut at all. Shock, some inner voice echoed within me. You're in shock.

"But—but I live here. You live in Boston. And—" I stumbled over the excuses we'd recycled all summer. The real reasons I'd jumped on that plane and broken it off. All the reasons this was never, ever going to work.

"Fuck all of that," Eric said softly, but his hands remained as strong as his gaze. The tenderness he'd only allowed to peek through occasionally this summer was completely unmasked. No filter. And it was blinding. "That shit doesn't matter in the end. It's simple, Jane. I love you. Do you love me too?"

"I..." I couldn't get my mouth to work, frozen as I was in his thrall. But as soon as my lips regained feeling, the word fell out instinctually: "Yes."

His eyes brightened. "Yes?"

I nodded, slowly at first, then more definitively. "Yes."

Eric sighed, long and steady. Then he pulled me close and stamped a harsh, torrid kiss on my lips that lasted only a few seconds but would tingle for hours.

"Good," he said as he released me. "Now, I have a plane to catch."

My jaw dropped as I stumbled back into the wall. My robe was now hanging half open, and I wrapped it up again. "Are you kidding? You're just going to drop that bomb on me and go? What kind of shit is that?"

The smile reappeared, the one I hated and loved at the same time—cocky, knowing, and utterly panty-melting. "I have to work, Jane. And so do you, right? Love doesn't mean asking each other to give up our lives, right?"

Oh, right. Work. That thing we were supposed to be doing round the clock as newly minted lawyers. My entire reason for breaking up with him to begin with. Fucking hell.

Every reason I knew this was doomed from the start raced back into my head.

"Hey." He took my hand again and pulled me close, weaving his fingers with mine. "You're coming this weekend."

It wasn't a request. So I simply nodded.

*He nodded back. "I'll send you a ticket on my way to the airport. In the meantime..." He gazed back toward my cousin's apartment. "Get that motherfucking swamp monster out of your bed. And in case we're not clear, from now on, no one else is allowed in it from now on. Your bed belongs to me. Just me. Understood, pretty girl?"*

*Like a puppet, I nodded again. How did he always manage to do this? Make me speechless while he commandeered my life? It was almost like I tried to say no to the man just to make him do it more.*

*"Until Friday night, then," he said with another quick, harsh kiss. "And, Jane?"*

*I swallowed. "Wh-what?"*

*"You better be ready to say sorry."*

*And then, he was gone, leaving me in the hallway to ponder exactly what he had in store for my redemption.*

———

I PLAYED a finger over my lips, like that last kiss was still stamped here. I had flown back to Boston as planned, and Eric had spent the entire weekend forcing me to "make up" for my mistakes. Making up that had included tying my hands and feet together at one point. Another time had involved handcuffs and a flogger. Lord, the boy had some moves.

But it hadn't lasted long.

That kiss might have tingled, but the red panties burned.

I frowned. Fuck him. Fuck whoever wore those polyblend monstrosities I found when I returned. And fuck the word *love*. Whenever Eric's natural charm and prowess distracted me, I needed to remember him for what he really was—a predator—and forget the tenderness I saw that day.

Still, I couldn't help looking for traces of it now. Eric didn't look away, but there was only his normal, stoic expression that was one-part nonchalance, one-part cockiness. No tenderness. No kindness. Not an ounce.

"Ironic," I murmured. "Yes, I see that now."

Eric sighed and turned back to the pictures. "Anyway, he was a good guy, I think. No matter what the papers said."

"The papers?"

He gave me a look. "Well, you don't head up a company like DVS without receiving some scrutiny. We're probably going to end up on Page Six, you know. And Grandmother will make sure the wedding takes up half the *Times* style section."

I balked. "Are you serious? I thought she was joking about my hair."

He nodded, looking annoyed. "Oh, I'm dead serious. Nina's a tabloid regular, and so are my second and third cousins. New Yorkers love 'socialites.' It's dumb, but the truth."

I made a mental note to do a little research into de Vries family news coverage. I wasn't sure how I felt about that, having my life plastered all over the papers. I remembered all too well Brandon and Skylar's brief foray with the press when Brandon had flirted with being mayor of Boston. Even now they were sometimes targets of the Boston tabloids, just by virtue of their wealth and Brandon's former notoriety. Skylar hated everything about it, and they'd sued multiple outlets for libel. It hadn't helped much.

"Why are you asking about all of this?" Eric wondered. "You never cared...before."

I shrugged my guilt away. I hadn't, had I? "Well...I am about to sign my life away to this family. I should probably know what I'm getting into."

He looked at me for an extended minute, to the point where I started to squirm. Sounds echoed from down the hallway, but he continued to watch me even as we returned to the couch.

"For the record," he said quietly, "I'd never ask you to sign your life away to anyone. Least of all me."

He offered a small smile, one that made me feel strangely warm in the pit of my belly. My mouth dropped as I searched for words to respond.

His grandmother entered the room with a creak of wheels as Garrett wheeled her in alongside her ever-present tank of oxygen, followed by a middle-aged man in an unremarkable gray suit. I assumed he was the family lawyer. Eric and I both took seats on the sofa next to Skylar while Celeste situated herself across the coffee table from us. Eric took my hand companionably in his lap. When I looked up in surprise, he just smiled, but the clear, earnest look in his eyes carried obvious meaning: *just play along.*

"All right, pretty girl," Eric murmured, and quickly mouthed "Sorry" when he caught my look of faux-admonishment. "Force of habit," he said. "Ready to get married?"

"Well," Celeste de Vries interrupted before I could answer. She wasn't quite the picture of elegance she had been last night. Her wig was gone, replaced by a light pink Chanel scarf that matched her beautiful suit separates. She took a siphon of oxygen but kept her stiff gaze on me. "We shall see about that."

# FOURTEEN

Two hours later, everyone was about ready to throw the entire deal out the window. Literally every condition that Skylar had added to the standard de Vries prenuptial agreement had been shredded by Celeste and her lawyer, who, as far as I could tell, basically served as a very expensive lap dog to his ailing mistress. Skylar herself had stopped looking like the formidable attorney she was and had transformed into an angry, bespectacled strawberry about forty-five minutes ago. Even Eric looked like he wasn't above murdering the old goat.

"Absolutely not." Celeste stated clearly for the tenth time in her sharp yet quavering voice. Her eyes pinioned Eric while she sucked on her oxygen. "I see no reason why the family should have to sacrifice millions simply because *you* decided to take a ride on the Yangtze River."

Her lawyer shook his head and buried it in his hands. He looked like he needed a stiff drink.

"I think that's in China, Mrs. de Vries," I corrected her. "Not Korea."

Skylar looked at me quizzically. She knew my knowledge of Asian geography was close to zip.

I shrugged. "I liked the book *Ping* when I was a kid."

Now everyone looked at me as if I was crazy.

"What?" I asked. "Cute yellow duck? Gets lost on the big bad Yangtze River? Spends the night out before he goes home and gets a spanking for being naughty?"

Of course, my eyes met Eric's right on the word "spanking." And of course his lips twitched in that delicious way. They had been for the last two hours. It was tempting. And annoying.

"Jane," Skylar whispered.

One look at her disapproving face, and I knew every dirty thought I had was scribbled over mine. And by Eric's raised brow, he could see it too.

I cleared my throat.

"Why don't you have a better lawyer?" Celeste demanded.

Skylar pressed her lips together.

Eric rolled his eyes. "For the twentieth time, Grandmother, I *am* a lawyer. Jane's a lawyer too. And Skylar and I are majority stakeholders of the same firm. I trust her to do this right."

"Well, perhaps you should reevaluate that, Eric," said the old goat as she shoved the papers back toward him. "Considering the way she managed to finagle herself into the Sterling fortune without any kind of proper arrangement, it's clear she's an expert in the art of extortion." The old woman's sharp eyes narrowed at Skylar. "I assure you, missy, that won't fly around here. My Eric's got a whole family to protect him against the likes of you."

Skylar's bright green eyes looked like they were about to spout flames. Eric groaned, and I just covered my face, trying not to laugh.

"I think maybe we should take a break," I said, reaching over Eric's lap to touch Skylar's knee. "Okay, missy?"

For whatever reason, I hadn't been terribly annoyed by the proceedings. Maybe I should have been—after all, I was the one being framed as a gold digger.

But the longer I sat with Celeste, the more I, well, felt kind of sorry for her. She weighed maybe eight-five pounds soaking wet, was clearly in a lot of pain, if the etched lines over her forehead were any indication, and genuinely seemed to want to protect Eric's interests when she was gone. The way she had forced him back into the last months of her life was awful, yes. But I wasn't sure I blamed her. She was dying. She was grasping for what little control she had left. And in the moments when he turned away, that mask of imperiousness dropped a little. Fondness crept into those beady eyes.

Somewhere in that icy, Chanel-clad heart of hers, Celeste de Vries really did love her grandson.

"It's already a privilege to marry into this family," Celeste continued as if I hadn't said a word. "I don't believe one needs a reward for doing so. Twenty million dollars, Eric? Really?"

"Jane and I never planned to get married," Eric said. "She's changing her whole life trajectory to make this happen on your time-line. Of course she should be compensated for it."

Celeste looked up at him with irritation. "You never wanted to marry? Well, then, perhaps you should be reconsidering your choice. I can think of at least five other girls you've known your entire life who would be more appropriate choices."

And there it was. She'd been dancing around it all day, especially after suggesting it multiple times the night before. I was in no way good enough for Celeste de Vries—after all, wasn't that why Eric had asked me to begin with?

Eric yanked on his tie. "I don't want to have this argument again."

"A break," I said again, this time louder. "I think I need some air. Mrs. de Vries, do you mind if I explore your balcony?"

She waved her hand at me, like I wasn't even worth the excess oxygen needed to respond. Well, fine. Maybe to her, I wasn't.

"Petri," I said, causing Eric to look up with narrowed eyes.

"Don't," he mouthed at me.

I just smirked. "Come on. Show me the view."

Celeste sat back in her chair, waving Garrett over to help her out of the room while Eric and I stood up. Skylar also excused herself to use the bathroom, and Eric and I walked out to the balcony that encircled the entire apartment.

Once again, it was a beautiful late spring day in New York. Below us, Central Park waved, and I leaned over the balustrade to watch a bunch of people flying kites by a pond.

"You need to stop sparring with her," I said. "For one, I think she likes it."

"Correction," Eric replied as he gazed out at the view. The top of the MET shone like a giant diamond below us. "She loves it. Grandmother always gets off on putting people in their place."

"Then we should go. This isn't working. She wants to see you married before she dies, and if it really has to be me—"

"It does."

I preened. Eric rolled his eyes.

"So, then, maybe we put our cards on the table and walk away until she relents. It might take the full six months, but at the end, she'll cave. Granny lust is a powerful thing."

Eric chuckled. "Maybe. But I don't like doing this without knowing you're getting your due. This is a lot I'm asking of you. It's fucking medieval."

I traced a finger around the carved stone railing. "Medieval would be if I brought a dowry. Unfortunately, all I have is eight hundred dollars in my savings account and a lot of student loan debt. She thinks I'm a social climber, and she resents me for it."

"She thinks you're a phase."

"Well, I am."

Eric watched me carefully while I toyed with a loose strand of my hair.

"What is that supposed to mean?" he asked.

I shrugged. "This has an expiration date. Maybe she knows it. Five years. The irony is that she laid the terms, right? Now she hates them because she can't tell if we're serious or not." I looked up to find him still staring a hole through me. "What? As soon as this is over, it's straight to the courthouse, right? And then you'll be free to bang whomever you want. Well...you'll still be free to do that anyway, but in five years, you can do it openly."

Eric opened and closed his mouth several times. "Jesus, Jane."

"What?"

He darted a glance through the window to where his grandmother had returned and was now sifting through the papers on the coffee table. She glanced up, and her face softened as it landed on him, then hardened on me.

Eric leaned in and kissed me.

"Oh my *God*, what are you doing!" I shoved him away by reflex. "I said no funny business!"

"You said no pretty girl bullshit," he corrected me. "This is not that."

"How do you figure?!"

He tipped his head, like I should know the answer. "You're right. She thinks this is transactional, and she's looking for more. Jane, you didn't touch me at all last night. Other than, you know, squeezing my hand off in the beginning."

I scowled. "Was I supposed to? I didn't realize playacting was part of the bargain."

Eric rolled his eyes. "When did you ever have to act with me?"

I pressed my lips together. He had a point. The guy might piss me off like no other, but I never faked it once with him. In any way. And that was saying something.

"Still," I said. "You can't just go around kissing me whenever you want, you caveman. You want something, you ask for it. It's called consent."

Eric exhaled forcefully. "You always have to make things so goddamn difficult."

"I'm pretty sure you brought this shitty situation to the table, Petri."

He looked up. "*Don't* call me that."

I smirked. "Then don't be an idiot."

He sighed again. "Fine. Jane, my grandmother is going to look up again in about another two seconds. When she does, will you please let me kiss you so she thinks we like each other enough to get married? And so she'll agree to the goddamn papers and give me access to my trust so we can get the fuck out of here?"

I paused. "Are you serious?"

He set his jaw. "As a heart attack."

I bit my lip. "Fine. Five seconds, no more. And keep your hands to yourself."

Eric sighed again. "Incorrigible woman," he muttered to himself.

"I'm sorry, what was that?"

In response, I was suddenly yanked to him by the waist.

"Jane," he said, "shut up."

And before I could come back with a slick retort, he kissed me again. And this time, I didn't fight it. His mouth fit to mine easily, forcefully, like he had been intending to match those puzzle pieces together all day. I sank into it, my body melting into the strong hands that held my waist. My lips opened, welcoming his tongue as it licked, twisted, twirled around mine. My hands slid into the short hair at the base of his neck, urging him deeper while his hands knotted the fabric of my jumpsuit.

I don't know how long it lasted, but it was a lot more than five seconds.

When he finally released me, one of his hands traveled up my side and cupped my face. I froze, caught in the unexpected tenderness as Eric's eyes traveled over my face, his thumb lightly brushing my cheekbone. We stared at each other for a good five seconds before he swallowed and stepped back.

I took a deep breath. "I told you to watch your hands," I said, somewhat more breathlessly than I intended.

The right side of Eric's mouth quirked as he patted his hair back into place. "I kept them above the belt." He glanced inside. "She saw."

Reality slammed down like a sledgehammer.

"You totally took advantage of me," I said.

"You liked it."

"You're an asshole."

He shrugged. "Maybe."

We stared at each other for a solid thirty seconds. This time, Eric looked away first.

"Come on, Lefferts," he said, taking my hand in his. "She's watching us now too. Let's go inside and finish this."

We walked back inside, where Skylar and the other lawyer were now bent over the document, listening to Mrs. de Vries rattle on about money.

"I don't care how 'in love' they might be," she said in a way that made her doubt clear, though I did notice her curious glance as we sat down. "Twenty million dollars is far too much."

"No, it's not enough," Eric put in. "It's twenty for the marriage. Another twenty if she gets pregnant."

I gasped. That was an addition I hadn't know about. "*Pregnant?*"

"You don't plan to have children?" The sharp edge of Celeste's voice had returned.

"I—I—I honestly don't—we hadn't really..." I looked to Skylar, who seemed to be trying not to laugh. I scowled. This wasn't funny.

"If it happens, it happens," Eric said, pulling my hand into his lap.

His thumb brushed over my knuckles, toying with my new ring. Celeste's eyes zeroed in on the jewelry.

Eric turned to me with a soft expression. "You deserve it, Jane."

"Forty *million*, Eric?" Celeste still sounded like she was about to choke. "Are you out of your mind?"

"I figure I'm exactly as sane as it takes to require someone to get married for money in this day and age."

I didn't know what to say. Neither did Skylar or the other lawyer, both of whom were now furiously writing on their copies of the prenups.

"Honestly, I would have offered her five times that if I had to,"

Eric continued. "It still would have been cheaper than bankrupting the rest of the family out of pettiness."

He didn't shout, but his words cut nonetheless. Eric almost never shouted. I could remember only a few times—and yes, they were directed at me—that I had ever seen him really lose his temper. Of the two of us, I was always the one with the sparks.

This was how rich people were, I was starting to learn. Speak softly, and carry a big, money-filled stick.

"And another thing," Eric continued in that same low, controlled voice, though his eyes flashed. "We're not cattle. I understand why you insist on this marriage happening right this damn second. I understand you're in poor health and you'd like this family to continue patrilineally. It's antiquated and idiotic, but I get it."

"Now, see here—"

"But *if* it's going to happen, it happens because Jane and I choose to make it happen." He squeezed my hand. "Consent, right?"

I didn't know what to say. As of last week, Eric and I had agreed *not* to touch each other that way. We had agreed this needed to be purely business. Now he was standing up for my right to choose, kissing me on balconies, and caressing my hand. It wasn't fair. The hottest thing in the world isn't watching a man sweat or work out or get all hot and bothered. It's not his abs or his pecs or whatever the hell else women ogle on romance covers. What makes superheroes so sexy is that they fight for other people. And after spending two hours watching Eric fight his grandmother over me...followed by that kiss...yeah, it was doing it for me. Big time.

Ovarian whiplash, plain and simple.

"If you're also doing this for the company," Celeste said, trying a new tactic, "you'll consider what a potential loss it will take when its new chairman marries someone like—"

My head shot up at last. "Like what?"

Celeste looked to me like she had just realized I was there. "Like you, dear."

We stared at each other for a long time. I tried not to look away first.

"Mrs. de Vries," I said carefully, holding up my hand when Eric tried to speak. "I've been listening to you crap all over me for the last two hours. Yes, I said crap. In a room full of priceless antiques and art. I'm aware that my very presence here violates your sense of grace and elegance. Every word out of my mouth disgusts you."

Mrs. de Vries opened her mouth but didn't argue.

"But maybe," I said, "maybe I'm doing this for him too. I'm not just some girl he grabbed off the street or one of those socialite chicks dying to sink their French tips into him. I've known Eric a long time, and I appreciated him well before I knew about any of this. So consider for a moment that maybe I wasn't intending to get married either, but I'm doing it to help. Because, well, I care about him. Very much."

I hadn't realized how true the words were until I said them. Maybe, somewhere deep down, some of those old feelings still existed for this man who drove me crazy. Maybe somewhere, I didn't hate him as much as I thought.

"I think you need to consider his happiness before your own here," I concluded. "If that's even possible."

Celeste narrowed her eyes, gripping the arms of her wheelchair tightly. "Eric," she said, "the family isn't going to pay millions so you can wed your little geisha."

My jaw dropped completely. "His *what?*"

This time she looked straight at me. "I have a reputation, my dear. What do they say? I call them like I see them."

"Grandmother!"

"Mrs. de Vries, that is *totally* out of line!" Skylar put in.

"Stop, stop, *stop!*" I cried out, finally standing up. I brushed down my pants, let the fabric settle, then glared at the diminutive old orc. My sympathy for her had evaporated. She really was awful.

"First of all," I said through clenched teeth. "Get your fucking cultural references right, lady. Geisha are Japanese, and I'm half

Korean. *Second* of all," I continued. "I might not be rich, but I'm a catch. I'm from a good family, I'm a decent person, I'm smart as fuck, and cute as a damn button. Eric was lucky to find me, and you should be so lucky to invite someone like me into this shitshow of a family. *Third—*" I took a deep breath. I was running out of steam, but her tightly coiled face was ramping it right back up again. "If you weren't so determined to rent your grandson out like a studhorse, maybe you wouldn't be in this situation."

"Jane!" Eric cut in, gesturing across his mouth that I needed to shut the hell up.

Unfortunately, I was on a roll. "Why don't you just do what the European royalty did, Mrs. de Vries? I've seen the family pictures. Eric's got enough extended family lying around that a few of them might want to procreate to produce the perfect child for you. Then you could just cut him out of the equation, right?"

"Jane!" This time it was Skylar who was yanking on my sweater.

"Or maybe," I rattled on, "you should just go full Egyptian. With technology today, you could grab a little of Eric's sperm, Nina's eggs, and *voilà*, perfect de Vries baby in one shot, am I right? All you need is a surrogate."

"JANE!"

Together, Eric and Skylar both yanked me out of my fury, bringing me back to a place of sanity. Slowly, I realized that I'd just recommended incest to my future grandmother-in-law. In her own home.

Oh. Dear. Lord.

I turned and found Eric staring at me in horror. I clapped a hand over my mouth.

"Oh, God," I said. "Eric, I'm..." I turned to Celeste. "I really am so sorry."

"You...you ungrateful little wretch." She coughed, then hacked, then pressed her oxygen mask to her reddened face, gasping for breath. Behind her, Garrett the butler shot daggers at me. Her lawyer looked like he wanted to disappear.

"Eric," I started again. "I'm so sorry."

"Just don't," he said as he stood up. He looked angry, but also exhausted.

*Well, that's what you get,* I wanted to say. Fucking hell, I knew it was a shitty outburst, but what did he really expect? He chose *me* of all people!

"I need a break," he said as if we hadn't just taken a few minutes. "I need some space." He swiped his coat off the chair and headed for the exit, turning in the doorway. "Grandmother, this is the deal. If you don't sign off, there will be no wedding. No church. No dynasty. And I'll be happy to tell Mom, Nina, Violet, and all the others that the reason they are all losing their inheritances is because you were too racist and stubborn to grant Jane the same exact prenuptial compensation that every other person who has married into this family has received."

My jaw dropped. I had no idea this deal was so...common.

"Now, Eric, please," Celeste started.

"Please nothing," he said quietly. And to me, his gaze was cold. Withering. "I'll see you later."

And then he left.

# FIFTEEN

I raced outside, but of course he was gone. I couldn't believe he had just taken off like that, left me and Skylar in the lion's den without him. Seriously, what kind of a dick move was that? Skylar and the lawyer stayed behind while I dodged banged around the maze of an apartment, hoping to catch him before the elevator doors shut, and then had to jog down forty-three flights of stairs. But Eric, the monkey, had slipped away by the time I made it all the way down.

"2310 Forty-First. That's Twenty-Third Street and Forty-First Avenue."

I turned around to find Gracie, the kindly doorman, leaning casually against the bricks.

"Aren't you hot in that thing?" I asked, gesturing toward the full uniform—and hat!—he was wearing despite the fact that it was at least seventy-five degrees outside.

Gracie shrugged. "You get used to it. Anyway, the address, that's where young Mr. de Vries dashed off to. I don't know what it is, but it's in Queensbridge."

I nodded and turned in the direction where I *thought* the subway was, but the second the words registered, I spun back around on my heel. "Wait a second. Isn't Queensbridge a housing project? Didn't Nas rap about it?"

Gracie gave a lopsided smile. He knew exactly what I was thinking. "I guess so."

Lily-white, Upper East Side born and bred *Eric* was hanging out where hip hop was born? There had to be a mistake.

"Well, to be fair, that area is really more Long Island City now." Skylar's dry voice interrupted us as she stepped out of the building. "Hipster central. Eric probably goes there for the five-dollar coffee." She gave me a long look. "Thanks for abandoning me up there, by the way."

I hung my head. "Sorry, Sky. I just—"

"I know," she interrupted, and the irritation on her face disappeared. "You couldn't have known either."

I turned. "Known about what?"

"The rumors. Brandon said people have been whispering about the de Vries procreating with their cousins for the last, oh, hundreds of years. They're probably a little sensitive about it."

I blanched. "Seriously? I'm actually marrying into an incest factory?"

Skylar chuckled and shrugged. "No more than say, Meghan Markle. It really is like the old European royalty, like you said. Limited gene pool, but they broke out of it eventually. Slowly, but surely."

"The British press hate Meghan Markle." I scowled. "And so do half the royals."

Skylar rubbed my shoulder. "You can still back out, of course. But you should also know that the second you two walked out, Celeste asked her lawyer to transfer Eric's trust into his name. You got what you wanted. The prenup. All of it. I'll draw up the final papers today."

I shook my head. "Then what the hell was all of that for? Why did the old miser have to put us through that entire song and dance?"

Skylar shrugged. "I wonder if she's feeling, I don't know...power-less, maybe. After you two left, she practically collapsed into her chair, and as soon as she gave her lawyer instructions, her butler rolled her into her bedroom. She's not well. She's desperate."

It almost made me feel bad for her all over again. Almost. Well, I did feel bad for the incest cracks.

"Shit," I muttered. "Looks like I have a mea culpa to make."

"Listen, Brandon and I have to get back to Boston tonight, but the hotel room is yours for the week if you need it while you find a place or figure out where you are living. I had assumed with Eric, but... What are you going to do now?"

"I need to find Eric."

Skylar nodded as if that was what she expected and pulled a piece of paper out of her briefcase. "Okay. Well, the grande dame asked me to give you your schedule for the next few months. As a condition for the prenup."

I frowned. "My *schedule?*"

It was a calendar of social events for the summer season—including an engagement party for me and Eric.

"What the hell is a white party?" I wondered as I looked over the paper.

"I'm guessing a party where everyone wears white. It's at their estate in the Hamptons, so maybe that should include swimsuits? I don't know."

"You better be coming to these too. God, there's more." Galas. Benefits. Luncheons. Mama Vader had my entire life booked from here until Doomsday. I looked up. "She was never going to say no. Look at this shit; she's got me tied up like a victim on railroad tracks. Skylar, I can't do any of this crap. I have to study for the New York State bar for the next two months."

Skylar just rolled her eyes. "Jane, be real. You're not going to have time to study for that. This wedding isn't just a marriage, you know. It's a public relations coup at a moment where corporations like this are facing serious public discord. I wouldn't be surprised if Celeste conducts some kind of nefarious takeover of the board while the shareholders are too interested in the wedding to care." She smirked. "Pink hair or not."

I pondered this for a moment—now I *really* needed to talk to Eric. This couldn't wait while he went pouting around the city. I signed on for a fake marriage, not a fake life. This could *not* happen.

"Okay, so, Long Island City," I said. "Can I take the subway?"

Skylar nodded and checked her watch. "Better grab a cab, though. It'll take you forever to get there from here at this hour." She handed me a fifty. "Just *take it*, Jane!"

"Thanks," I said. After all, I was kind of strapped.

———

THIRTY MINUTES LATER, I paid the cabbie and stepped out onto a fairly nondescript street just on the other side of the city. From here, Manhattan rose tall, almost close enough to touch. This was Queens, but only just. I looked around the block. Yeah, Skylar was right. Other than the familiar-looking tenement housing (hey, I used to watch MTV) rising over the heads of the smaller apartment buildings and warehouses, this pretty much was hipster central. I could throw a rock and hit guy in skinny jeans or a flannel shirt.

I looked up at the building that matched the address Gracie had given me and frowned. *Queensbridge Boulders* read the nondescript signage on the doors.

"Rock climbing?" I wondered. "Seriously?"

I put my hand on the door and pushed inside.

It was hard to call a place like this a gym. Really, it was a giant warehouse that jumped about a hundred feet toward the sky and took up about a full city block. Massive, really, by most large-city standards. The air looked smoky, like I'd walked into a fog bank. And from the tops of about twenty different walls hung multicolored ropes from which actual *people* dangled like marionettes while others scaled twenty-, thirty-, even forty-foot walls like monkeys.

"Take!" one man shouted as he lost his footing. My breath flew to my chest as he dropped a solid five feet before the person holding onto the other end of the rope yanked it taut, catching the man by his harness at the other end. His foot slammed against the wall while he dangled from left to right, swinging like a pendulum.

"Jesus fucking Christ," I murmured. Who in their right mind would do this?

"How's it going?"

I turned to the right, toward a guy with chin-length brown hair and a patchy brown beard. He looked like an extra from *Lord of the Rings*, but I couldn't deny the gun show. One and two, practically splitting the seams of his holey T-shirt. Okay, so maybe playing Spiderman did a body good.

I approached the desk and nodded toward the rest of the room. "What's with the smoke?"

The guy's face screwed up in confusion. "Smoke...oh, ha. That's chalk residue. It sort of gets into the air. We use it so our hands don't slip on the holds."

I glanced over my shoulder and caught one of the climbers dipping her hands into a bag on the ground. She rubbed them together, and a cloud of white powder emerged, then settled to the ground.

"I see," I said. "I'm sure it's great for the upper respiratory tract too, huh?"

"What?"

I shook my head and turned back to the receptionist. "Never mind."

He looked me over, as if he just realized I'd walked in this way. Yeah, yeah, yeah. I wasn't exactly a hobbit's dream girl. Well, I wasn't here to climb walls anyway. I was here to chew out a certain stuck-up Upper East Sider having a temper tantrum.

"So...can I help you with something?" he asked. Quick one, this guy.

I leaned over the counter and knocked my ringed fingers on the granite. The black diamond was particularly loud. "Do you happen to know Eric de Vries? Tall guy. Blond, handsome in an irritatingly debonair kind of way. Constant stick up his ass? I was told he was here today."

Immediately, the receptionist's face brightened. "Eric? Oh, yeah, he joined last week. Came in about thirty minutes ago. I think he's upstairs in the bouldering area. You can head up there to find him, unless you're planning to climb too..."

He looked me over doubtfully. I glared right back. *No, my jumpsuit isn't exactly made for strenuous exercise. Thank you and fuck off.*

"Thanks, Frodo," I said. "I'll head on up."

I made my way through the gym, trying and failing *not* to notice the way most of the men in there were extremely well-built. Okay, maybe I could get on board with this sport. Especially the way those cute little harnesses they wore framed their packages just right... maybe I did need to give rock climbing a try sometime...

"TAKE!"

I jumped as another person came flying off a wall, this time dropping almost twenty feet before the rope caught them. Yeah, fuck that. I'd take my exercise in the form of window-shopping, like God intended.

I found my way upstairs and entered another large, airy space bordered by climbing walls and covered with a floor that was basically made of sponge. It was like walking on a firm waterbed. These walls, however, were no more than about twenty-feet high, and people were scrambling up them without ropes, without *anything* to stop them from hitting the ground. And every so often, a person would lunge for one particular hold, their body swinging through the air like a damn chimpanzee. Multiple times they missed, and their bodies would hit the ground with a loud slap on the vinyl, where they would lie, recovering, for several more seconds before moving out of the way for the next climber to give it a try.

"Psychos," I murmured. Everyone in this gym was certifiable.

"Yeah, Eric."

"Get it, man. Do it."

I turned around to find a few people watching a blond man scaling a severely overhung wall on the far side of the gym. I moved closer—sure enough, this psycho was Eric.

"God, he's good," muttered one lady climber to another male spectator.

"I know," said the guy. "Did you see him flash that V-10? I've been working that problem for over a month."

Eric gave a loud grunt as he managed to wedge a rubber-guarded toe into a crack in the wall. I watched, transfixed, as he looked up the wall, where his fingers were crimped onto nonexistent holds at a forty-five-degree overhang while his legs dangled, and then found equally small holds to balance on. Clothed in nothing but a pair of flimsy athletic shorts, every single muscle was cast in high relief. Every. Single. One.

My mouth was suddenly very, very wet.

"Come on, Eric," cheered a few of the other people. "Finish it."

He pulled slightly on the holds, and every muscle in both of his arms looked like they were cut from stone while his toes found a couple of other nubs Then, with a cry that sounded like it was coming from a wild creature, he pushed off all of the holds at once and jumped *up the freaking wall* to grab for a hold at the top. His body swung wildly, but fought for control as he slapped his left hand over the right and held on with another yowl.

"Yeah!" cheered the climbers next to me, and several others who had been watching erupted into light applause as Eric dropped at least twenty feet to the ground and rolled onto his back, breathing hard. I waited a few minutes until he'd been congratulated by his audience, and then, as the small crowd dispersed back into the gym, I approached where he lay.

"Woo! Go, Spiderman!" I cheered.

His eyes were closed, and his fair face was flushed, sweat pouring down his forehead. Then his eyes flashed open, and what was there was pure...vitriol.

It was like a shot in the chest. A punch in the stomach. Lord, I had never seen him look at me with that kind of hatred before. Hatred...I supposed I had earned.

He closed his eyes again, and the mask resumed. "Jane."

I couldn't help myself. "Petri."

His eyes opened, irritation gleaming. Eric sat up as he massaged his neck. I winced sympathetically. Whipping his head against the mat, even if it was padded, would probably mean a nasty headache in about an hour.

"What are you doing here?"

I sank to my haunches next to him. I felt ridiculous. Out of place. Every person in here was dressed in completely no-nonsense garb. REI pants, shorts, or leggings. Chalk-covered T-shirts that looked like they'd been picked up at the Goodwill. And, of course, those silly little elf-shoes that apparently helped them scale walls. Meanwhile, here I was, in bright green and black, hair like birthday streamers, face full of my favorite makeup, including cherry-red lipstick. It was my usual look, but I felt more like an alien in this gym than I had last night.

"I came to look for you, of course," I said, tapping on my bottom lip as I looked around. "Nice digs you got here. But what's the point, if you don't mind me asking? All that effort to scale a wall to... nowhere? I don't get it."

Eric opened his mouth as if he wanted to argue—isn't that what I wanted too, deep down?—but something else completely came out.

"Do you have to wear that lipstick all the fucking time?" he demanded.

At first my jaw fell at his harsh tone, but a split second later, said lips spread into a smile. I shouldn't have felt so cocky, but god*damn* did I love it when he lost his cool. There was something so fucking satisfying about breaking through that apathy. About seeing him...*care*.

Besides, I was mad too. I didn't particularly care for being ditched. So instead of making peace, I leaned over him, smacking my lips in a way that made his silvery eyes dilate.

"You used to like my lipstick," I purred. "If I recall correctly, Petri dish, you liked licking it off."

Eric's nostrils flared as he swallowed hard. Fucking hell. What was I doing? Tempting fate? Why? I was the one who barred any of this crap with him, and here I was, goading him with everything I had. And yet...I couldn't stop. It was addictive, watching him unravel this way. It was sadistic, the pleasure it gave me. The power...

And then, before I could take the words back, his left hand snaked behind my head, taking a harsh handful of hair and suspending me there above him. He didn't hold me totally still, but I couldn't escape either. And goddamn if I didn't love it.

"Don't start something you can't finish," Eric said between gritted teeth.

My self-assured smirk wavered. "Oh? And what are you going to do about it?"

Behind us, another climber fell, but neither of us moved. His grip tightened, right on the edge of a pinch and legitimate pain. Right where he knew I liked it. Eric squeezed until my lips fell open, dropping all bravado, and my eyes widened. Half in fear, half in anticipation. *All* in lust. Just the way *he* liked it, the bastard.

*Fuck.*

"Jane, you know *exactly* what I would do," he said as he twisted my head, so I was now looking up at him. It was a subtle move, but established him firmly as the one in control.

I was trapped, but I wasn't exactly trying to get away either. In fact, I was pretty sure that if I could see my own eyes, they'd be dilated too. His eyes were still pinned to my lips. I couldn't help it. I licked them.

"Do you remember that night after the concert at Great Scott?" he asked in a voice that shook.

I remembered. Of course I fucking remembered. That was the night we hooked up—*really* hooked up—after graduating law school.

That night was burned into my memory forever. Sure, we had a brief thing during our first year of law school, but it wasn't until that summer, when we were both studying for the bar and running interference in Brandon and Skylar's relationship that things really picked up.

Yeah, I'll remember that night for the rest of my life.

"You teased me that night too, didn't you, Jane?" Eric reminded me. He twisted my hair a little more.

I sucked in a breath. "Did I?"

Our mouths were maybe an inch apart. At this point, I was staring too, unable to keep my gaze off that plump lower lip of his. So soft. So fucking suckable.

"You were dancing," he reminded me as his grip softened a bit. His fingers dug into the back of my head, massaging lightly, replacing that pinch of pain with a soothing rub. Again, my response was innate. I practically purred. It felt good, too good to move away.

"To every song. Shaking that sweet ass of yours. Shimmying your tits in every guy's face who wanted a look. Drinking way, *way* more than you should."

"Please. Like you weren't?" I countered, though my voice was breathy and light. Challenge him, always challenge him.

He tightened his grip again, pulling my hair into a tight knot. My eyes flew open as my thick frames tipped off-kilter.

"I was doing just fine, thanks, keeping you out of trouble," Eric growled. "But then you really fucked up, Lefferts. Do you remember? Do you remember what you did?"

A tiny muscle in the side of my neck fluttered, and Eric's eyes zeroed in on the spot. Slowly, the tip of his tongue traced the outline of his mouth. I had to physically restrain myself from yanking him down to lick it. *Fucking hell, Jane. What are you doing?*

But I couldn't stop. That was the problem. I could never stop with him.

"What did you do, Jane?" Eric shook my head a bit when I didn't answer immediately. "Tell me. Now."

"I-I spilled the beer," I stammered.

"That's right. You spilled the fucking beer. And where did you spill it?"

"All over my shirt." My voice was breathy, barely above a whisper. Barely recognizable.

"That's right," Eric said again. "All over your shirt. I could see everything, and so could everyone else. Your bra. Your navel. Your perfect round breasts, and those tight nipples that you love pinched. You made such a fucking mess. Like a bad. Little. Girl."

I mewled. I mewled, like a goddamn *kitten*. And then, because I couldn't *not* look, I glanced down and saw, to my simultaneous delight and horror, that Eric was sitting there with a full-mast hard-on, barely concealed by the bend of his leg. Most of the people in the gym were too focused on what they were doing, and we were in the back, somewhat sheltered by the overhanging walls. But if anyone cared to look, they'd have seen him standing to attention, right here in the middle of the floor. And me, of course, practically salivating over it.

But did I move away? Like I should have? Like I told him I wanted?

Not a fucking inch.

"Be honest," Eric said, his deep voice low, right next to my ear, so that only I could hear him. Shivers traveled down my spine. "Did you do it on purpose?"

"N-no."

His eyes closed when I stuttered again. He remembered too. He remembered that I only did that when he was undoing *me*. When my lust and desire was too much to take, and I started to lose the capacity to do anything else...but him.

Eric jerked my head again, slightly, so that no one else would notice, but hard enough that I mewled again at the welcome pinch. *Oh, this motherfucker.*

"You're lying," he said through his teeth. "Aren't you?"

He jerked my head again.

"Y-yes," I admitted, more of a breath than a word. "Yes, I am." Was I? Did it even matter?

"And you lied then too, didn't you?"

Another miniscule nod.

"And what did I do?" Eric asked. My hair, wound tight around his fist, hurt a little, but I didn't even try to fight it. "What did I do, Jane?"

My voice was little more than a whisper. "You punished me."

He licked his lips again. I didn't want to do anything else but kiss them.

"You were asking for it then," he said as he leaned over me and drifted his other fingers around my jaw. "Are you asking for it now?"

The muscle in my neck fluttered against his calloused fingertips. I was honestly scared of what I would say. My eyes drifted up and down his body, taking in his shirtless chest, biceps, forearms, one fully flexed from the grip in my hair. Lord, he had already been reasonably fit, but five years of doing *this* had made Eric into a work of art. I watched, transfixed, as a drop of sweat traveled from his neck over a perfectly sculpted pectoral muscle, catching in the light smattering of hair over his chest. *Fuck. Me.* I sucked hard on my bottom lip.

What was I doing? But the word came out anyway, as if my body were answering because my mind had stopped working: "Y-yes."

For a moment, it was as if the entire fucking gym faded away. I could see the future, each individual movement laid out, scene by scene, on a still reel of frames. Flip me on my back. Rip off my clothes. Drag me downstairs, use the ropes hanging from the ceiling to suspend me just the right height.

Tease me a little, then feed me his dick, one beautiful inch at a time. *Give you something for that smart mouth,* he'd say. Make me moan until he'd be shouting right along with me. Then clip me back up and fuck me hard enough against the wall that we'd both forget our names.

Just like last week.

Just. Like. Always.

*Thwack!*

A body slammed onto the crash pad next to us, yanking me out of my fantasy and back into reality. Eric's hand released my hair, and I fell back to my elbows, looking dazed as he scooted away, glaring at the intruder.

"Sorry, man." The climber picked himself up with a curious, friendly glance at me, then lumbered off to find another problem to try.

Eric shook his head, wiping his palms over his shorts as I got myself back together. I wiped the newly formed sweat off my own brow. Holy shit. What had just happened?

Eric looked at me hard, then picked himself off the ground.

"Give me ten minutes to shower and change," he said. "And then you can tell me what the hell you are really doing here, besides trying to drive me crazy."

# SIXTEEN

I waited in the lounge area by the front of the gym for about twenty minutes while Eric showered. When he reappeared, he wasn't dressed in the uptight pants or suit he wore to the office or his grandmother's, but in simple jeans, a plain white T-shirt, and Adidas shoes. New muscles aside, he looked much more like the younger man I had met in Boston eight years ago.

He pushed a hand through his still-wet hair as he approached. His mask was firmly in place.

"I'm hungry," he said. "Do you mind stopping for a falafel on the way back to the city?"

I shook my head, unsure of where he was at. "No, I don't mind."

I followed him down the street and stood patiently with him while he ordered.

"You want anything?" he asked.

I shook my head. "No, I'm not hungry."

He shrugged, picked up his food, and ate it right there next to the shop window.

"That's better," he said once he was finished.

We started walking down the block while he took an occasional drink from his water bottle.

"So, Eric de Vries gets hangry," I remarked. "I'll remember that next time you throw a tantrum."

I received another blistering look, but this one was tinged with humor. "It might have helped. But I think it was the part where you suggested I procreate with my family that tipped me over the edge." He took a long sip of water. "So, you want to tell me why you're here?"

I frowned. "Your doorman gave me the address. I—I wanted to say—well, your grandmother agreed to the terms."

"You could have told me later."

"Well, I mean...I also came to apologize, I guess."

He stopped again. "*You* came to apologize."

My mouth screwed up. "What? I can apologize. Like this: I apologize."

His face didn't move. "For what?"

"For...well, for implying that your family was a bunch of inbreeds, for one. I had no idea that was even a rumor, you know. I mean, I guess it makes sense, what with this country's obsession with eugenics, but still—"

"That's enough."

He started walking again. I didn't immediately continue, absorbed for a moment by the way he filled out his jeans.

"Stop staring at my ass, Jane!" he shouted without even turning around.

I snapped back into the present. How did he *always* know?

I caught up to him, practically having to jog to keep up with his pace. "You know, you could apologize to me too."

"Me? Apologize for what?"

"Well, for abandoning me to your grandmother, for one. I realize you warned me about wolves, but I didn't realize you'd be feeding me to them."

He stopped again and whirled around, almost smacking a passerby with his gym bag. "Are you serious?"

I folded my arms across my chest. "Well, yeah. Yeah, I am. It's not like you were exactly defending me in there. Your grandmother sat there and basically called me your comfort woman. Can you blame me for losing my temper after that?"

His brows screwed up in confusion. I sighed impatiently.

"Korean women were forced to be prostitutes called comfort women to the Japanese army during World War II," I said, filling him in. "I mean, she said geisha, but if we're going to use racist Asian sex-work jibes, she could at least be accurate."

Eric expelled a long breath.

"Look," I continued. "You can't do that. You can't just leave me to be attacked by your family and then get angry when I defend myself. I'm sorry I compared your family to the brother-uncle ancients, but she basically called me a whore, Eric. What was I supposed to do?"

"She's old," he said lamely. "You're supposed to take it, like everyone else."

"No, I'm supposed to get married. I promised to be your wife, not a shadow of myself. If staying quiet and perfect on the Upper East Side is what you're expecting, then maybe this arrangement really is a bad idea."

He took a handful of his hair and yanked thoughtfully. "That's not what I want."

"Oh, no? Then why does Skylar think I'm going to have to stop being a lawyer?"

At that he looked genuinely shocked. "What? When did she say that?"

"After you screamed out of the building. I mentioned I didn't have time for this psycho schedule." I pulled the now-folded piece of paper out of my purse and handed it to him. "Look at that. It's like a Jane Austen novel this summer. Like we're characters from Downton Abbey about to embark on 'the season.'"

Eric scanned the engagements. "Jesus Christ."

"She's RSVP'd us for all of them," I pointed out. "*All* of them. Your grand re-entry to society or whatever. Now, me, I was planning to study for the bar this summer and apply for some jobs around town. But I can't do that if we have to play Matthew and Mary Crawley." I snorted as a thought occurred to me. "You know, they were cousins too."

But Eric wasn't paying attention anymore. He was still looking through the list of events. "She knew I'd never budge," he murmured, more to himself than to me. He looked up with some curious satisfaction. "She had this typed before we even came over. It's on company letterhead."

I nodded. "That's what I thought. We had to endure all of that bullshit this morning for nothing."

"It was a power play. Meant to show us both who's in charge. But more importantly, this is a confirmation, maybe even more than a prenup."

He tucked the sheet into his gym bag, then turned to me. All traces of anger were gone—the mask was now tinged with hope. I thought.

"I don't want you to not work, Jane. And I am sorry about leaving you there. But you might...you might consider taking this time off, like Skylar said. It'll make it easier if you build some allies in my family."

I frowned. "Eric, I have to work. I have bills to pay. My student loan payments each month would pay the mortgage on a four-bedroom house in Iowa."

He paused again, right next to the subway entrance. The roar of the train below us sounded, and he shuttled me to the side as passengers started to emerge from the stop.

"Your loans aren't a factor anymore."

I frowned. "What do you mean?"

"I paid them off last week. As soon as you agreed to all of this."

My mouth dropped. "*What?*"

Now he was the one who couldn't meet my gaze. "It seemed like the right thing to do."

"Eric—holy shit—um, okay. Well, I guess we can take that out of the prenuptial agreement or whatever."

My hands were flapping around like wings—I had no idea what to do with them. After attending Northwestern and then Harvard, I owed the equivalent of a country house mortgage. My goal had been to work for another five years in public service so the loans would hopefully be forgiven, but who knew if I'd be able to get another job like that quickly. Now...now it wasn't even an option.

"Consider the next six months a break," Eric said. "A chance for both of us to reevaluate what we want. And next spring, if you still want to retake the bar in New York or Massachusetts, you can. We'll pay for you to take a class and do it right. In the meantime, you can decide if you still want to work at the DA's office again, or if you still even want to be a lawyer, or if you want to do...something else."

And there it was—that crazy ability of his to read my mind. He looked over my clothes, which he knew I'd made myself, and his hand fluttered out, almost as if he wanted to touch the green fabric. But instead of grabbing that, he took my hand instead and pulled me toward the train entrance.

"Come on," he said. "I want to show you something else."

———

WE TOOK the F train back into Manhattan and got off at Sixty-Third and Lexington, about twenty blocks south of his grandmother's building. But instead of walking there like I expected, Eric steered me toward the entrance to Central Park.

"Are you okay to walk?" Eric asked, gesturing at my shoes.

I looked down at my black ballet flats. "Oh, sure. I could walk miles in these." I loved fashion, but I hated uncomfortable footwear. It was a pet peeve of mine to wear "bloody shoes."

He nodded. "They're nice."

It's a weird feeling when a cute boy takes a moment to compliment your footwear. It's even weirder when it's someone who was ten seconds to taking you less than an hour ago.

Weird, but good.

I followed Eric into the park, and we meandered a bit, walking past some of the more recognizable elements. In all my visits to New York, I was usually too busy being entertained by Skylar's family or shopping to do the touristy stuff like walking by the lake or checking out the famous fountain. Eric narrated the landmarks, and like a good tourist, I took pictures. More than once, when he pointed things out for me to see, I caught him watching me instead.

"You're so funny," I remarked after he bought a pretzel and tipped the vendor about four times its worth. "You have all this money, but you never use it."

"What do you mean?"

"Well, for instance, coming here in a subway car that smelled like pee and sweat when you could easily call Smithers, your driver."

Eric snorted. "Should I ride around in a limousine like a Frank Capra bad guy? Live in a tower made of gold and sniff at the *hoi polloi*?"

I shoved him in the shoulder. "You know what I mean. Two-dollar pretzels instead of a ten-dollar baguette."

The closet full of custom-tailored suits that were definitely not from the Men's Wearhouse came to mind. His ridiculously picky tastes for fine coffee and liquor. Unless we were out with friends at Cleo's, the local dive bar where Harvard Law students hung out, I didn't think I ever saw Eric drink the cheap crap.

But those were a few idiosyncrasies. They weren't how he lived his entire life.

I didn't think.

Eric shrugged. "If it's good enough for everyone else, it's good enough for me."

It wasn't a bad argument. And I couldn't say I didn't like it.

"Besides," he said. "I have my weaknesses."

"Oh my God, don't remind me," I said. "Do you remember when I got you Dunkin' Donuts coffee that one morning?"

He chuckled. "Oh, yes."

—————

"HEY." I entered the apartment and closed the door with my hip. "Stop the presses! Literally!"

Eric turned around holding his fancy steel kettle in his hand. Behind him, his intricate coffee apparatus was set up on the counter, complete with beans ground and laid in a coffee filter over a glass container that looked more like it belonged in a laboratory than a kitchen counter.

"This isn't a French press," he corrected me. "It's a Chemex."

I rolled my eyes. It sounded like lab equipment too.

"What's that?" he asked as he walked around the counter, holding his kettle.

For a second, I didn't speak. Skylar was gone for the weekend, so Eric and I had the apartment to ourselves for once. Our study materials were strewn all over his normally impeccably clean living room, clothes were rumpled on the floor and, well, everywhere. Remnants of last night's reunion. And now he was standing in the middle of the kitchen in nothing but his boxers, his lean body filling things out way too well for a Saturday morning.

"Earth to Jane," he said, snapping his fingers. "Hello?"

I blinked. "Oh, ah. Sorry. Jesus, do you really have to walk around like that? It's distracting."

He smiled. That stupid, lazy smile that transformed his face from something close to ordinary to utterly heart-stopping. Lord, the man could work a grin.

"Is that so?" he asked. Then his eyes lit on the white bag and coffee tray in my hands. "What do you have there?"

I set the coffee and donuts on the counter. "Thought I'd save you the trouble this morning. That damn coffee contraption takes you about thirty minutes, and I'm sorry, but no joe is worth turning gray while I wait." I picked up my black coffee and pushed his toward him. "I even put half and half in there, just the way you like it."

Eric replaced his kettle on its electric heater, then picked up the disposable coffee cup dubiously. I watched as he held it up to his long nose, sniffed, then cautiously took a sip. He stood there for a moment, swishing it around his mouth.

"For fuck's sake, Petri, it's cheap coffee, not a fine Bourdeaux," I said.

He set the coffee back down and pushed it toward me. "That it's not. Thanks, but I'm good." He turned back to his setup on the opposite counter.

I stared at the cup. "Are you serious?"

He nodded over his shoulder. "It was really nice of you, Jane, but that's crap. Toss it out. I'll make you one too."

I gawked at him. "Um, excuse me? I bought you a gift. Don't waste your time with your science experiment, Eric. Just be a gentleman and drink the fucking coffee."

"I'm sorry, but no. I'll have a donut, though. Those look good."

"No coffee, no fucking donuts!"

I knew I was being irrational. But for some reason, it really pissed me off that he would choose his fancy fucking coffee over my gift. It wasn't much, of course. The entire meal had cost me maybe five bucks. But that wasn't the point. I had climbed out of bed—with legs that were barely working after last night's workout, by the way—made the walk of shame down to the Haymarket T-stop, and stood in line with every other hungover college student in Boston to pick up breakfast for this man. And this was the thanks I got?

Eric ignored me with a kiss on my cheek, then reached into the bag, pulled out an old-fashioned, and took a bite.

"You know," Eric said with a mouth full of donut, "next time you should just go to Mike's. It's just down the block, and their pastries are about twice as good. Coffee still sucks, but at least we'd have fresh sfogliatelle."

That. Was. It.

All at once, I dropped my arm across the counter and swooped both cups of coffee, the donut, the napkins, and the tray into the trash at the end.

"How about you, Mike, and your fucking pastries and fucking coffee go fuck yourselves," I said emphatically.

"Jane, come on. You're being ridiculous."

I looked up. Eric still stood there, shirtless and delicious, holding his half-eaten, equally delicious old-fashioned. Defiantly, I walked up, plucked the donut out of his fingers, then marched over to the trash and proceeded to rip the stupid thing to shreds and dump it in the bin with the rest of the stuff I'd brought.

"Oh, I'm sorry," I said as I dusted my hands off. "Did you want that? I guess it's for the best, since Mike's is so much better, right?"

Eric just narrowed his eyes and braced his hands on the counter. "Jane."

Shit. I knew that tone.

I stared at the floor. "We are not doing this."

"Jane."

I still didn't look up.

"Pretty girl..."

Fuck. Like it was on a string, my head tipped up, and just like that, Eric's eyes, bright and steely, flashed.

"You're going to pay for that," he said. There was no sign of that lazy smile from earlier. Now his expression was made of steel. And I knew exactly what that meant.

"Into the bedroom," he ordered. "Pants off. On your knees. Forehead to the bed. Don't. Fucking. Move."

I remained where I was for a moment more, my chin tipped up defiantly. I wanted to rip his head off for shunning my gift and tell him where he could stick his fucking orders. But just as badly, I wanted to run into the bedroom and do exactly as he said.

Well...maybe not exactly.

The bedroom won.

---

"I DIDN'T KNOW how to react," Eric said as he broke off a piece of his pretzel and handed it to me. When I took it, that lazy smile reappeared. So did the butterflies in my stomach. "No one had ever brought me coffee and donuts before."

"I can't believe that," I said. "You screwed half of Boston while we were in grad school, Casanova. You're telling me that none of them every brought you a little snack?"

"I think my reputation precedes me a little there," Eric said. "Contrary to what people think, my sex life was not *that* active."

I gave him a look. "You're so full of shit. I don't ever remember seeing you at a bar without leaving with someone. And from what Skylar said, you spent about half the nights of the week out of the apartment."

Eric shrugged. "Okay, sometimes it was too easy. But it wasn't always someone different. You make it sound like I had a new partner every night."

"Please, Petri dish. You didn't?"

He sent me a sharp gray look but chose not to respond to my goading. "Relationships aren't worth the stress, you know? The exciting part ends so quickly. Passion doesn't last forever."

I nodded. "Yeah, I hear that."

*Except with some, Jane Brain.* Ah, Dad. The voice of reason. I was wondering when he'd show up. *You do know one couple, at least,* he reminded me.

I considered Skylar and Brandon. The way he pulled her into his suite, so unapologetically in lust and in love with his wife. But they were the exception, not the rule. Most people didn't have that. Most people never would.

We paused at the edge of a gigantic lawn, watching contentedly as a young family chased their kids around the field. The four of them were so sweet: a man, a woman, and two kids, probably about five and nine. The couple was married—they both wore wedding rings that gleamed in the sun. When they sat down to rest, the man wrapped his burly arm around his wife's shoulder. She nuzzled into him, looking as though she belonged there.

I sighed. "How long do you think they've been married?"

Eric shrugged. "One year, tops."

"Come on," I said. "They have kids."

Eric shook his head. "I bet they're extended family. That couple hasn't been together for more than a few years. Newlyweds, for sure. No one with kids acts like that."

I started to agree, but suddenly I couldn't stand the thought of not knowing for sure. What if...what if Skylar and Brandon weren't the miracle I supposed? What if they were much, much more?

"Wait here," I said.

I handed Eric my pretzel and strode through the grass toward the woman. Her husband got back up and chased the kids again.

"Excuse me," I called as I approached.

The woman looked up. She had bright blue eyes and a warm smile against her almost-black hair. And it was then I noticed she was also in the middle stages of pregnancy. Her bump was freaking adorable.

"Can I help you?" she asked.

"I'm so sorry to intrude," I said. "But I was just wondering...how long have you and your husband been together?"

"Oh...a while..." She turned to the man running around with the two kids in the field and smiled at him. He waved at her and grinned right back. She giggled, then turned to me. "Nico and I first met... gosh...I want to say almost thirteen years ago now."

I choked. "Thirteen *years*?" She looked like she was maybe twenty-five. I looked out at the field. It was hard to say how old he was, but if it had been thirteen years... "So, those are your kids?"

She nodded. "Yep. That's my oldest, Mateo. He's almost ten. And that's my daughter, Coco. She's six."

"Wow," I said. "You do not look old enough to have a ten-year-old son."

The woman blushed. "Thank you."

"When are you due?" I wondered as she cupped her protruding belly pensively.

"Oh. In about four months." She sighed. "I'm a little nervous. We've...well, I've had a couple of miscarriages. And Coco's birth wasn't easy."

"Sweetie, you okay?"

The woman's husband bounded in, leaving their kids to continue playing. His touch floated over his wife, checking her everywhere, as if making sure she was whole. She shooed him off a few times, but the continued flush in her cheeks made it clear she liked his attention. I couldn't blame her. There was a preciousness about it that was endearing.

Most of all, I noticed the way his eyes didn't leave hers for a second. They were like magnets, drawn together, and when he gave her a kiss—quick and light, nothing untoward for a day in the park with family—it was evident from the way they both clutched at each other that there was *much* more where that came from.

After thirteen freaking years.

"So it is possible," Eric murmured behind me, having approached as well. I didn't have to wonder what he meant.

"I know," I replied.

The couple looked at us, as if they had just remembered we were there.

"Thanks," I said. "You have a lovely family."

"Have a nice day," said Eric, and the couple nodded before settling back on their blanket, absorbed in their children and each other.

I followed Eric off the lawn, both of us absorbed in thought for the moment. It wasn't until we had crossed the park completely and were standing on Central Park West that I thought to wonder where we were actually headed.

So I asked.

Eric turned with yet another lazy, stomach-fluttering smile. "It's just a couple more blocks. I wanted to show you our new apartment."

# SEVENTEEN

I followed Eric onto a relatively quiet block on what the signs said was West Seventy-Sixth Street. In contrast with the bustle of Central Park and some of the larger streets we crossed, this was downright idyllic.

"What neighborhood is this?" I asked as we passed several tall brick buildings and a bunch of Edith Wharton-style brownstones.

"The Upper West Side," he said. "I figured having the park between us and the family would be a reasonable buffer."

I chuckled. "You would be right." I gazed up and down the street, which was lined with bright green maples waving in the summer breeze. "Where are your offices again? Will your commute be bad?"

He laughed. "All the way downtown. But it will be fine. I don't want to live by Wall Street anyway." He stopped in front of a giant brownstone with L-shaped stairs leading up to a second-floor entrance. "Well, here we are."

I stared up at it in awe. "Please don't tell me this entire thing is ours."

"Jane, you know we can afford it, right? We could buy this whole block if we really wanted." Eric peered up at the building, but with a lot less dismay than I had. It was almost as if he were considering the possibility.

I swallowed. It was a funny thing, the money. We'd been tossing around the numbers like they meant nothing. Twenty million. Forty million. Seventeen billion. They were all purely theoretical. I still had less than a thousand dollars currently in my savings account. I was still staying with friends and, until a few days ago, my mother's couch. I still had no real place to live.

Until now.

"What if I didn't want to live in a giant house like this?" I asked, half joking. "Didn't you ever think of asking me, huh?"

"Jane, I'm about to inherit a seventeen-billion-dollar fortune. People are going to expect me to maintain a certain lifestyle."

I turned. "Do you actually care what people expect?"

Until now, I genuinely thought he didn't. Even in law school, Eric sort of moved to the beat of his own drum. It wasn't a particularly ostentatious drum. It was a drum that wore khaki pants and enjoyed a good vodka. And most of the time, the beat worked well with others. But it always kept its own cadence. Whenever I or anyone else dished out some ribbing, that drum kept beating, totally undisturbed.

I thought that was the entire point of this ruse, of asking me to be his partner in such an absurd crime. We both respected each other's rights to unique rhythms.

Eric examined me for a moment. "Some people," he said finally, then walked up the steps. "And don't worry," he said as he took a set of keys from his pocket. "It's just the top floor." He grinned. "If it still doesn't meet your requirements, we could probably buy the floor below us too."

———

"JUST THE TOP FLOOR" ended up being four bedrooms (including a giant walk-in closet in the master), two baths, a full dining room, living room, and massive kitchen. Plus exclusive access to the rooftop garden. In New York freaking City.

"Oh. My. God!" I spun around in a circle, my arms spread wide as I danced around the living room. "This place is huuuuge."

Eric leaned against the old fireplace mantle and crossed his arms, satisfied. A smile curved over his features as he watched me spin. "I'm glad you like it."

"Like it?" I asked. "I *love* it! You have no idea what kind of shoebox I've been living in for the last five years. My studio in Chicago wasn't even the size of the walk-in closet."

"I thought we'd need space," Eric said. "For those days when you can't take me anymore."

We meandered down the halls together, in and out of the other rooms.

"I figured you could use one of these as a design space or office or whatever," he said, gesturing toward one of the smaller bedrooms.

I ducked in. "Aww, you remembered."

"Do you still have that old sewing machine?"

I turned from the giant window that looked over the top of the neighboring brownstones. "Old Betty? Of course. I'd never get rid of her. She's a classic."

"I just remember her weighing about seventy pounds," Eric joked. "It was *not* fun helping you and Skylar move into housing third year."

I chuckled. "That's right, I forgot that you and that kid from the Stats department helped us move..." I snapped my fingers. "I can see his face. Lanky, a little on the shorter side. Nice ass, but kind of...calculating in bed. No pun intended. God, *what* was his name?"

"His name was Jordan," Eric said just a little shortly. But when I looked up, his face was as placid as ever. "I usually remember the people I bring home with me."

"That's because you never bring anyone home," I retorted. "You let them do the hosting so you could skip out in the morning. If you remember all of *your* conquests, Petri dish, then I'm the Queen of England."

His shoulders relaxed. "Point taken. But just for the record, you were the best I ever had, Jane," he said, his voice suddenly low. Almost taunting. "And I'd bet a lot of money the same goes for me."

I gulped. With a *lot* of difficulty. Just like that, every ounce of sexual tension from the gym was back, practically making waves through the air.

Was he the best I ever had?

*Of course he was, you fool. Head and shoulders above every man on that godforsaken list.*

Okay, so that was an open-and-shut case.

Eric cleared his throat. "If we're really going to do this whole platonic-roommates thing, it would be helpful if you'd make an effort not to be so..."

"So what?"

His gray eyes flashed. "Tempting."

"What-what do you mean?"

He tipped his head. "You were biting your lip again."

I swallowed again. "Please. I'm not the one walking around with a stepladder for a stomach these days."

A slow, lazy grin spread across Eric's face. "What, this?" He pulled up his T-shirt and gazed down at his six-pack as if he just realized it was there.

"Gah! Yes! Put those things away, de Vries! You're going to put my eye out with those edges!" I mimed like I was blocking the sun.

Eric laughed and let his shirt drop, somewhat to my disappointment. I could get used to looking at that kind of man candy on a regular basis.

"I don't know when you found the time to get so stacked in the last five years," I said. "I've been working like a maniac since we graduated. It's been insane."

The thought sobered me, but I didn't feel as sad as I probably should. I worked my keister off like any new lawyer—building connections and slowly working my way up the ladder of assignments. There were plenty of bad guys to prosecute in New York. But I didn't seem to care about getting any of them. Not here. Boston. Chicago. Not anywhere.

And I still hadn't really asked myself why.

We walked around the rest of the apartment, and I oohed and ahhed appropriately whenever Eric showed me a feature, like the newly stripped hardwoods, the refurbished crown molding, or balcony that opened off the living room over the street.

"I figured you could take the master, since you're the clothes horse," he said.

"Please, Petri," I replied. "Like you don't have at least a hundred different tailored suits in that icebox of yours in Boston."

"I'll have another closet put in."

I ignored the way my stomach flipped at the fact that we'd be sleeping in separate bedrooms. *Well, of course you will, Jane Brain,* said my father's voice, amused. *You wanted it that way, didn't you, kiddo?*

I walked around the room and stopped at the window. There were a few pedestrians making their way busily to Broadway or Columbus Street. Women pushing strollers, a mailman, more than one professional on their way to lunch. Everyone had somewhere to go.

"Eric," I said as I looked out. "I don't know what I'm going to do."

His footsteps sounded on the hardwood floors behind me, and when he came to a stop and looked out the window with me, he was just a *little* closer than socially acceptable for a platonic fiancé. Close enough that I could smell the fresh, rainy scent of his shampoo and the very light, dusky overlay of the cologne he preferred. I closed my eyes.

"You don't have to do anything, Jane," he said. "That's the beauty of all of this. You can relax. I'll take care of everything, and you can figure out your next step. And whatever it is...I'll support you."

I turned. "I don't *want* to do nothing," I pronounced. "I'm not looking to be your kept woman or whatever."

Eric's smile emerged again, crooked this time, like he was trying to fight it. "That's not what I meant."

"I certainly hope not."

He tipped his head. "Do you want to practice law still? From what I recall, you mostly came to Harvard because of your dad, right?"

I softened. "I didn't think you remembered that."

He propped a hand against the window, encasing me against its corner. "I remember everything about you, Jane."

For a moment, I couldn't breathe properly. That's what happens when you have six feet, two inches of beautiful blond man cornering you against a window on a summer day, gazing at you with the reminder that he once knew your entire soul.

*Oh, damn. Don't do this now, Eric. Don't make me fall in love with you again...*

"I never wanted to hurt you, you know," he said quietly.

Suddenly, I was bare. Open.

"But you did." I ducked under his arm and stepped away. "And I...I hurt you too."

When he looked up, his mask had dropped even more. His eyes flashed still, but with sparks of pain, not lust.

"Yes," he said honestly. "You did."

———

*"GOD, THEY'RE EVEN FUCKING RED!" I shouted as I ran around the apartment, trying to locate my things.*

*"Well, at least it's not a fucking person lurking around. I mean, at least you don't have to see the asshole who just fucked the woman you love like a used sex toy!"*

*I wasn't a violent person. I had a temper, sure, but generally it came out with words, not actions. Before I could stop myself, though, my hand flew out like a pinwheel, taking my body with it as I spun around and landed a hard slap across Eric's face.*

*"That," I seethed, "is the last time you will talk about me in that way. Ever."*

*Eric stood there, a statue while he pressed his hand to the now-reddened splotch on his left cheek. "Fine. By. Me," he bit out.*

*"I'm going to the airport."*

*"I'll call you a cab."*

*"Don't fucking call me anything!" I turned back to finish stuffing the few bits of clothing and makeup I'd scattered around his room. "Or anymore. Ever again."*

———

THE ECHOES of that fight seemed to invade this clean, new space. I hated the voices. I wanted them gone.

"You know, in spite of all of that, I've missed you."

Eric's voice chased the voices away, a soothing balm to their harsh blows. He walked toward me, and when I didn't immediately move away, his fingers intertwined with mine again, playing with them like laces on a shoe. His skin was warm, and this close I could smell that familiar mix of cologne, his soap, and something fresh that always lingered around him. Linen. Light.

"Eric..." I murmured.

"No, not like that," he said, though his face looked the slightest bit pained as he released my hand. "I mean as friends, Jane. We were already friends, even before things went south. Weren't we?"

I thought about it. We hadn't been particularly close, connected more through Skylar than anything. Sure, there had been that one hot month during our first year of law school, but we'd parted ways amicably that time.

*Well, as amicably as a bottle of wine and some tears required,* that irritatingly smug voice inside my head countered.

*Shut up, you.*

Still, he wasn't wrong. We'd spent countless nights in bars, study groups, classes, etc. together over those three years, always teasing, always laughing. Never hating like this. Whenever I thought about law school, there was always Eric. He had just always...been there.

"Yeah," I agreed. "We were friends."

Slowly, like he was trying to touch a wild animal, his hand rose up and floated over my face, almost like he was going to cup my chin again, but he didn't. It was a completely different gesture than his grab at the gym. This was tentative. Almost in awe.

"I almost kissed you today," he said, his gaze dropping to my mouth. "I really wanted to."

My lips fell open, as I found I needed to remind myself to breathe, as my lungs still weren't working properly again. "I know you did."

"I want to now," he admitted, his thumb just grazing the plump edges of my mouth. His tongue slipped out, and he licked his own lower lip. "But I won't. Not until you ask me. Not unless you want to."

I did want to. Every bone in my body was screaming for it. I had those memories too, the ones of him lifting me up, fucking me against everything and anything. The memories where I would rip his shirts off, take him in my mouth, take him *everywhere*, again and again until we were both exhausted of this constant, aching *need* we could never seem to be rid of.

It would feel so good to do it now. To give in.

But. That was just bodies. The hard part was what came after, and I had decided not to complicate things. What good would that do, especially when we were finally starting to get along again?

"I am not asking for that...now."

The last word fell out before I could help it. Like I couldn't quite eliminate the possibility.

Eric's eyes sparked, but he dropped my hand and stepped back.

He pulled the schedule out of his pocket and examined it again. These weren't just frivolous events, as he'd explained on our walk through the park. These were places for him to network. Understand the other ways the family business was run outside of the office. These events were where we would both make our debuts into this strange, archaic society of elites—Eric as its prodigal son, and me as his outsider bride.

It was important to everyone that we make a clean entry, in spite of my inherent shock value. Or at least participate.

"Jane, I didn't ask you to marry me so we could be lovers. Really. But I did ask hoping that maybe we could be friends again," Eric said. "I'm returning to this sharkfest alone. And I'd really like not to be."

We stared at each other for what seemed like hours. We were both at a disadvantage. I understood what he meant. To survive the next five years, we'd need to be a team. We'd need to be partners. Somehow.

For the first time, I really thought we might be able to do it.

"Am I going to have to...hostess...here?" I asked, gesturing around the apartment, if only to break the awkwardness. "You know, like Lady Crawley?"

I'd read enough period novels to know how it worked with aristocratic wives. And this might be twenty-first century New York, not Downton Abbey, but Celeste's dinner showed me that gendered labor wasn't exactly a thing of the past. I had a feeling that a lot of the informal duties would still fall on me.

But Eric, thankfully, shook his head. "Not here. If we do have to do anything like that, it will be at my cousin's, my aunt's, or my grandmother's, her health allowing. Nina and Aunt Violet will need to get used to it anyway, considering I'll abdicate this shit to her after the five years is up."

I snorted. He talked about being the head of a multinational corporation like it was the throne of England. But, I supposed, in a way it was.

"I want this place to be our sanctuary, Jane. Just yours and mine."

"Well, if that's the case," I replied, looking around. "No decorators, all right? And no icebox furniture. Just hand me a budget, and I'll deal with it. You'll like it, I promise."

"Jane. A budget? Really?"

Eric gave me a look one might give a small child who asked if ice cream was actually cold, or something equally banal. He reached into his wallet and pulled out a credit card, which he handed to me with a smirk.

I gawked. "Is this a black Amex?"

Eric nodded. "There's a number on the back for the concierge. Call them for literally anything you want. They'll pick up day or night. Oh, and here." He pulled out a business card, which I also accepted.

"Bridget McAvoy," I read.

"Our personal assistant."

I looked up. "We have an assistant?"

Eric chuckled. "We have a lot of things now, Jane." Tentatively, he reached out and ran his knuckles down my arm. "You're giving up a lot to do this for me. I'd like it if you'd enjoy the perks."

"Well," I said as I fingered the heavy metal card. "I suppose I will. Any requests before I go berserk?"

Eric grinned, and I almost fell over backwards. But before he could answer, his phone rang, a soft, quiet tune that sounded like Mozart. He pulled it out and frowned.

"Shit," he muttered. Then he looked up, almost worried. "I'll, um, be right back."

Without waiting for my answer, he left the room—left the apartment, actually. However, in his haste to talk to whoever was on the line, he'd left the front door slightly ajar, making his voice audible when I tiptoed out into the living room.

"I told you, I'm done with all of that shit, Jude."

I approached the door quietly, unapologetically eavesdropping. Hey, if the man didn't want me to hear, he should have shut the door.

"I've been out for ten years," Eric continued. "You can tell Carson and the rest of them too. I'm *done*."

There was a long pause while Eric's pacing increased.

"Don't tell me that," he hissed. "Don't you fucking tell me that. There's got to be a way out."

Another pause. His footsteps turned to stomps.

"*Fine*," he spat. "I'll tell them myself, at the next meeting..." He paused again. "Because I'm not at his beck and fucking call, that's why. If I have to go to this bullshit, they can wait too."

His footsteps drew closer, and I scurried back to the window seat that looked down on Seventy-Sixth Street.

Eric reentered the apartment, all traces of good will erased. The mask was firmly back in place—he was back to being the de Vries heir. My Eric—my friend—was gone.

"What was that all about?" I asked.

He just blinked and tipped his head toward the door. "Time to go," he said. "I have to get back to the office. Can you get this place sleepable by tonight? At least buy a couple of mattresses? I need to get the fuck out of the Upper East Side."

I flipped the black Amex card around with glee. "Oh, yeah. You leave it to me."

# PART THREE

## THE TURN

*Give me your lips now*
*That the danger is past, so*
*I'll find you at last.*

"Kiss"
—from the journal of Eric de Vries

## INTERLUDE II

T he long, sleek nose of the BMW turned down a dark street deep in the heart of New Haven. The car was black, and from his seat in the back, Eric marveled at the velvety silence of its drive. He had just exchanged the old Rolls-Royce for the bimmer, which was still black, but Eric liked to think was more modern. He hoped.

*What, you need another Batmobile, Mr. Burns? The old one wasn't creepy enough?*

Jane's voice rang through his thoughts, and he smiled to himself, remembering the night before. It had been nearly two months since they moved into the apartment on West Seventy-Sixth Street, living together as roommates with surprising harmony. The apartment in Boston had been emptied of his clothes and other personal things, but otherwise it would keep. After all, they had reason to visit, considering Eric still owned stake in his firm and Jane's best friends lived there too. Boston would still be home, although the new place was quickly turning into a close second. And Eric had never expected that.

Jane had adopted decorating and wedding planning as her new

full-time jobs on top of attending the few meet and greets arranged by Celeste. It had taken Jane less than twenty-four hours to furnish the two bedrooms with essentials to sleep, and within two weeks (with the help of Bridget), Jane had the entire apartment outfitted with an eclectic mix of their two tastes. Eric had never realized it, but Jane had an incredible eye for design. After taking a week to tour the port holdings of De Vries Shipping up and down the Atlantic, he had come home to find the entire space fully furnished with an even mix of modern and mid-century pieces—Danish-style armchairs paired with a gray velvet Chesterfield sofa, a teak credenza topped with Lucite lamps, an iron-wrought dining table topped with white marble, and eight red-upholstered Parsons chairs that matched the broad-stroked modern art behind them.

It was eclectic. It was modern. Colorful, but not gauche. Comfortable. Perfect.

Jane had looked up from where she lay sprawled on the rug, leafing through bridal magazines. She had tipped down her glasses (these ones were gold-rimmed), watched him take in the mid-century furnishings, the drink cart stocked with his favorite top-shelf vodka and gin, the bookshelves bearing his favorite literary masterpieces along with her substantial *Vogue* collection.

"I figured if you really were going to play Don Draper, you needed an apartment to match," she'd said.

He wasn't sure if it was relief, or the strange feeling of home-coming that made him want to fuck her right there on the plush, white alpaca. But that was a separate problem.

In the next several weeks, Jane had jumped into her duties with the grace of an experienced swimmer, going to nearly daily meetings with Nina, his mother, his aunt, and his grandmother. To Eric's surprise, when it came to Celeste, Jane apparently had the patience of a saint.

"I'm the daughter of Yu Na Lee Lefferts," she'd told him. "She is the *queen* of crotchety matriarchs."

And even more strangely, Celeste seemed to be taking to Jane too. Was she going to call her granddaughter anytime soon? Probably not. But sparring with Jane over her hair color, her clothes, or the minutia of the wedding seemed to make Celeste sit up a little straighter, flash her eyes a little brighter. Her appetite improved, and she was even going on her weekly trips to the MET again—often with Jane alongside. Her doctors were shocked.

Even Garrett the butler had taken to making sure Jane's favorite green tea was always stocked whenever she came to visit. And last week, when they had gone to the penthouse for dinner, Celeste had requested that Jane sit by her, Eric on her other side.

Not Nina and her husband.

Not Mother or Aunt Violet.

Jane.

It had caught everyone by surprise. Eric most of all.

And so, they had found a surprising rhythm there on the Upper West Side. Eric made them both coffee just after six and left to learn his family's business when Jane was just starting to rouse herself for a day learning the social side of the de Vries empire. When he got home, there would usually be another piece of furniture to admire or a new piece of art adorning the walls. They would chat over dinner about some other piece of the wedding that had come together that day. Both of them actually enjoyed cooking, so the hour between six and seven was generally spent trying out some new recipe or making something of their own, blending Eric's knowledge of fine French cooking with Jane's Korean recipes she had from her mother.

Eric smiled, thinking fondly of the night before, when Jane had insisted he add kimchi on top of the squid ink pasta he'd prepared.

———

*"JUST TRUST ME, you Philistine. It's going to be delicious."*

*"You can't put Asian pickled vegetables on a French butter sauce," he replied, being stubborn partially just to piss her off.*

*Jane flushed, her fair skin turning the color of a rose petal. It was fucking beautiful.*

*"Oh my God, Petri. Do you know anything about history? Go to literally any Vietnamese restaurant and enjoy the culinary fruits of colonialism. People have been mixing Asian recipes with French cooking since the day the frogs yelled 'Vive la France' in the middle of the rice paddies."*

*Eric just grinned. "Lefferts, your French is terrible."*

*"Guarantee it's better than your Korean," she countered. And as if it would prove her point, she shoved a bit of pasta with the spicy pickled cabbage into her mouth and moaned with delight. When she was finished, a drop of butter still clung to her top lip. "What? Cat got your tongue, Petri dish?"*

*This girl. This girl and her fucking attitude. Eric wasn't usually one to give people a taste of their own medicine, but Jane always could get under his skin better than anyone. Like she wanted what was coming to her. Like she wanted him to teach her a lesson.*

*She licked the butter off her lip. It was a slow, small movement, but watching that slip of pink trace over the decadent red pillow...*

*Eric had only been able to stare, completely transfixed while she tipped her glasses down. It reminded him of just how beautiful her eyes were without them—a gorgeous hazel that was a bit obscured behind the thick lenses. Eyes that opened very, very wide when she was flat on her back, legs around his shoulders, just as he was about to slide his—*

———

ERIC SHOOK HIS HEAD. She was right. This was going to work better if they could keep it strictly friends.

As soon as the dishes were done, he had left for the gym, scaled up and down every fucking wall in the place until his fingers were raw and his muscles too tired to even consider the leggy, carnation-haired bombshell on the other side of his bedroom wall.

It hadn't worked. He'd still jerked off in the shower. Twice.

Eric sighed heavily as the car rumbled through New Haven. It was getting more and more impossible to ignore. The strange thing was, the more comfortable they seemed to get with each other, the harder it became to fall asleep knowing there was only a few scant inches of plaster between them. Especially since neither of them had seemed the slightest bit interested in finding other company, despite having the mutually assured freedom to do just that. Eric had taken a walk several times over to Amsterdam Avenue only to find Jane sitting by herself in the same bar while she stared at a pint of cheap beer. Or she would prance into a lounge downtown to find him enjoying a finger or two of his favorite vodka. Alone.

Eventually they just started keeping their own fridge stocked and staying in, or choosing the bars together since they'd run into each other anyway.

It was just easier that way. Wasn't it?

So Eric had found himself faced with close to sixty straight nights of sleeping alone, sometimes stroking himself until he absolutely had to take his release in the bathroom or on his own stomach. And Jane was struggling too. He had even heard her through the wall a few times. He wondered if she still had the same collection of toys. A stupidly big vibrator for when she was alone, a smaller, bullet-sized one for when they were together, plus the one shaped like a clamp that would help them both out. A set of Ben Wa balls and a plug for when she was feeling particularly adventurous. He'd added others to the set when they'd been together. A flogger, small and suede with tiny beads of glass on the ends of the suede tassels. A feather duster, which was surprisingly fun to play (and torture) with. Several pairs of cuffs, two sets of nipple clamps, and a crop.

Eric adjusted himself. It had been a *really* long time, even longer since he'd touched anything like those accessories. It was only ever her who brought that side out of him. He'd never really stopped to ask why.

The car rumbled to a stop.

"Sir?"

His driver, Louis, was another replacement (since he wasn't interested in harboring any of Grandmother's spies, like Tony). Nice guy from Jackson Heights, and completely beholden to Eric after he had paid his daughter's school tuition on top of providing Louis with a generous salary. Private school in Manhattan wasn't cheap.

Jane still called him Smithers, though.

"Sir, we've arrived," Louis said with a tip of his hat.

Eric nodded. "Thanks. This shouldn't take long."

He exited the car onto Grove Street, which was normally quite busy, but at this time of night, between the deserted streets and the Gothic buildings of Yale across them, more closely resembled the setting of an Edgar Allen Poe story. He could practically hear a raven flapping above, quoting in its ominous rhythm: "nevermore."

He had tried to say that to Janus once. Apparently it hadn't worked.

Eric walked under the tall stone gate, stopping a moment to glare at the inscription engraved into the lintel: "The dead shall be raised." He rolled his eyes. Janus had always had a flair for the melodramatic, dating back to the society's inception. Laypeople assumed the slogan was just a quote from Corinthians, related to the fact that this was a burial ground. But in fact it was just another motto. A private joke at the expense of people in mourning.

It had been over ten years since he'd stepped foot into the Grove Street Cemetery, but Eric hadn't forgotten the way to the large tomb at the far corner marked only with the word *Portas* under a nasty, time-worn etching of a bearded man with two faces, similar to what was once on ancient Roman currency. Sort of hilariously heathen for a hill that was established by the finest Protestants New England had to offer. New Haven wasn't exactly a city on a hill, but it had a good legacy of theocracy too. Or maybe that was just to hide its dark underbelly.

Eric looked around furtively. The cemetery was usually deserted at one o'clock at in the morning, but that didn't mean the kids in New

THE HATE VOW   231

Haven didn't enjoy the thrill of hanging out in one of the oldest grave-yards in America.

When he was sure he was alone, he pressed the round stone at the corner of the tomb and watched the door slide open. He took one more look, then walked down the stairs spiraling into the heart of the hill.

The large, windowless complex at the bottom looked exactly the same. The brick wall of the main room was draped with crushed red velvet while deep leather Chesterfield couches and armchairs were set up around a crackling fireplace. A pool table stood empty, though Eric could remember plenty of times he'd lost thousands there. The stereo in the corner currently blasted the best of Glen Miller—it was like taking a trip back to the speakeasy age. A clubhouse where serious games were played, and even more serious decisions were made.

About ten men populated the room—a few enjoying the company of scantily clad women by the fire, others involved in a card game in the opposite corner. A few closed doors led to several bedrooms where some of the men would likely depart (if others hadn't already), and one that was affectionately called the War Room. What wars were waged there exactly, Eric hadn't stayed long enough to find out.

At Eric's entrance, all of the present members of the Janus Society looked up—some with recognition, others with confusion. All with open, yet suspicious curiosity.

"Hail the conquering hero!" A deep voice boomed from the circle by the fireplace. "Triton returns at last!" The dark-haired man with a goatee not unlike a pirate's stood up from one of the deep leather chairs, his hand firmly around the waist of a young woman who couldn't have been older than twenty.

"Still dabbling in sex trafficking, Jude?" Eric strode in, nodding to a few of the other men he recognized. There were several younger faces he didn't know. Those he did had changed a lot. They had all grown up since twenty-two. "That's a federal offense, you know."

There was a smattering of laughter around the room as the men returned to their games and women.

Jude pushed the girl off his lap so he could stand. He took Eric's hand, pulling him in for a hug and a hearty slap on the back. Remnants of cigar smoke and booze clouded the man. Eric resisted the urge to cough.

"We all do what we need for the society, brother," Jude said as he released him. "The girls have always been my contribution. If anything, this administration has made it easier to get away with shit just by virtue of their understaffing."

The other men around the room chuckled again. Eric did not. Nor did he take a seat.

Jude frowned. "Come. Have a drink. You used to know how to enjoy yourself, Triton."

Eric didn't move. "Why am I here, Jude? I left the society ten years ago."

Jude's frown lines deepened, then he snapped his fingers, and like that, the girls got up and left. Immediately, the other games and conversations ceased, and the other men in the room gathered closer to the fire. It was almost as if Eric was facing a firing squad.

"Carson wanted you to be welcomed back to the fold properly," Jude said. "That includes a gift in that suite over there, of course." He nodded toward one of the closed doors, behind which Eric knew there was a naked, beautiful, and most likely underage girl waiting to do any number of unmentionable things to him.

He still didn't move.

"It's also to reaffirm your...loyalty," Jude said, sitting on the arm of one of the chairs. "Carson wanted to make sure you didn't forget."

"Forgetting was a condition of my exit, wasn't it?"

"And yet you were able to find your way here, weren't you?" Jude replied. "It just proves the point: no one ever truly forgets Janus. Which is also why no one can ever truly leave."

There was a rumbling of approval around the room. The hairs on the back of Eric's neck stood up.

"I was allowed to leave before," he said slowly. "Why this? Why now?"

Jude shrugged and chuckled, as if he were speaking to a child. "You didn't just leave Janus, Eric. You left your entire world. Janus simply stopped summoning you because you were of no use to us anymore. However, your circumstances have changed. And so, we are happy to welcome our brother back to the fold. Along with your own...contributions. It's up to you if you choose to disregard our welcome."

The underlying threat fell on Eric's shoulder like a heavy mantle. Social ostracization. Financial ruin. Death. The costs of bucking Janus were severe. He had watched it happen before.

"Calvin hasn't been keeping up?" he asked. He would have been shocked if his cousin-in-law wasn't also a member. Nina's husband was as power hungry as they came.

"Triton, come now," Jude said as he pretended to adjust his tie. "You know contributions to Janus aren't always strictly business. We require personal attention. We are a needy bunch."

Another smattering of laughter. Eric stared, confused.

"We congratulate you on your pending nuptials," Jude prompted. "Tell us about the bride-to-be, why don't you?"

Eric scowled and folded his arms. "I'm sure you didn't summon me here for information that was in the *Post* last week, Jude." The damn papers had been all over Jane. She and her hair were sending New York society into a tizzy.

"Triton, Triton. You're still just as contrary as ever, aren't you?"

Eric couldn't help it. He rolled his eyes again. Jude was an idiot, enjoying the archaic code names all new recruits to the society were given once they were tapped during their final year at an Ivy. It was the main difference between them and school-centric societies, like Skulls and Bones. Janus cast its net wider. And as a result, it was much more powerful.

Since the days of his great-great-great-grandfather, a Janus founder with the name "Poseidon" (for the fact that his shipping business was seaborn), all of the de Vries men recycled names of offspring of the Greek sea god. Eric's was Triton, the trident-bearing son.

Beyond attendance of an Ivy-league school, the rules of Janus membership were simple.

You had to be male.

You had to be rich.

You had to be powerful. *Someone.*

An invitation to the Janus Society meant you had been identified as a potential gatekeeper of the world. No less than fourteen U.S. presidents had been members. More than half of the founding fathers. Governors. Senators. Heads of multinational companies or massive landowners. The members of Janus made the world turn.

Once, Eric had been identified as "someone." As had his father, his father before him, and nearly every man in the de Vries family since Janus had been formed in this exact tomb in the wake of the American Revolution, just after the yellow fever plague of 1795. It had been formed, like many secret societies, with the goal of puppeteering lines of power in this country, absorbed as it was with the new rhetoric of egalitarianism. But while most of the other societies had become opportunities for young co-eds to drink too much and prank their classmates, Janus had remained true to its mission.

Freedom was a farce in America. It always had been. Janus had made sure of it. Even within its ranks.

Eric ignored Jude's question. "Where is Carson?"

Jude just scoffed. "You know Carson doesn't bother himself with pleasantries like this."

"Carting me out here in the middle of the damn night is a pleasantry? Seems more like an inquisition."

"Not yet." Jude tapped his finger to the side of his nose and smiled. "This is just a friendly chat. A catch-up, if you will. So...let's catch up. The girl. Jane, isn't it?"

Eric narrowed his eyes. "Yes. What about her?"

"She's half Korean."

"You can't be serious. Is Janus really going to object on grounds of ethnicity in this day and age? What kind of archaic, racist bullshit is that?"

Jude tipped his head back and laughed, almost too loudly for the room. "Eric, please. Give us some credit. After all, Carson himself once married a Puerto Rican actress, didn't he? Race hasn't been an issue for Janus for at least thirty years." He looked straight at Eric, and any amusement in his face evaporated with the laughter. "It's not that she's half-Korean. It's that she's *this* half-Korean."

Eric's face screwed up with confusion. "What are you talking about?"

Jude nodded to the other men, who remained serious, then turned to Eric with a wry smile. "To be honest, Triton, I'm just the messenger. You keep calling me Jude, but don't forget who I really am."

Eric sighed. Jude's society name was Hermes, after the Greek god of trade—a messenger and a herald. Such was his role in the society as well.

All it meant was that Jude didn't know why Carson disapproved of Jane—just that he did, and Jude had been instructed to inform Eric. It was up to Eric to figure out why—or take the simpler way out and walk away from her, which was obviously what Carson wanted.

Unfortunately, things weren't that easy.

"Come, come," Jude said. "Now that business is over, let's enjoy each other's company, shall we, like the brothers we are. Bacchus blessed our cellars just last week."

Eric glanced at Finn Faber, otherwise christened Bacchus, after the Roman god of wine. His family owned half of Napa and vineyards all over the world. When Eric had known him last, Faber was only nineteen, still almost a boy. There was no sign of that naivety now.

"No, thank you," Eric said. "I should get back. I have...a lot to ponder, don't I?"

There was no argument in the room, but as Eric began to leave, Jude's voice beckoned again.

"Triton."

He didn't want to, but at the door, Eric turned.

One of Jude's sleek black brows raised. "My wife mentioned that we received the save-the-date for the wedding in the mail today." He examined his nails languidly, then looked up again. "If the proceedings continue, I look forward to meeting your...bride."

Eric swallowed, but didn't move, as much a statue as the other Greek and Roman gods placed around the room.

Jude tipped his head, the final indicator of his consent for Eric to leave, and also his power. "Until then," he said.

Eric left.

# EIGHTEEN

I stood waiting outside Sashay, an appointment-only bridal shop on East Sixty-Eighth Street, checking my watch every so often while I waited for Skylar to arrive. It was the week before the "season" in the Hamptons kicked off, and Skylar and Brandon were coming with their kids for the weekend to attend the white party that was also doubling as an engagement party for me and Eric at the de Vries compound. I was under strict orders from Gemma, the wedding planner, to choose my dress today before we left, which of course meant that I had to have the approval of Celeste de Vries, Heather, Violet, and Nina. Skylar just wanted to come along for the ride.

The Crosby-Sterlings' big black Mercedes turned the corner and pulled up alongside the curb. The back door opened, and Skylar popped out with a smile.

"Hey!" she greeted me.

"Red." Brandon's deep voice growled as he recaptured his wife's hand, pulling her back toward the car. Skylar flushed under the bright blue stare of her husband, who barely glanced at me. "Oh, hey, Jane. Red, come back here and say goodbye properly."

I tapped my bright red sandal on the sidewalk while Brandon

demonstrated what a *proper* goodbye meant, only then releasing his wife, who was suddenly quite flushed.

"Need a fan?" I asked as the car zoomed away.

Skylar did, in fact, fan herself, but she shook her head with a sheepish grin. "No, I'm fine now."

"Where are the kiddos?"

Skylar snorted. "At the hotel with Bubbe, probably watching too much TV."

"So, seventh heaven, then."

We approached the door to Sashay, and Skylar looked me up and down. "Look at you," she said with overt perusal. "Someone's been taking advantage of the local boutiques."

"I suppose."

I looked down at my clothes—the black, draping silk sundress I had actually made myself, but the fabric was the best I'd ever worked with. The shoes, though—those were legitimate splurges. Okay, so I had taken Eric up on his offer to continue sprucing up my wardrobe along with decorating our apartment and planning the wedding. He didn't seem to mind. In fact, he seemed happy every time I brought home another shopping bag, especially when it included a little something for him.

"You two seem to be getting along very well," Skylar remarked as we walked inside. She popped her eyebrows a few times.

"You look like a cartoon fox when you do that," I said. "And it's nothing, really. We're just...friends. It's nice."

*Yeah, friends who cook dinner together every day of the week. Who lounge around on the weekends, mooning at each other over cheap beer and cocktails. Friends who listen to each other get off through the walls after they say goodnight.* Eric tried to be discreet—I'm sure he thought I had no idea what he was doing with those thirty-minute showers of his, but the man hits things when he comes. You try not feeling uncomfortable when you hear a rhinoceros groan right when the wall pounds next to your ear.

*Uncomfortable? Try turned on, you junkie.*

All right…so maybe it made me want to do the same thing. While my libido seemed to have come back full throttle, I still hadn't gotten laid in over a month, and there was no reprieve in sight. Eric was right about Page Six. We had both been featured multiple times in the gossip column—there would be no side pieces in my immediate future, that was for sure. And the weird thing is, although I wanted to get some action, there was only one person whose action I wanted. The one person I had decided I couldn't have.

I wondered sometimes if this was all part of some nefarious plan of Eric's to get me back in bed. Masturbatory torture. Like some really fucked-up version of ASMR.

Well, it was working. I had never been so hard up.

"Sure," Skylar said as we entered the showroom, where Celeste and Nina were enjoying champagne while they spoke with Gemma. Heather and Violet were nowhere in sight. Heather only came to the wedding planning occasionally, but it was pretty clear on those occasions that Celeste viewed her somewhat as an outsider since she had married again. She was no longer a de Vries, and subsequently, not of much importance.

Nina and Violet, on the other hand, were blood.

"Jane."

Celeste beckoned from her plush chair when she saw me, her bright diamond wedding rings glinting under the chandelier.

If she didn't have the oxygen tank carted around with her everywhere she went, you would never have convinced me that Celeste de Vries was ill anymore. Today she had on one of her gorgeous gray wigs, and I had yet to see her with anything less than an original Chanel suit, her brittle nails painted impeccable mother-of-pearl pink.

"Afternoon, Mrs. de Vries," I greeted her with a polite nod. "Hi, Nina."

Even after a month of attending teas and dinners together, Nina Gardner née de Vries was probably the stiffest person I had ever met. She shared her cousin's coolness, but lacked his humor. Eric said she was two years younger, but she acted at least ten older because of her overall ice princess demeanor. I'd had at least three lunches with the woman, but it was clear from the beginning that she resented me for enabling her cousin to take away what she clearly thought belonged to her and her husband.

Well, maybe she was right. Even if, as Eric said, she had no idea that his inheritance was inextricably tied to the existence of hers.

"You remember Skylar, don't you, Mrs. de Vries?" I asked.

Celeste looked Skylar over like she was a stray dog. "Mmm. Yes. The lawyer, aren't you?"

Skylar nodded, doing her best to affect a genuine smile. It was kind of funny, because she was terrible at it. "Yes. And best friend."

"And maid of honor," I chimed in with an unnecessarily peppy tone.

"Will your husband be coming to the party this weekend?" Nina asked.

"Yes," Skylar said. "We'll both be there."

Celeste gave a nod of approval. I wanted to roll my eyes. Skylar's friendship was one of the few things I brought to the table in this world simply by virtue of her husband. The ladies who lunched weren't very discreet about the fact that they would love to jump Brandon's bones, and Celeste just liked the idea of associating with "good family," even if they were "new money."

"And when are you planning to change your hair color, Jane?" asked Celeste absently as she turned back to the pictures of wedding dresses Gemma had laid out on the table in front of her.

I touched the mostly pink locks I'd styled in haphazard waves over my shoulders. "Change it?"

Okay, granted, after two months, I was in need of a touch-up. My roots were starting to show, but the only reason I hadn't gotten anything done was because I couldn't make up my mind if I wanted to stay pink or go purple. Maybe even blue.

Nina made a noise that sounded a little like a snort.

Celeste just looked bored. "Well, of course, Jane. You can't stand next to a maid of honor with hair like that and clash so dreadfully."

Skylar and I considered each other as if for the first time.

"You know," I said. "I literally had not thought about that. But she's right." Skylar's hair was easily as bright as mine, only a mass of red and orange. We would look like Skittles next to each other in the church.

"Well, of course she's right," Nina put in. "Grandmother has impeccable taste."

Celeste looked at her granddaughter as if she were an insect she'd like to squash, not someone who'd just complimented her. "Yes, well. The fact remains that you cannot stand in the church next to each other looking like this. Orange and pink! Whoever heard of such a thing." She looked at Skylar. "Do you force your hair that shade as well?"

"Ah, no," Skylar replied. "This is my natural color."

"Is it? How...charming," Celeste said stiffly before turning to me. "Jane, you cannot walk down the aisle with hair like this. Come now, you must see reason."

It was hardly the first dig I'd gotten from Eric's family about my hair in the last two months. Actually, picking on it was one of Celeste's favorite pastimes.

*Ah, Jane,* she'd say whenever I entered a room. *I see you are as... colorful...as ever.*

*Indeed, Celeste,* I'd counter. *I thought your beige apartment needed something to brighten it up.*

Nina and Violet would always appear shocked, but I swore sometimes Celeste would hide a smile in her shriveled, painted lips. And then she'd turn to whatever it was we were planning that day and tell Garrett to bring me my tea.

The jasmine they served *was* excellent.

Before I could reply that blue would be perfectly complementary to Skylar's bright orangey-red, Gemma bustled around the corner with the store owner, Marisa.

"Jane," Gemma said, "Marisa and I have set up the final gowns in the back, if you'd like to come."

I followed Marisa to the giant dressing room in the back, where a rack of couture wedding gowns had been set up. This wasn't my first time at Sashay, but nothing had really worked so far. Today was the last day. It was fish or cut bait. Or, you know, whatever metaphor worked in this strange, fake wedding scenario I was living in.

Marisa helped me into the first dress on the rack—a sleeveless Badgley Mischka ball gown with about an acre of tulle expanding in either direction.

"Dear lord," I said as I looked at myself in the mirror. "I am a shower puff."

"Your waist is *so* small," Marisa said. "It looks romantic. And will photograph like a dream."

"Yes, I do think romance is largely determined by the number of hours it takes for a man to find his way under your skirt," I said, ignoring the fact that no one would be looking under mine on my wedding day.

"I'm sorry?"

I shook my head. "Nothing. Let's go put on the fashion show."

We went back out to the front room, and I dutifully stepped onto the pedestal in front of the mirrors for everyone to admire the dress.

"Oh, Jane," Skylar said as she stood up. Her mouth twitched, and I knew she was thinking of *her* experiences wedding dress shopping, when I made her try on every ugly gown in the place. "That's...that's a dress, Jane."

"It's stunning," Nina added.

"A bit gauche, though," Celeste added.

"Very gauche," Nina parroted. "Absolutely. Let's see the next one."

I nodded, waddled back to the dressing room to try on the next one, a mermaid-cut Vera Wang.

"I hate it," I announced as we walked back out. This was Nina's favorite on the list, and her face fell.

"It's absolutely *en vogue*," she protested. "Half the brides I knew last year wore dresses just like it."

"Well, then that wouldn't make it *en vogue*, would it?" I countered.

Skylar snorted.

I turned to Celeste. "Mrs. de Vries, I know you see it. This dress is made for someone with curves, which I am not. I look like a deflated balloon in this thing, and even if Marisa does her magic and takes it in, I still can't walk in it. Do you really want me to have to hop down the aisle at St. John's because I can't move my feet more than four inches at a time?"

Celeste looked horrified at the prospect of anyone hopping down the aisle at St. John's. "Absolutely *not*," she said. "Jane, you seem to know what works best on you. Show us the one *you* like."

Nina's mouth dropped, and I was smug. I had spent enough time now with Celeste de Vries to know that she hardly ever defaulted to anyone else's judgment but her own. *Point, Jane.*

"It's too bad your mom isn't here," Skylar remarked as I started to shimmy back to the dressing room. "Is she coming this weekend?"

When I didn't answer, she kept walking behind me.

"Jane. *Jane!*"

I scurried as fast as I could while wearing twenty pounds of leg-binding satin, but Skylar just followed me into the dressing room, where Marisa was waiting with the other dresses.

"No?" she asked.

I shook my head. "Let's try the Monique Lhuillier. Celeste liked that one the best."

Marisa nodded and started helping me out of the mermaid dress, forcing me to turn around to face my imperious best friend.

"Skylar, what is it?" I asked impatiently.

Her green eyes went big. "Don't give me that attitude, missy—"

"Missy? Someone has been on mom duty for too long—"

Marisa snickered.

"Don't change the subject," Skylar said. "Is she coming or not?"

"For what?"

"Oh, I don't know. Your engagement party?"

I frowned at my hands as I stepped out of the dress. "Ah, that's a no."

"And why is that?"

I accepted the last gown from Marisa, then stepped into it as she held out the fabric for me. "Well, it would be a little weird to invite her to an engagement party when she doesn't know I'm getting married."

There was a gasp from behind me. I looked over, where Marisa was shaking her head.

"*What?*" Skylar demanded. "How is it you haven't told your mother you are getting married in less than four months?"

I opened my mouth with a sharp retort, but found my bravado evaporated with my best friend. Well, of course. That's what friends were for, right?

I turned back to the mirror and examined myself in the dress. It was a monstrosity, actually. A giant, sugar plum fairy, skirt the size of China, marshmallow of a dress.

I giggled. So did Marisa.

"Jane!"

"Oh my *God*, Pollyanna, calm down. I was laughing at this ridiculous dress, not you." I turned back around. "Marisa, not this one. Not at all. Can I put on the Jenny Packham? That's my favorite."

Skylar smiled. "Okay, it *is* ridiculous. But, Jane, seriously. What gives?"

I sighed, then turned back so Marisa could help me unbutton the approximately fifteen hundred buttons running down my back. "I don't know. We've talked a few times. I told her I was just staying with friends. That I was thinking about taking a job here."

"Jane." Skylar was smart—she let her tone speak for her.

I pushed the dress off and stepped out of it, then stood awkwardly in my underwear while Marisa hung it up. There was a knock on the door.

"Jane?" asked Gemma. "Celeste wants to know if everything is all right."

"We have it," Skylar called.

Marisa handed me the sleek white Jenny Packham, which I stepped into with about a thousand times more ease that any of the other dresses. The silk was like butter.

I just smiled. "Skylar and I have the rest of this, Marisa. Thank you, though."

Marisa nodded and left me with my friend.

"I don't want to lie to her, Sky," I said quietly. "It's weird, you know? It feels like a play or something. Just make believe. But I can't do that with her."

Skylar didn't say anything, just stood patiently, waiting for me to continue.

I pulled the dress up and slipped my arms into the full-length sleeves. "My whole life, she was always straight with me, you know? She never hid anything about her life. Not the shitty little village she came from. Not the work she did to get out. Not how she met my dad. None of it." I sighed. "Did you know she was a bastard child? My grandmother had some kind of illicit affair, apparently, and had my mother out of wedlock. It was one of the reasons why they were so poor. It was a big deal back then." I sighed. "Apparently my grandma told my mother when she was practically on her deathbed. It was her shame that she carried her whole life. Before that, my mom thought her dad was just dead. I was maybe six, but my mom flew back to see her, and she told me right away. She said mothers and daughters shouldn't have secrets, and that we never would." I shrugged. "And we never did. Not until now."

Skylar moved behind me to help zip up the back of the dress. "Do you really think she would be that disappointed?"

"That I'm marrying a billionaire heir? *Ha*. Yu Na would probably fall over from excitement." I couldn't quite make the joke work. "But she would know in a second that it was fake. She'd...Sky, what if she thinks I'm shaming her, huh?"

Skylar frowned as I turned around. This was the question I'd been carrying around for the last two months.

"So...I'm saying this as someone who thought this was a terrible idea from the start," she began, tapping her lip. "But it's not the same thing. Not at all. For one, you're not being forced. You're giving your full consent."

I nodded. "That's true."

"And secondly, people get married for all sorts of reasons. You and Eric...well, I'm not going to pretend I like it, mostly because of how antagonistic the two of you are. But there is no rule that says you can't get married to someone to help them out. And really, that's what you're doing."

I gave a weak smile. "I appreciate that." I wasn't sure if I could accept all the altruism implied there, but it did make me feel better.

We both looked into the mirror where I stood in my dress. It was the one I'd fallen in love with from the start, kept on the rack every time despite all of the de Vries ladies' demands. It was simple and elegant, a white column dress with a high neck and long sleeves, conservative enough for the church with only a V-shaped back that nearly reached the small of mine—its only hint of sex that was still very church appropriate. It came with a train that was puddled around my feet, but I could imagine it spilling behind me, a cascade of white on the church stairs.

"Oh, Janey," Skylar murmured, then reached up to dab at her eyes. "You look...wow."

"I know," I said, staring at myself in the mirror. If I were thinking right, I would choose something else. Something that didn't feel like the only dress I'd want to wear if I were getting married for real. Something that helped remind me this was just a charade.

But as I looked at myself in the mirror, saw for once not a quirky, funky person, but a real beauty, pink hair and all, I knew there was no way I'd be leaving this dress on the hanger.

"Just...Jane, I think you need to call your mom," Skylar said.

"How are you going to feel if your own mother misses your wedding?"

I looked in the mirror and saw guilt written all over my face. Skylar was right. Maybe I didn't need to tell Yu Na everything about this arrangement, but I did need to tell her something.

When I turned back around, Skylar had already pulled my phone out of my purse. I dialed the number and held it gingerly to my ear.

"*Eomma*," I said, my voice so much quieter than I ever thought it could be. I felt like a little girl again. "*Eomma*, I have news. I'm getting married."

# NINETEEN

"So, your mom gets here when?"

"Tomorrow night," I said. "Her flight arrives at JFK at nine, and Eric's sending a driver to bring her out here immediately."

Skylar and I were driving up to the Hamptons. The engagement party was scheduled the following day, but Celeste insisted I arrive early with the rest of the family to help everyone "prepare" for the events. It was part of "hostessing," she said after making several more comments about my hair that even had Gemma looking embarrassed on my behalf. And since I was to be the new female head of the de Vries family—this was stated with no little disdain—it was imperative that I learn to do it right.

Which apparently meant learning to drink a lot of gin by the pool, wear a bunch of ice-cream-cone outfits, and look bored.

The "family" included Eric's mother, Heather, and her current husband; his aunt Violet and uncle Fisher; Nina and her family; plus a giant array of great-uncles and aunts, their kids and their kids' kids, all of whom would apparently fit easily onto the estate along with several sets of guests, including the Crosby-Sterlings. Brandon had driven the kids himself earlier so they could have fun at the pool instead of being stuck in the city. No doubt the ladies who lunched were more than happy to "hostess" him.

My mother was arriving the night of the party, hopefully in time to meet some of my to-be in-laws and get used to the idea that her daughter would be living like this for a while. I wasn't sure how she would respond. She wanted me to be well-off, of course. I knew that. But the kind of wealth the de Vries commanded was pretty much unfathomable to most. It would be overwhelming to anyone.

Eric had to stay at the office a bit longer. The plan was for him to arrive for dinner that night after I spent the afternoon welcoming the de Vries family's guests to their sprawling estate.

And sprawling it was.

"Holy shit," I murmured as David, Skylar's driver, took us down the last of several winding roads off the main drive toward the ocean. A massive house—if you could even call the shingled behemoth that —arose in front of us at the center of what had to be at least fifty acres of open property. We passed a full orchard, several ponds, two separate tennis courts, three pools, and multiple guesthouses before we came to a stop in the massive roundabout driveway full of very expensive cars. I spotted two Bentleys and one Maserati.

"Who needs that much horsepower?" Skylar wondered. "I'm fine with my Prius."

The house itself, though, was even more impressive. It was a huge white monolith, complete with massive Doric columns and windowed walls that extended endlessly in either direction. The gardens included rows of blooming roses, and I recognized one corner of the site of the family portrait in Celeste's sitting room. This wasn't a house, I realized. It was a palace.

David rounded the circular driveway and came to a stop in front of a cascade of steps from a grand main entrance. Garrett the butler emerged and walked briskly down the steps to greet us. Even in the warm July sun, he was still dressed in full tails and a stiff white collar.

"Ms. Lefferts," he droned as he opened our door.

"Do you ever get a day off, Garrett?" I asked as I got out, followed by Skylar.

The stolid old butler gave me a droll look. "Certainly not, miss. And I wouldn't want one, either."

"Garrett, you remember my friend and lawyer, Skylar Crosby. Her husband and kids should have arrived this morning."

"Indeed, they have. Shall I have your baggage brought up to your suites in the west wing?"

I nodded. Suites? Wings? I suppose that made sense.

"Sure," I said. "The suites work, I guess. Where is everyone right now?"

"The pool, miss."

"Wow," Skylar murmured as we followed Garrett up the steps into the house. Our feet rapped on the marble floors as we walked through a yawning entry hall lined with gleaming silver sconces. "This place is insane."

I gave her a funny look. "Sky, you do remember that you and Brandon are worth almost as much, right?"

She shook her head. "It's just a bank account, Janey. Our house is nice, sure, but it's not this place. It's not a castle."

And this house certainly was. After I prodded him for a tour, Garrett smugly informed us that the estate boasted seven suites across three wings, plus ten extra bedrooms, for a total of thirty-seven bedrooms in the entire place, on top of a separate servants' quarters in the basement, four living rooms, two game rooms, three kitchens, and a whole other bunch of rooms that I couldn't begin to remember.

He led us down a huge tiled hall that reminded me again of Versailles before taking us outside through the biggest French doors I had ever seen. We entered a massive pool area, complete with an outdoor kitchen on one side, another tails-wearing bartender on the other making cocktails, and several sets of outdoor furniture surrounding a huge kidney-shaped pool. Behind that, grassy grounds spilled toward the dunes and the Atlantic Ocean, the roar of which could be heard above the hum of people.

Garrett darted in front of us.

"Are you going to announce us like royalty, Jeeves?" I joked as he stopped by the pool.

"Ms. Lefferts and Mrs. Sterling," Garrett droned, and immediately turned on his stuck-up heel and reentered the house.

"Well, I guess that answers that question," I muttered as the other ten occupants around the pool turned to see who had arrived.

"It's Crosby," Skylar called, though Garrett paid her absolutely no mind. She shook her head. "Freaking patriarchy."

It was a bit much for a patio full of family. I spotted Nina and her husband at the far end with their daughter, standing with some of the other cousins and friends I had met at that first dinner. Everyone appraised us quickly and turned back to their gin and tonics, utterly unimpressed. On the other side of the pool, the older crowd was stretched out on loungers or drinking under wide umbrellas. A few people looked over their giant sunglasses at me with bored expressions before falling back onto their sun loungers.

Under a giant umbrella sat Celeste de Vries herself, fast asleep beside a tall gilded cage of birds. Mostly parakeets, from the look of it. They were all different colors, their chirps providing a little music to the otherwise humdrum scene. One chirped more loudly than the others, and Celeste gave a snort before sinking back into her nap.

Skylar immediately located Brandon in the pool, entertaining a bunch of kids. Once he spotted her too, he pulled himself out of the water. Several of the sunglasses—mostly females', but not all, I noticed—dropped again at the sight of his big body glistening in the summer sun.

"Thank God," Brandon said as he bounded over to us. "The party finally arrived."

I pushed my glasses down too. Skylar rolled her eyes. She didn't care if I inspected the man candy she called a husband, especially when said candy was six feet, four inches of stacked muscle. Brandon might have been forty-two, but he was a fox. A little too big for my taste, but nice to admire nonetheless.

"Jane, stop looking at me like a piece of meat," Brandon said as he toweled off.

"Then stop walking around looking like one," I retorted as I accepted his kiss on my cheek. "Get a beer belly like most men your age, why don't you?"

"I would if I thought my wife would like it."

It was sweet, but sort of nauseating. Okay, and maybe a little jealousy-inducing too. Would I turn a guy away if he looked at me the way Brandon looked at Skylar? Hard to say, since none ever had.

*Except Eric.* That voice inside was talking again—the one that kept telling me it was a bad idea to marry my ex, one of the only real relationships I've ever had.

A voice I'd been steadfastly ignoring.

*Shut up, you.* Great. This wedding was turning me into a schizophrenic. Fucking perfect.

"Jane!"

We turned to find Caitlyn Calvert striding across the patio, looking effortlessly beautiful. Her long, honey-brown hair fell in waves down her back. Hmm, looked like someone got herself a new ombré color job. Her open white kimono revealed a perfectly sun-kissed, Pilates-toned body clad in a blue and white striped bandeau bikini. She was preppy, cool, classic. Everything I was not.

"What a fantastic dress," she said as she delivered a few air kisses to me.

I looked down at the yellow wrap dress I had sewn last summer. It was one of my favorite things I'd ever made—square neck with pockets in the sides, plus embroidered red and black flowers over the A-line skirt. Cute, but not overdone. Next to Caitlyn, I felt like a peasant bumblebee.

"Hello," I said. "I—what are you—I wasn't expecting you here this weekend."

Caitlyn laughed, bright and airy in the sunlight. Two diamond tennis bracelets sparkled on her wrist—a lot different than the collection of leather and brass bands on mine.

"Oh, you're funny," she said. "I'd never miss the de Vries white party, Jane. I'm practically one of the family, remember? You'll soon discover that I'm pretty hard to get rid of."

"Like a yeast infection," Skylar whispered into my ear.

I snorted. Brandon looked red in the face.

"What's that?" Caitlyn asked.

"Ah, nothing," I said. "It's great that you feel so close to all of them. Maybe you can teach me how."

She smiled brilliantly. "Love to!" She turned to Skylar, who was looking her over critically. "And it's Skylar, right. B has been talking nonstop about you. I'm so glad we get to meet again."

Skylar glanced at Brandon. "Have you...*B?*"

The man at least had the decency to blush as he pulled his wife closer, apparently not caring at all if he got her sundress wet in the process. "Well, you're worth bragging about, Red."

Skylar softened. "It's nice to meet you," she said, shaking Caitlyn's hand when Brandon wouldn't release her.

Caitlyn turned to me. "No E?"

Skylar arched a brow at yet another letter-based abbreviation, and I bit back the urge to laugh. Was Caitlyn trying to advertise her knowledge of the alphabet?

"He's coming tonight," I replied.

"Well, good," Caitlyn said with a friendly smile. "We'll all have a little more time to get to know each other, won't we?" She winked at all of us, then sashayed back to Nina and the other cousins watching us.

"Where are the kids?" Skylar asked Brandon.

"Luis is napping in our room—Red, don't worry, there's a nanny up there—and Jenny's still in the pool with the other kids." He nodded toward their daughter, whose bright red hair glowed in a sea of blond.

"Brandon!" they shouted. "Come play king of the mountain!"

"Be right there!" he called back. He turned to Skylar. "You coming, babe?"

"Come on, Mommy!" Jenny's little voice rang out.

"Let me go change," Skylar said. "We'll go grab our suits and be right back."

Brandon jumped back into the pool with a howl that startled Celeste out of her sleep (though she fell right back in). But when Skylar turned to go inside, I was stuck in place.

"Janey?" she asked. "What's wrong?"

"Shit," I gritted out as I looked around the pool, struck by sudden realization.

Two things were immediately clear. One, I stuck out. That was nothing new, as Celeste had informed me at the bridal shop, but my pink hair was even more vibrantly odd-looking here than it was in the city.

That was uncomfortable, but I could deal with it. The other, unfortunately, I could not.

I turned to Skylar, my face already flushed. "I, um...I forgot something."

Her face screwed up. "What did you forget? Oh my God, Janey, you didn't forget your dress for the party, did you?"

I shook my head. "No, no, not that. I, um...okay, so I didn't realize there would be a pool here. And that people would be around it."

Skylar looked around. "You didn't bring a suit?"

"No, I brought a suit. But I'm not...prepared...to wear it. If you know what I mean."

Skylar looked at me blankly before realization dawned over her freckled face. "You are kidding me. You came to a Hamptons beach party without getting a—"

"Eh! Can you not yell it for everyone to hear?"

Skylar rolled her eyes. "You are ridiculous. Okay, fine. We'll get David and see if we can't find you a place in Southampton that will do a walk-in."

"I don't have time for that, Sky. Plus everyone is going to wonder where I went. It's fine. I'll just, I don't know, not wear a suit and manage."

"Jane, you're going to be on a beach for several days. Are you going to be the one weirdo who doesn't go in the ocean? It will be you, Celeste de Vries, and Eric's great-uncles, landlubber."

My horror must have been evident, because Skylar started to laugh. It wasn't funny, though. Eric's uncle Rufus had been known to cop a feel after he had too many gin and tonics.

"I'll just go into town and get some Sally Hansen at the supermarket or something," I said. "I can take care of this myself."

"Dude, you don't know if they are going to have that."

"Well, I don't have time to track down a stupid spa right now, Skylar!"

She shook her head, chuckling to herself. "Fine, fine. I have some you can use, okay. I was going to do my brows tonight, but I'll tweeze instead."

I looked at her hopefully. "For real?"

She grinned. "Yeah. What are best friends for, if not to share their extra waxing kits?"

# TWENTY

Thirty minutes later, I was standing in the bathroom of my suite. I was pretty sure that right now the entire kitchen staff of the estate was convinced I was a drug runner, considering the way I'd snuck Skylar's jar of wax down to the microwave and back. Nervous, I was. A ninja, not so much.

My underwear and shorts were in a corner by the enormous tub, and I was awkwardly balanced on one leg with my other foot propped up on the counter, spread eagle so I could examine the goods while I worked.

"All right..." I said as I dipped an applicator into the honey-colored goo. I stared at the directions. "Spread in a thin, even layer." I shrugged. "How hard can it be?"

Just as I was about to slap on a bit of the wax, a loud knock sounded at the door, startling me to the point where I tumbled to the ground.

"Shit!" I cried, checking that the wax hadn't spilled too. It had not, thank God. The applicator, however, was now stuck to the side of the toilet bowl.

"Shit," I muttered again, pulling it off. It left a giant wax blob on the side of the porcelain. Well, that was going to be fun to get off.

"Jane? Everything all right?"

I scrambled up. "Eric? Is that you?"

"Yeah. I decided to leave early. Can I come in? I want to talk to you."

I frowned at the mirror. "You want to come in the bathroom?"

"Oh. Right. I guess not."

There was an audible chuckle as I went about getting back into position. I tossed the old applicator into the trash and grabbed a new one, then dipped it in the warm wax again and set to work.

"Hey, Jane?"

"Hmmm, yeah?" I asked as I slathered a thick glop of wax on my inner thigh, right at my panty line. It felt pretty good, actually.

"Are you...there isn't anything I need to know about you before this weekend, is there? Something you should have told me?"

I froze, staring at myself in the mirror. How could he have known I hadn't waxed? Did Skylar tell him, that little snitch? "Ah..."

"Because you can tell me," Eric continued. "I wouldn't judge."

"Oh...no?" As carefully as I could, I continued applying the wax under my leg, balanced precariously with my heel on the counter. "Not bad looking, Lefferts," I told myself, admiring my reflection. Hey, it's a body part that should be admired. No shame in this game. "It's...nothing," I called back to Eric. "It's really nothing."

"Jane," Eric pressed. "Whatever it is, you can tell me."

I frowned at the mirror, trying to figure out how exactly I was going to do this as I pressed on one of the white woven papers. Clearly it wasn't getting the wax on that was the hard part. It was the getting it off. And I didn't have a snarky esthetician hovering next to my butt, ready to rip the thing away. All I had were my hands, coming from the opposite direction.

"Eric, I don't think you really want to know about this." I said, grimacing.

I reached under my leg and took hold of a strip. *Here goes noth-*

*ing*. With as much bravado as I could muster, I yanked on the strip and pulled as hard as I could.

*Rrriiiipppp!*

I stared at the mirror, my mouth gaping, frozen in an open, silent scream. I was basically the human incarnation of an Edvard Munch painting, right here in this Swarovski-encrusted bathroom. Holy *shit*, that hurt!

"Jane?" Eric was calling. "You okay in there?"

"JesusfuckingChrist," I whimpered to myself as I hopped around the bathroom floor, willing away the pain searing one half of my crotch. It wasn't like I had never waxed my eyebrows or anything like that before, but I was the daughter of an esthetician. I threaded, naturally. And since my adolescent acts of rebellion had consisted of shaving, not waxing (much to my mother's irritation), it had been well over fifteen years since I had come anywhere near this shit. Fucking idiot teenager.

"Why?" I whined. "Why would anyone do this to themselves?"

"Jane!" Eric's voice was growing frantic as he knocked on the door. "Jane, are you all right?"

"Fine!" I shouted back. "I just need a second."

"Jane, what's going on?"

Ignoring Eric's calls, I slapped more wax on the other side, being more generous this time. I didn't want this to take any more time than it had to.

"'Just like pulling off a Band-Aid,' she says," I muttered. "God, I am going to kill Skylar."

I could do this. I could be done and then I could go downstairs and enjoy the stupid party like a grown-up, Crayola hair and all. I just had to do it. Press and tear. Get this shit off, and then sneak out of this mausoleum to find someone who could do the job right. Like I should have done in the first place.

"Eeeee!" I squealed, unable to do it. Fuck. I really couldn't. It hurt *so* bad.

"Jane?"

*Fuck.* "Yeah?"

"Everything all right in there?"

No, it wasn't. I *couldn't.* But then I stared into the mirror at pitiful me. Lord, if the matriarch could see me now. *Put on your big girl pants, soldier.* I saluted myself in the mirror, pressed the paper over the spot, and pulled. And couldn't. Get. It. Off.

"OWWWWW!" I screeched as I toppled to the ground. "Fucking shit arsefuck *hell!*"

The harder I yanked, the harder the strip pulled on everything... else it was attached to. But nothing came off, and the more it all hurt.

"Jane? Jane, what is it!"

Before I could tell him not to, Eric slammed his shoulder against the door, once, twice, and on the third try, he blasted through the lock and toppled into the room, sending me, the box of papers, and wooden applicators off the counter, and my waxy mess of a cooch to the floor beneath him. In his light blue suit pants and white shirt, jacket and tie removed, he looked like he had come directly from the office. A light sheen of sweat gleamed on his forehead, and he had the hint of a golden five-o'clock shadow around his razor-sharp jaw. If I hadn't been so fucking mortified, I might have jumped him.

As it was, that was not the case.

"Oh my God, Eric, GET OUT!" I screeched, shoving him away and then scrambling up by the shower.

"What the hell are you doing in here?" he shouted, taking in the mess on the counter and floors and my Donald-Ducking naked ass with it. "What is that shit on the toilet? And why don't you have any pants on? And what the fuck is on your pussy?"

"GET OUT!"

When he didn't move, I grabbed the shower curtain behind me and whipped it around my front.

"Eric," I said.

His mouth twitched as he looked me over. "Yes?"

"Stop looking at me."

He did not.

I threw a hand towel at him, which he batted away. "Eric, can you *please* get the hell out of this bathroom and get Skylar?"

But he didn't move, instead his gaze focused on the spot covered by the shower curtain, which was clear, of course. "She was in the pool with the kids. Should I...should I get my cousin? Or Caitlyn? They were both down there."

"No!" I yelped. The last thing I needed was for the resident ice queen or Blair Waldorf to witness this atrocity. I had never wanted my mother so badly in my life. If anyone could fix this mess, it was her. "No," I said a little more calmly. "I just...I just need some help."

Eric tipped his head, and his mouth twitched again. No...no, I couldn't ask him. Could I?

*Well, it's not like he hasn't seen it before.*

I sighed. It was either that or send him with news of my shame to the cast of *The Great Gatsby* lounging around the de Vries estate. No. Thank. You.

"Fine," I said. "*Fine.* You want to know my secret?"

Eric leaned against the sink and crossed one ankle over the other, like he was settling in for a good story. "Please."

I rolled my eyes. "You could be a little less smug about it."

He didn't answer, just tipped his head and waited.

"I...I'veneverbeenwaxedandIdecidedIneededtodoitbecauseIdidn'tknowthiswasapoolpartyandnoweverythingisstuckandIcan'tgetitoff-STOPLAUGHING!"

But it was too late. By the time I was done spitting out my predicament, Eric was bent fully over, clutching his belly while he laughed so violently tears were streaming down his face and not a single sound could make it out.

"You're an asshole," I said bitterly as I clutched the curtain to my midsection. Not that it did any fucking good.

"Oh, shit!" Eric howled as he stood back up, wiping his eyes. "Oh, Jesus. I really needed that today."

"Ass. Hole. That's you."

"Oh, come on, Jane. It's hilarious. You have to admit."

I did not. And I would not.

Eric bent down and picked up the paper and applicators scattered around the floor, then set them back on the counter next to the hot wax that had thankfully not fallen. "I can't imagine what the staff was thinking when you snuck this in and out of the kitchens."

"No one saw me," I lied defensively. "I was like a cat."

"A cat with pink hair," Eric said. "I'm sure you were really stealthy. All right, Pink Panther, let's see what we have here." He picked up the box and read through the direction, his brow furrowing.

"Christ, Petri, it's not tort reform. You just reach down and yank," I said.

He looked up. "Is that why you were able to do it?"

"I don't have a good angle from here," I retorted, pressing the shower curtain over my waist more when he glanced down again.

Eric set the box back on the counter, then beckoned me over. "Come on, Lefferts. Let's have a look."

The smug look on his face almost had me screaming at him to get out again. But the desire *not* to be sticky and uncomfortable won out, and so I edged over to the counter, holding the edge of the shower curtain as far as it would extend.

Eric walked the other three steps next to me and tipped his head. "Drop trou, Lefferts. I can't help you if you're covering it up like the Amish."

I scowled at him. He just started laughing all over again.

"You are *never* allowed to breathe a word of this to *anyone*," I told him. "Promise."

He bit his lips, though merriment danced in his eyes. "Scout's honor."

"Were you even a Boy Scout?"

The grin widened. "No. I wanted to, but I wasn't allowed."

I cast my eyes to the crown-molded ceiling. "God fucking help me."

I dropped the curtain, then sat my naked ass on the counter, spreading my leg on the one side that needed the help while I awkwardly covered the rest of me with a spread hand. I'm sure you can imagine how well that worked.

"See that strip?" I asked. "I want it off. Then I can bury my head in the sand where it belongs."

"Yeah," Eric said in a tone that, right now, wasn't quite so merry. "I see it."

He bent down to examine the situation, and it was then I made the mistake of looking too.

There was Eric's face. Next to the unmentionables that I generally had *no* problem mentioning. Staring at them like they were a buffet and he was a starving man.

A flush traveled up my body, starting at my toes and reaching my head in just a few seconds.

I swallowed heavily. "Are you going to do anything?"

Eric looked up with a smirk. "I'm just enjoying the view." Moving slowly, his hand, strong and capable, pressed over the waxed paper, pressing it into the skin I'd just been torturing moments before. I sagged backward against the mirror and took a deep breath, staring up at the ceiling and trying to pretend like I wasn't in this position.

When he didn't do anything, I scowled. "You're being a pervert. Just pull off the damn strip, Petri dish."

"All in good time." He clicked his tongue, which, of course, only reminded me exactly what he could do with it. Bastard. "All right, I'm going to count to three and rip it off," he said as he secured a solid hold on the strip. "Ready? One—"

"YOOWWWWW!" I glared down at Eric as he tossed the strip into the garbage and then grinned up at me. "You fucker! You said three!"

He shrugged and stood up. "You would have flinched. Now, come here."

I wiggled around like a drunk two-year-old, dancing away the pain. "Fuck. *Fuck!* Why don't they tell you how bad that's going to hurt! Jesus, Eric, make it stop!"

The words flew out of my mouth, and before I could stop them, Eric grabbed my naked thighs, pushed me back onto the counter, and suddenly he was kissing me. His mouth was soft, pliant, and tasted mildly of the champagne that was already flowing like water by the pool. Before I could stop, my tongue slipped out to twist with his and my arms were tangled around his neck, urging him closer. It was a solid minute before I—he? One of us?—pulled away, leaving his lips slightly reddened with the remnants of my lipstick.

But something else hadn't pulled away.

I looked down to where his fingers had slipped between my thighs, coated with oil and massaging the slightly reddened spot where the wax used to be.

I shuddered. The arm around my waist didn't move. "You sneak. What—what are you doing?"

"The directions said to apply this right after."

Eric nodded at the small bottle of blue azulene oil lying innocuously on the counter, but he sounded as breathless as I felt. He was close—too close. Close enough that his mouth still hovered over mine, that I could still practically taste the sweet residue of champagne on his breath. I willed my arms to leave his shoulders, but they didn't. Instead, they just kept him close.

"I meant," I said, "what were you doing when you...when you kissed me?" *And why don't you do it again?*

A muscle in the side of his neck fluttered as he swallowed, staring at my mouth. "You asked me to make it stop. I did what I thought would work." His eyes flickered up, cocky and searching at the same time. "You used to say my kisses were mind-melting, right?"

The scents in the small room grew suddenly more pungent. The pine scent of the wax, of course, plus the lavender-scented oil. Him, of course, that always tantalizing mix of linen and cologne. And now, underlying those scents was me—the desire that had been growing for the last months. How many times had I imagined him touching me exactly like this while I lay in bed at night? How many times had I rehashed that last, crazy night together in Boston before we decided to get married? I would have expected the growing camaraderie between us to have numbed this strange, odd desire I always seemed to feel around him. But instead, the comfort of living with Eric had only seemed to make it worse.

I wasn't sure I had ever wanted someone this way. I wasn't sure I ever would again.

And that idea scared the crap out of me.

"I—I think that's probably good," I whispered, though he continued to rub the same spot. His fingers slipped down into the crease where my leg connected to my torso, tickling the boundary of where I still had hair—the place where things started to get *very* sensitive.

"Jane." His voice was a shudder—a deep quake that rumbled within us both.

I blinked. My glasses were literally fogging up. Carefully, I removed them and set them on the counter. This close, I could see everything about him with crystal clarity anyway. The question was whether that was even a good thing.

"Please don't tell me to stop," Eric whispered. His lips hovered maybe an inch from mine. Close enough that his breath was warm on my skin. "Will you...will you let me...God, I can't stop thinking about it. Can you?"

His fingers tickled closer, drifting over the sensitive layers of skin, hovering over my clit. I arched slightly. All the pain was gone, and now I just wanted to feel...well, I wanted to feel what I had only given myself for the past several months. Good lord, I was *dying* for it.

"You need to say it," Eric growled. He stared at his hand, completely absorbed with its progress. "I can't do this unless you say it. I promised."

"Eric..." My voice was hardly audible. I could barely think. "We shouldn't...right?"

"Right."

But he didn't stop. Instead, his fingers made contact, exploring the terrain—in just that spot—like he had never seen or touched it before. His touch was gentle, but every so often, his fingers would dip a little farther, a little farther, coating themselves with my desire. And every time I would shake a little more.

"I just want to see you fall apart, pretty girl," Eric whispered. His lips blew soft, hypnotic circles over my neck. "Please tell me I can at least do that. I know you need it, Jane. I have heard you...just like I know you've heard me too."

The tension that had been building for the last several weeks was suddenly unbearable. I stared down to where he obviously strained against the zipper of his pants. Like a woman in a trance, I reached down and unbuttoned his pants, then tugged down the waistband of his boxers to release him. My stomach clenched as he fell into my hand, heavy and solid. He was beautiful. So fucking perfect.

"Mmmph!" Eric's voice was muffled against my bare shoulder. "Jane!"

Through the window, I could hear the sounds of the growing crowds outside the window, the family assembling for dinner that night on the patio. But in here, I was consumed with the man in front of me, absorbed with the sight of his cock as I stroked him, watched it tremble in my hand.

Eric's fingers found my clit and pressed slightly as his cheek scratched mine. "Jane. *Please.*"

It was funny. Usually I was the one begging him.

"Okay," I whispered. "Let's fall apart."

No sooner had the words left my lips, then two of those dexterous fingers slipped into my waiting pussy. I arched into him, wanting to take him deeper, wishing on some primordial level that they were the throbbing cock currently in my hand and not just fingers breaking down my barriers.

"Fuckkk," I hissed as he curved them upward while his thumb clamped over my clit. They began to move in tandem, over that bundle of nerves that was desperate for this exact touch.

"You have no idea," Eric growled. "No fucking clue how bad I want you right now, beautiful."

My hand moved faster, and with a growl, Eric bent down and bit my nipple, right through the thin white cotton of my T-shirt.

"Ow!" I squealed, but with my free hand, I kept his head where it was, allowed him to suck and torture *just the right way* while his hand continued its other sweet torture.

"Oh, Ch-christ," I mumbled as the tension grew. And grew. "Eric...sh-shit! I'm...oh...my...God..."

"I want to see it, Jane," he murmured, though his own voice had long since lost its clarity. He buried his face into my neck, allowed his hips to move in time with his fingers, effectively fucking my hand the same way his fingers were fucking my pussy. He might have begged me in the beginning, but the man was completely in control.

"Eric!" I cried as my orgasm overtook me. Top to bottom, I shook, the high of his touch flying through my entire body with the force of a tidal wave. It wasn't just the effect of the moment. It was the effect of two full months of wanting this. Needing it.

Eric swore profusely as he thrust into my limp hand a few more times and then spilled himself all over my thigh, the crease of my hip, my lower stomach, and my pussy. I stared at the mess as my breath slowly returned to normal. I was in no hurry to clean it up. For some reason I liked it. I liked seeing the evidence of Eric's loss of control... all over me.

His lips found mine again with another kiss, this one sweeter, almost sad. "Jane." He pressed a towel to my naked lower half, covering up the remnants of his release.

The sound of my name pulled me closer to reality. We weren't supposed to be doing this. It was only going to make things messier. I broke the kiss, then took the cloth away and finished the job myself, hopping down from the counter and grabbing another of the towels hanging from the racks to wrap around my waist.

"Jane," Eric said again, beckoning me back to the moment.

But it had passed. I didn't know what it was exactly, or why, but I knew I didn't want to ruin whatever we had built these last several weeks.

"It's fine," I said, turning to the shower.

God, I was a complete fucking mess. My white shirt was damp over my braless nipple, my neck looked like someone had scraped a straight-razor over it, and my legs were a goddamn disaster. There was no way I'd be walking in a bathing suit around the pool. I needed to find a Mumu—STAT.

"Is there anything else I can...help with?" I didn't think he meant to sound so playful, but it did.

I glanced over my shoulder, but found I couldn't quite look at him.

"No," I said quietly. "I just need to clean up, and I'll be down for dinner."

I forced myself to turn around and look at him so he would see he hadn't totally broken down *every* barrier I had (he definitely had). Eric had already put himself back together—everything tucked and zipped away, every hair smoothed back into place. His bright white shirt didn't even have a single wrinkle. Meanwhile I probably had makeup smudged across my face like a battered clown, and I *still* wasn't wearing any pants.

"Okay?" I said, tipping my head toward the door.

He gave me a long look, sweeping his dark gray eyes over the messy contents of the bathroom, but landing back on me. Staying on me.

"Okay," he said finally, and then left me to ponder exactly what line we had just crossed. What we had just done.

# TWENTY-ONE

They weren't big things. They were little. Seemingly inconsequential. Not the kinds of pranks someone over the age of, oh, twelve would actually do.

It started with sand instead of salt.

The night Eric arrived, after the waxing debacle, we were eating dinner on the grand patio next to the west wing of the house. Maybe it happened after Eric had poured me my third glass of Sancerre and winked at me. Maybe it happened when he draped his hand over the back of my chair and traced circles on my shoulder for a solid five minutes while Caitlyn and Nina stared at us, stony-faced, from my other side.

Or maybe it happened when he caught me watching his full lips as he smiled, then snuck another kiss just because he could. Just because there was an audience, I supposed.

At the far end of the table, Celeste de Vries hid a smile behind her napkin and made another comment about my hair.

Eric tugged a strand and said he hoped I dyed it purple next time.

Everyone laughed, but his eyes shone. And my heart gave a big, chest-shaking thump.

I didn't know what was happening between us anymore. So maybe that was why, when I took a bite of my perfectly seared scallops, I almost didn't realize that someone had sprinkled sand over the top of them instead of salt.

"Everything all right?" Eric asked. He still hadn't moved his arm from around my shoulder.

I wanted to ask him why he was touching me like that. We had agreed to be somewhat affectionate around his grandmother so she wouldn't think this was a complete farce, but he hadn't stopped touching me all night. Gripping my thigh, caressing my fingers. Some weird door had opened, and Eric was charging through it. But I had no idea where it started. Was there a lock? Had I inadvertently tossed away the key?

His eyes, so gray and deep, seemed sincere in their concern. The mask had dropped again.

I blinked, staring at my food. Took another forkful and examined it. Yeah, that was definitely sand, not salt.

Luckily, pushing one's $39.99 per pound food around seemed to be a normal habit at this table, so I wasn't alone in not finishing my plate. I was just probably the only one who had actually wanted to consume all of its contents.

"Don't give her a hard time, Eric," Caitlyn called out. "She's got a wedding to prepare for."

"I'm fine," I said as I took a bite of potatoes, which were thankfully sandless.

Eric pressed another kiss to my shoulder and went back to his food. I shivered and stared at mine, unsure of what to do.

"Gordon's food is *so* heavy, isn't it?" Caitlyn said conspiratorially as some of the other serving staff whisked away our still-full plates.

"Gordon?"

She smiled. "The cook, silly. He's been with the family for years. I swear, the scallops were swimming in so much butter, I'll have to double my trainer's hours next week."

"There was a lot of butter," I said, more wistful than not. I wouldn't have minded the butter. All of it.

Was it the kitchen staff? Or the other girls, Nina, and Carly, one of Eric's second cousins, winking at Caitlyn across the table?

"Everything all right?" Eric asked for the fourth time.

"I..." I started to tell him what I'd eaten, but ended up remaining quiet. I honestly didn't know, and I wasn't about to make a fuss. They wouldn't do this. Not now. Not after I had spent months at this point trying to endear myself to a family that really didn't seem as given to drama as Eric had described.

Whatever happened with his fiancée seemed like a long time ago now.

"Well, good," he said as the salad course arrived. "I just hope you're getting enough to eat. You barely touched the fish, and beurre blanc is one of Gordon's specialties."

"Oh, E, be reasonable!" Caitlyn cackled, reaching around my shoulder to touch Eric on the neck.

He grinned. My stomach turned to ice.

"Jane has a wedding to prepare for," she said. "For my last one, I didn't eat for a month so I could fit into my dresses." She winked conspiratorially at me.

On the far end of the giant dining table, Skylar glared at Caitlyn. "How many times have you been married, Caitlyn?" she asked casually.

"Just twice," Caitlyn said through a thin smile. "Sometimes it takes a moment before you find the right one. Isn't that right, E?"

Eric shifted uncomfortably. "I suppose." He took a long drink of his wine.

"It's too bad your wedding won't be a quieter affair," Caitlyn continued as she toyed with her beets. "Since, Jane doesn't seem to be one of those appearance-driven types. Lucky her. Wouldn't it be nice if we all lived like that?"

I put my fork down on my plate. What in the hell?

"Actually, Jane's got a pretty amazing eye," Eric said. "You should see what she's done to our apartment, Cait."

"Is that right?"

Eric nodded whole-heartedly and smiled at me in a way that made my chest bloom. "It's amazing. She does the same thing with clothes. You know she designs, right?"

Caitlyn looked me over with renewed appraisal. "Really?"

I nodded, somewhat shy. "I do. I made this dress, actually."

"She made her dress for the party," Eric continued to brag.

From down the table, I caught Skylar watching him over the rim of her glass as she elbowed Brandon in the side.

Eric just looked at me. "She's really talented."

I didn't even know what Caitlyn said next. All I could see was the way Eric continued to hold my gaze like I was the only person in the room. And the only thing I could think about was the way I couldn't stop looking back.

A plate of fresh, impossibly green spinach salad was placed in front of me, and the scallops and dresses were forgotten as Eric slipped a hand under the table to clutch my thigh again, his fingers drifting just above the spot he had touched much more intimately only an hour or so before. Unable to help myself, I lay my head on his shoulder, and I thought I could feel his smile against my hair.

"Thanks," I said, quiet enough that only he could hear.

A brief, but tender kiss was pressed to my forehead.

"Anytime, Lefferts," he said just as quietly. "I got your back. Don't forget it."

I sat up and turned back to my food, relieved to find that there was no sand on my salad.

But when I took a drink of my wine, it suddenly tasted like vinegar.

———

THE NEXT DAY, after spending the morning playing croquet with the Crosby-Sterlings, I returned to my room to find that all of my shoes had gone missing. Every single one. The only thing that remained was a crudely drawn map. A treasure map of the sort small children make when they pretend they are pirates. It took a while, but eventually I found them in a pile on the beach, close to a half-mile away. Buried in the sand with a sign over them in clumsy letters that read "X marks the spot."

"Buried treasure," I said to Brandon, who had walked with me out to the crime scene. I hadn't bothered to tell Eric, not wanting him to worry. "You know, like a pirate digging for gold? It's actually kind of witty."

Brandon squatted down and helped me dig shoe after shoe out of the dune. Nothing was too severely damaged, though they had been there for hours. I was mostly pissed off that the Jimmy Choos I'd purchased for the engagement party were left by the saltwater for so long. Leather shrinks, you know.

"I'm more concerned that whoever did this thought it was a good prank," I said as we trudged the shoes back to the house. "It took too long, you know? And the gold digger reference is kind of obvious, isn't it?"

Brandon didn't look amused. "Jane, who doesn't want you here? This isn't just a prank."

I looked down at my armful of shoes. "Um...well, how about everyone?" I tried not to sound bitter.

"Celeste seems to like you," he said. "And I have it on good authority that she pretty much hates everyone."

"She hates my hair," I said as we maneuvered around a big driftwood log.

"Yeah, but that's pretty obviously in a loves-to-hate sort of way."

I pondered that as we continued past kids flying kites and other people sunbathing on the wide, white beach. Finally, we reached the trail that led back to the house, and Brandon followed me between the grassy dunes.

"It's just a prank," I said. "No harm, no foul, right?"

Brandon glanced at me over an armful of shoes. "I think the real concern is why you felt you needed ten pairs of shoes for a weekend getaway."

I shrugged, clutching my favorite gold strappy sandals to my chest. "A girl has to have options, you know."

———

I HAD HOPED that would be it, but when I returned to my room, there was another surprise. Brandon and I dropped my shoes in the closet only to find a giant pile of dirt on the bed, along with a shovel. And a note that read, *Happy digging."*

Brandon shook his head. All humor had deserted us. "I'm going to get Eric."

He left, and I didn't argue as I surveyed the mess. There was at least five pounds of sandy soil in the middle of this pristine bedroom. I glanced around. It wasn't anywhere else. Not in my closet—all my clothes seemed untouched. And there was no trace of who might have done this. No silly map or drawing. Nothing.

But as I approached the pile, I noticed something peculiar: it gleamed.

"What the hell is that?"

I looked up. "That was quick. Did Brandon find you?"

Eric shook his head as he strode into the room somewhat sweaty, dressed in a white polo and shorts, carrying a tennis racket. Whatever he said, he seemed to be getting back into the groove of family routine more smoothly than he'd initially let on. Tennis whites looked damn good on him. Plus, I saw him at night, fingering the pictures scattered around the house and in our room. There was a part of him that missed being a part of this massive clan after all these years.

But he was still wary. Especially in moments like these.

I stood up, revealing the mess, too preoccupied to notice the way his polo shirt stuck to his body. Sleeping one room away from the man had been nearly impossible last night after our strange interlude.

"What *is* that?" he asked again, oblivious to my gawking.

"It's dirt," I said. "And..." I bent down. "Well, if it's not gold, it's supposed to be, mixed in. It's almost creative, actually. This is better than the shoes. Or the sand. Although now I'm wondering if that sand was supposed to be gold as well. I didn't look very closely. It might have been camouflaged by the butter."

"Jane, what are you talking about?"

I sat on the edge of the vanity across from the bed and recounted the pranks of the last twenty-four hours.

"Who did this?" His voice was sharp, demanding. Almost like he blamed it on me.

I shrugged him away. "How would I know? There are about twenty-five people staying in this house right now along with a whole menagerie of children. Honestly, it's just as possible one of the kids overheard someone else using the term and decided to play a little joke. Haze the newcomer or whatever."

I looked away, not wanting to show how much that idea hurt. I'd been getting along with the kids here more than anyone else aside from Celeste, thanks to Jenny, my goddaughter. That they would be this cruel felt pretty shitty.

"That still means that someone has been saying those things, Jane," Eric pointed out. "It's not okay."

"Hey." I reached out and touched a hand to his sleeve. His arm was tense—very tense.

Eric looked down at my hand, then back up at me. And then, before I could stop him, he slipped his hand behind my neck and kissed me, hard and fast. So quickly, that by the time he finished, I had only just registered what was happening as I stumbled back and my legs hit the bed.

"Sorry," he said as he released me. "I just had to. You're a brick, Jane," he uttered. "Fucking amazing."

He stared at my mouth, like he wanted to do it again. Hell, *I* wanted him to do it again. That little interlude in the bathroom hadn't done a damn thing to stifle this utter craving I was dealing with. But we still hadn't talked about what happened last night. Instead, we'd both fallen into our separate beds with wine-addled good nights. I couldn't speak for him, but I wasn't sure I was ready for where that conversation might go.

"Eric..."

"I know, I know," he said, stepping back with a rueful shake of his head. "You gotta give me these moments, Jane. I can't always be as in control as you."

I frowned. *I* was the one in control? Most of the time when he was around, I felt two seconds from spinning out.

"Well, if we're not going to confront anyone, what do you think about getting out of here for the afternoon?" he said, interrupting my thoughts. "I could use a break from these assholes. You look like you could too. Want to go into town while we have someone clean up this crap?"

Relieved, I nodded. "Oh, hell yes. I'll meet you in the car in thirty minutes."

———

ERIC TOOK a shower while I pulled on a pair of cutoff shorts, a boatneck striped shirt, and tied my hair up with a red scarf, Bridget Bardot style. With my oversized glasses and a pair of espadrilles, I thought I was making the vintage look work for me in the Hamptons.

Apparently not. As I circled a hedge on my way to wait for Eric near the garage, the voices of several women floated over the roses.

"Mother can't be serious," remarked someone I recognized as his aunt Violet. "She's really going through with a full engagement party? Wedding? The whole nine yards for...*that?*"

"He seems to like her." That was Nina. Considering how icy she had been to me for the last month, it was somewhat of a relief to hear that she saw the merit in Eric's and my charade. Or at least wasn't overtly hating on it. Perhaps she wasn't the prank culprit.

"And that atrocious hair," said Violet. "She looks like a character from that game the grandchildren play. What is it called? Candyland?"

"Violet, we've *all* seen that hair," put in another woman whose voice I didn't know. "All of Manhattan has seen that hair for the last two months."

"Dreadful, isn't it?"

There was a brief eruption of laughter. My stomach knotted up even more.

"It must be killing Celeste to have had her little game backfire like this," said the unfamiliar voice.

"What do you mean?"

"Nina, please. She never had any intention of Eric actually *marrying* that harlot. The entire point was to bring the boy to his knees. Make him beg for a way out. If I know Celeste, she was planning the whole time to trade the five-year contract for a ten without a marriage requirement."

"I see." Nina's voice sounded less than enthusiastic about that idea.

"The sad thing is," started another voice I knew. Caitlyn Calvert's cloying, dulcet tones would be recognizable anywhere. "Eric doesn't realize what marrying someone like that will do to the company. What will the shareholders think of a chairman married on a lark to someone like that? The company is going to lose half its value if he's even voted in at all. Isn't that what you and Calvin have been saying, Nina?"

Though I didn't hear Nina's response, there was a chorus of agreement.

"Oh, I know," said someone. "We've already asked our broker to sell our shares in DVS."

"Mark my words. If the two of them are in the style section looking like that, DVS will be bankrupt before next year."

And so they continued. And with every comment about all the ways I would be the death knell of the shipping dynasty Eric was pledging his life to save, I shrank more into the pink and green roses.

The more I looked around the idyllic paradise, the more I felt trapped, like one of Celeste's pet birds.

I turned toward the parking lot and crept away as quietly as I could. I didn't want to hear any more, since their words were already sinking like rocks into the pit of my stomach.

Was I really that bad for Eric? Part of my appeal had been my shock value—I knew that. But if I was going to cost *him* so much, was it really worth sticking it to his family?

I approached the car where Eric stood waiting and greeted him with few words. Suddenly, I was no longer sure I wanted to be a tool for such vengeance—or its backlash.

# TWENTY-TWO

After spending thirty minutes in the car together, Eric and I parted ways almost immediately upon parking in the business district of Southampton. We each needed time to ourselves, apparently, to think about what was happening—both the rising sexual tension we couldn't quite get rid of, but also the strange events of the last twenty-four hours.

I for one couldn't knock those last bitchy words of his female relatives out of my head.

"You knew they wouldn't like me," I kept trying to tell Eric as he steered his uncle's Bentley *way* too fast around some of the streets toward the main drive. "We knew this was going to happen."

I hadn't told him about the ladies' comments, but he was still upset about the rest of the pranks.

"I...I know," he would respond each time, but nothing more than that as he would grip the steering wheel harder and whip around another turn.

So, I spent the afternoon alone, poking in and out of stores, eating a few too many pieces of saltwater taffy, and picking up some odds and ends. A bracelet for my mother. A gray and red tie, plus a hat that I knew would look gangbusters on Eric. And, when I spied a drugstore on the corner...some hair dye. Two types, so I could make a choice. I could retouch my roots myself with a bit of bleach and some pink, or, with the other box, I could just dye everything black again and start from scratch.

By the time I popped into a bookstore at the end of town, I still hadn't made a decision. Not as I poked through the fashion section looking for inspiration. Not as I paged through my favorite Mario Testino photography books. And not as I rounded a corner to find Eric standing in poetry.

From his place near the window, the sunlight cast a warm halo around his concentrated form, shimmering through the edges of his T-shirt, but making his body, arched over a book, look more like a candlelit statue than a man.

I considered cracking a joke about reading old white men, but found I didn't want to. I had actually always loved it when Eric recited poetry to me. And he looked very beautiful—and peaceful—standing there reading it. Actually, the fact that we both enjoyed certain things just because they were beautiful was one of the few things we had in common.

As I approached, I found he was actually arrested with Edith Hamilton's *Mythology*, with another book tucked under his arm. So much for old men.

"Sudden craving for classical Greek mythology?" I asked.

Eric started, the book falling open to the section on Poseidon. "Ah, yeah. Reviewing, I guess."

I snorted. "For what, work? Why would you need to review Greco-Roman folklore?"

He clapped the book shut and set it on the shelf. "Call it curiosity. What have you been doing?"

I shrugged. "A little of this, a little of that."

He looked down at my bags. "More shopping?"

I didn't mention the dye. "Well, yes, but it's for you, actually."

"For me?"

I smiled. "Yeah. I saw this, and I don't know, I just thought you might like it." I pulled out a straw fedora with a black band around the middle. "For the sun. I noticed you didn't have a hat this morning when we played croquet."

"Thanks." Eric accepted the hat curiously, examined it for a moment, then put it on.

I wasn't sure I'd ever seen Eric actually wear a hat, even during the most frigid winter months in Boston. He was one of those people who wore his thick, close-cut hair as it was because it likely provided more than enough insulation.

But the second he put it on, it was like his smile—it transported him back to another time where no man walked around without something on his head. Eric suddenly looked mouthwateringly like a character out of a Hitchcock film. Like Cary Grant. Errol Flynn. Paul Newman. Classic, tall, and full of charisma that practically made the entire store sparkle around him.

"How do I look?" He tipped the hat jauntily to the side, and I had to look away.

"You, ah, it looks pretty good," I said as I studied the spine of the book under his arm, then immediately regretted it as I read the name out loud: "*Poetica Erotica?* Going for the old-school porn, I see."

When I looked up, Eric wore a self-satisfied smirk. "Vintage hat, vintage porn," he said.

I almost fell over.

"Are we feeling a little hard up there, Petri?" I asked as I ran my finger down the shelf. "It's been a while since you refilled your dish, hasn't it? Is that why you can't stop kissing me?"

When he didn't answer, I finally looked up. He was *not* amused.

"What do you think, Jane?" he asked with a voice that was suddenly steely. His silvery gaze pinned me into place.

"I—I don't know." All my attitude flew right out the window.

Eric tipped the hat up so I could see his entire expression, but really, I was entranced with those fingers. Those long fingers that less than twenty-four hours ago had been between my legs...making me moan...making me collapse. And then those lips, which had stamped two solid kisses on mine within the last day as well. My mouth tingled. *Fuck.*

"Really?" he asked. "You don't know?"

I swallowed. "Well...no. I guess not. You walked away pretty easily last night, didn't you? And it's not like you said anything else afterward. And then in the room earlier..." Lord, I really could not help myself.

"I walked away." Eric studied me for a minute, then closed his eyes, like he was praying. "Sometimes, you really..." He drifted off, like he refused to complete the thought in his mind, much less out loud.

*I really what?* I wanted to scream. *Tell me now! Tell me if those kisses rocked you like they did me.*

"Want to hear a poem?"

I blinked. "Talk about an about face, Petri."

"I used to read you poetry all the time."

"Yeah, but that's because you were trying to get some."

"Who says I'm not now?"

*What?*

I rolled my eyes, forcing myself not to fold. "God, just when I think you have style, you lay a corny line like *that* on me."

Eric grimaced, but instead of coming back with another sharp retort, just opened his mouth and intoned:

> *A sudden blow: the great wings beating still*
> *Above the staggering girl, her thighs caressed*
> *By the dark webs, her nape caught in his bill,*
> *He holds her helpless breast upon his breast.*
>
> *How can those terrified vague fingers push*
> *The feathered glory from her loosening thighs?*
> *And how can body, laid in that white rush,*
> *But feel the strange heart beating where it lies?*

*A shudder in the loins engenders there*
*The broken wall, the burning roof and tower*
*And Agamemnon dead.*
*Being so caught up,*
*So mastered by the brute blood of the air,*
*Did she put on his knowledge with his power*
*Before the indifferent beak could let her drop?*

When he finished, he looked at me, cocky and full of pride.

"Big deal," I said. "So the English major memorized 'Leda and the Swan.' Everyone knows that one."

"Everyone does not. Least of all you, Ms. Fashion Design."

"Hey, I majored in economics, asshole, and I took a few lit classes like everyone else at Northwestern. I may not be able to recite it all by heart like you, you big dork, but that poem is seminal." I tapped my knuckles on the bookshelf. "You know, if you're looking for advice on how to woo the ladies, I probably wouldn't start with a poem about rape."

Eric grimaced. "No, I wouldn't. Although it depends on the lady."

"That it does. What would it be for me?" I should have regretted the question, but I didn't. I wanted to know. Or maybe, a small voice said, *you want to know if he still knows how to do it. Oh, who are you kidding? Of course he does.*

He examined me for a second, then opened *Poetica Erotica* to a page he'd apparently marked. He stepped closer, and with a smirk, caged me against the bookshelf.

"What are you doing?" I asked suspiciously, trying and failing to ignore the drift of cologne that suddenly floated around me.

"Jane, just shut up and listen." Then he leaned close and intoned the poem next to my ear:

*Teach me to sin—*
*In love's forbidden ways,*

*For you can make all passion pure;*
*The magic lure of your sweet eyes*
*Each shape of sin makes virtue praise.*

*Teach me to sin—*
*Enslave me to your wanton charms,*
*Crush me in your velvet arms*
*And make me, make me love you.*
*Make me fire your blood with new desire,*
*And make me kiss you—lip and limb,*
*Till senses reel and pulses swim.*
*Ay! Even if you hate me,*
*Teach me to sin.*

———

*"HERE,"* Eric said. *"And here."*

His big hands covered mine as he placed each on top of the wide wooden headboard above his bed. I watched, transfixed, as he threaded the two pieces of silk through the eyelet hooks that were drilled into each side. They were delicate, almost unnoticeable before today.

"I wondered what those were for," I said as he began wrapping one piece of silk around my wrist, tying me to that side. "I thought you liked to hang Christmas lights or something, like college students in their dorms."

I snorted to myself. The idea of Eric doing something so pedestrian was truly laughable.

Eric laid a kiss on my shoulder. "I put them there for you, pretty girl," he murmured.

It was so unlike him. Most of the time, our interactions were playful, contrary, or somewhere in between. Tenderness wasn't in Eric's lexicon.

"I—" I didn't know what to say to that. To the kiss. To the other silk scarf that he was now tying around my other wrist, pinning me to the headboard. After that, a third piece of silk wrapped around my eyes, blindfolding me to the room.

Eric tugged my ass toward him so that I was leaning toward the wall comfortably, but also displayed for his pleasure. Immediately, my skin tingled with anticipation.

"Hush," he said as he slipped one hand between my legs to tease the slickness there.

"That feels good, doesn't it?" he asked as he toyed with my clit.

I nodded as I pressed my face to the wall, sinking into the pleasure. This wasn't new. He knew how to touch me there like he was playing an instrument, knew how to read my body's cues like he was reading one of his books. Who would have ever thought it? Pretentious, calculating, unflappable Eric de Vries. The best I'd ever had.

"How about that?" he asked as he slipped his thumb into my pussy, effectively holding both points of pleasure in his grip while his other hand massaged my skin.

"Ummmm." Words were starting to fail me now. It was happening faster than ever these days. I was hot before I got to the place to see him, and by the time we tumbled into the apartment, I was already halfway to orgasm. It was Pavlovian, really. Just the thought of the man made me want to come.

Eric chuckled, low and wise. "I'll take that as a yes." He continued his massage, internal and external, driving my pleasure in a slow, simmering frenzy. I couldn't take much more of this...until he forced me to.

His other hand squeezed my ass, then slid to the middle, where slowly, surely, his thumb teased that other entrance, the one most people never dared to cross. I froze, lip clenched between my teeth, as the digit worked its way in until he had me effectively clasped between his two hands. His cock brushed the inside of my thigh as he leaned over me.

"And this?" he asked, his deep voice suddenly hoarse.

"Mmmmm," I said. "Yessss."

*He continued to work both entrances, manipulating the energy coursing through me like I was a puppet, and he was my master.*

*"Take it," he instructed me. "Feel it. Feel the way I control every fucking inch of this body."*

*"Are you trying to teach me to behave, Mr. de Vries?" I asked, though my voice had lost its bite. I could hardly think of anything other than the feel of him behind me, pressing between my legs, a threat, a taunt, a stroke of desire. I was certain it would just take once to undo me completely.*

*But instead, he removed his thumb from my ass, and his cock replaced it, finding its seat in my darkest place, one slow inch at a time.*

*"No, pretty girl," he said with a guttural sigh as he slid in completely. "I'm teaching you to sin."*

———

"JANE? *JANE.*"

The snap of a book in front of my face yanked me out of the past, and I blinked to find Eric watching me with a wry, amused expression.

"Everything all right there, Lefferts?"

I readjusted my glasses. "Um, yeah, sorry. Just got...lost there for a second."

I stared at the ground, examining the uneven wood slats beneath my feet. Lord, even our feet were so different. My toes were painted in ruby-red polish and wrapped in my black espadrille wedges, pointed toward his light gray boat shoes. The idea that we might ever fit together permanently seemed even more ridiculous than those women had inferred.

But really, the bigger surprise was how disappointed it made me feel.

Two fingers slipped under my chin and tipped it up. Eric studied my face for a long time, his deep gray gaze penetrating me to the bone.

"Hey," he said. "It's going to be okay."

Like a book. That's how well he could once read me. How could I have forgotten?

"How do you know?" I asked, trying and failing not to sound pitiful. "How do you know it will be all right?"

His thumb brushed gently over my bottom lip as his expression softened. "Because they're just kids," he said. "They don't know you like I do. Not yet."

*Oh.* He thought I was upset about a few stupid pranks. He had no idea how deep it really went.

His hand dropped from my chin. "Your mom arrives tonight?"

I nodded. "On the seven o'clock. She should be here by nine or maybe ten, when the party is going. I told her to dress for it."

"Good." Eric took a breath, then expelled it, long and low. "Jane, we need to talk," he said quietly. "Things have...things have changed."

I swallowed heavily. Yes, they certainly had. "Okay," I whispered. "But not now."

Eric studied me a minute more. "Tonight? After the party?"

I nodded again. "Yes. Okay."

# TWENTY-THREE

At approximately seven o'clock, there was a sharp knock on the bathroom door in Eric's and my suite.

"Jane, you all right in there?"

The bookstore had cast another awkward glaze over the remainder of the afternoon, and so after Eric purchased the mythology book and *Poetica Erotica*, we drove back to the house in relative silence without commenting on so much as the fine weather.

The poem continued to echo. Teach me to sin? This man had taught me to do so much more than that, many times over. And I couldn't shake the look in his eyes when he'd asked to talk. He was scared. Almost mournful. Like he didn't know what I was going to say.

The thing was, I felt the same.

What if this conversation didn't lead to the beginning of something, but the end?

Upon our return, Eric was swept off by some of his family to talk more business (it appeared to be impossible to leave the office in Manhattan). The caterers, band, and valet had been setting up all day, and most of the women—Skylar included—had already disappeared to prepare for the party that was about to happen, and Celeste had also adjourned for a nap.

And so, just as I was watching from the bathroom window as car after car bearing white-clad guests arrived in the front drive, I was also running very late. I had retreated to my room for an hour after arriving, staring at the boxes of dye, trying to make a decision. I didn't want to embarrass Eric. And I had some things to say too. And when I said them, I wanted to put my best foot forward. I just didn't know what that was.

Finally, I closed my eyes, stuck out my finger, and jabbed.

Well, sort of.

"I'm fine!" I called out as I clutched my newly rinsed hair in its towel. "But I'm going to be a while. You might want to use another bathroom."

"What?" Eric called. "Jane, you've been in there for over an hour. This thing with my uncle took for fucking ever and I need to shower too."

"Well, you're going to have to wait, de Vries," I called back as I unwrapped my head and shook out my newly dyed locks. "Perfection takes a minute." *I still need a haircut*, I thought with satisfaction, *but this should shut some mouths.*

"Jane!" There were several more knocks. I tried to ignore them, but when he didn't stop, finally, I stomped over to the door.

"*What?*" I snarled. "You can't use one of the other forty-five bathrooms in this palace?"

I flung open the door to find Eric standing with his forearm balanced against the top of the doorframe like he owned the place. Which, I guess, he did. Motherfucker. What *was* it about men that made them look so hot when they stood that way? Was it a genetic thing? Did they have a secret orientation in ninth grade where they were taught how to light women's panties on fire with *posture*? Mine were already done for, thanks to this bastard. He didn't need to keep driving me to the point of frothing.

The thought made me irrationally angry.

Eric's cocky smile dropped immediately to a frown. "What the hell did you do to your hair?"

I touched the still sopping wet locks that dripped all over my shoulders and tried to ignore the horror on the man's face. "Well, thank you for noticing. Yes, it *does* look good, thank you. God, you're such a fucking gentleman, Eric."

I turned back into the bathroom and faced myself in the mirror. Yes, I did look different. Or, I guessed, more like myself? At least the self of the last five years.

"It's black."

"Observant too."

"Let me rephrase," he said as he strode into the bathroom with me. "*Why* did you do that?"

He pinned me against the counter with his interrogation. And, of course, reminded me acutely just what he had done to me last night. What was it about us and bathrooms?

I toed one foot into the tile. "I just... Yeah. Well. I just thought... I needed a touch-up anyway, and...listen, I just don't want to ruin your business with my Candyland hair, all right? Between my big mouth and my weird clothes, I'm embarrassing enough as it is."

It was hard to admit. I'd been plowing through my life for the last twenty years doing my damnedest to embarrass anyone stuck-up enough to care about things like hair or dress codes. But the women were right. As much as I liked streaking my hair with five different colors or the idea of wearing combat boots with vintage Mugler, it wasn't going to do me any favors in this world. Not as a lawyer. And not as Eric's wife either. If everyone acted like the women in Eric's family, it was only going to push people away. And for some reason, I didn't want to do that with Eric. Not this time.

*We need to talk*, he'd said. Yeah, I had some things to say too.

*So long, tie-dye hair. It was nice while it lasted.*

"Jane."

Eric's hands clasped my shoulders, fingers slipping a little on my damp skin. He pulled me close enough that I could see the flecks of gold embedded in his brown-gray eyes. *Huh.* I'd never noticed that before. So that's why they always shined like coins.

He raised a blond brow. I bit my lip.

"For the record," he said. "I liked the hair."

"Um, okay."

"I never asked you to change it."

"I know you didn't."

"But you did anyway."

I took a deep breath. "Yes. I did." *No. For the love of God and your own fucking dignity, keep the next question to yourself, Jane.* But I couldn't help it. "Do you like this too?"

For a long time, he just looked at me, his gaze searing my skin with that unreadable mask of his. But then, just as I was about to turn away, he reached out and took a lock of wet hair, trapping it lightly between his fingers and pulling. Just a little.

Then, instead of answering, he blinked. "Jesus, Jane. You're not even dressed." He dropped his hands and checked his watch—a shiny, unobtrusive Rolex that was quietly expensive. "We have to be downstairs in about thirty minutes. People are arriving, and you're not even close."

I opened my mouth to tell him not to nag, but I knew better. Eric knew exactly how long it took me, on average, to do my makeup. He was well within his rights to worry. I still needed to blow out my hair, do my makeup, and put on my dress. Not to mention I probably needed to double check that my mother's room was ready before she arrived in a few hours.

We stared at each other for a long time, and it was only then that I got a really good look at him. Eric wasn't the only one who had gotten cleaned up for tonight. He was still wearing the shorts and casual T-shirt from earlier, but while we were out, his blond hair had been trimmed and shaped to his scalp, and the extra sun he'd gotten this morning had mellowed into a sun-kissed glow. Behind him, a pristine white suit hung from his bedroom door. I shook my head at the mere idea of him in it.

"Jane."

"Hmm?"

Eric looked me up and down. "You, um, going to put some clothes on?"

I glanced down and realized I was still in nothing but my towel, which was dangerously close to slipping off, and sopping wet hair. "Oh. Crap. Yeah, of course."

But instead of leaving or stepping aside so I could get to my room, he took a step forward, backing me up against the counter.

"Eric, what are you doing?"

"Sometimes," he said in a low, foreboding voice, "sometimes I think you do this on purpose."

"Do what?" I asked, unable to keep the quaver out of my voice.

"It's like you know," he says. "You know when I've had the kind of day or week where everything goes wrong. Where everyone at work or the penthouse or *somewhere* has *something* to say about how I'm supposed to live my fucking life. And then just when I think I have you figured out...you completely change directions." He picked up a piece of hair again and fingered the wet strands. "Like this."

"What-what's so bad about dying my hair?" My voice had faded to a whisper.

"Nothing." My back was touching the counter as he crowded me against the marble. "Except that it drives me crazy."

His gaze dropped to my lips.

"Eric," I said. "You said we need to talk."

"We do," he said. "But I need to do this more."

And then he kissed me. But it wasn't a kiss like the other night, some desperate attempt to distract. Nor was it like this afternoon, when he was overcome with gratitude and had to get it out.

This was a kiss that was filled with only one thing: desire.

He kissed me, and I kissed him back, opening my mouth, my

tongue, my neck, my face, everything to him. And then his hands were also everywhere, pushing my flimsy towel to the floor and clasping me against his body so he could run his calloused palms up and down my slick, bare back, slide over my ass, run up my waist and over my breasts and stomach until I moaned, loud and animal, into his mouth.

"Jane."

His mouth dipped, teeth grazing my neck, and he dropped lower and pulled one nipple between his teeth. This time there was no cotton barrier. He pulled.

"Ah!" I cried at the sudden pain, but arched into it nonetheless. A shock of desire ran from my chest directly between my legs, and when Eric pressed his large body between them, I bucked into him, eager to welcome him, however I could.

"Fucking *hell*, Jane," he grumbled against my skin as his hands memorized every inch of me they could. He grabbed my ass and lifted me back to the counter, back to the spot where we had been only twenty-four hours before.

His mouth found mine once more, sucking, biting, tormenting until we were both out of breath, gasping into each other's mouths like we were drowning in the same small ocean.

"You have no idea," he said hoarsely. "No fucking *clue* the kinds of things I want to do to you right now."

"Oh, don't I?" I said, eyeing him. One touch, and I'd probably melt. But I felt like some kind of wild animal, like I was just as likely to bolt as to break.

He seemed to know it too. Slowly, one of his hands left my waist and traveled up my torso, hovering over my naked skin but never completely touching. It floated over my stomach, my breasts, sternum, and finally up to my neck. But skin only met skin again when his fingers encircled my neck, holding me in place with an offer that was also a threat.

*I own you*, his touch seemed to say.

*Yes, you do.*

I reared further, but only in expression. Because he did own me. I couldn't move.

"No," he said with a calmness that was nowhere to be found in the stiff, tensed posture of the rest of his body. "You don't."

Still holding me perfectly still, he bent down, and his mouth brushed over mine. His lip wedged between my teeth, and I bit it. Hard.

"Ahh!" he cried, but didn't pull away. Instead, the hand around my neck squeezed.

"Ssssss!" I hissed, but I practically came right there. My legs splayed open. I had never wanted him—or anyone else, for that matter—more.

The kiss continued as we bruised, punished each other. But his hand didn't move from my neck, keeping me firmly in place, squeezing more tightly whenever I wriggled or if I even touched him. It was a hint of what was to come, if nothing more. A threat. A rejoinder. A promise.

And then, just as suddenly, he released me, leaving me panting there on the counter as he dragged his gaze up and down my naked body.

"Selkie," he whispered, almost resentfully.

"Wha-*what?*" I was almost too out of breath to say anything more.

Eric shook his head, but didn't stop staring. "Mythological creatures. Keats writes about them. Others too. Seals in the water, but women on the ground." He gestured vaguely at my wet form, the water that still dripped from my sopping hair. The damp stain on his shirt. "They bewitch their lovers."

We stared at each other while the drips hit the floor.

Drip.

Drip.

Drip.

I bit my lip. Eric exhaled heavily.

He opened the bathroom door.

"I'll get ready in another room," he said. "But tonight, Jane. Tonight, we *will* talk."

And then the door closed, leaving me to touch my lips, close my eyes, and imagine once more what that conversation would entail.

# TWENTY-FOUR

"Okay."

I finished putting in my contacts, then touched up my eye makeup, which was just a ring of thin eyeliner and mascara. Then I stood back from the full-length mirror to look myself over. My now-black hair lay in tousled barrel curls around my shoulders, pinned back from one temple. My dress, the white, drop-waisted affair draped lazily over my hips with a perfect "don't give a fuck" attitude. No jewelry except my engagement ring and a leather and sterling silver cuff.

Clean. Cool. I nodded with approval. "Perfect."

There was another knock at my door.

"Eric, I'll be out in a second," I said irritably. Lord, was he back already?

"It's not Eric."

I walked over to let in Skylar, who stood there looking a damn vision in a simple white slip dress and shawl, her red hair braided heavily over one shoulder. A pair of diamond studs gleamed from her ears along with her engagement and wedding rings. Aside from those small touches, the only real signs of my friend's wealth was the impeccable fit of her dress and her personal grooming. Even after marrying into billions, Skylar had kept to herself. Simple. Elegant. Down-to-earth. I loved her for it.

She gawked as she got a look at my hair. "Well, that's a change." She strode into the room. "Thought I'd come check on you," she said. "Eric's downstairs asking about you. Again."

I smiled as I walked back to the mirror. "Thanks. What do you think?"

Skylar looked me over, whistling as she did. "You know, you kind of fit into this life."

I looked at her through the mirror, disbelieving. "You're kidding."

She sat down on the bed. "No, I'm not. I mean, I just remember how uncomfortable I used to be even visiting Brandon's house. You've just...I don't know. You've acclimated well."

I snorted. "Tell that to Eric's family, please."

Skylar frowned. "Why? What's going on."

I cringed. "Brandon didn't tell you?"

She shook her head. "We were at the beach with the kids most of the day. What happened?"

So I did, starting with the weird pranks that morning and the comments I'd overheard before Eric and I left for town.

"We could sue them," Skylar said when I was finished.

"For what?"

She shrugged. "Emotional larceny?"

I snorted. "Okay, Andy from *Singles*."

"I just think it's bullshit. And you guys aren't even going to talk to anyone? These people are supposedly here to celebrate *your* engagement. And instead, they're dumping dirt in your bed."

Skylar glared at the now-pristine mattress. I looked with her. The staff had done its work, but I still wasn't sure I wanted to sleep on it.

"The thing is," I said. "I thought things were going well, relatively speaking. Celeste has actually been looking me in the eye when she talks to me."

"Is that why you dyed your hair back to black?

I shrugged. "My roots were showing anyway." To avoid the pity in Skylar's eyes, I started the process of putting on my lipstick. The last step. The only bit of color in my outfit.

"No glasses?" Skylar asked.

I turned, blinking heavily. "No. Not tonight."

"But you hate contacts."

I shrugged. "Well. I wanted to make a good impression tonight. I'm tired of sticking out like a sore thumb. I think it will help Eric if I don't look too Debbie Harry when I meet his family's entire social group, you know?"

"That's...generous of you." Skylar watched as I drew on a deep, almost purple-red shade, slightly softer than my usual fire-engine red, but no less vibrant.

"There," I said. "All done." I turned around. "What do you think?"

It had taken me almost two months to make this dress. Initially, I'd found a vintage Halston that I considered wearing, but needed to take in. The fabric ended up being damaged in the back, so instead, I'd dismantled it and created something of my own. The sheer, minimalist midi skirt fell to my calves, with a boatneck bodice patchworked with white silk and charmeuse that draped around my torso to the drop waist. Not exactly Stepford wife, but it was still couture, technically. Times two. And still me. A labor of love—more work than I'd even considered with my wedding dress. And I was glad, because if things were about to change with Eric the way I thought they might, there was potential that tonight might even mean more.

"Janey, you look stunning," Skylar said honestly. "I love what you did with your hair, black or not."

I examined my nails, which I'd repainted this morning with shiny black polish to match the black leather cuff. I couldn't let go of that edge, just a bit of hardness. I'd never done it in court, and I wasn't going to start now.

"You and Eric...it's not just an arrangement anymore, is it?"

I looked up. "How did you know?"

Skylar rolled her eyes. "Jane, I do know both of you pretty well. Something was different this morning at breakfast. Last night, even. Both of you were different. More...relaxed somehow. Am I right?"

I twisted my mouth around. "Honestly, I don't know. But maybe..." I looked up. "Maybe I hope so."

Skylar smiled. "Good. Just don't mess it up this time by being so damn stubborn, all right?"

I scowled, even though I knew she was right.

"Come on," Skylar said, linking her arm with mine. "Let's go make your society debut."

———

THE PARTY WAS ALREADY in full swing when we rounded the staircase into the main hall and exited the French doors onto the patio and lawn. Really, party was a misnomer—this thing was a fucking ball. The entire pool area had been completely cordoned off, and on the wide green field next to it, a giant outdoor extravaganza had been set up. This included a dance floor, a full band, several drink and catering services, about three dozen tables, and several other more casual seating areas, all lit by suspended twinkling lights, tasteful candlelight, and eons of fragrant lilies. It looked like...well, it looked like a wedding. Except all of the extremely wealthy guests milling around the party were also wearing white, not just a bride.

"I still don't know what the point of this is," Skylar said. "An annual party where everyone wears something virtually guaranteed to stain by the end of the night? Why?"

But I was too entranced by the scene to make snarky comments with her. "Because it's beautiful, Sky, that's why," I said. "And because they can."

"Jane?"

I turned to find Celeste de Vries being wheeled slowly toward us by Garrett, dressed in his customary black tails. Like everyone else, she was completely decked out in white, a frothy confection of breezy silk that matched her curled white wig and satin slippers. Tasteful diamonds swung from her ears, matching a delicate pendant at her neck. Her gray eyes—so like her grandson's—sparkled sharply under the night sky.

"Good evening, Mrs. de Vries," I said, fighting the urge to bow to the clan matriarch. "You look a vision tonight, if you don't mind me saying."

I held out my hand. For a moment, she examined it, and then accepted it with a light squeeze before letting it go.

"Your hair," she remarked. "It's..."

"It needed an update," I said, patting it again. "I thought with the wedding coming up, perhaps something more...classic...was in order."

She looked at me with something approximating approval. "Indeed."

"Have you seen Eric?" I asked. "Is he down yet?"

Celeste nodded, though she still seemed to be absorbed with my new appearance. "Yes," she murmured. "Just by the dance floor. I believe he was looking for you."

"Thank you," I said. "And, Celeste, thank you for sharing your party with us this evening. I couldn't imagine a better way to celebrate my engagement to your grandson."

Skylar looked at me curiously.

Celeste nodded again. "Indeed," she said. "I couldn't agree more."

She ordered Garrett to wheel her to another set of guests, and I watched them until Skylar elbowed me in the side.

"Ow! What?" I rubbed my ribs. "Do you have knives on those things or what, Sky?"

"Look," she said.

I followed her hand to where Eric and Brandon stood next to one of the drink bars, both of them tall, blond, and filling out their clothes better than just about any other men at the party. Both held drink glasses—Brandon a brown liquor, Eric with his standard vodka martini. But while Brandon was busy chattering away, Eric didn't seem to be listening. Instead, he was staring at me.

In a sea of white, he still managed to stand out. Tall and lean, with his blond hair combed back from his face, Eric was the picture of summer in an Italian-cut, white linen suit and matching shirt, cognac-colored wingtips, and blue-gray tie around his neck. Everyone around him seemed to disappear into shadow as I approached. The man gleamed. An angel in white with a deliciously dark interior. But really, even that part of him glowed to me.

"Jane," he said with a small shake of his head. Tentatively, he reached out for my hand. I let him take it, absorbing the warmth of his fingers, the familiarity of his touch. It was innocent, but carried so much. Brandon and Skylar glanced between us.

"Should we go check on Jen and Luis?" Brandon started to ask, but Skylar was already tugging him away.

I turned to Eric. "You, um, you look really nice."

Eric pulled on his tie—the tie I had bought him just last week. "I had some help."

I smiled. He smiled back. Both of us were so unaccountably shy.

*Just say it!* I wanted to yell. *Whatever you want to talk about, just say it!* Was it because I was afraid he would ask to go back to what we once were? Utter those three little words he had said before? The ones I had fled with such terror?

*I won't run this time.*

Wouldn't I?

Slowly, he lifted my hand to his lips and pressed a sweet, slow kiss to my knuckles before pulling me close.

"You're a fucking vision," he said, his voice humming. Then his finger tipped my chin to look at him straight. "And don't let anyone make you forget it."

I pressed my lips together, afraid that if I opened them, I'd kiss him right there and wouldn't be able to stop.

"Thank you," I whispered.

Eric just smiled, and I felt my whole body glow like one of the twinkling lights above us.

"You know, we actually are supposed to dance at these things," Eric said, somewhat jocularly as he set his martini glass back on the bar. He tipped his head toward the dance floor, which was currently populated mostly by people over the age of fifty-five.

I bit back a smile. "Senior special?"

His own smile grew in response. "I thought you liked going against the grain, Jane."

I full-on grinned. "Okay, but fair warning, twinkletoes. I have absolutely no moves."

At that, Eric yanked on my arm, sweeping me in a sudden arc against his chest. His other arm wrapped immediately around my waist. "Don't worry," he said as he started to move. "I'll lead. All you have to do is follow."

It was only supposed to be one dance, but it turned into two. Then three. As the big band behind us continued to play jazz standards and I increasingly suspected I was living inside an F. Scott Fitzgerald novel, Eric moved me around the dance floor with sure, graceful steps, not even making a sound when I stepped on his feet. Twice.

"I didn't expect it," he said as he turned me under one arm and caged me against his chest.

"Expect whaaaat," I drawled as he flung me out with a smirk before pulling me right back. I felt like a rag doll—and I kind of loved it.

"How well you fit here," he said. "In this life."

I glanced around. "You're kidding."

He shook his head, and the overhanging lights twinkled in his eyes. "I'm not. You do, Jane. Pink hair—well, used to be pink hair—and all."

I scoffed. "Skylar said the same thing. Weird."

"Well, she would know. She still struggles with this world. You...I don't know. I'm impressed."

I considered the events of this morning. Over the last few months, his grandmother and his family had been stiff, but never totally mean. They weren't the horror he had led me to believe caused Penny's death. Maybe the sand, the shoes, the little bit of hazing were just his family's way of welcoming me into the fold. Maybe tonight could really be the start of something special.

"I don't know about that," I argued, more for the sake of arguing than anything else. "Look around. I see maybe four other Asians, and everyone else who *isn't* white is the help, right? And no one here has pink hair, glasses, or anything else."

"Well, neither do you, now." He sounded almost sad as he said it.

I looked around. I looked at literally anything but him. But as his steps slowed to a gentle sway, I could feel that penetrating gaze of his aching for me to meet it.

"Jane," he said. "I..."

"May I cut in on your friend—oh! Oh, Jane, my goodness. Your hair!"

Eric and I both turned to Caitlyn, who looked stunning as usual in a flowing white gown covered with intricate beading. It brushed the tops of her French-tipped toes as she walked. It was very...bridal.

"I thought it was time for a change," I said, touching my hair.

"Jane likes variety," Eric said, pulling me back to his side when I tried to step away. "I like it too."

I looked up at him gratefully. His mouth curved into that smile I knew and...loved, once upon a time.

*Who are you kidding? Once? Try now.*

"Well," Caitlyn interrupted my internal dialogue. "The request still stands."

Eric blinked. "What request?"

"The dance, silly." She turned to me with shining eyes. "We learned together, didn't he tell you? Our parents made us take gobs of lessons when we were children, right, E?"

Eric just nodded. "That's right. I forgot about that."

I frowned. He *forgot* about "gobs of lessons?"

"Did I ever tell you about Eric's and my first kiss, Jane?" Caitlyn sighed. "When we were seven, the instructor taught us dips. And he surprised me—when we finally got it, he landed a kiss right on me." She giggled with the memory. "You know, for a long time, I was convinced he was my Prince Charming. Childish dreams, huh?"

I didn't say anything, fighting back the desire to scratch her perfect-looking face. But even worse—Eric didn't either.

Caitlyn held out a perfectly manicured hand. "For old times, Des?"

Eric looked at her hand. "Oh. Yeah, sure."

I watched, somewhat dumbfounded, as Eric's hand left my waist. Caitlyn winked at me and then allowed Eric to guide her onto the dance floor. The band was playing jazz standards, and he was actually a really good dancer. So was she. Whereas he had been leading me around in a tepid box step to avoid my two left feet, with Caitlyn, he could move freely around the entire floor to the point where eventually, people moved to the side to give them free rein. They twirled, spun, and laughed all over the floor.

"Don't they make a lovely couple?" someone whispered behind me.

"She makes *so* much more sense for him than that horrible pink-haired woman," replied another. "I wonder if that's why nothing has been formally announced yet. I haven't seen her, have you?"

"Celeste must be holding out," said the first. "I would."

And to my shame, I didn't turn around to correct her. Instead I watched, twirling the engagement ring that suddenly felt loose, as Eric's face continued to light up. Fought the dread rising in my belly as everyone clapped and closed around the couple at the end of the song. And stared, in horror, as Caitlyn leaned in and landed a kiss on Eric's lips.

"Jane?"

I turned. Skylar stood behind me wearing her own expression of concern.

"What is he doing?" she asked.

"I—I don't know," I said, realizing that a host of tears were threatening to explode. "Sky, I..."

She nodded. "Come on."

With my friend's arm securely around my shoulders, I was ushered through the party.

"Ah, shit!" I cried as I tripped over a chair leg. I caught myself on Skylar's arm, but in the process, one of my contact lenses fell out. "Fuck!" I shouted, catching the ire of a few older party guests. "My contact. Shit, I can't see."

"Come on," Skylar urged. "Let's get inside. You can get your glasses."

I followed her around people, but when we rounded a hedge toward the main house, Skylar dropped my hand. Half-blind as I was, I realized only too late why.

"SPLASH!" cried the little voice as they threw several containers of bright red paint at me.

I looked down and found my dress—my hand-sewn, personally designed, one-of-a-kind dress—completely doused. The thick paint, which seemed to be the kind kids used in classrooms, oozed down the white in thick, sanguine globs.

And I began to shake.

"Oh my *God!*" crowed a woman in a short sequined number as she teetered by on four-inch heels, escorted by yet another white-tuxedoed male.

"Wow," he said with a smirk. "That sucks."

"Cait is going to *love* this," she crowed, and they headed back into the party to spread the news.

I turned to Skylar, who only stood there, her hands over her mouth.

"Sky." I reached out. "Help."

She took my hand again, careful to keep a wide berth.

"No," I said, now choking on the sobs stuck in my throat. "Not—not the house. Too many people. And I'll—I'll get red everywhere." I couldn't bear for these people who seemed to prey on weakness like raptors on mice to see me crying.

Skylar glanced around. "Well, there's the beach. But, Janey, your dress—"

"Fuck my dress, Sky," I said. "Just get me out of here."

"Jane!" Eric's voice called as I turned back to the crowd, doing my best to ignore the increasingly audible laughter as more and more people caught a look at my dress. The world was half-blurry with only one contact in.

I looked at Skylar, unable to focus. "I'm going to run," I said. "Please keep him here."

"What the hell!" Eric shouted. "What the fuck just happened? Who did this?"

"Jane," Skylar's voice floated up from somewhere, but I couldn't tell, as it was swallowed in laughter.

Here I was. Jane Lee Lefferts.

Half-Korean daughter of Yu Na Lee and Carol Lefferts.

Lawyer.

Seamstress.

Smart-mouth.

Laughingstock.

I just shivered, no longer able to hear the laughter or Eric's shouts over it. And then I took off toward the beach.

# TWENTY-FIVE

"Jane!" Eric shouted, his footsteps thumping over the grass after me. "JANE!"

*No.* The voice inside whispered, yet somehow was louder than the sobs I could no longer stop. I swiped viciously at the tears, kicking off my shoes so I could run. The party—the lights, the music, the cackling voices—fell away as I approached the beach, diving into the narrow path that ran through two grassy dunes toward the open ocean. The paint on my dress dripped all down my legs and my feet. I looked like the victim of some heinous crime. Maybe like a woman who had just had a miscarriage, or suffered something even worse.

*Penny in the tub.*

I had never seen what the girl looked like when she ended her life, of course, but I'd imagined it plenty of times after Eric told me. Too late, I wondered if this was all a threat. Harbingers of things to come if I continued to sully this world with my messy, imperfect existence.

Either way, I was a disaster. Anything but the impeccable vision of pristine, perfect white the evening was supposed to be. I didn't belong here.

"What are you doing out here?" I cried over my shoulder, though I didn't stay for an answer.

I didn't want Eric anywhere near me. I could easily picture him, storming behind me in his linen that never wrinkled, hair perfectly combed. Eric. Mr. Poise. Mr. Together. He was everything I wasn't.

"Go!" I cried, flapping my hands at him as I ran. "Go dance with your Lucy. Go back to those people. Go back to where you belong!"

But he didn't listen. His feet pounded through the sand, urging me in front of him. So I kept on. Past a rickety white fence marking the path through the dunes. Past the rows of driftwood swept in from previous storms. I ran clumsily, kicking up sand until I reached my goal and pelted straight into the water.

"Goddammit, Jane!"

Eric's voice was broken, and I glanced behind me for just a second to find him dancing along the shore as the ocean crashed in front of him. I had long since lost my other contact lens, and now he was a blurry mess as he started taking off his shoes, hurling them, along with his jacket, onto the dry sand behind him.

I turned back to the waves. Everything seeped into everything else. Even me.

"Fuck! Jane, WAIT!"

*No,* I thought as I floundered farther into the chilly ocean. If this would keep him away, I'd do it. I didn't care about the fact that the salty Atlantic was ruining yards of gorgeous fabric. That red was spilling out from the skirt like ribbons of blood or that the new black dye would probably run off my scalp in torrents. Every part of me was basically being robbed by the ocean. And it could have it. I didn't care anymore.

Was this what Penny had felt like? She had done this for years, not months. How many times had she been sabotaged this way? High school...college. She and Eric had been together a long time. I wondered vaguely if she had only considered suicide after they got engaged, or if it had started before then. If these people only let their crazy out when their property was truly threatened.

The ocean came up to my chest, pulling hard, splashing on all sides. For a second...just a second...I wondered if I should let it take me too.

"Jane!"

Just as I reached the edge of the sandbar, my arm was grabbed from behind, and I was jerked back. Eric found his footing and pulled me close, anger splashed across his beautiful face right along with the surf. His shirt and pants were ruined as well, the pure, wet white completely transparent in the night. His five-o'clock shadow glimmered under the starlight.

"Oh, God," I whimpered as I crumpled against him. He was so warm, a solid island in this frigid sea. "Why? Why did you follow me out here? Did you come to see me fall to pieces too?"

The anger melted off Eric's face, but instead of being replaced by his normally cool mask, all I saw was sorrow. Pity. I hated it.

"I'm sorry," he called over the surf. "I'm sorry I ever brought you here. You don't deserve this. What those jackals did to you. I'm sorry I ever asked you to do any of this, Jane."

His regret, his utter realization that I was so wrong for this place in spite of what he said earlier, broke me even more. The sobs crashed through me right along with the surf, and I fell backward into the waves.

"Jane!"

Eric dove after me, catching me under my back and lifting me above water. When we emerged again, we were both soaking, our white finery pasted onto our bodies, a watery parody of silk and linen.

"Let me go!" I screamed. "I don't want to do this anymore! I don't want to be a sideshow! Some freak your family will titter about over Manhattans for the next twenty years. Some fucking lark for *you* while you're presiding over your fucking company! You can take your twenty million and shove it because I'm *done*!"

"Is that what you think I'm going to do?" Eric yelled. "You really think that's what I think of you?"

"I don't know *what* you think of me anymore," I sobbed. "You're so hot and cold. You're nice one day, and like an ice cube the next. But you were straight with me from the beginning, Eric. You asked me to do this because I'd piss off your family, and I can take the abuse, right? Well, turns out you were only right about one of those things. Because I'm not fucking cut out for the other. I'm just not!"

"That's fucking it." When I tried to turn away, he reached out and grabbed my wrists, holding me in place so I couldn't run. "Listen to me, goddammit!"

My face turned from side to side, a pathetic headshake. He shook my arms right back.

"Jane," he said. "Jane, look at me!"

His voice commanded me to stop. And damn me...I did as he ordered.

His gray eyes were big. So open. So wide.

"Why do you think I call you pretty girl, Jane?" he asked. "Why?"

The tears poured. The ocean and I were one. I could feel nothing else.

"I don't know," I wept. "I never knew. Was it a joke? I know what we look like together. We are the oddest couple in the entire fucking world. The freak and the playboy. It's like pairing Jackson Pollock and Leonardo da Vinci; e.e. cummings and Shakespeare."

"But it's all still art, Jane. It's all still poetry."

I shook my head. "It's too different. *We're* too different. I'm not good enough for this world, Eric. For—for you."

In my mind's eye, I could see my father shaking his head. He would have never allowed me to talk like this.

*Oh, Daddy*, I thought. *Where are you now?*

"Goddammit," Eric said again between rough, harsh kisses that scraped up and down my neck. "You never fucking listen, do you? You never see what's in front of your fucking eyes."

"My eyes? My *eyes*?" I laughed, the sound choked. "Do you not see what I did for you tonight?"

I yanked on his hair, forcing him to look down at me. His expression razed everything.

"Look at you," I continued. "You're perfect. You're *so* beautiful. But me...there's too much ugly in my pretty."

"If that's really what you thought, you haven't been paying attention," Eric cut back with a face full of fire.

"Wh-what?" I asked, disbelieving.

"I call you pretty girl," he said slowly, "because you're fucking magnificent, Jane. The best things in the world aren't perfect. The most beautiful things have a little bit of dirt."

"Stop." Every touch of his was splintering through me. Every word shattered.

But he didn't stop. Instead, he framed my face with his big hands, diving deep with his stormy eyes and holding me still. "I call you pretty girl because you've *always* been a work of art to me."

I searched his face for evidence of a joke, anger, *something* that would show me that truth I knew to my core: that he was lying. That he had never thought of me that way and never would.

I was nothing to him. A bit of fun, right? Just a challenge, entertainment at best.

But there was no sign of anything other than concern. Adoration. Maybe even...love?

He pulled me closer, dragging me through the water, and bent down.

"D-don't," I whispered.

"No," he said, his voice somehow low, but still thundering over the surf. "I'm done respecting your fucking boundaries when it comes to this. You want to walk away from me after tonight, Jane, *fine*. I won't come after you. But I'm not letting you go without telling you in no uncertain terms that I'm in love with you. I'm crazy about you. I knew the second you walked into that fucking bar, all the way back when we were practically just kids, that you were the only one for me."

I shook my head, teeth chattering. "N-no. It's not true."

"It is true. You stunned me then. You stun me now. You'll stun me every day for the rest of my life, because it's not what's on the outside that does it, Jane. It's what's in here. You're not just my pretty girl. You're the most beautiful fucking person I know, inside and out. And I *love* you. I never stopped."

My mouth dropped. I hadn't dared hope for those words for years, and now here he was, saying them out loud. And I couldn't believe it. "No, you c-can't."

Eric's face was fire. "Don't tell me what I can't do."

And then he kissed me again. Despite the cold water washing over us both, the kiss burned, through the waves, through my clothes, down to my toes that were starting to numb, to my fingers that began to wrinkle. It was a kiss that seared straight to my soul, branding me the way that only Eric de Vries could ever do.

I kissed him back. I did more than kiss him back. I opened myself to him for the first time in years—maybe ever—letting him inside not just my heart, but my soul too with every biting, nipping, tongue-deep kiss we gave, awash in each other just like the waves all around us.

"Come," Eric said after he had taken his fill again and again. And before I could answer, he bent down and slipped a hand under my knees and swept me into his arms to carry me back to the beach.

"Seriously?" I joked, unable to help myself even though I was still hiccupping through my tears. "We're going to damsel-in-distress this moment? I can walk, you know."

"Jane," he said, not yelling, but not particularly gentle either. "Shut up."

So I did, while he carried me out of the water, hoofed us both back up to the beach while streams of water fell from my drenched clothes. The red paint blended onto his immaculate whites, turning us both aglow in rosy pink to match our chilled skin.

In our frenzy we had been washed at least a hundred feet down the beach. The party glowed in the distance, but we were out here alone with nothing but the stars and the ocean to witness this moment.

"Come here," Eric said as he dropped to his knees, laying me carefully down on the hard, semi-wet sand, just a foot or two from where the surf washed up around us.

"Are you going *From Here to Eternity* on me, de Vries?" I teased, though I feared he would say no. I felt so fragile I would break if he even took one step away.

"Hush," he said as he covered my mouth again, then reached down and literally tore my skirt apart, one wrenching rip up the center so that I was bared to him completely from the waist down.

"I need you," he said. "Every fucking inch of you, pretty girl. No arguments."

His words, seemingly cold and harsh, were naked with their truth. He didn't just want me. He needed me. Like, I realized, I needed him.

"If that's how it's going to be," I said as I fingered his sopping wet shirt, "then it's my turn too."

I grabbed the collar of his shirt with both hands. Eric met me with another bruising kiss. I bit his lip. He groaned. And I tore his designer shirt open, scattering buttons into the sand.

"Fuck!" he shouted as he collapsed over me, his desire throbbing through his wet clothes. His fingers dug into my hips as he ripped my underwear off, and he bent, burying his face between my legs.

"Jane," he breathed. And then he feasted.

"Ahh!" I cried toward the sky as his tongue began to explore. He devoured me like a starving man, licking and sucking, teasing that most sensitive spot, lifting my hips to him as if I were being served on a platter. I arched back, taking his sweet torture. The world was open and wide around us, and yet I could sense nothing but this moment, his touch, his mouth,

And then, I couldn't take it anymore. I needed more than just one part of him. I needed all of him.

I shoved hard on his shoulders. He fought it for a moment, wanting to continue his work. But then he sat up, eyes gleaming, full mouth glistening.

"Come here," I ordered, pulling on the soaked tie that still collared him in spite of his open shirt.

"*Don't* tell me what to do," he snapped again, but covered me nonetheless. My hands slipped all over his dripping wet chest, his body glistening under the moon. Eric was a star, shining in the dark.

"Eric," I whispered, unable to think anything else but his name.

"Come here," he whispered, "my pretty, luminous, fucking beautiful girl."

He reached down and released his cock, hard and long against my thigh. And before I could say anything else, he slid home, filling me completely with his light, his love. With all of himself.

His name was lost on the waves as I called it again and again, a cry as guttural as the gulls flying over us, as the roar of the ocean crashing on the beach, just as he crashed into me.

"Say it," he demanded as he drove us both closer and closer to home. "Say it, Jane. I need to hear you say it too."

When I didn't respond, his movements stopped. I moaned my discord. Eric pushed up on his elbows so I could see his face clearly. The moon cast a shadow over the square lines of his jaw, the hollow of his cheeks, the straight line of his nose. I stared, transfixed. Because if I was a work of art, then this man was an utter masterpiece.

"Say it," he whispered again. "Please."

I opened my mouth. There was nothing else I could do but obey.

"I love you, too."

Eric shuddered. And then he drove forward with a howl as ancient as the world itself. The abyss we had both dug for years opened up between us. And we toppled into it together.

# TWENTY-SIX

The entire beach, up and down every dune, was dark before we returned to the house that night. Or, as we both suspected, morning, since the sun was starting to glow by the horizon as we stumbled down the path again.

Now both of us were a muddy, sandy mess. My hair was a water-logged, salty, sandy black-running disaster, and even Eric's short hair was still plastered with sand too, along with his now-sludge-colored pants and demolished shirt.

"Celeste," I said. "Do you think she's mad we ran off?"

"Honestly," he said, "she's probably more upset that we weren't there for the announcement."

I looked up. "You think she still made it?"

Eric nodded. "If there's one thing I know about my grandmother, Jane, it's that she hates missing her schedule." He gave me a curious look. "Actually, I think she likes you."

I blinked. "You know, for a while, I thought so too." I looked down at my skirt. A lot of the paint had been washed away, but there was enough of a stain that I still looked like an accident victim. We both did. "Now I'm not so sure."

Eric grimaced at the remnants of paint. "I'm sorry about that. We'll figure out who did it."

"It's okay," I replied quietly. It wasn't, but I wanted to move past it. The closer to the house we came, the more mortified I felt, remembering how I had broken in front of all these people. Why had my bravado deserted me when I needed it most?

"It's not," he said. "They're fucking vultures. And I'm sorry you've been alone with them for so long. They don't deserve you."

He stopped walking and pulled my hand to his lips, feathering over my knuckles and lingering over my ring.

"We could bypass the house completely," he said. "Hijack my uncle's car again and take off for the city. No one would even know we were gone until morning."

I giggled. "We'd probably ruin the interior in these wet clothes."

"I'll buy him a new one." Eric smiled wickedly as another thought occurred to him. "Or you could just take them off. I wouldn't mind looking at you naked for a few hours back to the city."

I had to clear my throat as his teeth lightly bit my knuckles. The thought was tempting. But before I could answer, a bit of light glinted at his neck. A necklace I hadn't noticed before when we were caught in the throes of passion.

"What's this?" I asked, reaching up to touch the small medallion hanging from a thin gold chain.

It was also gold, so it shined despite a layer of grime of the type that took years and years to build. It looked like a coin, but not one I had ever seen before. There was a man with two faces looking in either direction, each side wearing identical laurels. Likely a facsimile of something Greek, or maybe Roman. But very unlike Eric, with his penchant for more modern fashion.

Eric stood up straight again, then covered my hand—and the pendant—with his. "It's nothing," he said. "Just an old necklace I found in my dad's things."

I frowned. "I didn't think you were into antiques."

In return, I got a bright smile. "I guess I've been surprising you a lot tonight, haven't I, pretty girl?"

The name reignited the embers in my belly all over again. "I guess you have, Petri."

He slung a heavy arm around my neck and pulled me into his side roughly. "You're going to pay for that later."

The fire in my belly glowed. "I love you, Eric."

He looked down with genuine surprise, but I found I wasn't. The words were already out there. The dam had been breached. And now it was easy to identify that warm feeling that spread through me whenever he was around. It was simple. Love. It just was.

*Glad you finally figured it out, Jane Brain.*

My heart twisted a little at the echo. If only Eric could have met him. Dad would have liked him, I'm sure.

Still wrapped up in each other, we trudged back onto the lawn, where the remnants of the party were still being dismantled. The band and guests had long since gone, the caterers had packed everything up, and right now the dance floor was being taken apart, piece by piece, under the still-glowing lights strung from pole to pole.

"Well, this thing is definitely toast," Eric remarked, shaking his waterlogged Rolex.

I looked at it sadly. It was a very pretty watch. "Can I have it?"

He looked at me strangely. "What for? There's no way it's going to work again."

"It's still a beautiful watch. And I don't mind things that are a little broken."

"Is that so?"

Eric stopped in the middle of the grass. He turned to me while he removed the expensive timepiece from his wrist.

"Consider it yours," he said with a quirk of his mouth.

I watched as he slid it over my wrist and fastened it there. It dangled loosely—Eric's arms were much bigger than mine—but his large hands wrapped around it, clasping it into place.

"Jane Lee Lefferts," he said softly with shining eyes. "Will you marry me?"

I looked up. Would this man never stop surprising me?

I genuinely hoped he never would.

"Ah, I think you already asked me that question..." I said, but the joke was cloaked in a whisper.

He massaged my hand between his two, brushing his thumb over the shining black diamond on my ring finger while the other held the oversized watch in place. Of the two, the watch seemed more important.

"I did," he said, and when he looked up, his eyes glittered like the stars in the sky. "But I'm asking again. No contract. No time limit. Just me. Just you. Will you marry me?"

For several moments, I couldn't speak. Aside from this ridiculous agreement, I had never really considered marriage, and I was sure that Eric hadn't either. We weren't the marrying type...were we?

"Eric, are you...are you sure?" I looked down at my ripped skirt, which I had clutched in one hand to keep the wind from blowing the fabric apart. I grappled for each rented side again, not particularly caring to show the remaining waitstaff my newly waxed nether regions.

But instead of answering my question, Eric sank slowly down to the grass on one knee and spoke.

> All that touches us, you and me,
> takes us together, like the stroke of a bow,
> That draws one chord out of two strings.

His deep voice sang through the air, holding me still with its lyrical quality. He took a deep breath. "That's Rilke, you know."

"You never give it up, do you?" I jested lightly.

Eric stood back up, and his arms folded around me. This time, I didn't fight it. I was too relieved. Too starved.

"It means, 'what speaks to you here, speaks to me. It's always been, and always thus will be.'"

I tipped my head. "More Rilke?"

For that, I was rewarded with a distinctly crooked smile. His long nose touched mine, and something in me exhaled. "De Vries."

I opened my mouth, prepared to launch a new quip. But none came out.

"But...but look at us." I gestured down at our ruins. My shredded, stained clothes, his torn shirt. The sand that plastered everything. "It's one thing to love a mess, Eric. It's another to pledge your life to it."

But Eric's smile just broadened, that curious smile that lit up his face and turned it into something truly extraordinary. "I want to make a mess with you for the rest of my life, Jane," he said. "Not just for the next five years. For always." He leaned down. "Say yes," he said, his salty lips cool against mine.

I inhaled his fresh scent. I could stay here forever.

*Well, then. Why don't you, kiddo?*

It wasn't exactly my father's permission, but it was the closest I'd ever get.

I blinked. My eyes watered again, but this time with tears I had never known before: tears of happiness.

"Yes," I whispered as I pulled Eric close. "Yes, I will marry you."

———

SOMEHOW, we made it all the way back to the house, arms all around each other, laughing and whispering as we stumbled across the lawn, catching the curious glances of the staff members whenever we paused for another kiss or brief tumble.

"Upstairs," Eric murmured against my lips as we turned one corner toward the stairs of the west wing. "I need a shower more than my life right now. Preferably with you in it."

"Oh, really?" I said, though I couldn't stop stealing kisses for myself. "And what are you going to do up there?"

"Well, first I'm going to wash the sand out of my ass," he said, suddenly walking a little bow-legged, as if to emphasis his discomfort. "And then I'm going to make you pay, like I said."

"Pay? For what, Petri?"

"For all those fucking years without you." He delivered a loud smack to my ass that echoed up and down the marble halls. "And for that stupid goddamn nickname."

"Oh, come on, my little test tube. It's cute now." I bit my lip with glee. "You'll never be rid of it."

I jumped as his hand found my ass again with a loud, wet slap.

"Just try it," he said with a steely look that made my stomach flip in the best possible way. "Say it again and see what happens to you, pretty girl."

I opened my mouth, enjoying the look on his face as he waited for the words to drop. Dared me to say them. Challenge him.

"Whatever you say," I said. "Petri di—"

"Jane?"

I jumped in Eric's arms, then whirled around toward the familiar voice. Eric stilled and looked over my shoulder.

"Who is that?" he asked.

My vision was still blurry—only Eric, close as he was, was crystal clear. The rest of the house, cast in the shadows of early dawn, was still unfocused, and so was the small figure slowly walking down the steps of the grand staircase.

But I still would have known her anywhere.

"*Eomma*," I said softly. "You made it."

One, two, three more steps, and she stood at the bottom so we were eye to eye. Close enough that I could see she was wrapped in her favorite mauve robe, the terry cloth one that was frayed at the bottom because she rarely bought anything new for herself. Her makeup, however, was still done, and her short black hair was neatly combed. I wondered then if she had ever gone to sleep. And without her daughter there to greet her.

Some daughter I was.

"Jane," she said. "I arrived at nine, but they said you were gone. Where have you been? What happened to you?"

My mother's gaze traveled over my wrecked dress, my wet, faded black hair, my uncharacteristically makeup-less face, now that it had all been washed free with sand and ocean. Concern radiated from her tiny body.

"I—we—"

My head hung. I didn't know what to say. All I could feel was shame. How had they treated her? I didn't even want to imagine how she had fared at the party without me.

I could imagine her in the hired car, face full of shock as she had rounded the circular driveway and taken in an estate overrun by rich, white, gleaming people. I had told her about the party, but who knew if she had come dressed for it, scatterbrained as she was these days. Who had welcomed her? Had anyone brought her to her room? Told her what happened to me? Made her, the mother of the bride, feel at least somewhat comfortable in my absence?

Or, considering the company, very uncomfortable?

I was a terrible, terrible daughter.

"Mrs. Lefferts." Eric's voice was stiff and polite as he stepped around me, gracefully pulling his torn shirt closed. He walked with his shoulders straight, head tall. Like the aristocrat he was, no matter the mess. He held out a hand. "I'm Eric de Vries, Jane's fiancé. It's... it's a pleasure to finally meet you."

Yu Na's sharp, quick gaze traveled over Eric too, taking in his height, his bearing, his clothes, and resting on his face.

"I'm so sorry we weren't here to receive you properly," he continued. "You can blame it on me for distracting Jane. I was—she was—" Unable to procure a decent excuse any better than I could, he shrugged boyishly. "Sometimes we get a little wrapped up in each other," was all he could say with a sheepish smile. "Your daughter is very absorbing."

I grinned.

But my mother wasn't amused. "This party...this house...it belongs to you?"

She wasn't asking because she was impressed with its size, though she likely was. It was more because she wanted to know he was for real. She had been shocked when I'd informed her over the phone of the pending nuptials—even more when I told her who Eric actually was.

Eric smiled. "It is, Mrs. Lefferts. And Jane's too, soon enough. Which, in a way, will also make it yours."

My mother turned to me with even more shock. Clearly she hadn't really considered what "billionaire" meant when I told her about Eric's company. She didn't have internet. She probably had thought a shipping company was just a bunch of trucks rented out to Walmart.

"I'm so sorry we weren't around, *Eomma*." I reached for her arm, but she shied from my touch. I couldn't lie. It hurt a little.

"Did my grandmother make the announcement?" Eric wondered. "We weren't here when that was supposed to happen either."

"Yes," my mother said numbly, her eyes still fixed on Eric. "She did. Everybody drank champagne and laughed. Because you were not there."

My face wrinkled, and Eric swore lightly under his breath. Of course they laughed, the overgrown hand puppets. Of course they all thought it was just *hilarious* that the bride and groom had gone missing for the big announcement. I'm sure Celeste was pleased with us as well.

But I didn't care about that right now. All I cared about was the reaction of the only other person in this castle I could call my blood. Things between Eric and me were finally real. I didn't have to lie to her anymore. About any of it.

And so, I desperately needed to know:

"Is that...is this okay, *Eomma*?" I ventured.

At first, she opened her mouth, and I knew she would say yes. Eric had charmed her the way only he could, and there was no way my mother would ever disapprove of a life that would keep her and her only daughter in comfort many times over.

But then her eyes landed on the pendant swinging from Eric's neck. As he leaned over, the light from the first rays of the sun caught on the edge, sparking in the middle of the empty hall.

My mother's eyes widened.

"No," she said, shaking her head slowly, back and forth, stepping back on the stairs. "No, it is not."

# PART FOUR

## THE RELEASE

*Her eyes are moons,*
*glassy and bright.*
*Her body, a cross,*
*shimmers in light.*
*Slung on the floor,*
*a hand, a blight,*
*drips love, adored.*
*Oh, bloody night.*

"Elegy"
—from the journal of Eric de Vries

# INTERLUDE III

"**O**kay, Mr. de Vries. Hold still."

Eric looked down at the tiny tailor who was currently adjusting the hem of his tuxedo pants for the last time. Maceo had been flown in just for today to finish up the custom Ferragamo. It was against the house's policy to let anyone but his staff work on the couture, but Eric didn't give a shit. Maceo had been adjusting his inseams for ten years. He was the only one who knew how to give the hems of his pants just the right break.

"Sorry, Mace. Do what you need to do."

The wedding was in one week. Somehow in the two months since the white party, everything had fallen into place. Everything was ready for what really *had* turned out to be the biggest day of his life.

Well, almost everything.

Eric pulled out the small Moleskine notebook from his jacket pocket and reviewed the latest iteration of his vows. Even though he and Jane had agreed they wouldn't write their own vows, he still couldn't stop scratching them out. For what, he didn't know. It was just something he had to get out.

So, he'd been trying to write them since that last night at the Hamptons, before he and Jane had stayed up for several more hours trying to convince her mother he wasn't a malicious monster out to ruin her or her daughter.

That fucking necklace. He'd taken it on a whim after going through his father's things. His mother had presented him with the box a week before the engagement party. The last remnants of a man long dead. The golden heir to the de Vries family whose legacy Eric had inherited the second the sailboat was pulled into the storm.

*Things to wear for the wedding,* she'd said. *Things he'd want for his kids.*

It was clear from her face that she didn't want them anymore.

He had recognized most of them, of course. The diamond cuff links. The wide gold wedding band. The collection of tie clips. Taking them felt morbid, but at the bottom of the box was the necklace—an actual gold Roman coin bearing the double faces of Janus on one side and its motto on the other, strung with a thin gold chain. *Noctis silentio tuetur.* Silence protects the night.

Maybe it was because he wanted to assure himself that he was doing the right thing. That he could tell the society he had done his due diligence when he ran several different background checks on Jane, even hired a private investigator to dig up anything about her and her family. There was nothing, of course. Jane was quirky, but other than having a string of boyfriends that Eric wouldn't have minded squashing under his thumb, she was clean. And so were her parents. Yu Na was a housewife and sometimes nail technician. Carol Lefferts had been nothing but a mild-mannered VA psychologist.

Eric winced, as he did every time he thought of Jane's deceased father. There was a part of him that hated doing this without either of their fathers there. Mother was no help at all. She had no thoughts about Jane—really, she had barely any thoughts about Eric's life at all. She was no longer a de Vries, and Celeste made sure she knew it.

But Jane had loved her father, just as Eric had loved his. He wished desperately he could have met the man when he had the chance. He would have liked the approval of the first man in Jane's life.

And so, thinking of his own father and his promise to Janus to learn about his bride's supposed shortcomings, Eric had lifted the medallion out of the box and clasped it around his neck. And it had been fine until Yu Na had seen it.

For the rest of the night, he and Jane had talked in circles trying to convince her mother that he wasn't some terrible person out to hurt her daughter. She had insisted on leaving immediately, and so, as soon as Jane and Eric had changed out of their clothes and packed their things, the three of them had taken a car sometime past five back to Manhattan. Yu Na never explicitly said the name Janus out loud, but Eric would have wagered half his fortune that she knew what it was. Or at least knew *something* about it. Enough to be scared.

———

*"EOMMA, this is ridiculous. It's a necklace! It belonged to his father. That's all."*

*From the armchair in their suite, Yu Na turned to Eric with wide dark eyes. It had taken all of their patience to get her back upstairs, since at the first sight of the stupid medallion, she had demanded a cab back to the airport.*

*Eric eyed her from his seat on the matching sofa. He was desperate to get out of this sandy, chafing mess, but instead he had to sit here and take the third degree from Jane's mother while Jane herself tramped around like an extra from the* Night of the Living Dead. *She still looked beautiful, of course. That dress, which had been unique and stunning, just like her, when it was dry, was somehow more tempting when it was pasted on her long, lithe body like papier-mâché, its ripped, stained skirts notwithstanding. With her newly dark hair slicked back and the last remnants of her makeup ringing her eyes, Jane looked like some kind of gothic maiden about to be consumed by a monster. Eric shifted uncomfortably and looked away. It would really be better if he didn't have those kinds of thoughts at the moment.*

*He turned and found Yu Na eyeing him again. Fucking hell, the woman could probably disintegrate a statue with that stare. He was learning very quickly where Jane got her stubbornness. Yu Na didn't let go of things any better than her daughter. She looked a lot like Jane too, though shorter and more compact. Jane's height, Eric thought, must come from her father's side of the family.*

*"Where did he get it?" she demanded for the fourth time. "The father. It's bad luck, a two-faced demon around your neck. Bad luck to wear that for a wedding. Where did he get it?"*

*She asked him repeatedly, never satisfied with his answer of "I don't know" or "his jewelry box." Because he couldn't tell. He couldn't breathe a fucking word of Janus to anyone. Bad things happened to people who did.*

———

IN THE END, Jane, in her ignorance, had done the lion's share of the work for Eric. She had pointed out all of the antique attributes of the necklace, demonstrating her handy knowledge of fashion as she pointed out the other qualities of the chain, the setting, and the other things that clearly made it a valuable piece of vintage jewelry, not the marker of a dangerous man.

"It's an heirloom, *Eomma*," she kept saying. "I bet it's been in their family for generations. Like the locket you gave me from Korea, right? Do I know everything about it either? I can't even read Korean!"

With every statement she made, Eric felt a curious mix of gratitude and guilt. For Jane's safety, he chose to focus on the gratitude. And somehow, everything had come back together, right down to Yu Na coming around on him, even before she went back to Chicago later that week. She had stayed in the apartment on Seventy-Sixth Street with them, watching Eric like a hawk in the mornings and the evenings—did the woman *ever* sleep? She was always up before him and the last in the living room when he went to bed—but otherwise spent her time with Jane and Celeste as they continued to plan the wedding. Jane took her to several tourist destinations around the city, and by the end of the week, Yu Na seemed plenty pleased about her daughter's sudden nuptials.

But every now and then, even on the last day, her gaze would linger about two inches below the half-Windsor knot Eric preferred. And Eric would blink and smile blandly, trying not to press his hand to the spot where his necklace still hung.

In the weeks following the white party, the news of Jane's embarrassment had also spread like wildfire, of course. They'd never figured out who told the kids to throw the paint. Caitlyn and Nina swore up and down that it wasn't them or any of their friends. Eric, for his part, believed them both. Grandmother just seemed too frail these days to have much of a taste for masochism, and she seemed just as upset as Eric when she finally understood what had happened. Besides, Nina's style was more cutting comments than outright sabotage. And Caitlyn had never seemed anything but nice to Jane. Eric couldn't believe it was her.

And so, because of the lack of resolution, Penny had been haunting his thoughts more frequently these days. Everything seemed to be building, but it didn't feel like a celebration. It felt like a storm.

"It just needs to be over," he said as he looked at himself in the mirror. "We just need to move on."

"I'm sorry, sir?"

Eric looked down at the tailor at his feet. "Sorry. Nothing. Everything all right, Mace?"

"It looks good to me," said another voice behind him.

Eric frowned at the tailor. "Who is that? The shop was supposed to be closed." It was one of the perks of being a black card carrier—being able to shut entire stores down to do things like this, even when you wanted to bring in your own tailor instead of using theirs.

"Hello, Triton."

Eric's eyes narrowed as Jude Stevens, otherwise known as Hermes to those in the Janus Society, appeared behind him in the mirror.

"Jude. What are you doing here?"

Jude shrugged his wide, sloping shoulders that were neatly clothed in a crisp gray Oxford shirt. He looked like any other businessman on the street just getting off from work. Eric knew he was not. Jude's family was in trade, mostly with Southeast Asia. Hence the supply of Thai girls for the Portas meetings, among other things.

"What else?" he said. "I'm here on business, Triton."

Eric tensed while Maceo looked up quizzically.

"We're not supposed to use those names outside...the gate, Jude. You know that."

Jude shrugged again. "He won't talk. And apparently, neither will you." He looked sharply over the tuxedo. "You were supposed to call it off, Triton."

Eric turned to the tailor. "Mace, would you excuse us for a few minutes, please?"

Casting an irritable look at Jude, the tailor nodded and obediently left the room. Eric waited until the heavy door to the boutique's office slammed shut before turning to Jude.

"You told me to be careful. Not to call off my fucking wedding."

"I thought the implication was clear. Your little concubine isn't what she seems."

Eric narrowed his eyes. "I looked into it. I couldn't find anything. Her life is pretty simple, and her parents are spotless. More than yours. How does your dad like being disbarred, by the way?"

Jude's eyes narrowed. Neither he nor anyone else in the Stevens family enjoyed talking about his father's disgrace. Owen Stevens was one of several lawyers convicted for insider trading a few years back in a major scandal on Wall Street. He had not only had to serve eighteen months at the Suffolk County Jail, but was also stripped of his license to practice law.

"My father's...disgraces...have nothing to do with yours. Or hers."

"And what exactly has Jane done?" Eric pressed. He remained on the tailor's stand, giving him a solid six inches over Jude's six feet. "Top-performing student. Northwestern and Harvard. Straight and narrow prosecutor. Oh, wait. Maybe *that's* why you don't like her. Think you might follow in your dad's steps, Jude? Well, she's not at the DA's office. Yet. You still have some time."

Jude rolled his eyes. "I assure you, that's the least of my worries."

"She doesn't even have pink hair anymore," Eric said. "I don't see a problem."

He smirked. Jane had promised to dye at least some of her hair back before the wedding, provided it wouldn't be damaged too much. He really *had* been upset when he saw what she'd done to it. It wasn't that the black didn't look good—she looked as beautiful as ever, to the point where, over the last two months since the engagement party, he could hardly believe she would really be his.

But it was true. Somehow, this wild creature would soon belong to him.

Jude showed no sign of letting up as he pushed off the mirror.

"I'll say it clearly," he said. "So there's no confusion. This is straight from Carson. Do not marry the girl, Eric. She's off-limits. Literally anyone but her."

But that was precisely the problem. There was no one but Jane.

"No," Eric said simply. He couldn't be clearer than that.

Jude's generally placid face tensed. "If you don't, Carson is going to get involved."

"Let him."

Jude stepped back, worrying his jaw as he examined Eric anew. "I see." His tone was calm, but the man's expression had assumed a new, almost metallic countenance.

Eric didn't like it. Especially since he knew exactly what kind of attention he was begging for. Carson was a bully, used to having his way.

*For Jane*, he thought to himself. He needed to think of something for her.

"Look," he tried again, affecting a more jocular tone. Jude was the kind of man who wanted in his heart for everyone to think he was their friend. "There's got to be something. Jane is just a woman. Carson doesn't need to be bothered with her. There has to be something he wants. Shares, maybe?" He could hardly believe he was trying to barter his fiancée's freedom with whole parts of the company, but here they were.

Jude's brows crinkled as he looked Eric over, as if he were trying to determine whether or not his proposal was real.

"No," he said. "I don't think so."

"Come on," Eric tried again. "There has to be *something*. Carson isn't completely unreasonable."

A slow smile spread across Jude's face. "That's a thought," he said to himself before looking back at Eric. "There's a shareholders meeting next week for DVS, isn't there, Triton?"

Eric frowned. "There is."

"You're going to announce something. A merger. With one of the Indian shipping conglomerates, rumor has it."

Eric's frown intensified. "I can neither confirm nor deny that, Jude. You know that."

Jude crossed his arms and leaned against the tri-part mirror, affecting a smug grin. "Maybe you should. Maybe if you did, and *maybe* if you informed Janus of which company it's going to be, that would be enough to convince Carson to let off. He's fairly attached to this issue at the moment, but fortunately *this* particular knowledge might convince him to...lighten up."

"That's...isn't that exactly what sent Owen to jail, Jude?" Eric asked, his mouth suddenly dry. "I'm surprised you're even asking me this." He glanced behind them. The fire door was still shut behind Maceo.

"Oh, Triton. We do a lot of things within Janus that would send many of us to jail if this was a fair world." Jude rapped his knuckles on the side of the mirror. "Lucky for us, it's not." He tipped his head. "I suppose it really just depends on how much you love the girl. How much she's worth."

Eric swallowed. The coin around his neck hung heavy. The small book of vows in his hand was even heavier.

"All right," he said in the end, because there was really no other choice. "But do *not* write this down."

# TWENTY-SEVEN

"I don't think that's going to work," I said to Gemma as I pointed to a particularly bad combination on the seating chart. "I'm all for integrating the families, but we can't have my mother's cousin from Seoul sitting next to Eric's great-uncle Rufus. He's a World War II vet who still uses the term 'Jap' in polite company." I didn't mention the fact that Rufus had, within my hearing, also asked Eric if he *really* wanted his babies to have yellow skin. Yeah, I was marrying into a real treasure trove.

My wedding planner nodded. "Keep the racist uncle away from, well, everyone." She switched the sticky note bearing Rufus's name with Eric's deaf second cousin, Marcia. "That ought to do it. So, have you and Frederick finalized the look for the big day?" she asked with no little glee.

I nodded. Frederick was *very* mad at me for destroying his beautiful dye job with boxed crap and had insisted on coming out to fix it before the wedding. I was glad, and so was Eric, who had also insisted that I at least put some color back in.

"It wouldn't be you without it," he'd said.

I had to agree.

"Freddy's plane arrives at nine tomorrow morning. Then he'll fix my hair, and we'll do the dry run before Skylar picks me up for the bachelorette party."

Gemma sighed. "I'm jealous. But you just leave everything to me. Sunday is going to be perfect, I promise."

Before I could answer, the front door of the apartment opened, and Eric swept in along with the last remnants of an Indian summer. A couple of orange and red maple leaves fell from his shoulders as the door swung shut, and his golden hair, which had been growing, stuck out a bit, like he'd been running his hands through it. He looked disheveled. And delicious.

"Hey," I greeted him. "How was the fitting? Did Maceo finally get your hems the way you want them?" I said it as a joke. Eric had generally been pretty laissez-faire about the wedding with every aspect except one: his tux. The man was an absolute tyrant when it came to fit, and he literally had only one tailor he trusted with any of his pants.

But he didn't answer as he dropped his briefcase on the ground and stripped off his jacket. I watched with some concern as he yanked on his tie and let the custom Armani fall to the ground.

"Bad commute?" I tried again.

"You," he said as his eyes found me. In five long steps, he strode across the living from and pulled me from my perch by the breakfast bar, wrapping me up in a kiss that blacked out the room completely.

Five seconds later, he released me, both of us breathless.

"Well, hello to you too," I said, pulling playfully on his tie. I wiped the remnants of my lipstick from his mouth with my thumbs, though I almost didn't want to. I sort of liked the look of his lips post-ravishing.

At last, Eric's mouth quirked to one side as he pressed his forehead to mine and exhaled through his nose.

"You smell good," he said. "Like silk and lavender." He inhaled deeply.

"Rough day?" I murmured.

"You have no idea." His gray eyes closed for a moment before he stood up and turned, somewhat sheepishly, toward Gemma. "Sorry about that. I, ah...just needed a moment with my fiancée."

Gemma didn't exactly look put out by the display. "I think that's my cue to get out of here for the night. Jane, I'll run the final seating arrangement by Mrs. de Vries, but I think we're all set. I'll have your dress sent to the apartment tomorrow morning so you and Frederick can make sure your hair matches the dress."

People have no idea what goes into a multi*million*-dollar wedding. No. Idea.

I nodded. "Sounds good, Gemma. Thank you for everything."

"You know, I have a talent," she replied as she packed up her stuff. "In the days before the wedding, when it's all stress and no fun, I can always tell who is going to make it and who isn't." She winked at us both. "You two have the goods."

Eric's arm tightened around my shoulders, strong and possessive. I hummed into his side. I couldn't help it. I was all gooey and lovey these days.

Since the white party, things had been good. Really good. Eric had gone on an absolute rampage after we returned to the city trying to find out who told the kids to dump paint all over me, but no conclusive answers were found, so we let it go. And in the meantime, we had assumed a somewhat normal rhythm—he went to work and the gym while I spent my days sewing, half-heartedly studying for the next New York State bar exam, and wedding planning with Gemma. We barely even fought anymore—or if we did, it was on purpose. Like when I called him Petri dish, and he said I looked like Joan Jett (why he thought that was an insult, you tell me), and we ended up naked on the kitchen counter.

The only thing was...well, when I dropped that piece of pasta on his shirt, I had expected something more than being pinned to the table, you know? At least a swat on the ass. Maybe a few restraints. The man was a genius with his hands (and tongue), but I hadn't seen his creative side since...well, since that night in Boston.

The door slammed shut behind Gemma. Eric turned to me with steel in his expression.

"Hungry?" I asked, batting my eyelashes.

"Starving." He grazed his mouth around my jaw, and his teeth worried my earlobe. "I want to put this fucking day behind me."

I inhaled sharply. "I just ordered Thai. It'll be here in about forty minutes."

Instantly, I was lifted off my stool. "That's enough time."

"Time for what?" I asked coyly. "I'm game, but you should know I just had my nails done today. I don't want to fuck them up."

I was joking, of course, but he seemed a little tense. Okay, a lot tense. Which only made it too fun to mess with him.

Eric carried me into his bedroom—well, ours, now that mine mostly just served as a closet—and dumped me unceremoniously on the four-poster bed.

"Hey!" I scrambled up indignantly. "What's with the sack-of-potatoes treatment?"

He yanked his shirt out of his pants. "I'm not really in the mood for jokes tonight, Jane. Right now, I just need you naked and willing."

"Well, I hate to tell you, but dumping me around like farm produce isn't the best way to achieve your goals."

"Deal with it."

"Hey!"

A second later, I was flat on my back, and Eric had pounced on top of my legs, trapping them between his strong thighs.

"I need to know one thing," he said crawling over me.

"Wh-what?"

He stilled, pinning me into place with his body. "Are you worth all this bullshit?"

"I..." I honestly didn't know how to respond to that. Where was this coming from?

Eric exhaled. Then he pushed himself up. "I'm going to grab something from the closet."

"Is that so?"

He turned from the doorway to his walk-in, shirt open and his tie hanging down both sides, framing a set of tantalizing abs and a chest that looked like it had been chiseled from marble. I drooled.

"Just sit up and get undressed, pretty girl. Otherwise there are going to be fucking consequences."

*Oh.* We stared at each other for a full ten seconds as his tone sank in. *He* was back. Not mild-mannered Eric, but Mr. de Vries.

Well, fuck me silly. Or at least, I hoped he would.

I cast my eyes down, almost by instinct. "Of course, Mr. de Vries."

"Good," he grunted, and left.

When he returned, I had shucked my comfortable red harem pants and black tank top. Eric strode back into the room wearing nothing but a pair of black boxer briefs, holding his tie and something else in his other hand.

He eyed me. "I said your clothes were supposed to be off."

I looked down at my plain black bra and underwear. "They are off. These are underwear."

His eyes flashed "You're always misbehaving, aren't you?" he asked. "You make everything harder than it has to be."

I screwed up my face. "I do not—"

"Don't fucking argue with me," he snapped with a sudden smack on my ass.

I stilled, enjoying the thrill that ran down my spine.

"You going to behave?" he asked, his voice low and foreboding.

Slowly, I nodded.

"Safe word?"

I rolled my eyes. "They shouldn't really call them safe words anyway, considering people use them when they don't feel the slightest bit safe. They should be called 'stop words.' Because when you use them, you should want everything to stop. And if I wanted that, I wouldn't be here in the first place." A thought occurred to me. "Maybe you want to stop. Maybe *you* need a safe word."

Suddenly, Eric's breath was hot against my ear, as a hand wrapped lightly around my neck.

"When did I *ever* want to stop with you?"

I opened my mouth to argue...but found I couldn't. At least not when we were here. Not when we got going. What made Eric and me so fucking infuriating in real life was electric in bed. Or the foyer. Or the living room couch.

"Erie," I whispered. "As in the lake."

"Good girl," he murmured. The hand at my throat released, slipping over my shoulder and down to stroke my ass, my legs, then disappeared. "Now come here."

Obediently, I rose from the bed and came to stand in front of him at the foot. He turned me around so that I was facing the bed, him at my back. His hand swept my hair around one shoulder, giving him access to the other side.

"Don't fucking move unless I tell you," he warned as he pulled my arms behind my back. With quick, sure movements that I could easily imagine him practicing at the gym with all those ropes, he tied my wrists together, binding them securely at the small of my back, then gently turned me back around to face him.

"Kneel," he ordered.

"But—"

Another quick smack landed on my ass. "What did I fucking say?"

"Okay, okay!"

Another smack. That one tingled. I quickly sank to my knees and watched as Eric pulled down the elastic band of his briefs. His cock fell out, heavy and waiting. I licked my lips. He hissed.

"Open your mouth."

His face glowed in the cool city lights shining through our window. It was the only light in the room. I obeyed, savoring each inch as he fed himself into my mouth.

"God, you're so fucking beautiful like this, you know that?" he whispered. "With your eyes all big, my cock between those luscious lips." He pulled out, then slowly slid it back in with a shuddering breath. "Fucking stunning."

I moaned, sucking on him like candy. He pushed in further. In and out, slowly fucking my mouth. I wiggled on my knees. I loved this, but I wanted more.

His fingers lightly slapped my cheek. "I said don't move."

I stilled, obediently letting him take his pleasure. There was something about seeing the raw desire etched across his chiseled face, ruining the careful mask he wore most of the time. I might have been the one on the floor, but we both knew who was really in control here.

Eric pulled out. "Get up."

Silently, I rose on unsteady legs.

He took my jaw and kissed me, long, languid, even lovingly before he bit my lip sharply enough that I winced. A pang of desire stole into my belly.

"Open your mouth," he said quietly. My lips were already open, but I widened them. Eric held up the other thing he had retrieved from the closet.

"A ball gag?" I smirked. "What else have you got hidden back there?"

"One day, maybe you'll find out," he replied as he held it up. "I find myself...browsing for things..." One blond brow quirked. "Just for you."

My mouth dropped further. Eric smiled, removed my glasses, and placed the gag in my mouth.

I stood patiently as he buckled the soft leather around the back of my neck. It wasn't uncomfortable—the ball was fairly small with a few breathable holes through it, and the leather harness was soft enough that it didn't cut into my skin.

"Perfect," Eric said, satisfied.

I would have loved to make a comment about enacting the patriarchy by silencing his woman, but, of course, I was literally silenced. And really turned on.

*Oh, the irony.*

"On the bed," he ordered. "Head down. On your knees."

With a defiant look that was about all I could manage with my mouth plugged and my hands tied up, I turned to the bed and followed his instructions, kneeling on the mattress and laying my head to one side. The mattress shifted as Eric followed, taking his place behind me. His hand slid up the back of one thigh and then my ass cheek as he slipped a few fingers under the hem of my underwear.

"These," he said, "are going to have to go." And before I could nod, he ripped the thin cotton in half, literally tearing it up one seam.

"Mmmphm!" I cried out—or at least as much as I could.

Three hard smacks landed on my ass in quick succession, making me jerk. "Next time you'll do what you're told."

I stilled, closing my eyes as his hand slipped over my skin, soothing what now tingled fiercely. Lord, I loved his touch. Harsh. Soft. No matter what.

His hand floated lower, and one finger slipped inside my pussy, gliding in and out until my hips started to move with it. It felt good—*oh*, it felt good—but Eric wasn't in the mood, apparently, to let me off that easy.

His hand left. I moaned in disappointment.

Another hard smack. I jumped.

"I told you," he said as he seized a handful of my hair. "Not a fucking sound." His other hand left my pussy and slid under my chest to lift me so I was propped on my knees, balanced backward against his solid chest.

"Do you feel it?" he demanded between clenched teeth as he cock nudged my entrance, then pushed in, one solid inch at a time. "Do you?" He shook my jaw. "Yes or no?"

I couldn't talk—obviously—so I nodded fiercely. *God*, I felt him. I could feel nothing else.

He slammed in the rest of the way, tossing me forward but for his other arm caging me against him.

"Again?" he asked as he pulled out, slowly.

Again, I nodded violently. I wanted it as many times as he was willing to give it.

He lunged. I flew. He caught me. Again and again, just like he said, until we rocked back and forth together in a vicious, luscious cycle of power and play.

*Eric!* The shout rang through my mind instead of off my lips, condemned as I was to relative silence. But as if he could hear me, one hand gripped my hair and yanked me back against his chest so he could tickle those full lips against the soft skin just under my jaw.

"It's fucking killing me that I can't kiss you right now," he said, his voice gravelly, raw. "I want to mark these lips so no one else could ever fucking *think* of touching them." He released my hair and traced a finger around the top of my mouth. "So fucking beautiful."

In he slammed again, tossing me forward against his other arm. He rammed into me mercilessly, driving us both further toward that familiar cliff. My eyes squeezed tight, and I soon forgot all other obstructions. My bound hands ceased to matter, nor did the ball between my teeth. All I could sense was him. Feel him. Need him.

*Eric.*

And then, with a light slap, his fingers found my clit. Pinched. Rubbed. Squeezed.

Done. I was done as a muffled yowl erupted from the back of my throat, muffled by the gag but siren-like nonetheless. His name vibrated through me since I couldn't shout it aloud, and I fell forward as he relaxed his grip, collapsing onto the bed in a heap of shivers while wave after wave of my orgasm crested through me.

"Jesus, *Jane!*" Eric barked as he thrust forward again and again, his hand meeting my flesh in time with his ferocious thrusts until his body released its own fury. We both fell against the mattress together, shaking and groaning, the sweat glistening on our bodies as we melted into one indeterminate mass of pleasure.

Slowy, slowly, I came back to consciousness as kisses trailed over the back of my shoulders. My hands were released. I reached up to unbuckle the gag, but Eric was already there to free me.

"Thank you," he whispered as he lay his head on my breasts and inhaled, long and low while his hands stroked my skin, my naked body, memorizing its lines and curves. "I needed that."

I sighed and wove my fingers into his hair, cradling him close. "We both did," I replied. I had a feeling we probably always would.

# TWENTY-EIGHT

S ometime later, after a quick nap, a solid meal of chicken curry and larb gai, plus a second round of "Mr. de Vries Returns to the Upper West Side" (this time involving scarves instead of his tie, plus a riding crop he'd apparently been saving), I found myself lying in bed, watching the flickering lights of the city outside the big bay window as sleep closed in.

I was sated. Worn out. Completely and utterly blissed out on this man's chest.

Well, not completely. Something was still bothering me.

"Eric?"

The hand toying with my hair paused, then twirled another strand. "Mmm?"

"What was all that about?"

His hand stopped moving. "What do you mean?"

"Don't get me wrong. I loved it. Needed it. More, please and thank you."

Eric's chest rumbled with pleasure, and he smiled sleepily up at the ceiling. "I needed that too." Then he kissed the top of my head. "I think I need you, Jane."

He traced a finger down the line of my stomach and up between my breasts, cupping one lazily under his palm. I was glad he seemed to like them as they were. There wasn't much to enjoy, but he appeared to be happy with them.

"What happened tonight?" I asked quietly.

Maybe now that he had gotten his frustration out of his system, he'd actually talk to me. That was the one major issue with Eric. He never talked.

He sighed. "It's nothing."

I bit back a sharp retort, propping myself up on his chest to look straight at him. "It's not nothing. When you left this morning, you were basically a Wham! song. You were walking sunshine. You returned a storm cloud. Something happened."

His mouth quirked again. "You sound like an A.A. Milne story."

"I do not." I whacked him with a pillow, which he parried easily to the side, laughing. The sound warmed the entire room.

"You do. Winnie the Pooh and Tigger too, right?"

"Shut up!" I grabbed another pillow and smacked him again with it, but he tossed it away and rolled on top of me.

"Okay," he said as his mouth found mine. "I will."

I let him kiss us both breathless once more, but when he started to grind into me in that familiar way again, I pressed a hand on his chest. This wasn't sex as catharsis anymore. It was sex as evasion. And I wasn't okay with that.

"Eric," I said as gently as I could. "Seriously. What happened?"

He sighed, dropped his head onto my shoulder. "It really doesn't matter."

"Yes, it does. It matters to me."

He didn't reply for a while, and for an infuriating second I thought he might ignore me. But finally, he spoke against my neck: "Do you trust me?"

My hands wove into the short hair at the base of his neck. For some reason, the question sent a weird vibration down my spine.

Love, we seemed to have. We didn't say it all that much—neither

Eric nor I were particularly ooey gooey people. It wasn't one of those words I wanted to throw around all the time, like when you walked out the door or said good night. No better than a common greeting. I did love him—and that was hard enough to wrap my head around. But trust...I wondered if that part took a little longer to build than a few short months. Especially considering we had both sort of mutually agreed to sweep the past under the rug.

"I'm...getting there," I said honestly, wincing as I caught the hurt look on his face.

"Really?" he asked. "After all this time?"

I wanted to say no. I wanted to say everything was fine. That the past was in the past, and there was nothing to do about it. But he knew, just as I did, that eventually the bloom would fall off the rose here. Would he still be this devoted, this focused on us then?

Would I?

"I worry," I forced myself to say.

"About what?"

"About...you. Me. Us. Trying to do this whole 'for life' thing. What if...what if it's not enough? What if a secretary at your office starts to look better than the crazy chick you have at home? What if you pass one of the thousands of models who roam the streets of New York like antelope and realize you could do so much better? What if one day you want another red thong in your bed instead of plain cotton underwear?"

I gestured at the underwear now lying on his floor. Again, Eric jerked, like I'd just hit him in the gut. But he didn't deny the possibility.

"I'm sorry," I said quietly, looking away so he wouldn't see how much his reticence hurt. "But it's the truth. It's what I wonder sometimes."

He pondered that for a bit, but didn't stop touching me. I took it as a good sign.

"Okay, how's this for truth?" He kept his hand clasped in mine while he played with my engagement ring. The black diamond shone bright under the lamplight, an unlikely beacon. "I'm not exactly excited about the idea of your bachelorette party this weekend myself."

I frowned. "My bachelorette party? Why?"

"Because." His fingers tiptoed up my arm and started drifting over my lips again—they were, he'd told me, both his favorite part of my body and what aggravated him the most. "You and I used to be cut from the same cloth, weren't we? What were you doing in Marleigh's the night we got engaged?"

I avoided his gaze. We both knew what the other was doing that night. Eric had asked me to marry him—a fake proposal, but still a proposal—and not a week later, both of us were cruising for a hookup. Cut from the same cloth indeed.

"Did you...the past five years..." He worried his lips, trying to pick his words carefully. "Was it still like law school?"

We both knew what he meant. The two of us enjoyed reputations for being the most "fun" members of our little crew. Together, yes, but mostly apart. I had a different date almost every weekend. I don't know how Skylar put up with the merry-go-round of men that traveled through our apartment for those three years. She was a good sport. Half the time she helped me shovel them out the door.

Meanwhile, if I had a dollar for every girl I saw Eric leave with... well, maybe I wouldn't have had to get married for money. He had a reputation then and now as a genuine lothario. There probably wasn't a woman under the age of forty in Boston who didn't know his skills in the bedroom.

And yet, I wasn't going to apologize for my life or make him apologize either. Men have plenty of sexual partners, and they're praised for their virility. Women just get called sluts, and that I was not. I was single, young, healthy, and more interested in school than in a relationship. Why couldn't I have fun on my terms? Just like him?

Eric lay there without a shred of judgment on his face. I waited for it. It never came.

I swallowed. "Well, I mean, I was mostly single. And focused on work. So...yeah. Yeah, it pretty much was the same as back then. Mostly casual. A few short-term relationships, but nothing major. And nothing at all after my dad died."

"Nothing?"

I swallowed. "Wow, I guess we're really going down the truth rabbit hole, huh?"

He squeezed my hand. "Tell me."

I squirmed uneasily, but he wouldn't let me sneak away. "Well, after he died, the lights kind of went out, if you know what I mean."

Eric nodded with understanding. "Yeah. Grief can really fuck you up."

I squeezed my eyes shut. "Yeah. It can." Some people want to embrace life when they are close to death, but I just wanted everything to fade away.

*If you look for the clouds, pumpkin, they'll usually show up.*

I blinked. I wasn't hearing Dad's voice as often these days. It was almost like he was leaving me be, knowing I was finally in a good place.

"And after that..." Eric prodded.

I sighed, finally looking at him again. "Well, that was about the time you showed up at the salon, stalker. And then you were at the bar...it had been almost a year when we...at your apartment."

That crooked smile emerged. "Really?"

I hid my own grin. Unsuccessfully. "Don't be too proud of yourself. It would have happened sooner or later. You just happened to be in the right place at the right time."

But Eric just lay back, folding his hands behind his head looked *very* smug. "I brought you back to life, didn't I?"

"Stop."

He turned, eyes flashing with mischief. "You were a ghost until you met me, weren't you?"

"Shut up!"

Now he full-on laughed, then rolled over to cage me against the bed, framing my face between his forearms.

"I love it," he said gently. "You brought me back to life too, Jane. When I started at Harvard, I was so fucking angry at this world. But you...shit...I don't think I would have made it if I hadn't known you."

He delivered a sweet kiss and then rolled back to his side of the pillow, as if he knew I had reached my maximum capacity for mushiness.

"And what about since?" I asked, not wanting to be the only one humiliated here.

He blinked as his indiscernible mask resumed its place as he started playing with my hand again. "About the same as you, I guess. Without the nine-month grieving period."

This was uncomfortable. I had yet to meet a single man who could stand to hear about his girlfriend or significant other's sexual or romantic past. It was kind of sad, really. Here I was, lying next to a man with whom I was about to share a life. And I wanted it to be a *whole* life, I realized. I wanted him to know everything there was about me.

"What's your number?" I asked suddenly.

Eric's fingers froze over my knuckles. "Ah..."

"I'm serious," I said, wiggling my hand away. Eric took a firmer hold of my wrist.

"Jane," he said, looking uneasy. "You don't really want to know that."

I scowled. "Don't tell me what I don't want to know, Petri dish. Come on, now. I'm curious. How many, ah, specimens have you collected in your lab?"

"Jane."

His reticence, of course, only made me push harder.

"Thirty?" I asked. "Forty?"

His face remained blank.

"I'll tell you mine if you tell me yours," I offered.

At that, the mask cracked. One eyebrow rose. "Really?"

I nodded. "Promise."

He examined me for a moment, like he wasn't sure where this

was going to go. Then, with a regretful expression, he leaned down and whispered the number in my ear. My eyes popped open.

"That's *it?*" I yelled.

He fell onto his back looking embarrassed. "What do you mean, 'that's it?'" he asked. "I've been told by plenty of people that's quite a lot."

"Oh, do you go crowing your number out everywhere, Petri? Should I buy you a jersey so you can show it off around town?"

He just rolled his eyes. "Come on, Jane. You promised. Your number for mine. What is it, hot pants?"

"Hot pants?" I practically screeched. "That's what Hooters waitresses wear! What kind of nickname is that?"

He looked way too pleased with himself. "If you're calling me a fucking lab experiment, the least I can do is make fun of your underwear. You like those little underwear shorts—I'm pretty partial to them myself, by the way. I'll have to replace those ones I tore off you. But now that I know it bugs you, the name's here to stay, I'm afraid. So, come on, hot pants. Fess up."

I bit my lip. Now I really didn't want to tell him. But a deal was a deal, and I wouldn't back out now.

I bent down and whispered it.

Eric blinked, surprised. "No shit. You almost had me. Down by one, Lefferts. Nice."

I backed away. "Are you appalled?"

He frowned, shaking his head. "Why would I be appalled? Sort of the pot calling the kettle black, isn't it?"

"Well, maybe," I said. "But you can't be ignorant. There's this little thing called a double-standard in the world, and it's pretty fucking obvious when you compare men and women's sex lives."

Again, he just shrugged, in his fantastically privileged yet beautiful way of disregarding things he didn't personally find important. "We might have our insecurities, Jane, but I know one thing. I'm the best lay you've ever had."

Eric de Vries.

Cocky bastard.

Body for days.

Best I ever had?

I looked him up and down. *Oh hell, yes.*

His cocky smirk told me he could see my thoughts plainly.

"Don't worry," he said. "The feeling is definitely mutual, pretty girl."

I punched him in the shoulder. He just laughed and pulled me close.

"And the bottomfeeder in his Calvins?" he asked, recalling the visitor from that terrible day at my cousin's apartment in Chicago. "Where is he in your lineup?"

I swallowed. "Eric..."

"Out in the open, Jane. Like you said."

I stopped wriggling. "Fine. Um...about two-thirds of the way through, I'd guess."

"You don't know?"

I elbowed him in the gut. "Would *you*?"

He chuckled, then pulled me onto his chest, so he could stroke my back meditatively. I thought everything was all right until he spoke again. "You wouldn't...tomorrow night...you wouldn't want to get out there again, would you? See what other dirty jeans are left in the city?"

He was trying to sound light-hearted, but fear laced his words. The same fear that often struck mine. Was *that* what was driving all this delicious possession tonight?

I pushed up so I could look down at him directly. "Eric, you can't possibly think I would do anything like that now. Do you?"

*Of course he does. Just like there is still a part of you that wonders what he'll be up to this weekend too.*

"I didn't say it was a rational fear." With one hand, he toyed with a loose black wave that spiraled over my shoulder. "Any more than your fear of a red thong is rational."

"It *is* rational—" I started to interrupt, but he just shook his head.

"Jane, it's irrational because it's not going to happen, not because I don't get it. I saw your face when you found that shit. Just like I'm sure you saw mine when I found that jackass in your apartment." His expression stilled. "I'll never fucking forget hurting you like that, Jane. Never."

I swallowed. I remembered his face too. The gut-wrenching combination of surprise, fear, anger, and sorrow when he heard the voice behind me. And then the way he had processed it. Taken it in stride. Stayed, let me explain. And wanted me anyway, in spite of what I'd done.

Eric did always have more grace between the two of us.

"I'm sorry," I said honestly. I wondered now if I had ever said it. I was ashamed it was even a question.

He pulled me over him so I covered his beautiful body, splayed on his chest, nose to nose. "Me too," he said. There was no threat, no authority in his voice. Just plain adoration. Love.

That, maybe, I could begin to trust.

"You weren't my first," I said quietly as I lay back down on his chest. "But, Eric...I do hope you'll be my last."

His broad hands traveled up my spine, spinning locks of hair around his fingers and off again. "Me too, pretty girl. Me too."

# TWENTY-NINE

"Ah...*ah*...girl, stop *moving!*"

Frederick finished the last of my blowout, which he had curled into haphazard, tousled waves. It was my favorite kind of haircut since I had grown my hair out long—a little shaggy in the front so I could get my Chrissie Hynde on for a night out, but long bangs that would cooperate nicely with the formal updo I had to wear with my dress.

"You owe me so many cocktails after this," he informed me as he twirled the streak of deep, bright crimson he'd put at the base of my neck. "No one else but *moi* could have put this color back in your hair without making it fall out. Boxed dye. I still can't believe you would do that to my masterpiece."

"Well, it had been a few months," I protested as he brushed the cuttings off my shoulders and onto the living room floor before he spun me toward the large mirror mounted on one of the bearing pillars. "My roots were showing."

I didn't mention that I'd also bowed to the pressure to conform. Freddy, with his skintight vinyl pants and fifteen separate piercings—

two of which were currently evident through his shirt—wouldn't get it. It was funny. Once I wouldn't have thought I would get it either.

"Girl, isn't your man heir to the damn earth? The answer is to fly home and have me do it *right*."

Frederick finally pulled the cape from around my shoulders, releasing me from the chair while he swept the cuttings. I catwalked to the mirror over the fireplace, inspecting the cut. Some might say it was risky to get a haircut this close to my wedding, but this was Frederick we were talking about.

"You're right," I said with approval. "I should have come to you from the start." I turned around, practically skipped over to Fred, and wrapped him up in a hug. "Thanks, my friend."

"Girl, you know I got you covered," he said. "Just say you'll let me put you in my book, all right? And tell the damn papers *loud and clear*, okay?"

"What's she going to tell the damn papers?"

We turned around to find Eric entering the apartment looking as dapper as usual in a navy suit and bright blue shirt. I grinned as the fire in my belly lit all over again. I was starting to wonder if this would ever get old.

Then he frowned as he strode toward me. "What happened? Why is it still just plain black?"

"Oh, no, he did *not*..." Frederick murmured under his breath while he finished cleaning up.

"It's there," I said. "I promise. It's just underneath the black. I figured I wouldn't piss Celeste off *too* much."

"Let me see."

I pulled my hair over one shoulder to show him the scarlet stripe in the back. Eric reached out a hand tickling the back of my neck as he wove his fingers around the colored lock. He tugged on it a little, and his eyes brightened, clearly reading the thrill that traveled through my body.

"Well, that's some heat if I ever saw it," Frederick said as he started packing up his equipment. "Honey, is it all right if I leave this here for the weekend, or are we getting ready at the hotel?"

My eyes still glued to the man examining my hair like it was a deadly weapon, I shook my head—as much as I could against Eric's grip. He pulled tighter. "No, you can leave it here. We're meeting at the hotel, but I can bring it."

Frederick glanced between Eric and me locked in our silent standstill. "I better take it. Something tells me you're only going to remember every other word of this conversation."

Eric finally smiled. "You know, we could have our own celebration in here," he purred as he leaned in, tracing his nose down my bared neck. "Go out. Pretend we're still single. Give each other a solid one-night stand. Or three." His teeth found my earlobe. "Just like how we started, right?"

I shivered, but not because I was cold. Three days away with my friends or three days of pure sex with Eric? It *was* sort of the perfect way to get lost in each other, which we hadn't really been able to do...well, ever. Despite living with each other for the last several months, it still felt sometimes as if I was only getting to know him. His hours at the office took him away from the early morning until seven or later, even on Sundays.

But instead I pushed him away. "I think that's what the honeymoon is for."

In return, I received a sharkish grin. "Oh, I'm counting on that, Lefferts."

"Where is the big location?" Frederick asked as he finished. "Tell me it's Mustique or someplace like that, and I might slap you. The royals vacation there, you know."

I smirked as Eric hopped onto a bar stool behind me. This week, Freddy sounded almost more Scottish than English. Eric wrapped me in his arms, trapping me between his legs.

"It's not Mustique," he told Frederick.

"Good. If it was, I don't know if I could be friends with my girl anymore. Too fabulous. The envy alone might kill me."

"My uncle owns an island in the Bahamas, so we're going there," Eric offered, like he was presenting a different sort of cocktail when a standard martini was turned down.

If looks could kill, we would have been dead. I just giggled while Frederick shoved the last of his equipment into his bag, muttering something about "rich damn white people" and *Pirates of the Caribbean* under his breath.

"All right, baby cakes," he said as he headed out. "I'll see you Sunday morning, bright and early. We've got work to do, so make sure you don't party too hard this weekend, you hear?"

"See you, Freddy."

I accepted my hairdresser's kisses to my cheeks, and chuckled when Eric took one too. Frederick loved flirting—boys, girls, it made no difference. And Eric, unruffled as he always was, took it all in stride.

After Frederick left, Eric and I sat for a moment, enjoying each other's company in silence. It was hard to believe the big day was almost here. We'd have some time to celebrate our last bit of freedom, meet up for the rehearsal dinner on Saturday, and the wedding on Sunday. Both of us knew it would be a blur, so it was nice to have a second to decompress before the insanity really began.

But despite an entire night's worth of catharsis after Eric arrived like a storm cloud yesterday evening, I couldn't shake the feeling he was trying to chase something away through sex. His thirst was basically unquenchable last night—even after our little heart-to-heart, he couldn't be sated.

I closed my eyes with the memories. Hot wax. Cool breath. Eric was getting more creative, and I was responding.

He kissed me again, this time with a bit more urgency now that we had no audience. The tension from last night reappeared, and goose bumps appeared up and down my arms.

"There's more where that came from, pretty girl," he whispered before tracing my earlobe with his tongue. "I just need twenty minutes."

For a second, I forgot to breathe. But before I could answer, my phone buzzed on the counter. I checked the screen. "Too slow, Joe. She's almost here."

Eric swore under his breath. But then his phone buzzed too. "Fucking hell. Brandon just pulled up too."

"Can I just say, I think it's pretty funny that your former boss is your best man?"

Eric shrugged. "I have other friends. You've met them. But Brandon and Skylar are some of the few people who've known us through everything. I thought it fit."

I nodded. "It does. I'm glad."

After we grabbed our overnight bags and locked up the apartment, we walked down to the street hand in hand, ready to party until the rehearsal dinner on Saturday night. Brandon was taking the boys—which included Eric, a few friends of his from school and Boston, Calvin (Nina's husband), and a second cousin—to Vegas for the next few days. Skylar, meanwhile, hadn't yet divulged what she had planned for my big night(s). I just knew our party was somewhat smaller, with her and the rest of the bridesmaids: Suejean, our friend Cherie from Harvard, and Nina. Since Suejean wasn't able to take the time off for the bachelorette party, it was just the four of us.

It was such a strange feeling, I mused for what might have been the millionth time. All my adult life, I had been kicking men to the curb quickly—either I ran out the door, or they did. But with Eric, I didn't want to let go. I didn't like the idea of being without him for even a few nights.

I also didn't know quite how I felt about that, marriage or no.

Brandon was waiting outside a large SUV on the curb. His giant body (the man was built like a tree) towered over the top of the car while he chatted with Steve Kramer, one of our friends from law school.

"There's the man of the hour." He greeted us with his usual effusive charm, his slight Boston accent coming through. "Vegas, here we come. I got some serious shit planned, my friend. Jane, don't be surprised if this bastard doesn't remember half of the next few days."

"Just get him back in one piece, Sasquatch," I shot back, earning a dirty look from Brandon and a snort from Eric. I turned to my soon-to-be husband. "Have fun with the boobs and the prostitutes and the gambling. If you're smart, you should catch Cardi B. But really, try not to get chlamydia before our big day, all right?"

I tiptoed up and gave him a brief, benign peck on the lips, then turned quickly, not wanting him to see the genuine fear that had crept in. It was a joke, the Petri dish thing. That was all in the past now.

*Sure...*

"Jane."

Before I could step completely away, I was yanked back into Eric's arms for the kind of kiss that would stop traffic. When he was done, all my doubts had disappeared, and he framed my face with his hands, forcing me to look at him directly. Fear, yes, but mostly adoration shone clearly through those deep gray eyes.

"I love you," he said, serious and still.

I blinked away the tears that pricked suddenly. "Eric, I—"

"I know," he cut me off. "I just wanted to say it." He released my face and smacked my ass a little harder than was necessary, earning some laughter from the SUV. "Have fun. Don't do anything I wouldn't do."

I quirked an eyebrow. "So what does that really leave off-limits?"

Eric grinned as he backed away toward the SUV with a boyish shrug. I felt like the whole street lit up from his charisma.

"I'm not worried, pretty girl," he called out. "Because when I see you next, you're going to become my wife."

Before I could reply, a big black limo pulled up behind Brandon's car, and Skylar bounded out, a tiny ball of red-headed energy.

"Ah!" she cried as she caught sight of Brandon. "*How* did you beat us here? You had two other people to pick up, and we left at the same time!"

Brandon chuckled. Everyone did, actually. Skylar's competitive streak was legendary, as was the fact that she could never best her husband.

"Two words, Red," he said. "Express lanes."

Skylar groaned, then turned to me with a fierce hug, hard enough to lift me off the ground.

"Wha!" I cried. "Need to breathe here!"

Skylar dropped me. "Sorry. I'm a little excited. It's been a really long time since I've had a single night away from the kids *and* the ball and chain, much less a whole weekend."

"Hey, I'll show you a ball and chain," Brandon protested, but quieted when Skylar sent him a look. "All right, all right, we're leaving."

Eric waved, disappeared into the SUV, and we watched the boys leave before Skylar turned back to me.

I bit my lip with glee. "I cannot *wait* to see what you have in store, Sky."

She grinned. "Okay, but before we get in, I have to tell you something. I didn't really have a choice here, so don't get mad."

"Mad about what?"

"I had to ask—"

"Surprise!"

Skylar and I both turned to find the back window of the limo rolled down, and none other than the face of Caitlyn Calvert popped out.

"Jane!" she cried, as always, a little too happy. A little too thrilled to see me. "I hope you don't mind, but Nina said I could crash the party. Spa weekends are my absolute fave, and I haven't been to London in forever!"

I smiled as politely as I could before she slid back inside to gab with Cherie and Nina.

Skylar turned back to me with a less than thrilled look on her face. "Well, now that the *other* cat is out of the bag...are you mad?"

I shook my head, too excited to be pissed off. I knew my friend.

Inviting Eric's ex...whatever you'd call her...childhood bestie with a minor crush? Skylar wouldn't have done it without some pressure, probably from Nina and Celeste. But it didn't matter. Caitlyn was a harmless, pearl-clutching nothing. And nothing was going to ruin this weekend. I'd be sure of it.

# THIRTY

**M**y best friend knew exactly how to spoil me.

Two days later, Nina, Caitlyn, Cherie, Skylar, and I had crossed the Atlantic to good old London town, where we were pampered at a spa in Kensington, lounge-hopped around Notting Hill, went sightseeing and flea market shopping, before pub-crawling in Camden. Skylar rented a big townhouse in Notting Hill for our home base. We were constantly on the move, and I had three full days of bliss with my best friends doing all the things *I* loved.

It would have been great, if not for one thing.

Caitlyn freaking Calvert.

The girl would. Not. Stop. Complaining.

First, it was the house— "Oh, honey, if you'd just told me this was all you could get, I would have borrowed my aunt's flat. It's a penthouse right on Hyde Park, you know."

Then it was the spa— "Were we unable to get in at Madame Ducos's? If I'd known, I could have made a call. You really have to know someone to get in."

And then it was the food. The drinks. The shops. The streets.

Too salty. Too weak. Too cheap. Too dirty. For every idea Skylar had, Caitlyn had a better one that she would mention, but only after there was nothing to be done about it. The girl was the "should have" queen.

But more than that, considering how everything Skylar chose was so acutely tailored to my personal tastes (I happened to like pub food, cheap beer, and thrift shopping, thank you very fucking much), Caitlyn's passive-aggressive comments really seemed to be geared toward me.

By the time we settled into the third pub in Camden and I had put down my third Guinness, I was done putting up with the woman, done with the Upper East Side, done with doubting whether or not every move I planned to make was wrong. And I was *really* done with questioning why Eric—who had left with those three little words I always wanted to hear so much more than I let on—would want someone like me to begin with.

Done.

And so, more out of spite than anything else, after Caitlyn's final jibe about Camden—"if you'd only told me, I could have gotten us West End theatre tickets instead of winging it around these types"—I grabbed the first mohawked Brit in the bar and asked him where the best place was to go that night for a really great time. Which was how we found ourselves at the end of a particularly "dodgy" (in the words of Mr. Mohawk) part of Brixton, going to see the best Clash cover band I had ever heard. And that was saying something—I had a minor obsession with The Clash. The look on Caitlyn's face as we walked into a club full of punked-out Brits was worth every other second.

"I swear to God," Skylar muttered as we both watched Caitlyn tiptoe cautiously through the bar, as if she was trying to keep its inhabitants from sullying her cream-colored, Donna Karan sweater set. "If Miss Priss doesn't shut the hell up, I'm going to duct-tape those injected lips of hers shut."

I snickered. "I'll help you out, sis. Daisy Duck needs to be *quiet*."

Skylar laid her head on my shoulder. "I'm sorry I said she could come. I just knew you wanted to make good with your in-laws, and Nina really seemed to want her along. I think she's a little intimidated by you."

I considered Eric's cousin as she joined Caitlyn by the bar. I still hadn't gotten a good read on Nina despite the countless breakfasts, luncheons, or other little meetings we'd shared with her grandmother over the months. She mostly just treated me with indifference. She was polite, of course. Never rude. I also knew that she and Eric never talked unless they were at some of the few family events we'd attended through his grandmother. But I knew nothing of what kind of relationship they had, even before Eric had left his family.

Nina's pearl necklace glowed in the dark light of the club, and I couldn't help feeling a *little* satisfaction with how out of place she and Caitlyn looked. While Skylar, Cheri, and I were dressed for dirty dive bars in ripped jeans, greasy hair, loud mod makeup, and in my case, big combat boots, Nina and Caitlyn looked like they'd walked right off a Madewell catalog shoot. For the first time in months, I wasn't the odd one out. It felt...good.

The opening band kicked in as the crowd began to cheer. Nina and Caitlyn turned, clutching the rims of their vodka sodas like they had never held plastic cups in their lives. Skylar gestured toward the top of the club, where a number of tables were open. I nodded. Yes, that was a good idea. Nina and Caitlyn would probably enjoy looking down at everyone and cackling while Skylar, Cherie, and I danced below. Good for everyone.

On the balcony, we rounded into a booth. Nina examined the tabletop distastefully, and sat back as far as she could from its edge.

"This place is...an interesting choice," Caitlyn remarked as she looked around. "I wonder whether they have ever cleaned the floors."

"Here we go," Skylar muttered, though I elbowed her in the side.

"It's fun," I said. "This band is supposed to be great."

"I bet they'll be awesome," Skylar said. "Remember the band that played the night you and Eric became...you and Eric?"

I snorted. "Of course! How could I forget? That night was such a disaster."

"What happened?" Nina asked. She really hadn't said much over the weekend, but right now, she looked legitimately curious exactly about how I had ended up with her cousin. Eric and I had been feeding his family very blasé lines about meeting in law school, never really going into detail about those first, explosive interactions.

"Well, Eric and I were tagging along with Skylar and her husband when they were first dating," I began.

"Lord, I remember *that* mess," Cherie snickered, earning an elbow from Skylar. "What? You clearly ended up all right."

I giggled with her. "More than all right. They make everyone want to vomit. The man would run through fire for you without thinking twice."

Skylar just preened, looking more than a little self-satisfied. "Like Eric would for you?"

I blushed. Caitlyn looked like she wanted to throw her drink in my face.

"So anyway," I said, deflecting, "I had tickets to another Clash cover band in Boston and forced everyone to come with us," I continued. "But back then, Eric and I didn't really get along."

"Really?" Nina asked. "But he's so...well, everyone loves Eric."

There was something in her voice that didn't sound exactly happy about that.

"Everyone *does* love Desi," Caitlyn agreed, disintegrating the mood. "How could you not? He's an absolute doll."

Nina's expression turned blank. Not for the first time, I wondered how much of her and Caitlyn's friendship was sustained based on Caitlyn's fondness for Nina's cousin rather than because of Nina herself.

"I think you can love Eric without thinking he's perfect," I said. "I certainly don't. Actually, he's kind of an uppity pain in the ass a lot of the time."

"Poor Des. Must be hard to come home without anyone in his corner," Caitlyn said in a teasing tone that still managed to cut.

"Or maybe it's good for him," Nina said, looking at me with something approximating warmth. "Sometimes it's good to have someone in your life who humbles you."

Again, I couldn't help wondering why she thought so.

"Anyway...maybe it was the drinks," I said. "Or the music...or maybe it was something in the air that night. But for whatever reason, we couldn't stay away from each other. We kind of crashed. Or clashed, if you know what I mean." I winked. Okay, so it wasn't my best joke. But give me a break, it was my bachelorette party.

Nina offered a shy smile. Cherie giggled. Caitlyn looked disgusted.

"And it was meant to be," Skylar said, looking pleased with herself for saying so. "You guys didn't know it then, but you were so good for each other. Anyone could see it."

"But tonight's not about that," Caitlyn interrupted once more.

We turned to her, a little confused. "What do you mean?" I said. "It's my bachelorette party. We are literally celebrating my pending nuptials, right?"

"Silly me, I thought we were helping you bid farewell to this life-style. That's why we're here, isn't it? It's not like you'll be able to attend 'soirées' like this once you and Eric are married."

I frowned. "What do you mean? Eric doesn't care if I go out. Half the time he comes with me."

Caitlyn snickered. "You're joking. You realize that with Celeste's health the way it is, Eric will officially take her place on the board of directors at DVS, and from what Nina says, they'll vote him in as chairman on the spot. Isn't that right, Nin?"

Looking like she had sucked on something sour, Nina nodded, but didn't make eye contact with me.

"You can't possibly think that the chairman of a multibillion-dollar company could ever be seen attending this kind of establishment," Caitlyn continued. "For one, he'd be a major target of people like this."

A look at Nina and Skylar told me they both thought Caitlyn's assessment was correct.

"This family comes with a lot of...responsibilities," Nina admitted. "But you do seem to be doing well with them."

"Just keep the paint away from the kids, right, Jane?" Caitlyn jeered, earning a sharp look from Skylar that quieted her down. My best friend did have freaking daggers for eyes when she wanted to.

Cherie looked confused. "What?"

I shook my head. "Nothing, nothing." I was too worried about Caitlyn's thoughts to recount that terrible night.

"A game," Skylar announced abruptly, clearly wanting to help. "Jane loves drinking games—shut up, you do. We haven't played any yet, so let's have some fun, huh? Let's see, what's a good game?"

"Yes!" Cherie rejoined. "Let's do it!"

Caitlyn rolled her eyes.

"Relax, Sky, don't hurt yourself. I got this." I looked over my glasses around the table. "How about a little 'Never Have I?'"

"No!" Skylar moaned. "You *always* win that."

I just grinned. "Of course I do. But I'm the bride, and I get to choose."

"Oooh, yes," Cherie said, turning to Skylar. "I'm going to make you fess up, mama."

"What's 'Never Have I'?" asked Nina.

"Oh, N, it's that silly game where you say something you've ostensibly never done, and if other people have, they drink." Caitlyn looked at me. "Did I get that right, J?"

Again with the letters. It's the same number of syllables. Did she just not like pronouncing more than one consonant at a time?

"Yes," I said. "That's right. But let's make it more interesting. If you *have* done it, I want the stories. Sound good?"

Everyone around nodded their assent.

"Okay, I'll start," I said. "Never have I...been on a yacht."

Next to me, Cherie scoffed. "Girl, *please.*"

But Nina, Caitlyn, and Skylar (with a dirty look at me) all took sips of their cocktails.

"One of Brandon's friends at the Cape," Skylar muttered. She clearly didn't like being grouped in with the other wealthy women at the table, regardless of her and Brandon's money.

"Gosh, which time?" Caitlyn supplied, looking at Nina. "Both our families own them, right, Nin?"

Nina just nodded. "Our uncle took it down to St. Thomas last year, Jane. Otherwise I'm sure you would have seen it by now."

I nodded. Okay, so I hadn't planned on feeling like the loser on that one.

"My turn," Skylar stepped in again with a sly look my way. "Never have I...had a one-night stand."

I rolled my eyes and took a long drink of my beer. "You bitch. That's like shooting fish in a barrel."

Skylar just smiled smugly, and Cherie laughed.

"Caitlyn! Really?" Nina stared at Caitlyn, dumbfounded as her friend took a long sip of her drink.

"What?" Caitlyn said when she finished. "I can't have a little fun?"

"When was it?" Nina pressed.

I sat forward. I had to admit, I was kind of interested in hearing about Ms. Priss's escapade.

"It was...oh, I don't know, four or five years ago. Right after Grayson and I split. My second husband," she told those of us not familiar with her entire marital history. "Nina, it was when we went up to the Cape to stay with Kevin McCartney and his parents, do you remember?"

Nina nodded. "But...you were with me that whole week. When could you have had a one-night stand?"

"I went into Boston for the weekend, do you remember? I wanted to do some shopping on Newbury and meet up with a few friends. Little did I know, I'd do just a bit more than that."

"Who was it with?" I asked curiously.

Caitlyn smiled, looking very much like a cat who ate the canary. But before she could answer, the Clash band started to play below— beginning with a fan favorite that's pretty much guaranteed to get anyone to dance, "London Calling."

I jumped out of my seat. "Dance time, bitches. Come on, we're going. No excuses."

Nina and Caitlyn demurred, choosing instead to remain in the booth and watch while the rest of us piled downstairs as the crowd began to cheer.

"Oh, I'm going to miss this!" I shouted as Skylar, Cherie, and I started to get completely and totally down. I didn't have the best moves, but I had never cared about that when it came to The Clash.

"Janey, don't believe those bitches up there," Skylar called over the noise. "Eric knows who you are. He wouldn't want to marry you otherwise."

I shrugged, already getting lost in the music. I didn't want to think about that right now. I just wanted to have some fun.

"Wanna dance, love?" A hand slid around my waist, and I turned to find a cute, hipster-looking guy with thick glasses and ironic suspenders, grinning at me. "You got some moves," he said in the thickest Cockney accent I had ever heard. And this one wasn't fake.

"I don't think so," said a familiar voice. "She has a date. Doesn't she?"

I turned around to find the very last person I expected to see. Eric, glaring at the guy with a face like thunder, stood behind him, with Brandon and the other groomsmen flanking his sides like the cast of *Reservoir Dogs*.

"What are you doing here?" I shouted even as I threw my arms around him. He squeezed me tight, then kissed me, hard.

He looked tired and uncharacteristically rumpled in a wrinkled chambray shirt and black pants, his blond stubble having grown out over the last few days, and his normally combed hair a wreck.

Brandon shook his head as he greeted Skylar.

"Most desperate motherfucker I ever met." He picked up his diminutive wife for a kiss. "One game of craps, in and out of a strip club, moaning and groaning about Jane the whole fuckin' time until finally I chartered a plane just to shut him up."

She just smirked up at him. "I'm sorry, but how many times did I find you waiting for me in random places when we first met?"

Brandon just ignored her comment. "He was a mess. I've never seen him like this. Did you know Springsteen was playing at the Grand? I got us all front-row tickets!"

I couldn't hear what happened next, though I guessed it was some kind of snarky comment about Brandon's love of the Boss from Skylar the music snob. I was also too wrapped up in my own husband-to-be to worry about it.

"You came for me?" I couldn't *quite* keep the squeal out of my voice. This was supposed to be our last hurrah, but it was impossible to ignore the fact that I had missed my man. A lot.

Eric grinned, that curiously potent smile of his lighting up the dim club. He grabbed my waist and pulled me to him, his lips meeting mine in a haze of vodka and joy.

"What do you think, pretty girl?" he said, his voice scratchy from the effects of alcohol and lack of sleep.

"How many have you had?" I wondered as I traced his stubbly jaw with one finger.

"Enough to stop worrying about it."

I stepped back and looked him over. He did look a bit of a mess, but his eyes were sharp enough, and his smile was wicked. I sucked on the edge of my beer bottle meditatively. Yum.

"Jane, don't do that."

I sucked harder. Eric's eyes flashed.

He yanked me to him again. "If you don't stop, I'm going to dump that beer on you all over again. I can't believe you went out looking like this. Without me." Eric's eyes roved hungrily over my body, taking in the short black skirt, combat boots, and admittedly low-cut shirt I had worn for the night. Okay, so I wasn't exactly the picture of a prim and proper bride-to-be.

I pushed up my glasses and swallowed. Jesus, his gaze practically melted, it was so hot. How did he do that?

"Jane." Eric's hungry expression burned. Everything else seemed blurry. He didn't have to say anything else—his desire was palpable.

I grabbed the lapels of his shirt. "Come with me."

Eric followed me doggedly through the crowd, upstairs, and past the few remaining people still in their seats. We ignored Caitlyn and Nina's curious glances, and when Caitlyn shouted, "Hi, Des!" far too loudly, it was like she didn't exist.

Instead, we tumbled down a dark hallway, eclipsed by shadows as I tore at Eric's shirt and he ripped at my clothes. In less than five seconds, he had my skirt over my hips, I had his pants shoved down, and the man was inside me, pinning me against the wall while he rutted like an animal.

"*Fuck*, Jane," he choked into my neck as he sank in. "Fucking hell!"

"Shhh!" I admonished, even while my head was banging against the wall like a drum. "Oh my God, ohmyGod, *Eric!*"

His hands gripped my thighs like vises, spreading me wider, forcing me to take him as deep as he could go. And that was pretty damn deep. Like, to my limit. Eric wasn't a small man, if you catch my drift.

"Touch yourself," he ordered as he drilled into me. "Make yourself come, gorgeous. I'm not going to last long, but I can wait for you."

"Uhahhhh!" I moaned as my fingers found my clit and started to rub. Eric hissed as he sensed their presence. It was my gift, I supposed, that my pleasure seemed to intensify his.

"Do it," he gritted out. "Let me feel it. Come, pretty girl. Squeeze my dick as hard as you fucking can."

To other people, his orders might have sounded ridiculous. Cheesy. Completely unrealistic. But something about the vulgar words coming out of Eric's generally composed mouth undid me. Every. Fucking. Time.

"ERIC!" I shouted as a lightning-quick orgasm streaked through me, arching my body against the wall

One hand left my thigh, and before I could register it, Eric delivered a quick, sharp slap across my cheek. I shook that much harder, then moaned into his mouth when he kissed me, grunting, groaning, and shaking as he came too.

"Jane." The word was a shudder, barely anything more. My limbs turned to noodles as he ground out the rest of his release. There was nothing holding me up but him. His arms. His cock. His body.

And yet, in the back of a crowded club, in the darkness of this grimy corner, I had never felt more sated or more safe.

"That," Eric said as he finally released my legs to the floor, "was for going out in that getup without me. It's been too long. Not fucking fair, Lefferts."

I looked down as I pulled my clothes back into place. "This? You miss this?" I wasn't exactly the picture of beauty right now. More like a punk girl in mourning. Considering Caitlyn and Nina's comments earlier, it was more apt than I'd realized.

Eric tipped my chin up so I looked into his eyes, then delivered a soft kiss to my lips.

"This was who I fell in love with, Jane," he reminded me. He reached behind my head and pulled on a few strands of the new red streak. "Don't forget that, will you?"

It took me a second to regain my breath. I hadn't realized how much I needed him to say that until now. "Okay," I said. "I won't."

That grin reemerged—the one I was starting to think was now reserved only for me. Hmmm, maybe we could do round two right now.

"Come on," Eric said, grabbing my hand. "I hear our song. I want to dance with the hottest girl in the club."

"'Rock the Casbah' is our song?" I asked incredulously as I recognized the familiar keyboard licks. "Why? I know we were at another

Clash cover show when we hooked up, but why this one? It's not exactly romantic."

"No, it's not," he agreed amiably. "But it was the song that was playing when I realized how I truly felt."

"Oh." I couldn't argue with that. "Well, then, sir. By all means. Lead on."

# THIRTY-ONE

"Thank you for coming! Sky, I'll see you at the hotel in the morning, okay?"

I waved at the last of the bridal party who had attended the small rehearsal dinner. Eric wrapped his hands around my waist from behind, setting his chin on my shoulder as we watched our friends depart the private room of the Waldorf Astoria where Celeste had hosted the dinner. Outside, the lights of midtown Manhattan glinted like stars. Since Eric's arrival in London, I had felt nothing but the bright halo of love surrounding us. Now, less than twenty-four hours from the big day, we had to say good night.

"Finally," he said as he buried his nose in my neck. "Are we done with this circus yet?"

"Stop," I whispered, though I couldn't hide my smile. "People are looking."

Celeste glared disapprovingly from the far end of the table, where Garrett was helping her into her wheelchair. I was honestly surprised that she had even made it. Nina mentioned the night before that she had been upping her pain medications lately.

"Let them look," Eric responded as he continued to nuzzle.

"Also, I need a legitimately good sleep tonight. I have a whole styling team showing up to my suite for pictures in the morning, and I do not plan to have suitcases under my eyes for the *Times* style section, thank you very fucking much."

"Screw 'em," Eric growled. "Tonight's the last night I have a fiancée, and I'm being forced to spend it without her. These antiquated traditions are ridiculous."

I smiled, feeling my cheeks heat up at the idea of exactly what we could do to celebrate the occasion. Hmmmm. We'd spent the previous night in London reminding each other of everything in store for later, but it wasn't enough. Not nearly.

I turned in his arms. "I'll make it up to you when I'm your wife," I said, delivering a chaste kiss that seemed to disappoint him. "You get two weeks with me on that island. No work. No people. No annoying family. Just you, me, and whatever, ah, toys you decide to bring from the closet."

At that, I received a wicked grin. "I already sent a whole suitcase ahead of us."

"Ahead?" I gaped.

Eric nodded. "The second the fucking reception is over, we're getting out of here. No stops. I'm ripping that dress off you in the air, pretty girl."

I shivered at the idea. Mile high club with Mr. de Vries? *Yes, please.*

"Eric! Eric, do you know these men?"

We both turned at the sound of Celeste's withered voice that still managed to squawk. She looked very, very tired as Garrett pushed her around the table. She had taken to wearing a full nasal cannula extending from her nose and attached to her ever-present oxygen tank, and it looked like she had lost more weight. That didn't stop her, however, from showing up to each and every event in her Chanel finest. Tonight, it was a tasteful shift dress with suede pumps and the biggest diamond earrings I had ever seen. Begrudgingly, I had to respect the old sociopath.

Celeste de Vries was a grande dame in every sense of the phrase.

Eric turned toward the two men in beautifully cut suits who stood at the entrance of the private room. They looked about his age, with their wealth and, well, whiteness, practically glowing out of their perfectly tailored suits in the dark room.

One of them, whom I christened "Chad" in my head, raised his hand in greeting.

"Shit," Eric muttered under his breath. "I'll be right back."

Before he left, I tugged on his hand. "Hey. Everything okay?"

He reared back at me, almost as if he was startled by my presence. Which was odd, since I had just been wrapped in his arms.

"Go keep your mother company for a bit," he said, and strode toward the visitors without another look.

Frowning, I moved back to the other side of the table, where my mother was sipping on her cup of lukewarm green tea. She had been very quiet for most of the night, kept company primarily by Cherie, my second cousin, Suejean, and her mother, Ji-yeon, the only other family who had been able to make the trip here for the wedding. My side of the aisle was going to be woefully underrepresented.

"Did Suejean and Auntie leave?" I asked as I sat down.

My mother nodded as she folded and re-folded her napkin. "They went back to the hotel. I waited for you."

I nodded. "Thanks. I'll just be a minute. Eric is saying goodbye to some people, and then you and I can probably leave too."

She nodded again, but didn't say anything. I frowned. My mother was many things, but taciturn was not one of them.

"*Eomma*, are you okay?"

She looked up, as if startled by such concern. A pang of guilt shot through me—I hadn't been doing the greatest job of caring for my mother, had I?

"I just wished Daddy could have been here," I continued wistfully. "To walk me down the aisle. He would have liked that."

It was the one thing I had refused to be supplemented by the de

Vries family. Tradition dictated that *some* man be present to give me away at the altar, but the idea of one of Eric's uncles doing the job just seemed strange. The reality was, there was no one to give me away but myself. I'd walk that long line alone.

My mother just stared at her tea, looking troubled. I winced. I should have known better. Of course she was probably missing my father too. Christmas, birthdays. They had been hard for the last year, and would continue to be for a while, especially at major moments like this.

There was a scuffle at the far end of the bar.

"I *got* it." Eric floated above the fray, a little too sternly. "You can tell Carson to mind his own business, all right, Jude? This doesn't concern him."

My mother and I both watched as the other two gentlemen backed off, hands held out in a joking surrender. They spoke, but I couldn't make out what they were saying.

"You really love him?" she asked, almost hopelessly.

I nodded, focusing on the warmth that pooled in my belly at the thought of it. "I do, *Eomma*. I really do."

She sighed. It was resigned. Painful.

I tried to think of something to say that might comfort her obvious anxiety. She, however, was still staring at the men, one of whom was gesticulating wildly, baring a small bracelet with a gold token in the middle. Vaguely, I thought it looked a little like the medallion Eric wore on his father's chain.

Eric scowled darkly, then followed the men outside.

My mother stood up with sudden vigor. "Time to go."

I frowned. "*Eomma*, we aren't going yet. Eric will be right back, and then we can go to the hotel. I want to say goodbye to him first, since I won't see him until tomorrow."

"No," she said, turning to leave. "No, we have to go right now, Jane." But not, apparently, out the main exit.

"*Eomma!*" I shouted as she disappeared through the service doors. I took steps after her, but was stopped by Celeste's voice.

"Jane?" she called. "Jane, where are you going?"

"I'll, uh, be right back!" I called back to her before I followed my mother through the back entrance of the restaurant and into a deserted alley. I paused, looking from side to side until I spotted her small, solid form trotting down the sidewalk toward Times Square.

"Hey!" I shouted, jogging after her. "*Eomma*, wait!"

She slowed as I approached, but didn't stop walking.

"What is the goddamn deal?" I asked. "Where are you going?"

"Back to the hotel," she snapped. "And you should too. It's late."

"*Eomma*, stop. *Eomma*!"

I pulled on her sleeve, finally forcing her to halt.

"You cannot marry that boy!" she shouted before spouting a torrent of Korean.

"*Eomma*, come on," I tried to cut in, though she didn't stop. "*Eomma*, I can't understand you. What the hell is going on? I thought we covered this at the engagement party. Why can't I marry Eric?"

"Because he doesn't know who you really are!"

I took a step back. "What...what do you mean?" Something told me a knee-jerk reaction here was inappropriate.

"Jane...my sweet Jane. Oh, Jane." Yu Na looked up and down the street. But there was no one walking in this quiet alley.

"*Eomma*," I said slowly. "What's this all about?"

She stepped into a stream of light shining from a lamp on the corner. "Oh, Jane. Your father...Carol...he was not." She buried her face in her hands. "He was not your real father."

The words were like sucker punches to the gut, one after another. "What—*what*?"

She sucked in a deep breath like it was physically painful. I took another step closer.

"*Eomma*," I said. "Tell me right now. *What* are you talking about?"

When she looked up at me, a tear tracked down her face, a silvery line across her rouged cheek. "It was...it was when I work for the airline," she said. "You remember, I was in the first-class section. A lot of men. A lot of rich men."

I screwed up my face. "What?"

"There was a group of us," she continued. "We...we were poor, Jane. We need money to send our families. And these men, they liked us. They invite us their hotels. They give us money if we..."

I couldn't speak. If I was hearing this correctly, my mother was telling me that she had, at one point, participated in some kind of low-level prostitution ring in Korea. *My* mother. Yu Na Lee Lefferts, pious church attendee and queen of chastity. A hooker.

"Sometimes they just want dinner," she whispered. "Sometimes they want more. Sometimes we say no. Sometimes...sometimes we say yes."

I honestly felt like my head was going to explode. Korean culture dictated, even now, that women remain "pure" before marriage. That my mother would have flouted that so deliberately in the eighties was almost unthinkable. "So you're saying...you're saying my real father was one of them?"

Miserably, she nodded. "When I find out I am pregnant, it was when I meet your father, Jane. Such a nice man. On vacation to Korea and Japan. He...he ask me to dinner. I think he is like the others, but he is not. He was so nice..."

Her voice drifted off. I stared at her like I was just meeting her. I guessed, in a way, I was.

"He fell in love with me, Carol did," she said. "And I fell in love too. So when he ask me to leave with him, to come to Chicago...I said yes. It seemed like the best thing."

I pressed my hands on either side of my head. This hurt. Every part of it hurt. Carol Lefferts. Daddy. The man who had raised me. This couldn't be possible. It *couldn't.*

And yet.

*Come on, Jane Brain. You never knew? Never once wondered?*

My wider eyes, hazel, not brown or stormy blue. My unruly hair, when both my parents' was straight and sleek. My slim, almost lanky height at over five-eight, while the two of them were compact and solid.

I turned to my mother, seeing the truth all over her face and finally believing it myself. "Did he know? Did he know the baby wasn't his?"

My mother jerked her head up. "Of course I tell him! What do you think I would do?"

"Well, I don't know, do I?" I exploded. "You didn't tell me, did you?"

Her face crumpled, miserable. "I didn't mean to," she whispered. "No one ever knew."

"What was his name?" I asked. "What did he do? *Eomma,* who is my real father?!" I was becoming almost hysterical as the reality of what she was saying sank in.

"I don't know!" she cried. "I don't know. They don't tell us their real names, Jane! He say his name is John, okay? John. But otherwise, I don't know anything else! He was rich. He was handsome. He have dark, curly hair like you, and his name was John. Otherwise...he left, and I don't know what happened to him!"

We stared at each other, the both of us trying to work through this impossible situation. How could she do this to me...now?

The question begged a different one.

"What does this have to do with Eric?" I asked, almost afraid to answer. "Why don't you want me to marry him?"

She swallowed, and for the first time, the fear I had seen that night in the Hamptons stole back into her eyes.

"That necklace he has," she said. "The bracelet on that man's wrist. You see it?"

Slowly, I nodded. "We've been over this. The necklace was a gift. An antique."

"It's a marker," she said clearly. "The man—your father—he wears one too, just like it. So did some of the others with him. They all wore them that night."

"Eric got it from his father," I said, and then revulsion rippled through my entire body. "Are you saying..."

"*No.*" Her response was quick, and brutal. "No, no, no. I saw a picture of Eric's father. No, that was not the man. I know it was not him. I would never forget."

Relief flooded through me as my heart slowed its tempo. Jesus, *that* was close. And disgusting, even the thought.

"But whoever that man was, Jane, I know this." *Eomma* paused, glancing back toward the streetlights like she was afraid someone would jump at us from around the shadowed brick corners. "The men who wear that jewelry, they are not good men, Jane. Your father...not a good man, Jane. He was bad, very bad. And if Eric is one of them, maybe Eric is not a good man too."

———

WHEN WE REACHED THE HOTEL, we disappeared into our rooms without exchanging much more than a few words. My mother was angry that I refused to take her concerns seriously. I was furious that she had kept half of my genetic code a secret for thirty years. You know, potato, po-tah-to.

But once the door of my room closed, the gravity of her disclosures raced through me all over again, and I began to cry—great, heaving sobs that shook me from head to toe. I collapsed on the floor, shaking hard as my glasses bounced onto the carpet. What was I supposed to do now? What in the *hell* was I supposed to do?

A knock on the door interrupted my keening.

I rose, thinking it was Skylar, but when I opened it, found Eric fussing with his shirtsleeves, his forehead wrinkled slightly with worry.

"Hey," he said. "Where did you go? I came back and they said you and your mom took off through the service entrance—whoa."

My tearstained face seemed to be enough of an answer, because without a word, he barged in, pulled me into his arms, and steered me toward the bed. He settled me on the end, then crouched between my knees so he could look up at me, clasping both of my hands.

"Tell me what happened," he said in that gentle way that somehow still commanded obedience.

I hiccupped. And then I recounted the entire exchange in the alley.

"Jesus," Eric murmured after I was finished. He rubbed his cheek with a stunned expression. "That's...insane."

I nodded. I was starting to feel numb. "Honestly, I don't think she ever would have told me if it hadn't been for you. And really...that's almost worse, you know? Not that this thing happened, but that she was so determined to keep it a secret."

He had removed his tie before coming, and his bright blue shirt had been unbuttoned just enough to reveal his collarbone and the glint of a thin gold chain draped over it. I reached in and pulled out the gold coin that hung there, brushing my thumb over the engraved, two-faced image.

"It was this again," I said. "She said she saw this on one of the men you left with tonight. And that the man who—well, my real father, I guess—wore a necklace like this."

Eric's eyes popped open. "She thinks—"

"No, no, no." I shook my head furiously. "Thank fucking God for that, no. We're not committing any Ancient Egyptian inbreeding here."

Eric relaxed visibly and exhaled. "I legitimately thought my heart stopped for a second."

"Gives new meaning to your Petri dish, doesn't it?"

For that, I received a sardonic look, complete with a raised brow. I contemplated jumping him on the spot. But I had other questions. And so, apparently, did he.

"Do you...Jane, if it's too much, would you prefer to postpone?" Eric rubbed his cheek again—it was a habit I'd noticed whenever he was a bit uncomfortable. "We can call it off. This is a massive bomb you just had dropped in your lap. I wouldn't blame you for wanting some time to process."

"Eric, do you have any idea how much this wedding cost?"

I didn't even want to say. It was utterly obscene how much Celeste was spending. I had tried to talk her into cutting back, but she had waved me away like a pesky fly every time.

Eric just shrugged. "Whatever it is, I doubt it's putting that much of a dent in our accounts."

"Your family could probably fund, I don't know, ten African orphanages with the money going into this wedding. All of New York is turning out to watch the de Vries heir marry the weird Asian girl. It's the event of the year, or so I've been assured by at least a hundred people." I shook my head. "We can't pull out. I won't do that to you or your family."

It was strange, but I'd actually developed a minor fondness for Eric's shrewish old grandmother. Celeste was a little nuts, it was true. Sick with power, maybe. But there was some love in her dying wish to see her favorite grandchild married and happy. If Eric and I were what we had been six months ago, I'd probably still hate her for forcing him into it. But as it was now...a part of me was sort of grateful she had done it. I'd still be toiling away in Chicago otherwise.

I also wondered if she knew him better than he thought she did. Maybe Celeste knew Eric wouldn't just choose anyone for this task. Maybe she knew he'd marry for love anyway.

Maybe, I thought optimistically, that was the entire point. Her real dying wish was to make things right with her grandson the only way she knew how.

Regardless, there was still one more thing I needed to know.

"You don't...you don't have any more secrets from me, do you?" I asked. "Eric, if you do, I need to know now."

Eric looked at me for a long time, his gray eyes swirling like storm clouds. Then he framed my face with his large, graceful hands, cradling it toward him.

"You see everything about me that matters, Jane," he said in a low, clear voice. "There would never be any point in keeping the stuff that doesn't."

We watched each other for several intense seconds, as if waiting for the other to break. But no one did.

"Well, then," I continued. "The show must go on. I'll walk myself down the aisle. My mother will keep her mouth shut. And you and I...well, if I don't know who I am right now, at least I know tomorrow I'll be your wife. That's not changing, right?"

Eric smiled, and I closed my eyes, basking in that glow. I inhaled his warm, familiar scent of soap, cologne, linen, and man. God, he always smelled so good.

I opened my eyes. "You should probably go. It's almost midnight, and it's bad luck for you to see the bride on your wedding day." Normally I wasn't superstitious, but after everything that happened, I figured we needed as much luck as we could get.

Eric stroked my face and tucked a loose strand of hair behind my ear. He smiled again, and I felt that glow inside me light a small, warm fire.

"I'll see you down the aisle...pretty girl."

# THIRTY-TWO

"Jane! Look over here, honey. No, not directly at the camera. Just over my shoulder. Yes, that's right."

I turned obediently, following the instructions of one of the three photographers who had been assigned to follow the bridal party around all day while we prepared for the big event. It wasn't exactly the most relaxing process in the world.

My mother sat in the corner, studying her nails, which she had actually manicured for the day. It wasn't something she typically did, considering that she spent most of her time with her fingers immersed in acetone. For the wedding, she wanted to look her best, though all morning she had been doing everything she could to remain a wallflower. Out of fear or spite, I didn't know. I wasn't sure I cared anymore.

The thought of my dad jabbed my heart. The more I thought about it, the more I was mad at him too. He was a wonderful father to me, but both of them had engaged in this deception. They were both liars. They both should have told me.

*Then what would you have done, Jane Brain? This doesn't change anything about who I am to you.*

"Jane, don't you *dare* move," Frederick ordered as he stood back to apply yet another layer of hairspray. I closed my eyes and tried to ignore the voice in my head and the cacophony around me.

The conflicting directions were just the start of the morning's chaos. Murphy's Law appeared to be in full effect this fine Sunday morning.

First, one of the heels on my shoes broke, so one of Gemma's assistants was sent to open Bendel's at seven in the morning to locate an extra pair of white pumps that would match the white of my dress. It took two trips to satisfy my wedding planner. Jenny, Skylar's daughter, then misplaced the basket of rose petals she was supposed to carry, sending Gemma into a tizzy and her other assistants all over town trying to find a new one that would meet Celeste's requirement of tasteful, yet moneyed. Whatever that meant.

On top of that, my cousin, Suejean, ended up getting food poisoning from some bad nuts she purchased yesterday in Central Park, so she was married to her toilet, leaving me without a fourth bridesmaid. And, according to Celeste, having four attendants with five groomsmen simply wouldn't do.

"Found someone!" Nina announced as she entered the suite that had been designated as ground zero for wedding preparations. "And, as it happens, she's exactly your cousin's size, Jane."

I turned from my seat at the vanity to see Caitlyn Calvert following my future cousin into the suite along with another woman carrying a small brown bag.

"You gotta be kidding me," Skylar muttered under her breath while she turned *Frozen* on for Jenny as we finished getting ready.

"Oh, not Debbie Downer," Cherie rejoined from her place on a settee.

"'Let it go,'" I sang in my best, partly tone-deaf Elsa impression. Skylar chuckled, and Jenny grinned.

"Jane!" Caitlyn delivered a pair of air kisses to me, pushing past Frederick and the makeup artists like they weren't even there.

I grimaced in her cloud of Chanel No. 5. "Hi, Caitlyn. Thanks for coming."

"*So* lucky I happened to stop by to see N, isn't it?" she asked with far too much enthusiasm. "Saving your big day! You'll owe me, won't you?"

It was meant to be a joke, but I couldn't help wrinkling my nose a little with distaste.

"Of course, we don't know if I'll *really* be able to fit into her dress exactly. I did see your cousin at the rehearsal dinner, of course, and to be frank, she could probably use a few barre classes or so."

"Suejean is a neonatal surgeon," I replied dryly as I closed my eyes to have shadow applied. "Doing squats isn't really high on her list of priorities since she's usually busy saving babies."

"Happy, ladies! We're looking *happy*, darlings!" cried the photographer.

Caitlyn just flipped my comment away with a delicate hand and examined herself in the mirror behind me. "Well, you know the real secret is just doing them whenever you get a spare moment. I got Nina to start doing them when she brushed her teeth at night, and by last summer, she had a bikini body for the first time in years!"

"What's a bikini body, Mommy?" asked Jenny as she turned from the TV.

"It's a body with a bikini on it," Skylar replied drily.

"Do I have one?"

"Not unless you're wearing a bikini. Just pay attention to *Frozen*, babe." Skylar glared at Caitlyn, who was now observing my dress obliviously.

"Lord, this child," Cherie muttered under her breath before taking a long drink of champagne.

"Oh, I wouldn't do that if I were you," Caitlyn said as I followed suit.

I lowered my glass and looked up so the makeup artist could finish applying my mascara. "Pray tell, why not?"

She tapped her nose. "Don't want to be red in the face in front of the cameras, do we? I saw you at your bachelorette party, Jane. One drink, and you turn into Bozo the clown! We don't want that, especially since you fixed your hair." She broke into giggles, as if the idea of me with a red nose was the funniest thing in the world. She turned back to the window. "So this is the dress, I suppose?"

As Emily, the makeup artist, finished putting the final touches on my cheeks, I looked over at the long white confection hanging from the window dressings. It was the last thing I would put on. "Well, yeah. I don't normally walk around dressed like the ghost of weddings past."

"You're good," Emily said as she pulled back the blush. "You look great, Jane. And the dress is perfect."

Caitlyn cackled. "Oh my goodness, you are just the sweetest. Well, it's nice. Very...nice. Did you sew it yourself? You're very brave."

Skylar practically growled from where she and Cherie were zipping each other up into their blush bridesmaid dresses. "It's a custom Jenny Packham, Caitlyn. Couture. They flew it to London to be redone especially for her."

"Did they really?" Caitlyn fingered the end of the sleeve. I fought the urge to swat her hand away. "I suppose when things are last minute, beggars can't be choosers, can they. When life gives you lemons, right? You are doing amazing things with what they gave you, Jane."

I just stared. "Wow. Thanks."

"You're welcome!" Caitlyn grinned like she hadn't just given me back-to-back underhanded insults. "Now, where is my dress? I brought my seamstress to help fix it."

I opened my mouth to tell her where she could shove her seamstress, but decided to keep my thoughts to myself. After all, she was doing me a favor. Without her, we would be one bridesmaid short, and Celeste, given her frail state, probably couldn't handle the horror.

"It's fine," I said. "Nina, can you show her where the dresses are?"

They walked out into the next room, leaving me, Skylar, and Cherie to finish getting dressed.

"Two more shots," said the photographer. "Just...like...that." A flurry of clicks sounded as he took his last photographs of me looking at myself in the mirror.

"Darling, you look incredible," Frederick remarked as he floated his hands around my head. Today's accent was closer to Cornish, if anything. "If I do say so myself. Some of my finest work."

It was hard not to feel a little smug. I did look amazing.

"You do look beautiful, Jane," said my mother in a small voice from the corner, where she had been watching the interactions with Caitlyn sharply.

I turned, the smugness dying.

"Thanks, *Eomma*," I said quietly.

She stood and brushed her hands down her muted navy dress. To Celeste's utter irritation, Yu Na had refused the services of any of the stylists employed for the weekend, stubbornly preferring to wear her own clothes to the ceremony and reception. I was glad, almost proud of her for it. My mother refused to be anyone she was not, refused to be made up like a doll.

*Like you are now?*

That independence was a characteristic we had once shared, I thought with some regret as I looked over my carefully coiffed body. I reached up and touched the back of my head where the red stripe was. It was supposed to show during the ceremony. Wasn't it?

"Jen, go with Auntie Cherie, okay? Daddy's waiting for you downstairs with the other groomsmen and Luis. We're going to get started soon," Skylar said, breaking the silence. "Jane, I'm going with them to make sure everything is settled, and then I'll help you into your dress, okay?"

She ushered the others into the next room, where Caitlyn and Nina were waiting in their bridesmaid dresses too. The styling team, photographers, and the seamstress followed them out. Eventually I stood there, alone.

I shivered, examining myself in the mirror. I was still only clad in a satin dressing gown that Celeste had insisted on as part of a proper trousseau. I didn't even know people still had those. With my face done up and the simple diamond earrings she lent me dripping from my ears, I looked the picture of a polished, nervous bride.

*Oh, God.* Could I really do this?

There was a knock at the door.

"Jane?"

I turned at the sound of the familiar deep voice, then practically skipped over to the door, which I opened a crack.

"What are you doing here?" I asked, immediately putting myself on the other side of it when I fully realized who it was. "No, don't come in! It's bad luck!"

"You don't really believe in that sort of thing, do you, pretty girl?"

I smiled. No, I didn't. But on the other hand, so much had gone wrong today.

"What is it?" I asked. "You're supposed to be on your way to the church. Your grandmother is going to keel over if things don't start on time."

There was a chuckle, but instead of Eric answering, a small, folded piece of paper appeared by the edge of the door.

"I know we decided not to do our own vows," Eric said. "But I wanted you to have something anyway."

I took it, unfolding the paper slowly. It was ripped on one side, like it had been torn from a book. "What is this?"

"Read it," Eric said. "It's not much...but it was in my head. I wrote it for you. Something to think about with this bullshit pomp and circumstance."

I squinted at the uneven scrawl. I sort of loved his handwriting, actually. For all his polish and poise, Eric's letters were absolute chicken scratch. The one part of him that was as messy as I was.

*Vow*

*Pretty girl. Woman. Siren. Fiend.*
*She with her*
*Lipseyescheekshairlegspussyskinshouldersarmsbreaststhighsback*
*But more than that her*
*Mindgazehumorsmartstonguewordstalentkindnesscandor*
*Makes me*
*Crazydevotedfrustratedsated*
*Inloveinlustinheatintrustin*
*All you are, Jane, all yours.*
*This is my*
*Hate vow*
*Sex vow*
*Love vow*
*My vow is that*
*Forever*
*Always*
*I belong to you.*

I touched the words, muddled and messy. This wasn't a neat sonnet, like the ones he sometimes read me, but its chaos fit the emotions that so often overtook me—us—when we were together.

"I love it," I said. "Eric...I..." I turned to the door, suddenly desperate to see him. Look into those eyes and see for sure that this wasn't a dream or an act.

"I love *you*, Jane," he said solemnly, like it was an oath, not just a statement.

His hand appeared at the door, reaching out, begging for me to take it. So I did, and he squeezed, tight enough that I wouldn't forget.

So I squeezed back. "I know, Petri dish." I said, imagining the look of mock outrage mixed with humor all over his handsome face. "And I love you too. Now get to the church so I can tell you to your face."

———

"OKAY," Skylar said about fifteen minutes later when she returned to the room. "Everyone is off to the church. There is a car waiting downstairs for you. We just need to get you into your dress, and off we go. I'll carry your train."

I nodded, standing from the bed and taking down the dress. "Let's do this."

Skylar helped awkwardly as I stepped into the gown. I looked at myself in the mirror while she zipped it up from the back, staring at a woman I barely recognized.

My glasses were gone, replaced by contacts for the big day. Gone was the thick black eye makeup I generally preferred, the bright red lips, the black clothes, the chunky boots. I looked like a stock model, a picture out of *Vogue Bride*. Demure. Poised. Maybe even a little faceless.

"Wait," I said. "I need something from my purse." I beckoned toward it, scared to move in my pristine dress.

Skylar retrieved the purse, and I pulled a tissue, some lipliner, and tube of lipstick out of my makeup bag.

"Ah, your signature color," Skylar remarked as I wiped away the tepid rose Emily had applied. "Of course. It's not really you without it."

I smacked my lips in the mirror. "Damn straight." I started drawing on the liner while Skylar watched, absorbed.

"I still miss you doing my makeup for me in college," she sighed. "Every time I try to use liner, I look like a clown."

"Brandon likes you natural anyway," I said. "Any time you wear a skirt, he barely notices your face."

"Hey! I resent that!"

I grinned cheekily and continued applying the lipstick. But just as I was finished drawing on the familiar red shade, the other door to the suite opened, and the voices of Nina and Caitlyn entered the hotel room.

"I think she's already left, Cait," Nina said. "We really need to go if we're going to be on time. Grandmother detests people who are late."

"I know I left my phone here somewhere," Caitlyn replied. "It's just...shoot, where *is* it? Help me look, N."

Skylar and I rolled our eyes at each other while the other women looked around. Neither of us spoke, not wanting to beg another dressing down from Caitlyn.

"I still feel like I should tell her," Caitlyn said as they moved around. "Isn't it sort of the same thing as walking around with spinach in your teeth? The nice thing to do is to say something, isn't it?"

"I suppose..."

"I feel sorry for her otherwise. If I had something on my shirt, I'd want to know. And if my fiancé slept with someone else, I'd want to know that too."

There was some murmured response that I couldn't quite make out.

"Jane," Skylar whispered, but I gestured for her to remain quiet. I wanted to hear the rest of this fucking conversation. That is, if they were going to continue it.

"Well, it was so long ago, though," Nina said. "Five years. I doubt it really matters now."

"True," Caitlyn said. "I wish I'd never left Boston after that night. Maybe then he would have asked me to help with this ridiculous charade instead of an Alexa Chung wannabe with bad hair."

There was a long sigh. "It certainly would have made things easier for everyone. Grandmother *hates* that red stripe, even if she came around to her."

There was a harsh giggle. "Do you know I purchased the *worst* set of lingerie for that night, N? Penny told me once that Eric liked things a little racy sometimes—sorry, I know he's your cousin, but you don't care, do you? All those years, and he never thought of me as more than a friend. So, I figured what would be less Park Avenue than cheap red panties, right?" Caitlyn scoffed. "Looks like he wanted that sort of thing permanently. Well, he'll tire of her soon enough. They always do."

Red panties. Boston. Five years. My skin iced over, a sudden tundra thin enough to crack. Skylar's big green eyes flew open.

"Ah ha! Found it!" Caitlyn crowed. "Okay, Nina, we can go. Relax, why don't you."

Their footsteps clipped out of the room, and the door slammed shut, echoing for a few seconds in their wake.

"Oh, Janey," Skylar started. "Do you...do you want me to call Eric?"

Her voice was scared. She knew what this meant. She knew what this meant to me. She also had no idea what I was going to do.

All my fears about Eric, his past, my past, came flying back. But they settled around one fundamental fact:

He lied.

*Do you have any secrets?* I asked him. *Anything you haven't told me? Anything I should know?*

I closed my eyes, willing the volcano that was exploding in my chest to calm. Down.

"No," I said in a voice I didn't completely recognize. "It's time to go."

# THIRTY-THREE

The cathedral was a beast. It was a monolith of Anglican pageantry on the Upper West Side, and I had it on good authority (meaning Celeste) that it was the largest Anglican church in the world. The de Vries were Presbyterians, of course, having descended from hordes of good Dutch Calvinists. But the entire city was turning out for this wedding, and it was only the best for the de Vries golden boy, their prodigal son, returned to take over the family throne. And the best (and biggest) was St. John the Divine.

"Are you ready?" Skylar whispered as she took Brandon's arm in front of me. The rest of the bridal party had already taken the long walk down the aisle.

Stone-faced, I nodded. "Go," I said. "I'll be fine."

Skylar gave me another worried look, then turned and began walking to the crossing with her husband.

"All right, Jane." Gemma appeared with a headset attached. "Go bridal march," she said into the mic.

The organs began and the choir started singing a different hymn, their voices raised louder, vibrating through the stone walls. And in that moment, I felt for the first time what I was really marrying into. A complete and utter spectacle, all of it designed to show one thing: power.

Gemma looked at me. "Your turn, beauty. Here we go."

It was one hundred and forty steps from the lobby of the church, past uncountable apses, row upon row of New York's elite, down the long, almost interminable knave to the crossing of the basilica-designed cathedral. The arched ceilings yawned above me, with stained glass windows sparkling beyond them and Gothic-style gargoyles at the top, portending some strange kind of doom from beyond. I felt like I was walking to my death, not to a new life. Not for the first time, I wondered if I was truly crazy for doing this.

At last, I reached the crossing, where an elevated platform had been set up in the center so that people in each arm of the basilica and the choir at the head could watch from every direction.

Eric stood next to the minister, watching me the entire time with an expression of awe. His traditional black tuxedo with thin peak lapels and just a hint of tails over the Italian-cut pants was tailored to perfection. *He* was perfection.

I couldn't have hated him more. And it wasn't until I reached him that he must have seen that in my face.

"Hey," he whispered carefully as he took my arm and guided me up the steps. "Everything...everything okay?"

I swallowed, unable meet his eyes. I could do this. I could get through this charade. We could fight after. Now was not the time. I could do this...

I couldn't do this.

"I know," I whispered, just under the hum so only he could hear me.

"You...know?" His eyes were shifty.

"I know everything," I hissed, gripping my flowers so hard I could feel the stems cracking under their satin bindings. "About you. And Caitlyn. And those red. Fucking. *Panties.*"

I spat the word, startling the minister who approached.

"Jane?" Skylar touched my elbow from behind, where she stood with Jenny. "Is everything all right?"

But I didn't look at her. I didn't look at Brandon either, who frowned over Eric's shoulder while holding his son's hand. I could only see Eric—his deep, silver-gray eyes, the way his brows knit together, and then the way clarity passed over his face. The truth of the statement as it registered.

"Shit," he whispered, with no apparent regard for the church. "Jane, I—"

"Are we ready?" asked the minister.

"No," Eric snapped. "We need a minute to talk." He jerked his head toward an apse behind us. "Over here."

I scowled. "Eric, I am standing in a thirty-foot train that has been perfectly placed over those steps and takes at least five people to move properly. I am not moving *anywhere*."

He glanced toward the crowd, where people were already watching us curiously, wondering about the obvious delay. "Jane, come on."

"How could you?" I hissed through my teeth, trying and failing to maintain an even tone.

"Ms. Lefferts, really, if you need a moment—"

"No, it's fine, Reverend," I cut the minister off again. "We'll continue. Mr. de Vries here just needs to understand one thing."

But Eric just glared. "Jane, I'm only going to say this one more time. Pick up the goddamn train and follow me." And then, without waiting, he turned on his patent-leather heel and strode off toward one of the doors that exited the main altar where we stood.

The crowd watching us immediately started to jabber, and past Skylar's shoulder, Caitlyn tried and failing to hide a grin. The reverend turned to me questioningly.

"Sky," I whispered.

"Right here, Janey."

"Grab my train, please." I turned to the reverend. "We'll, um, just be a minute."

"Brandon!" Skylar hissed as we trotted off. "Take the kids, and entertain the crowd."

Brandon gave her a look like she was crazy, but turned to the filled pews as we trotted in the direction Eric had gone.

We found him pacing a smaller chapel that jutted off the main altar.

"You want me to stay?" Skylar asked. She looked like she would rather do anything but.

I took the fabric out of her hands. "No, it's fine. We'll be right out."

She gave me a look that was utterly disbelieving, but sighed and left.

Eric turned from his place under a stone saint as the door shut behind her. "Jane."

"Don't," I said, holding up a manicured hand. "I honestly don't want to hear it. I'm so over this shit, Eric. So over it. It's five years old. It's done."

"It's not done. You're obviously still pissed off about it." He shook his head like he couldn't believe it. "About something that happened five years ago. It's unbelievable."

"You think I'm mad because you slept with someone five years ago?" My voice shot up an octave with incredulity. "God, you're really that fucking clueless, aren't you?"

I strode in the opposite direction, unable to face him. Instead, I came face-to-face with a statue of a noble-looking dude labeled "King Eric IX."

"Arggh!" I screamed at it. "Of fucking course!"

"What the hell is wrong with you?"

I whirled around. "I'll *tell* you what is wrong with me, you pedantic, patronizing, sociopathic *liar*! Caitlyn. Fucking. Calvert. And her tiny red thong. That was balled up in your fucking sheets the night I came back for you. It's not the fact that you slept with someone, you asshole. It's that you slept with *her*. And you. Never. Told. Me."

As I spoke the words, the color in Eric's face drained, making him look a lot like the statue behind me.

"Jane," he started.

"Spare me."

"Jane."

"Stop."

"*Jane.*"

"Shut up!" I screeched. "For once in your fucking life, take your smug, condescending remarks and shove them straight up your entitled ass, right along with the stick that seems to be permanently lodged there!"

I paced around the room, tripping on my train and alternately kicking it out of the way. The edges were already getting smudged with the grime from the stone floors. It seemed to fit the utter illusion of this day. We looked so perfect from far away, but up close, it was a fucking mess. And there was nothing beautiful about it.

Eric took a tentative step toward me, his shiny black shoes clipping on the hard floors. "Jane, you have to let me explain. Jesus, it was *five years ago.*"

"I asked you. Last night. Do you have any secrets, Eric? And what did you say, huh?"

His arms flew out. "Jane, this isn't a secret. I honestly just didn't think it mattered."

"Didn't think it mattered? Eric, that passive-aggressive bitch has been trying to weasel her way back into your life since you showed up. I'd bet ten dollars it was *her* who got those kids to throw paint on me. Honestly, I bet she knew I was in the hotel room the entire time she gabbed to Nina about her little affair with you."

"It wasn't an affair," he said. "And may I remind you that you and I were split up—by *your* choice, I might add. Why doesn't that ever get through to you! Am I supposed to tell you every goddamn woman I've fucked in the last five years, Jane? Or the last fifteen, for that matter? You already know it's a long fucking list, sweetheart!"

"You're disgusting," I spat. "And missing the goddamn point, as usual. I don't care about any of those women, Eric. But you know what I do care about? Honesty. I care about my partner being straight with me. With him telling me the fucking truth instead of lying to my face!"

"I didn't tell you because I knew you'd fucking react like this!" he exploded. "You'd blow it out of proportion, just like you did back then, and we'd be right back at square one." He started pacing around. "Honestly, Jane. It's like you don't care about anything from the past four months. You don't fucking care about *us*, you're so willing to throw it away!"

I gaped, wishing I had something else to throw at him. "Don't care? Are you serious right now? Look at me! Look at this!" I gestured up and down at the dress, my face, my hair, the entire church. "This isn't me, Eric. Does this *look* like someone who doesn't fucking care?"

"I never asked you to do any of that, did I?"

"You didn't have to. Not in so many words. God, look at me. I look like a mannequin, a fucking shadow of myself. I'm literally a person in black and white."

"I told you to put your hair back the way it was," Eric retorted.

"It's not just about the hair, though, is it? You've been pleased as punch every time I've gotten along with your family. Well, playing that game has required some chameleon skills, asshole. And you haven't exactly been complaining about any of it, either. 'Pleasantly surprised,' you said, right? Happy that I was fitting in."

"Jesus *Christ*, you really are determined to take everything out of context, aren't you?" Eric rubbed his hands over his face and groaned. "Fucking nightmare."

"Nightmare of your own making, I'd say."

He looked up with new resolve. "Look. I didn't ask for this giant circus of a wedding. I didn't ask for the ninety-foot dress or the fifty-person bridal party or a ceremony in the biggest church in the world. I just wanted you, Jane! That's it!"

He roared every one of the last words, his words echoing off the hard stone walls and floor. But none of them mattered. All I could see

were those stupid red panties. And now, of course, the utterly punch-
able woman who wore them.

"Well, you can't have me," I said at last, taking a firm grip on the
back of one of the old wood chairs to stay in place. "Not now. Not
ever."

His face dropped. Legitimate, real surprise replaced all his frustration. "You're kidding. You don't mean that."

"All I've done is try my hardest to fit in," I said, biting back tears.
"And I didn't just do it for you—I did it for me. I didn't want to be a
big fucking joke to you or your family. So no matter what they did—
the backstabbing comments, the weird pranks—it didn't matter,
because in the end, I knew if I could win you over, I could do the
same with them. Turns out, the person who thought I was the biggest
joke of all was you."

"Jane, stop. You don't mean that."

"Don't tell me what I mean, asshole."

"Come on!" Eric shouted. "This is ridiculous. It's ancient fucking
history, and we have *moved on*. I love you, Jane! Doesn't that mean
anything to you? Did it ever?"

"I don't know what it means anymore."

"Why? Give me one good reason why something that happened
five *fucking* years ago should be this important."

"Because you broke my heart!" I screamed.

"Well, YOU BROKE MINE TOO!"

We stood, seething at each other, unable to tear ourselves away,
but unable to forgive either. In that moment, the fury fell out of Eric's
eyes, replaced with utter, heart-wrenching despair. I choked, unable
to breathe, trying my hardest to swallow back everything I'd just
yelled at the top of my lungs.

I tried to shake everything away like a bad dream. That's all it was
anyway. That's all any of this was.

"I don't know why I do this to myself," Eric said, his voice
dropped again, low, despondent. "I must be a fucking masochist. I
keep trying to make it work with you, but I should have known you'd

do this again. Find some excuse. Some fucking reason to pull the rug out from under me all over again."

"Excuse me for not wanting to love a fucking liar and lothario," I snapped. "If you want someone who's willing to let you manipulate her for the rest of her life, you should have done what was expected of you in the first place and given this ring to Caitlyn Calvert."

In my frenzy, I yanked the engagement ring off my finger and hurled it at him. The ring bounced off his chest and to the floor in a series of light tings. Slowly, Eric dropped to his knees and picked it up, then held it up in a parody of another proposal.

"Put it on," he ordered in a voice of steel.

"No."

Eric stood. "So this is how it's going to be? You want to end this? Now?"

I gulped. Was that what I was doing? In front of five thousand of New York's finest?

"If you do, that's twenty million gone, Jane." Eric held out the ring, pinched between two fingers. "Not to mention Nina's inheritance. My aunt's and my mother's. Countless cousins, relatives, not to mention hundreds, maybe thousands of people out of work if Grandmother actually sells off all her shares." He let the ring roll into the palm of his hand. "Think about what you're doing."

His voice was hard. Cold. Completely devoid of any emotion. It was the one thing that told me the last months were erased. We were back to where we started. If I did this, it would be nothing but a transaction. A deal, just like he promised.

I stared at the ring for a long time. Watched the bright, sparkling diamonds reflect prisms of light to the edges of Eric's hand while the black stone in the middle seemed to consume all light at the same time. For a moment, I wondered if it would consume me too. Like the ocean. This city. This man. This life.

*Breathe, peanut. Think about what you're doing.*

But for once, the calm, soothing voice of my father only made things worse. I shuttered him away. After all, he was nothing but a lie too.

I looked up. "Okay."

"Okay?"

"Yes. But it's not for the twenty million dollars," I said. "It's because I won't let you or your family toss red paint on my dress again."

Eric shook his head as I took the ring and slid it back on my finger, wishing it would disappear.

"I'll say the vows," I said. "But I'll hate every minute of it."

# THIRTY-FOUR

I don't really remember the beginning of the ceremony. I don't remember what the minister said. The scripture that he and the other speakers intoned. Or the hymns from the choir behind us. I don't remember anything but Eric's stormy yet unwavering gaze, forceful and unforgiving under the cold, stony light of the cathedral as the minister asked us to swear our intentions for each other.

"Jane Lee Lefferts, will you have this man to be your husband; to live together with him in the covenant of marriage? Will you love him, comfort him, honor and keep him, in sickness and in health; and, forsaking all others, be faithful unto him as long as you both shall live?"

I nodded. My jaw felt like it was made out of metal, a trap that couldn't be pried open.

But at last, I said what I had to say.

"I will," I stated, loud and clear, but through my teeth.

"And, Eric Sebastian Franklin Stallsmith de Vries, will you have this woman to be your wife; to live together with her in the covenant of marriage? Will you love her, comfort her, honor and keep her, in sickness and in health; and, forsaking all others, be faithful unto her as long as you both shall live?"

Eric stared at me for a long time, long enough that I wondered if he was actually going to say it or cut and run.

"I will," he said, and his words fell like anvils at my feet.

The officiant turned to the congregation and requested their witness, to which they all replied another resounding, if slightly confused, "We will." Then he looked back to Eric and me. "Now, you will speak your wedding vows."

Eric took my hand, clasping it gently between both of his as he spoke the traditional Protestant vows we had both agreed on, repeating after the minister's quiet voice:

"In the name of God, I, Eric, take you, Jane, to be my wife," he began in a voice that shook slightly. "To have and to hold from this day forward, for better, for worse, for richer, for poorer, in sickness and in health, to love and to cherish, until we are parted by death. *This*"—he seemed to say it with extra emphasis that made me want to step away—"is my solemn vow."

I stared for a long time. I couldn't speak. I couldn't breathe, and it wasn't just because of the dress.

"Jane?" the minister prodded gently. "Would you like to say something to Eric?"

I switched hands, ignoring the way his larger one felt between my two. I spoke in a voice that sounded as hollow as the church, light and echoing. Full of nothing.

"In the name of God, I, Jane, take you, Eric, to be my husband, to have and to hold from this day forward, for better, for worse, for richer, for poorer, in sickness and in health, to love and to cherish, until we are parted by death. This is my solemn vow."

My voice cracked over the last word, and in the front row, my mother dabbed her eyes with a handkerchief. I sniffed.

"Jane," Eric whispered.

"Don't," I warbled. I couldn't cry now. I wouldn't.

We moved through a terse exchange of rings. I stared at the

gleaming metal as it slid over my finger, then watched numbly as I slid on Eric's solid platinum band. I spoke the words I had somehow memorized over the last weeks, but I couldn't for the life of me understand now. Symbol. Love. Ring. Wed. What did they mean anymore? What had they ever meant?

When we were finished, the minister took my right hand and Eric's left and put them together. Eric's ring was cool against my skin. My chin quivered.

"Now that Eric and Jane have given themselves to each other by solemn vows, with the joining of hands and the giving and receiving of rings, I pronounce that they are husband and wife, in the name of the Father, and the Son, and the Hol—"

"Wait!"

A man's voice called like thunder through the cathedral, rolling over the drone of the minister, cutting off his final words.

"What the fuck..." Brandon muttered.

"*Who* is that?" Skylar said sharply.

"Oh, shit..." Brandon muttered as he saw who approached. "Titan?"

Eric turned sharply to his best man. "You knew?"

Brandon glowered. "I was tapped at MIT. I went halfway through initiation before I met this asshole and cut out."

Skylar popped over my shoulder to glare at her husband. "What? What initiation? What are you talking about?"

Behind her, Nina's mouth dropped, though she quickly picked it up and resumed a placid expression. In the front row, I caught twin expressions of horror cross the faces of Celeste, Violet, and Heather as they watched the man striding down the aisle. All of them looked like they had just seen a ghost.

The speaker approached, flanked by several others, all of them white, wealthy, and dressed in more exquisite suits, like everyone else in the church. He was older, with a head full of shiny, almost unruly salt-and-pepper hair, and a nose like a hawk. He approached the altar like he was completely in the right to stand there with us, with seemingly no care for the five-thousand-member audience.

"Eric," said the man.

Eric sighed. "Hello...Carson."

From her seat in the front pew, Celeste stood up, holding her oxygen to her face as she sputtered. "Jonathan Carson, how *dare* you! Leave at once!"

The man didn't turn back to the old woman. He was the only man in the church—maybe the only person in New York—who didn't respond to her commands. "I've come to protect my best friend's son," he said without turning. "It seems he's made a grave mistake today, and we're here to rectify it."

"You shouldn't be here!" Celeste called, and Heather beside her seemed to think the same thing.

"What...what do you mean?" I whispered. Something was wrong. Something was very, very wrong.

In the front row, my mother slowly rose, clutching her handkerchief. Too late, I realized she had been crying through the entire ceremony. Now she just looked terrified.

"John?" she called in a small voice that reached us nonetheless.

The older man—Carson—turned slowly, locating the source of the voice. "Hello, Yu Na."

"John."

My mother pushed herself up from her chair with great effort. Slowly, she approached the crossing, her gaze flickering between me, Eric, and this strange man.

"What are you doing here?" she asked.

"I think the real question is what are *you* doing here, Yu Na?" Carson said. "Especially with her. You were told to stay out of my affairs. Did you think this was the way to do it?"

"John. *John.* I tried, I really tried—"

"It doesn't matter." Carson turned to me and nodded, like he was meeting me in a dance out of a Jane Austen novel, not interrupting my wedding. "I suppose now I shall meet my daughter. Hello, Jane."

My jaw dropped. For once in my life, I couldn't speak.

"Perhaps another time we shall meet properly," Carson continued. "Unfortunately, now is not that time. Your fiancé needs to come with us. Now."

Eric puffed his chest up, recovering his voice. "I'm not going anywhere, Carson," he said. "I heard Janus's—well, your commands—and it doesn't matter. I married her anyway. The minister just said the words. The license is signed. It's done."

But Carson didn't move, didn't even seem phased.

"Eric," I whispered to the man still holding my hand with a death grip. It was funny. Five minutes ago, I was dying to be rid of him. Now I only wanted to keep him close. "What is going on?"

Carson just cocked his head like you would to a trained dog. Then he opened his mouth and uttered two words: "*Deorum vocas.*"

Eric shuddered, then emitted a long, low sigh, like a balloon slowly draining. He turned to me, slowly, and for a minute, his eyes closed, as if he were in pain.

"I'm so sorry," he whispered.

And then he dropped my hand and followed the man out of the church, leaving me standing on the altar alone.

The doors echoed behind them when they slammed shut. And then chaos erupted.

"What do you want to do?" Skylar asked as people rose from their seats, chattering, pointing at me, many already moving toward us.

"I—I don't know." I turned to the minister. "Am I married? What just happened?"

But the poor man looked just as stumped as I was. "I—I don't know. We didn't technically finish..."

"Am I married?" I asked again, to the ushers, Brandon, Skylar, my bridesmaids. Even that smug bitch, Caitlyn Calvert. "Am I married? Someone, tell me!"

But before someone could, there was another cry from the front row.

"Help!" someone shouted from behind the throngs of people.

"Someone, call an ambulance!"

"Is there a doctor in the church?"

"Grandmother!" Nina jumped off the steps and ran down to the first row. Some of the crowd moved aside to allow her to access her grandmother, who lay passed out in her chair.

"Celeste!" I flew down the steps, ignoring the yards of fabric billowing behind me. I reached the frail old woman, slumped in her seat, and placed two fingers at the side of her neck where her pulse should have been.

"Oh, God," I whispered as I looked at Nina. "Oh, God."

...

...

"She's dead."

## POSTLUDE

*A flash of red*
*Your lips, her clothes.*
*Her blood. Your blood. Life, just life.*
*Moments three, in which I'm caught*
*A flea in the web of your spider thoughts.*
*But it wasn't until you released me*
*With a slap,*
*A curse,*
*(Give me your sex, your worst.)*
*That I knew to be free*
*Was so much worse a trap*
*Than you had ever been, my love.*

— "Lost"
from the journal of Eric de Vries

He couldn't think about her. He couldn't even say her name. He wondered if he would ever see her again. And a part of him, the best part of him, truly wished he wouldn't.

That was how Eric knew he loved her.

Jane.

Jane Lee.

Jane Lee Lefferts.

Was she de Vries now? He hoped not.

Again, that love shined through, even in the darkest moment of his life.

Because really, he only wanted the best for her. Even if it cost him everything he had.

———

**To Be Continued in THE KISS PLOT.**

**Coming June 29, 2019.**

**Preorder here: http://bit.ly/TheKissPlot**

To receive a first-alert about the next book of Jane and Eric's story, subscribe to Nicole's newsletter at bit.ly/NicoleFrenchNewsletter

**While you wait**...see how Jane and Eric met in the Spitfire Series, Brandon and Skylar's story. Book I is FREE here: https://www.nicolefrenchromance.com/spitfire

# ACKNOWLEDGMENTS

First and foremost, to all of my readers. I dedicated this book to you because I can't even count how many of you have emailed me and messaged me, begging for Jane and Eric's story since I linked those three rough chapters to the end of Legally Ours, over a year ago now. It's been a long wait. I hope you think it's worth it. And I REALLY hope you're not to mad about the cliffhanger. Because it's me, right? You know what you were getting into.

Secondly, to Danielle and Patricia, who read every chapter of this book as I was writing, offered praise and cheer, ever confident in my abilities even when I was not. Patricia, Eric is all yours, girl. You earned him. Thank you both for your tireless support.

To my dear, dear friends in the author world, without whom I would never be able to last in the landscape of social media: In particular, Jane, Harloe, Kim, and Laura: you are my sisters in this strange, strange business. I cannot wait to squeeze all of you tight. Thanks for indulging my curmudgeonly moments and for not putting up with my shit. Also, thank you to Ava, Sierra, and Claire for being such lovely souls who have allowed me to get to know you and your talents. And to the wonderful authors in the Do Not Disturb Book

Club, the Private Party Book Club, the Romance Support Group, the Emerald City Author Chicks, and the Spring Fling Anthology: I am SO delighted to continue these beautiful collaborations with all of you. Thank you for your support.

And of course, to my husband and kids. The Dude is an everlasting source of inspiration for these men. I'm lucky to have him, and even luckier to have his support for this venture. My three kids provide uncountable moments of inspiration and levity. I do this for myself, yes, but also for all of you. You are my heart.

# ALSO BY NICOLE FRENCH

**The Spitfire Series**

I had a plan.

Finish law school. Start a job. Stay away from men like Brandon Sterling. Cocky, overbearing, and richer than the earth, he thinks the world belongs to him, and that includes me.

Yeah, no. Think again.

It doesn't matter that his blue eyes look straight into my soul, or that his touch melts my icy reserve. It doesn't even matter that past all that swagger, there's a beautiful, damaged man who has so much to offer beyond private planes and jewelry boxes.

But I had a plan: no falling in love.

I just have to convince myself.

**Book I is available FREE: bit.ly/LYwide**

**The Discreet Duet**

I was broken. A mess.

So what should I want with this man? We had a connection, sure, but overall, he was nothing but trouble.

Will Baker was grouchy. Arrogant. A total loner. He had serious control issues, and was waving every red flag known to man..

And yet.

Since we met, it felt as if the universe itself was tilting on its axis, trying to knock me into him. I couldn't stay away from him, even if I tried.

We might have been too broken for anyone, but together, we seemed whole.

Once upon a time, I wanted the spotlight.

He gave up his life to escape it.

Now the question is...can we remain discreet?

**Start the duet here: bit.ly/DiscreetBook**

**Broken Arrow**

**Discover the Layla and Nico real first meeting in a FREE *Bad Idea* novella.**

They call me every name in the book, and every one is true.

Violent. Criminal. Bad news.

And if they're lucky, I'll take my anger out on a punching bag instead their faces. If they're lucky.

Then I meet her. Sophisticated. Successful.

More culture in her finger than I have in my entire body.

She says I have more to offer the world than my fists. She says I can pick my own direction instead of taking the one I'm given.

But tell me, beautiful, how do you do that, when you don't know where to go?

How do you find the right path when your compass is broken?

**Download Broken Arrow FREE here: bit.ly/BrokenArrowGiveaway**

# ABOUT THE AUTHOR

Nicole French is a lifelong dreamer, Springsteen fanatic, and total bookworm. When not writing fiction or teaching composition classes, she is hanging out with her family or going on dates with her husband. In her spare time, she likes to go running or practice the piano, but never seems to do either one of these things as much as she should.

For more information about Nicole French and to keep informed about upcoming releases, please:

Visit her website at www.nicolefrenchromance.com/.

Check out Nicole's Goodreads page: www.goodreads.com/authornicolefrench

Want to hook up with other Nicole French readers or interact with the author? Join Nicole's reader group, La Merde.

Made in the USA
Coppell, TX
19 February 2020